Praise for Keith Melton's *Blood Vice*

"Enthralling! ...will hook you in the first paragraph and keep you ensnared throughout... The paranormal has never been so sexy and ruthless... The realistic inside look into the mafia is fascinating... Blood Vice is a paranormal work of art."
~ *Teagan, BookWenches*

"...[T]urf war dramas, vampire politics, women with big guns, and other fun stuff to make sure that this one doesn't have a dull moment... Blood Vice is a charming fast-paced and action-packed tale that allows the bullets to fly free and the blood to flow..."
~ *Mrs. Giggles, www.mrsgiggles.com*

"...I ended up really loving this story...It's one of the better Urban Fantasy stories I've read this year."
~ *Anna, Anna's Book Blog*

"...well-written ...a fast-paced and complex story from beginning to end."
~ *Scandalous Minx, Literary Nymphs*

"...[T]urf wars and politics going on, but they're like the spice to the action. This book was really fun to read and time just flew by for me. I cannot wait for the next book."
~ *rbm00, Urban Fantasy Fan*

"[Karl and Maria] are a powerful duo with great chemistry."
~ *NeNe, Fallen Angel Reviews*

Look for these titles by
Keith Melton

Now Available:

The Nightfall Syndicate Series
Blood Vice (Book 1)

Nightfall Wolf Clans Series
Run, Wolf (Book 1)

Blood Vice

Keith Melton

A Samhain Publishing, Ltd. publication.

Samhain Publishing, Ltd.
577 Mulberry Street, Suite 1520
Macon, GA 31201
www.samhainpublishing.com

Editing by Sasha Knight
Cover by Anne Cain

First Samhain Publishing, Ltd. electronic publication: February 2009
First Samhain Publishing, Ltd. print publication: December 2009

Dedication

To my wife, Ana. Your hard work made all the difference.

Chapter One:
Opening Gambit

*"Add thy name, O sun, to tell thee how I hate thy beams,
That bring to my remembrance from what state I fell..."*
—Milton, *Paradise Lost*

It was a beautiful night for murder, but wet work was wet work and had to be done regardless of conditions. Still, Karl Vance had time to appreciate just how crisp the autumn air had become as the wind pushed up the side of the building and buffeted him where he stood on the rooftop ledge, watching. On the horizon, the silver blade of the moon sliced through a dark cloud. Around him, Boston sprawled in every direction, its lights drowning out all but the brightest stars.

A car pulled into the parking lot below him. A silver Mercedes AMG. The one he'd been waiting for.

Karl had a SIG-Sauer P-226 9mm in a holster beneath his left arm. In the right pocket of his cargo pants he could feel the weight of the silencer pressing against his leg. He'd mate them in a little while, but not yet. He had plenty of time.

Plenty of time.

The Mercedes parked and three men got out. He recognized them, by face and reputation, all of them made men in the Lucatti crime family. The driver was "Frankie Lost" Carrara, the Lucattis' most feared enforcer. Supposedly, he'd earned the name for his ability to make his victims disappear. The fat man in the tracksuit was Jimmy Fucci. The one climbing out of the backseat and adjusting his sport coat was Jimmy de Carlo.

Why Don Alberto Ricardi wanted this piece of work done

didn't matter. This was business, nothing personal. Even the eighty-five thousand he'd been paid to make it happen mattered only in the abstract. Still, the fact that he was allowed wide leeway in how it went down was an important fringe benefit.

The sound of their heels on the asphalt rang in his ears like gunshots as they made their way toward the front door below him. He could hear one of them laughing—the harsh sound rolling through the parking lot and echoing off into the darkness.

They entered the apartment building and he lost sight of them. No matter. He knew where they were going. He closed his eyes and listened, sorting through the city sounds as he allowed the men time for the ride up the elevator. A plane overhead, inbound for Logan. The sharp, staccato sound of a small dog barking. Two blocks over, a stereo booming rap music. Nothing amiss.

Time to go to work.

He turned and began to scale down the side of the apartment building. The brick felt cold to his fingers, but it didn't slow him. He kept to the shadowed side of the building, away from the moonlight.

"Frankie Lost" Carrara was the most dangerous of the three, a man who had once put six bullets in an informer and then ripped out his tongue with pliers and shoved it down his throat. He had to die first and die fast. Jimmy de Carlo was no saint either, but he was second in line. He ran numbers for a Lucatti capo named Tazetta and sometimes did side jobs leaning on underpaying "clients". Rumor had it he once made a guy swallow twelve of his teeth, one by one, after he'd knocked them out with a cue stick.

Fat Jimmy Fucci was by far the least dangerous and the poorest of the three. He burned his money gambling as fast as his fat hands grasped it. Tazetta had paper on him for bad bets that would've ensured Fucci spent the rest of his life crawling around with two shattered kneecaps, except that Fucci was a made man. So instead he spent almost all that he earned keeping up with the vig—Tazetta's back-breaking loan interest—on the debts he owed. Hence the rundown apartment he would soon die in.

Fucci's apartment was on the fifth floor. Karl paused outside on the narrow window ledge and *listened*. He could easily pick up the sound of their voices through the glass.

"Nowadays who can afford to drive one of those? Gas prices are kicking my ass."

"You mean to tell me you wouldn't take one of them Escalades because *gas* costs too much? I oughta kick your ass."

"I told you. Things have been tight. War's bad for business."

"What are you? A fucking economist? You're killin' me."

"Hey, Jimmy, do us all a favor and shut the fuck up."

Karl moved slightly to the left from where he clung to the bare brick wall so he could see inside. Beer bottles lined the tables and gathered in clusters on the marred hardwood floor. Curling centerfolds of nude women hung from the walls. A playing card, a square mirror and a small bag of cocaine lay on the coffee table in front of an expensive high-def television. No religious icons and no silver, though. That was good.

The three men stood close together in the small room. Even through the glass Vance could smell the blood in their veins.

Jimmy Fucci sat on the stained sofa near the mirror. He picked up the playing card with fingers like a balloon animal and began to cut the coke into even lines, tapping the card on the mirror to shake off clinging dust. He leaned low and snorted a line, then sat up quickly and gave himself a shake, like a dog running out from the spray of a fire hydrant.

Dammit, Karl hated cocaine. His eyes moved to de Carlo, standing with his arms crossed over his blue sport coat. It would have to be him.

Karl moved out of sight. Carefully, he drew out the silencer, pulled the 9mm's slide back, and screwed the silencer onto the threaded barrel. There was an old legend that Karl Vance's kind couldn't pass into a house without first being invited. That was bullshit.

He stepped in front of the window, brought his fist back and rammed it through the glass. The window shattered, frosting the air with slivers that glinted in the light of the bare ceiling bulb. He hit the carpet and rolled, blades of glass cutting wounds on his face and hands that healed as fast as they were made. He came up in a crouch and lifted the SIG-Sauer, the pebbled stock rough against his pale hand.

Frankie Lost reacted first, his hand sliding toward his waistband. The SIG hissed twice, the ratchet-click of the pistol action the loudest sound in the room. Frankie staggered back

11

and fell over the arm of the sofa, a hole in his forehead and one in his chest.

The air was suddenly drenched in the smell of blood, so vibrant that Vance could almost taste it. He stood slowly, smoking pistol in hand, his gaze trailing over the blood spatter on the walls.

"You *bastard.*" De Carlo clutched at the weapon beneath his coat, but Karl took two steps, moving so fast he doubted de Carlo's eyes registered anything but a blur, and slammed the man in the gut, doubling him over. As the air whooshed out of de Carlo's lungs, Karl slipped his hand into the man's jacket, grabbed the butt of his pistol and sent it spinning out the broken window. Then he turned to Fucci.

Jimmy Fucci stared at him as if he were some kind of acid trip nightmare. Snot streamed out of one of his nostrils. "Oh God don't—"

Karl's pistol whispered again. Jimmy Fucci slumped over on the couch and didn't move.

Karl turned to Jimmy de Carlo, who had staggered back against the wall and was staring at him with fear in his eyes and his lips skinned back into a snarl.

"I heard you once made a man eat his own teeth," Karl said.

"What the fuck do you know about that?"

Defiant. Even now. That was good.

One of Karl's fangs peeked out of his smiling lips. "I'm going to show you something new about teeth." He grinned even wider.

Jimmy de Carlo started to scream.

The church of St. Rosa was empty, its rose window and stained glass dark. A small, wrought iron cross sat atop the spire, lifted against the stars. To Karl's eyes, the cross burned with a pure, blue-white light that had nothing to do with reflected moonlight. Staring directly at it caused too much pain, as if somebody were slowly and steadily pushing a thumb into his eye.

He kept well away from the borders of the holy ground, which he could see smoldering like blue coals, the shimmer completely enclosing the hundred-year-old church and the small cemetery beside it. Standing this close felt like holding a live wire—the closer he got to the church, the more current ran through it. He wanted to be gone, the sooner the better.

The weight of obligation made him stay. The short, cobblestone street was empty, and few of the surrounding buildings had lights on. At the bottom of the street, traffic occasionally zipped past, even at this late hour. He knelt on the sidewalk, in the shadows between streetlights, and prayed for the souls of the men he had killed.

It felt as though he were sending radio messages out into the void of space, hopeless of ever receiving a reply, but he did it anyway. A ritual was a ritual. Sometimes the details of the faces had already begun to fade from his memory, smearing like ink in thinner. He'd seen a lot of death. He couldn't be expected to remember them all.

He prayed for their souls, but he did not pray for forgiveness. What would be the point?

For a few moments longer, he endured the pain, almost welcoming it. Then he stood and vanished into the darkness, while behind him, the cross continued to blaze its holy light against the backdrop of stars. The stones of the old church said nothing.

Five hours until dawn.

Karl slid open the balcony door to his twenty-first-floor apartment on Beacon Hill and stepped through Xiesha's wards of protection. The hair on his arms and the back of his neck lifted as he passed through. This close, the vibration of the ward was very strong, almost uncomfortable.

No lights were on in the apartment, but the surrounding lights from downtown, the Financial District and Chinatown provided more than enough illumination. He stepped to a small decorative table that held a Mikasa crystal bowl filled with filtered water. The water was cool on his hands, and pink with blood after he washed.

The air in the room shifted the tiniest fraction and the temperature dropped a few degrees. He sensed Xiesha enter the room, though she made no sound.

"Welcome back, Master," she said.

"What did I say about that word?" He dried his hands on a towel and turned to her. "How many times do I have to ask?"

Xiesha bowed, her form a faint shimmer in the darkness.

Her beauty was haunting, her dark eyes intense. Those eyes had always seemed more *there* than the rest of her, crackling with power like arcing electrical wires. She wore her long brown hair in a braid over her shoulder, and her pale skin glowed softly in contrast. Tonight she wore the red and black kimono, the one with the tail-eating dragons. She was currently obsessed with the Orient. Twenty years ago it had been Africa.

"I don't understand your discomfort with it." Xiesha's voice was soft, almost a whisper, but musical, as if tiny bells chimed as she spoke. "You are my Master, after all."

Except he wasn't. A long time ago, he'd saved her from the Order of the Thorn. Crossing an ancient religious order that hunted supernatural creatures was no small risk. To repay her debt she'd chosen to guard him during the daylight. But the term master was entirely her choice.

He unstrapped the shoulder holster and moved toward what had once been the dining room. He'd converted it into a small library, with teak, floor-to-ceiling bookshelves holding hundreds of books. Everything from linguistics tomes on modern slang and dialect to volumes on string theory, evolution and the relative nature of time. He'd read them all.

Relative nature of time. Between killings, all he had was time.

He walked into the kitchen and set the pistol on the kitchen counter, near Xiesha's crystal scrying bowl and her necklace, which resembled the design on a peacock feather. A small mound of gray ash and another of salt sat on white filter paper near the sink. Beside them stood two jars filled with amber and green liquids, things he did not recognize and didn't really care to know about.

"Any luck?" he asked. She had located Jimmy Fucci's apartment by scrying when Karl's street contacts had come up empty. Now he had her searching for someone else. Someone he wanted to kill for purely personal reasons.

"Not yet. I'm sorry. He masks himself too well."

He'd figured as much, but he nodded in thanks anyway. Someday things would be settled. Soon.

He left her in the kitchen and walked to where his laptop sat charging on a glass end table next to the leather couch. The blue glow that bathed the room as he powered up reminded him for a fleeting second of the blue-white glow of the cross and that spike of pain in his eyes. To his relief, the blue glow disappeared as the loading screen gave way to the desktop—a wallpaper image of the eclipsed sun. He smiled slightly. What delicious post-modern irony. Nosferatu of the digital age.

One new email, from the Ricardis. Five hours until sunrise and they wanted to meet, tonight. That didn't give him a lot of wiggle room before dawn, and dawn was something he never played around with.

But he didn't have much choice. The message had been sent to him only a half an hour ago and ended with a cryptic promise of profit, enough to make it worth his while. He'd heard that before. No mention of the hit they had ordered, though he'd no doubt be asked about the results. The middle sentence had a cell number for him to call.

"Will you be in for the rest of the night?" Xiesha asked from the doorway.

"No. I have to go out again."

"Business?"

"What else?"

She smiled, her dark eyes suddenly playful. "Be back before curfew...master." Then she withdrew with a bow, shutting the door behind her.

It was a wonder he tolerated it. He guessed seventy-five years of service had earned her the right to be impudent.

He moved out onto the balcony and looked up at the cold stars gleaming overhead. The skyscrapers of Government Center and the Financial District rose off to the east. The Zakim Bridge spanned the Charles River like an illuminated sculpture with an electron flow of traffic streaming along its lanes. He could just see the dome of the State House, and beyond it, the dark swatches and bisecting lighted paths of Boston Common. The night breeze brought him a riot of sounds and scents. Car exhaust and the faintest whiff of garbage from far below. The young couple two apartments over were making love again. His next-door neighbor, the lady lawyer, was warming a bottle for her newborn, and he could hear the child's impatient whimpering. His mouth curved into a smile.

He dialed the cell number and waited.

"Yes?" a male voice said.

"This is Vance."

"I see. Thank you for calling. Mr. Ricardi would like to meet with you, if you have the time."

Very polite. Not exactly what he was used to. "I have some time."

"Excellent. He would be most pleased if you would meet with him at the Riddark Hotel restaurant. He will be holding a table."

"Very well."

He flipped the cell shut and slipped it into his pocket. He chose a suit. Armani. Gray, double breasted. It wouldn't do to show up in his bloodstained work clothes. Neither would it do to bring a weapon to a meeting with a boss.

He left through the front door for a change, the pistol still lying upon the counter.

He hardly needed it to kill people, anyway.

The Riddark was all ritz, ten floors of opulence near the waterfront, but its walkways were empty of bellhops and most of its windows were dark. Trees lit from beneath by spotlights ran in ranks across the width of the hotel. Even the cigarette urns had been turned into *objet d'art*—basins of white sand ensconced in wrought iron that twisted upward like flowers straining for sunlight. The effect was ruined only by the scores of crushed cigarette butts drowning in the sand.

Empty velvet-roped queues stood sentry before the restaurant entrance, but he slipped past them. Inside, the chairs were all stacked upside down upon the tabletops. The chandeliers were dark, no gleam in their crystal teardrops. In the far corner, one of the cleaning crew ran a floor polisher.

A tired-looking maitre d' hurried toward him, greeting him with a wide smile that didn't quite cover up his desire to be somewhere else. The maitre d' led him through a short hall off the main dining room. A man—dark-haired and linebacker-big in a well-cut Italian suit—stood guard at the entrance to the private dining room. He stopped the maitre d' and patted him down, and Karl watched the maitre d' pale as the man's huge hands slid up under his arms and down his sides, searching for hidden weapons or wires.

When the guard was done, he turned to Karl and shrugged, seeming to say *You and I both know the drill.* Karl allowed the same pat down, and the guard came up empty and seemed satisfied. As if guns were the only dangerous things in the world.

"You may head right in, Mr. Vance," the man said. "The room's clean."

Karl nodded and went inside.

The private dining room held a table for four, with a small centerpiece of opening roses, red, white, peach, in a silver vase. Oil paintings of Venice streets hung on the walls. The light cascading down from a delicate chandelier was dimmed, so that shadows pooled in the corners of the room. The maitre d' pulled out Karl's chair, poured him a glass of wine and then withdrew.

Alberto Ricardi was in his fifties, with short silver hair as carefully arranged as the roses. Time had been less kind to his face, carved with creases and lines. A scar traced along one eyebrow, adding fierceness to his brown eyes. Popular Ricardi legend held that he had killed his first man at fourteen. A real early bloomer.

Ricardi wore a charcoal suit, double-breasted Armani, excellently cut. His necktie was red silk, an upside-down blood exclamation point running from his throat. He smelled faintly of expensive cologne. He stood and extended a hand and a smile.

"Mr. Vance," he said, "always a pleasure."

Ricardi spoke with no hint of accent, Italian, Boston or otherwise. Perfect broadcast English, no doubt honed in his days at Boston University. Every bit the successful businessman.

"The same, Mr. Ricardi." Karl glanced at the young woman seated next to Alberto. She stared back at him with large dark eyes. The resemblance to Alberto was there—family, certainly, maybe a daughter. He'd heard Alberto had a daughter he doted upon, who'd also gone to BU. This might be her.

Karl smiled at her. "I don't believe I've had the pleasure."

She had very full lips, and when those lips curved in a smile it lit up her entire face, making her look achingly young. Her eyes were bold and intelligent and watched him with interest.

"This is my daughter, Maria," Alberto Ricardi said. Karl could feel the weight of his stare. Considering.

The purple and black dress she wore covered her to the neck, but the skin on her throat seemed to glow softly in the dim light from the chandelier and candles. His attention jumped from her throat back to her eyes.

"Miss Ricardi. An honor."

She turned to her father, and her smile was a little bit wicked. "It's nice to meet a gentleman for once."

Something in her look stirred Karl's desire. A vampire's lusts were certainly not limited to blood alone.

"He's always been that way," her father said, but he seemed less pleased. Perhaps he regretted bringing his daughter after all. So what game was this, then? Was she bait—a pretty face to sweeten the deal? That didn't make any sense. He'd found *mafiosi* to be extremely protective of their sisters and daughters. She wasn't part of the business side of the family, that he knew of, anyway.

Her large dark eyes were fixed on his. "Thank you for coming on such short notice, Mr. Vance."

"Certainly. Your father is an old friend." An exaggeration. Alberto had done a few favors for him after the destruction of the Mancino crime family, and Karl had paid him back ten times over by pulling off near-impossible jobs. Much of the Ricardi rise to power was linked to Karl's participation, and both of them knew it.

"I know you're a busy man," Alberto Ricardi said, "and I'm sure you're wondering why we've asked you here. But first, are you hungry? They have decent chicken Parmesan, for Americans. Sadly, we can't all be Italian."

"I've already eaten, thank you."

"To the point then. We've had a long and mutually beneficial relationship with you." Alberto lifted a wineglass in salute.

Karl mirrored the salute, but said nothing.

"Now I have a business proposal." Alberto let the words linger as he took a sip of his wine.

Karl's gaze danced over to Maria for a brief second and then back to Alberto. He raised an eyebrow. Alberto smiled—almost a smirk. Maria frowned and anger shimmered like heat in her eyes.

"She's ready," Alberto said. "She graduated with top honors from BU. She knows everything about our books. I've schooled her in many things, as if she were my son." He paused. The silence became uncomfortable. Five or six years back his son had crashed his BMW into a concrete pylon at ninety miles an hour. Alcohol and cocaine.

Outside the private dining room Karl could hear the conversation between the maitre d' and the cook in the kitchen. They were talking softly about how much they were being paid to keep the restaurant open. Mr. Ricardi's bodyguard shifted in his seat, his suit rustling against the back of the chair.

Alberto stirred himself again. "Are you familiar with the *ronin*, Mr. Vance?"

Where in hell had that question come from? "A little."

"You've always reminded me of them."

"In what way?"

"Masterless samurai. Roaming. A warrior without direction."

"I see." A recruitment attempt.

Maria watched him closely. Her dark brown eyes reflected candlelight, seemed almost to glow, but the anger in them had faded. He closed his eyes for a second, driving away memories and the taste of blood.

"You play your cards close, Mr. Vance," Mr. Ricardi said. "I admire that. I always have."

"As do you."

For a moment they all stared at one another across the steadily deepening silence. Maria took a drink of her wine. The light flashed off her diamond earrings. Karl watched the muscles in her throat work as she swallowed.

Mr. Ricardi smiled at him. "Is it done?"

Karl lifted his wineglass and looked at it, wishing the red inside were something else. *The man changes topics with the abruptness of a car wreck.* "Of course. Is that what this meeting is about?"

"Not at all. When have you ever failed me?" He rubbed a hand across his mouth and sat back in his chair, staring at Karl with sniper's eyes. "Do you know why I had those men removed tonight?"

Karl set his wineglass down. The crystal chimed softly. "I have a few guesses."

"Care to share them with me?"

"Pre-hits and escalation. No made men had died until tonight, and Frankie Lost was their Hannibal Lecter with a pistol." Made men had taken the *Omerta* oath of silence and were the backbone of every crime family, worth far more than the hundreds of disposable associates. Killing one would be enough to earn serious retaliation. Killing three...

Alberto grinned. "Precisely. Some Lucatti dealer lost his hand when we shoved it in a lawn mower, but what the fuck is that? Nothing. Small-time, petty stuff, all of it. The Lucattis are happy to erode my territory without firing a shot. I need a shooting war to stop them. Without Frankie Lost, they'll have a harder time keeping their peckers up for the fight I'm bringing. Pull a sparkplug and you stop the motherfucking engine."

"You'll definitely have a shooting war now."

"Indeed I will," Alberto said. "Do you think me bloodthirsty?"

"Does it matter what I think?"

Alberto laughed. "I guess it doesn't. I can no longer suffer this *provocation* by that ignorant, knuckle-dragging motherfucker running the Lucatti *borgata*. And despite the hand-wringing in New York about territories, tithes and troubles, I know gradual strangulation when I see it. We'll end up like the Mancinos unless we defend ourselves."

"You don't have to convince me."

He'd heard the basics through his street contacts. The uneasy peace had started to unravel over a year ago. A Ricardi-run Super Bowl betting ring had been forcibly taken over by Lucattis, costing Alberto hundreds of thousands. A few trucks had been hijacked by the Lucattis in Ricardi territory, and a bunch of Ricardi owned and operated Joker Poker video gambling machines had been busted up all over the city. The Ricardis had retaliated in kind. Things had deteriorated from there.

Maria leaned forward. The candlelight made her face look valkyrie-fierce. "Only we Ricardis stand in the way of their push for Boston. If we weren't pushing back, they'd control the entire city. It's a matter of survival."

"So what would you like from me?" Vance asked.

"I mentioned the *ronin*," Alberto said. "We want you to be part of this."

"I'd be pleased to help. You know my prices."

"I want more. I want trust. You hate the Lucattis."

"True. But this is business."

"I admire that." Ricardi turned to his daughter. "A man who

can keep things from getting too personal. None of his decisions are based on emotion." He laughed. "You can tell he's not Italian."

Karl waited.

"My daughter has a plan to take the Lucattis down quickly. A long, drawn-out war is bad for business. Everybody's on the mattresses, in hiding, instead of out earning."

"Attack the money," Maria said. "Dry up their cash flow. Economics, not people."

"Then you don't need me. I'm...a people person."

"My father thinks you have the talents I need. A hundred percent success rate. No witnesses. You keep your mouth shut—it's like you're a ghost."

A ghost. He didn't know whether to feel amusement or despair. Perhaps in the end it didn't really matter.

"It would be cheaper to use your own people."

"Let's just say there are some extenuating circumstances," Maria replied.

By which she might've meant that Ricardi soldiers chafed at the thought of following a woman. Or they didn't trust their people for the work. Either way it added up to more complexities than he liked.

"So will you join us in this?" Alberto Ricardi asked. "I promise you enough motherfucking Lucattis to keep your gun warm, and sugar enough to sweeten any pie."

"You have my attention. But the devil's always hiding in the details."

"All I want is a vow of loyalty from you to the Ricardis—a promise that you belong to us, at least for this war, maybe after. Go on the record with us. You'll work with my daughter. She'll choose the targets, you destroy them. Simple. I'll give you a hundred large to ease any transitions."

A hundred thousand to give up his independence? Almost an insult. Karl began to stand up. "Thank you for the wine, Mr. Ricardi."

"Two hundred thousand, then," Alberto said, frowning. "And I'm very generous to those who work for me. There'll be other bonuses."

"Please, Karl." Maria reached out and touched his hand. She didn't flinch at the coolness of his skin.

He paused, smothering a twisted smile at Alberto Ricardi's tight-lipped reaction. But it was not for him. He would be happy to work job by job for the Ricardis, but he wouldn't be bound to anyone. Never again.

"No, thank you." He took a step toward the door.

"Alejandro Delgado sends his regards," Alberto said softly.

Vance stopped. "Where did you hear that name?"

"It was a message sent from Stefano Lucatti. They remember you. I've heard rumors Stefano had brought in a specialist, some Spaniard—posturing, I guessed. But from your face, I think there's something more."

Alejandro Delgado. May God damn him forever.

Karl smiled. No teeth, but Maria favored him with a piercing, evaluating look, and Alberto frowned as if a tame dog had suddenly growled back.

"If Delgado sends his regards," Karl said, "then I have little choice but to accept your offer."

Maria and Alberto raised their glasses in salute. Karl sat back down and raised his own.

Over three hundred years of blood between Delgado and Karl, and now Delgado had finally returned to Boston.

The hour had come to finish it.

Chapter Two:
Second Salvo

Maria had left messages on Karl Vance's voicemail all day long, until she could dial his number from memory. He finally returned her call an hour after dark, which left her none too pleased. Waiting was about as thrilling as plucking eyebrows.

"Meet me at Purple Shamrock," she said, fighting to keep the irritation out of her voice. Purple Shamrock was a club in Quincy Market. Nice and crowded and anonymous. "You know it?"

"Yes."

A thrill traveled up her skin at the sound of his voice, and she shook her head in annoyance at her reaction. He had one of those deep voices, dark almost, as if the words had weight in her ear. His voice had lingered in her mind long after their first meeting.

"Be there at ten thirty," she finished and hung up before he could read anything in the sound of her own words. She'd hate herself if she were developing some schoolgirl crush. This was all business. Business, dammit. He was a tool, a weapon, and she was here to aim him in the right direction.

She arrived early, waiting in the car a short distance from the club. Club goers surged back and forth in a long line waiting to be let in, while Maria watched bouncers sort through them like they were separating laundry—this one goes in, these two stay out, and on and on. Meanwhile others stumbled out of the club buzzing on alcohol and sex. She knew the feeling. She'd toured her share of clubs, including this one, often enough.

Be nice to dance for a while.

She could hear the bass beat whenever the club doors opened. The sound of overloud talking and laughter drifted like smoke to the car. Did Karl dance? Somehow, she couldn't picture it. Maybe the waltz or something. No, the tango...

She checked her watch. Ten thirty-five. Dammit.

The car door opened and Karl Vance slipped into the passenger seat of the Ford Taurus she'd borrowed for the night. The seats groaned against his dark leather jacket.

"You're late." She lit a cigarette. The flare of flame made the pupils of his blue eyes contract, and she suddenly had the image of some huge predatory cat staring at a solitary jungle campfire from the deepest shadows. She shook her head to clear it.

He smiled a little. "Your watch is fast."

"Doesn't matter. Did you bring anything? A tool?"

"Nothing," he said, looking at her closely. "You didn't say to come heavy."

"It doesn't matter. No shooting tonight, I hope to God. Just reconnaissance."

Vance turned to look out the windshield, evidently expecting her to get on with it. She tossed the cig, put her hand on the keys and then paused. It was strange. She'd felt something about him in the restaurant days ago, again, a kind of weight to him, as if his body had more density than any other object around. As if it had magnetism, gravity that drew and held the mind. And here it was again. Weird.

She turned the key and started the engine. Of course, there were rumors about him too. He was a mercenary Satanist doing side jobs to pay gambling debts and to collect blood for profane rituals. He was some ex-Navy SEAL who'd been court-martialed for killing his commander and had faded into the criminal underworld to escape justice. He'd been on the grassy knoll in Dallas. Some people would believe anything.

He glanced over at her and raised his eyebrows in silent question. He was very good looking in a European kind of way. A refreshing change after some of the yaks who worked for her father. Faces like the bottom side of a garbage can. And not to mention minds riveted on booze, tits and which rival they wanted to crease.

Well, it came with the territory.

But this Karl Vance was well spoken, when he actually bothered to speak. He'd been pretty damn abrupt so far tonight.

"Call me Maria and I'll call you Karl and we'll save time," she said.

"All right."

She pulled out into traffic, headed down Union Street to Lynde, leaving the burning smears of neon light behind. She hated to drive in silence, and the radio sucked in this piece of junk. So she'd make conversation. Great idea. Make the ride seem quicker.

"Where'd you go to school?" she asked.

He was quiet for so long she wasn't sure he'd answer. "What makes you think I'm a college boy?" he finally said.

"I heard you use words with more than two syllables at dinner. Not everyone in our line of work can do that."

He laughed. It was a surprisingly gentle sound. "Hard to get much past you. What did you say you studied?"

"I didn't say." She lifted her chin, glancing at him. "Accounting."

"I see how that could be useful," he said, and she grinned. No jokes about bean counters even. Score another point.

Karl resumed staring out the windows as they drove. She tried to think of something witty to say and couldn't. The streetlights flashed overhead in rhythmic pulses, and buildings cut dark shapes against the sky. Somewhere off to the south she could see a searchlight sweeping back and forth across the clouds. Some club no doubt.

A half hour later and far from the main arteries through the city, she edged the car to the curb and killed the lights. She unzipped a duffel bag she had in the backseat and brought out a Bushnell night vision scope.

She stared for a few minutes through the scope at the eerie, ghostly green world of light amplification. Katz Collision and Auto Body Repair had alley access with multiple garage bays. Joseph Katz ran the shop and paid twenty to thirty percent cuts directly to the Lucatti family on stripped parts. Frames were sold to a scrap yard also in the pay of the Lucattis—with no titles, of course—and crushed and shipped out to Japan. The Lucattis got a sip of that cream too.

She handed the scope to Karl, who took it without speaking. While he watched, she broke down the information she had on Katz Collision. She even knew which cop on the Auto Theft Division was on the payroll.

"So what do you want done?" he finally asked.

In the alley, a BMW Z4 M Roadster slid through the darkness with no headlights. A garage door rolled up, grinding and clattering, and the silhouettes of three men appeared briefly before the car slid inside and the bay door rattled shut again.

"I want Katz clipped. Make it a recognized hit—no body hiding, no creative dismemberment. Then burn the place to the cement."

"Security?"

"Some muscle off and on. The hired help might pitch in. Avoid them if you want," she said. "Or take them all out. It doesn't really matter as long as Katz dies and the place burns."

"When do you want it done?" Karl glanced at her and again she felt that heaviness of his gaze. It moved across her face like a lover's touch, slow and deliberate.

"As soon as you can."

"Then drop me off at Franklin Park. I have some business to attend to first."

"You'll be in contact?" she asked.

"You'll know when I'm done."

She considered demanding more, but something gave her pause, and her snappy reply died stillborn on her lips.

Strange.

She started the car and pulled slowly away from the curb, but she didn't turn her headlights on until she was half a block away. They made the trip to Franklin Park in silence. He left with a brief goodbye and the shadows seemed to swallow him.

Curiouser and curiouser.

Karl smelled the other vampire first. The stink of death was hidden beneath a mix of other scents—cinnamon, old blood, wet soil and a darker, more animal smell. The musk of the lion's den, of the stalking wolf pack, of the lone predator stealing through the jungle. Not a human scent by any stretch.

Karl closed his eyes and focused all his power and senses on the night. He hadn't returned home after his ride with Maria. Instead, he'd thought to touch base with a couple of contacts he'd made over the years and see if he could learn more about this war. Maybe hear things untouched by Ricardi slant. Things they didn't want him to know. He'd been on his way to Hyde Square to find a squealer called Little Ricky. And then, the scent...

There. He could sense the vampire a half mile, maybe more, to the southeast. If the vampire hadn't left a scent trail, Karl might not have noticed him. The vampire was partially shielding himself, so that in Karl's mind the sensation of him was a cold, black pulse sweeping across Karl's senses like radio waves from a pulsar. The partial shielding might have been enough to mask it from him at this distance, but the scent made Karl focus, and once he turned all his senses to finding the other vampire, there was little hope the flawed concealment would continue to mask it from him.

He set out toward the southeast, focusing in on that pulsing darkness. A young vampire, almost certainly. No experienced nightwalker would ever make so careless a mistake as to hunt without completely concealing his presence. Unless it was a trap.

It took only minutes to cover the distance, sprinting across rooftops and power and cable lines. He slowed down as the feel of the other vampire grew close. He could smell only the one—a male. Again, unless it was a trap. Scents, like that cold black presence, could be masked with skillful use of a vampire's powers.

Karl crouched at the edge of a large auto parts store above the twin security lights that blazed down into the adjacent parking lot of a chain motel. Anyone who glanced his way was likely to be light-blinded. The second vampire felt very close, hidden in the shadows somewhere in the half-filled parking lot. There were lampposts, but the arc-sodium lights cast pale orange pools that didn't push back the darkness very far.

He heard the high heels first. *Clack, clack, clack* on the asphalt. A jingle of keys, quickly silenced. Karl leaned forward, peering toward the sound. A moment later, a young woman came around the corner of the motel. She hurried along, increasing her pace. Her hair blazed a sunset of yellow and orange when she passed briefly under a lamppost, and he saw how pretty she was, how young. Nineteen, twenty at most, dressed in a dark suit that accented her figure, elegant and tasteful. She glanced left and right and behind her as she walked. Her keys glinted as they poked out from between her fingers. A cautious girl, and that was good, but keys wouldn't save her from what waited in the shadows.

Karl scanned the parking lot again, his vampire sight piercing all darkness. Nothing. But the sense of that other vampire was stronger than ever. He glanced at the young woman. Her face was the face of every girl who had mysteriously disappeared—of every girl he'd ever found pale and dead through the centuries.

He stood to his full height. Hundreds of smells continually flooded his senses, everything from the stink of death from the other vampire to the thick scent of spilled motor oil. A thousand sounds broke against him—the woman's heels striking the asphalt, the irritated buzz of a flickering light, traffic, someone cursing in Spanish, and in the distance, the long mournful howling of dogs. Perhaps that was what had made the woman cautious—the howling, a sound that shivered down the spine like an icy finger drawn slowly down the back.

There. The other vampire was crouched in the shadow of a black SUV. The vampire's pale red eyes glowed from the heart of the shadow, tracking the young woman with the greed of a lioness eyeing a gazelle.

Karl jumped from the roof of the auto-parts store, landed silently in a crouch and then sprinted toward the girl. When he moved this fast, the world scrolled in fast-forward in front of him, while the woman's movements were slow, advancing frame by frame.

The vehicles opposite her provided him plenty of cover as he slowed and changed direction, moving parallel to her. She hadn't seen him, he was certain of it, but she began to move faster. Her heels *clack-clack-clack-clacked* now, almost as fast as her heartbeat.

The woman would pass very near the SUV. Karl changed course again, cutting directly toward her, pushing himself harder, faster.

The other vampire saw Karl approaching his prey and his eyes flared a deeper red. His lips pulled back from his gleaming fangs. He crouched, gathering strength to spring.

From this close, Karl could smell the blood in the young woman's veins. Warm. Rushing through her body as her heart thundered away, life in liquid, a heart-blood sacrament.

The woman glanced back at Karl an instant before he reached her. Her eyes widened, poured full of sudden terror, and her mouth dropped open. The spiked fistful of keys came up. She drew in breath—he could hear it skating across her white, even teeth.

Karl launched himself past her and into the leaping vampire, driving him into the asphalt, rolling, tumbling, shoving a hand up under the vampire's chin to force back those striking fangs. He wrapped himself around the other vampire like a python.

The woman staggered backward a couple of steps, key-spiked fist still held high, her other hand lifted as if to push them away, back into the darkness from which they had come.

Karl looked her in the eyes. "Run," he said softly.

She kicked off her shoes—one spike-heeled pump sailed past like some strangely shaped bird and hit the side of the SUV with a clunk—and then she sprinted away as fast as any human he'd ever seen.

The vampire made another wrenching lunge toward her, trying to free himself of Karl's grip. Karl grappled with him, twisted around and shoved the vampire's arm upward at a vicious angle and heard bone shatter. The vampire grunted, writhed like a snake and tried to sink his teeth into Karl's throat. Karl drove his head forward, smashing his forehead into the vampire's lips, splitting them open. Thick black blood seeped out of his mouth.

The vampire twisted again, ripping its arm away. Karl felt the arm dislocate, but the vampire gave no sign of noticing. Karl shot out his other hand and seized the vampire's ankle.

"You fucking traitor," the vampire said, claws scrabbling on the asphalt as he tried to drag himself free. "She's mine!"

The vampire spun and lunged at him again. Karl punched him in the eye, rocking his head backward. The vampire shook his head, but finally yanked free of Karl's grip. With a snarl he was up and moving at vampire speed in the direction the woman had run. Karl sprinted after him, shot his hand out and seized the back of the vampire's neck.

The vampire thrashed as if he were a feral cat held by the scruff, desperate to bite Karl's hand. Karl spun, wrenching the vampire around, and hurled him into a cinderblock wall. The

29

vampire turned in midair. Instead of slamming into the wall headfirst, he impacted with his feet and launched himself back at Karl.

Karl dodged aside and slashed the vampire's face and body as the vampire flew past, opening that pale skin with his claws. The vampire shrieked, setting all the dogs to howling louder than ever. A moment later several lights came on in the motel rooms.

The vampire tumbled away, rolled to a crouch, and then stood slowly. The deep wounds in his face and chest seeped that stinking black blood. If Karl had brought one of his silver knives, this would've been over already. The hard way always took longer, and there was usually a bigger mess in the end.

Karl snapped his fingers, and all the surrounding arc-sodium lights went out, masking the parking lot in darkness. A touch showy, but what the hell. Newly spawned vampires were always impressed by that kind of tripe.

"Those fingernails of yours fucking sting," the vampire said. He was shorter than Karl, stockier, dressed in all in black. His ghostly pale hands and face seemed almost to glow against the night sky. Broad face, but his cheeks were flayed open and one lip hung in tatters, turning what might have been a plain face on a human into a grotesque nightmare on a vampire.

"Where's Delgado?" Karl asked.

"Never mind him. That bitch was *mine.*"

Karl considered him. "What do they call you?"

"Farrell." Big grin, showing off his teeth. "I'm a nasty bastard."

"No doubt."

Farrell heard the contempt in his voice. "You fucking kill-stealing piece of *shit.* They told me about you."

"Who told you?" Karl took a step toward him. To his credit, Farrell didn't back away.

"The Master told me. He tells all his children about the Traitor." Farrell began to laugh—an empty, echoing cackle that might have come from a crazy old man. "The Master has plans for you."

"Care to share?"

"And ruin the surprise? Not even." Farrell laughed again, and this time a gush of black blood hit the asphalt, splashing across the yellow parking lines. The dark blood steamed, but Karl knew that if he were to touch it, it would feel cold, like ice. Farrell stared at the splash of blood and frowned.

"Doesn't feel so nice to bleed out, does it?" Karl said.

"Why ain't I healing?" Not quite a plea, but the bravado was gone.

Karl smiled. "Your Master didn't teach you much. Supernatural wounds don't heal quickly." He waved a dismissive hand. "You may start to grovel for your ersatz existence at any time."

"Fuck you."

"Not the most eloquent last words ever, but since you don't get a tombstone, I guess it doesn't matter."

The smell of sudden fear. It poured off Farrell—a prey smell that had Karl's lips peeling back to reveal his own fangs in anticipation.

"I just wanted to eat—"

"She was innocent."

"What are you, a fucking superhero? The Master said you—"

"It doesn't matter what he said. I'll slaughter all his children and then cut out his silent heart." Karl paused, cocking his head. "I'm sure Delgado mentioned that we don't get along...?"

Farrell stepped backward. His eyes flicked around the empty parking lot. Sirens had begun to wail in the distance, and they joined with the howls of the dogs, filling the air with a soundtrack for the end of the world.

The glow in Farrell's eyes had lost some of its shine. "I got friends on the way."

"Not in time," Karl said, almost sadly.

Karl stepped toward him again. Farrell raised his hands and moved back. "I never hurt that girl."

"It doesn't matter."

"Come on, man." Frantic now. "A guy has to eat."

"I wonder how your blood will taste? No matter how sour I find vampire blood, I always relish it far more than human blood."

Farrell suddenly held his ground and his claws cut black crescents out of his fingers. Then he tensed, cocked his head

31

slightly, as if listening to a voice Karl couldn't hear. Was Delgado giving his endangered servant a last message?

The sirens drew closer.

The distant look in Farrell's eyes vanished. He smiled at Karl and then laughed.

"You act like a savior," Farrell said, "but you're really just another killer, just like us. You feed on the cattle just the same."

Karl said nothing. Watching. Waiting for the play.

"You can't save anyone," Farrell continued. "Not the humans. Not yourself. The Master is laughing at you, Traitor. You—the deluded death angel doing the Lord's work. The Master killed all your friends. And he wants you to know that now he's here for you."

Farrell hurled himself at Karl, slashing with his claws and snapping with his fangs, driving Karl back. Karl dodged aside from one flurry of strikes, but found himself with his back to another large SUV. When Farrell attacked again, Karl slipped under a swipe that would have flayed him from shoulder to shoulder. Instead it sliced a deep gouge in the side of the SUV and sent a splash of sparks raining to the asphalt. The SUV's alarm began to wail.

Karl launched himself up out of his crouch. He swung both hands upward, and his claws hissed like arrowheads as they cut through the air and into Farrell's undead flesh. Cold blood flowed over his fingers.

Farrell staggered to the side, clutching the wounds, his face a pale mask of agony.

The sirens were very near—discovery very close.

Karl moved in, drawing back his arm to sever the other vampire's head from his shoulders. Farrell locked eyes with him. His red eyes flared, like laser points.

Farrell hurled himself forward, mouth wide, claws reaching for Karl's throat. Karl leapt to meet him head-on. Farrell twisted aside before they collided, swiping his black claws at Karl's eyes.

Karl's counterstrike was too fast to see, but he felt the shock of resistance as his claws sliced home. He landed behind Farrell, turned his head and looked over his shoulder to where the other vampire stood very still. No sound came from Farrell's lips, only a gurgle instead, like air in drainpipes. Farrell's head toppled backward off his neck. Black blood bubbled from his throat and poured slowly down his chest, smoking when it pattered to the asphalt.

Karl spun around and drove his clawed hand into the other vampire's torso from behind. He seized the icy cold and utterly still heart in his hand and squeezed. The heart exploded. Farrell's body convulsed, and began to disintegrate into black motes, like onyx snowflakes. They swirled away in the wind, changing again into gray ash before disappearing. Nothing was left. Even the blood spatter had smoked and vanished.

The vampire's words drifted back into his mind: *The Master is laughing at you, Traitor... You can't save anyone.*

Tonight, at least, he had saved one.

Red and blue lights flashed across the parking lot. Police cars roared into the lot so quickly they rocked on their springs and their tires screeched.

Karl turned and fled as fast as he could, cloaking himself in shadows, wrapping himself in the night. No reason to bother with the church. No point in praying for the soul of a vampire.

Chapter Three:
Internal Politics

Maria was dreaming of the ocean, standing on black sand and staring at waves gently curling under a brilliant sun, when her cell phone began blaring Black Sabbath's "War Pigs". It had been so damn amusing a week ago when she'd downloaded it, but now it destroyed her dream beach like a napalm strike. She lifted her head to find that she'd drooled on her pillowcase. Attractive.

"Yeah," she managed to say into the phone. She sat up in bed and immediately regretted it as her head threatened to implode. She hadn't gotten in until after two last night. It had better be Karl Vance telling her that Katz was dead.

"Maria," a calm voice said. Not Karl.

"Who is this?"

"It's John."

John Passerini. Underboss of the family. Shit.

"Is my father okay?" she asked. John had never called her on her cell before.

"He's fine." John's voice was flat, almost emotionless. He'd talked that way as far back as she could remember. Angry, happy, bored—all the same even tone. "Nothing to worry about. But I want to see you. If you have time."

Implying that she should make time. An easy thing to resent, but Passerini couldn't be ignored. She was due to reconcile her father's books today, but that could wait. Really all she was doing was waiting for a single phone call. But not John's.

"Sure, John. Where?"

"I'm taking my kids to the aquarium today. If you could meet me there in..." He paused, and she could imagine him glancing at his Rolex. "An hour, that would be great."

That gave her less than twenty minutes to get ready and out the door. Rush hour was over, but with all the construction downtown, getting to the aquarium that quickly would be iffy.

Like she had much of a choice.

"I'll be there," she said, and hurried for the shower.

She made it, but barely. Road construction was a bitch—the Big Dig was a plague from God on Massachusetts. Atlantic Avenue was down to one lane, and she considered driving her Mercedes off Long Wharf to end her misery.

She hated to leave her car in a public parking lot, but she had little choice. At least getting her parking validated at the aquarium would offset the plundering a bit. Parking lots... She had to get into that racket. Pay an attendant minimum wage to collect the ridiculous rates and watch the cash roll in. A nice source of legitimate income for herself and her father if she set it up right.

There she went again, her mind wandering off in every direction. The call from John had upset her more than she wanted to admit.

More cash to get inside the aquarium. He couldn't just meet her in the Common? She glanced around for John Passerini but didn't see him on the ground floor. Son of a bitch.

She paused at the rail above the rock formations and illuminated pools where penguins frolicked. A woman in a wetsuit was giving a speech to an elementary school class clustered around the glass rails. Aside from the class, the place was mostly empty, the few families and couples inside were spread out along the walls of tanks. So much the better. At first she'd thought John nuts to pick so public a place for their walk and talk, but perhaps she'd been wrong. It was random, impossible for the feds to wiretap on short notice, lots of ambient noise, lots of space.

So what did he want?

They called John Passerini "The Cleaver" because he came from a long line of butchers, not because it was his weapon of choice or anything. Her father had made him underboss eleven years ago, back when a RICO indictment against Stefano

Lucatti had sufficiently weakened their hold to allow the Mancino and Ricardi families to make some headway. Boston wasn't New York. There wasn't enough room for two families, much less three. The Mancinos and Ricardis had allied against the Lucattis, and aided by the silence of the New York families who were dealing with RICO indictments of their own, they managed to hold their own. Until Stefano Lucatti beat the RICO rap on a hung jury and turned his attention to wiping out the Mancinos.

She'd been a teenager back then, more concerned with the phone and music than the machinations of all the men who often gathered at her house, talking to her father in the den. She couldn't even remember when that hard look had settled into her father's eyes. To her, it had always been there.

Maria turned back to the penguins and leaned against the glass rail. A penguin flapped its stubby wings, cocked its head, and shot into the water like a black bullet.

She'd never been "made", of course—that wasn't for women, God bless testosterone-influenced thinking—but she guessed she qualified as a high-ranking associate. Technically, even the greenest soldier in the Ricardi family outranked her, and that was bullshit. But the fact that she was the only daughter of the Boss of the family gave her leverage. Her skill with money gave her more.

Still, this thing with Karl Vance would punch her card forever—if she handled it right. It had taken a long time to bring her father around to agreeing in the first place, and now, she suspected John Passerini—Mr. Butcher's Boy himself—wanted her to stop.

Like hell.

And where the hell was he anyway? She glanced at her watch. He had to be here by now. Maybe he'd arrived ahead of her. She began to walk around, looking for him.

A huge cylindrical tank several stories high rose through the center of the aquarium, filled with fish and plants and rocks. She found John standing on the ramp, watching the fish circle endlessly. He turned toward her as she approached around the wide curve of the ramp. His skin was olive Mediterranean, with thick black hair graying at the temples and disconcertingly intelligent eyes. He wore dark slacks and a charcoal gray Brioni suit jacket. His shoes were leather

Salvatore Ferragamo loafers. He was alone and way overdressed.

"Where's the rest of the family?" she asked.

"Tide pools. The kids wanted to touch something slimy."

"So what's on your mind?"

John stared at her, put his hands in his pockets and frowned.

"I heard from your father," he said after a moment. "He decided to let you get your own hands slimy."

Look at that. She was fucking psychic. "And of course you disapprove."

He turned back to the fish. A particularly ugly one cruised past—something that looked as if it had been hit with a shovel. Several times.

"Why can't you be happy with what you have?" he asked. "This isn't some fucking game."

"How many times have I heard that before? Everyone's all chuckles as long as I'm making them money and keeping my mouth shut. But the moment I want to *do* something, it's all about keeping the womenfolk safe."

"If you play, you're a target. No one wants to see you hurt."

She laughed. A mother and two young kids walked past, headed up the curving ramp. Maria kept silent until they were gone, staring instead at the massive skeleton of a whale hanging from the ceiling, dangling out into space.

"You don't care if I'm hurt," she finally said. "What do you really want?"

His tone never changed, sounding almost indifferent to someone who didn't know better.

"That's not fair," he said. "I've known you since you were a little girl. You have a talent—you make us legal money hand over fist. Is there anyone else in the family who can do that as well as you? No. But there are plenty of wiseguys who can pull a trigger."

"Bullshit. I'm not a fucking bird in a cage. If we don't stop the Lucattis, they'll crush us. It's only a matter of time."

"And you're the only one who can stop them, that it? You gotta show you have balls? You wanna make your bones here? I would've worn cheaper shoes if I'd have known there'd be so much bullshit."

"Don't throw that at me." She had to work to keep her voice down. More fish circled, slicing through the water like swords. "We're talking about the fucking future of the family, John. It's all hands on deck, break out the mattresses. If we win, Boston's ours. You think we've been making good money in the last five years? Imagine if we double or even triple it."

"You were always too bright for your own good. Bright enough to get yourself into trouble. Your father told me how you blackmailed your way into the family. He was so fucking pissed, but he ended up laughing about it too. Proud of you."

She didn't know what to say to that so she kept quiet. He didn't look as if he were paying her a compliment.

"A man in my position has to be practical. What do you think it'll do to your father if something, God forbid, should happen to you?"

She heard the unspoken. Her brother was already dead. Her mother's death was a vague memory, but her brother's death still had that rubbed-raw pain that burned worst in the long stretch between two a.m. and dawn.

Bastard. Using that against her.

"I don't want to stand on the sidelines," she said. "I want to play a role in bringing down the Lucattis."

His eyes hardened. "I'll fucking repeat myself for you. What do you want to prove? That you're tough? You looking to earn your stripes? Earn that button?" He shook his head in disgust. "You'll never be made. I'd have thought that would be clear enough by now, but I guess I'll have to spell it out. You're not going to be the one running this family when your father's gone."

"Well, fuck you. My brother would have been, and I'm better than he was. Smarter. Why shouldn't I?"

"I'm next in line," he said, softly.

"Only if the captains raise you up. If I'm making them the most money, I think they'll follow their wallets."

"Naïve, Maria. They'll never follow a woman."

"Is that all you wanted, John?" She stabbed her words at him as if she were thrusting with a dagger. "Big fucking masquerade about caring for my safety when you really want to make certain your own rising star has a clear path."

"You're irrational."

"You're an asshole."

They stared at each other for a long moment.

"I've said what I had to say." John shook his head. "It's a mistake, letting a girl try her hand in this. Bringing in an outside gun is another mistake. I'd hoped you would be reasonable."

"You threatening me now?" Her heart began to beat even harder and she had to force herself to keep breathing slowly. She'd love to be able to laugh off a threat from John Passerini. Unfortunately, that had never proved wise to anyone.

For once his tone dropped that strange flat quality. His words were softer, and he even gave her a small smile. "No, Maria. We both want what's best for this family."

"What's *best* for the family is taking Boston for ourselves. Let's not get distracted by petty bullshit."

She turned away before he could answer and left him standing in front of the thick aquarium glass, as swarms of circling fish swam by, all empty eyes and silence.

Maria fumed all the way to the parking garage. She'd known it was there, that fucking misogynistic, patriarchal bullshit, but this was the first time anyone had called her out. And it had to be John, one of the most influential men in the family.

Dammit.

She picked up her phone to call Karl and then put it down. Ten minutes later it was back in her hand and she had dialed his number. She let it ring twice before she hung up. Get a grip. He'd said he would tell her when he was done. She had to delegate.

Be a lot easier if she were doing things herself. Then she'd know right away.

That was a stupid thought. Her, doing wet work...

She dialed his number again and got his voicemail. Did he never answer his fucking phone? She left a message for him to call immediately and hung up. She needed the Katz thing done as quickly as possible. She needed some success to bring to the table, otherwise, she might just find herself frozen out of the inner circle completely.

Karl Vance knelt beside a weather-stained air conditioning unit and looked down on the closed bay doors of Katz Collision and Auto Body Repair. The air had bite to it tonight; there'd be autumn frost before the dawn. He kept crouched down to avoid cutting a silhouette against the stars. Dawn was ten hours, forty-seven minutes away. Plenty of time.

Two days had passed since he had killed that sireling of Delgado's. Two days since he had sat in Maria's car outside the chop shop and sensed the heat of her blood through her skin and kept himself in line by will alone.

Focus.

The fact that she had left him six increasingly irritated messages didn't help. He hadn't returned her calls yet—had left the cell at the apartment, in fact. No distractions.

This particular job was all the distraction he could tolerate. Wasting time stalking some nobody when Alejandro Delgado was out there somewhere. The Ricardis had no idea what they were up against, but he couldn't tell them and they wouldn't believe. The irony had that sharp twang that made it perfect.

Katz was inside. Karl had seen the man enter earlier and the face matched the picture Maria had handed him, dragging jowls and all. Three other men were inside, dismembering cars. He could hear the hiss and burn of acetylene torches and the grinding shriek of metal cutters. He counted three distinct voices, plus Katz, despite the rap music booming in the garage area. They were alternately bitching about the Red Sox and bragging about women.

Hunger awakened within him, making his skin feel as if it were pierced by a million cold needles from the inside out. He hadn't fed since de Carlo. He'd been burning too much power lately—he'd need to feed again, soon.

Karl slid through the shadows and climbed down the cinderblock wall, making no sound. He could have flooded the alley with fog to cover his movement—there was enough moisture in the air tonight. But fog was a trifle too...Hollywood.

He crossed the alley so quickly and quietly he didn't even startle the stray cats feasting out of the dumpster behind the deli. He halted and crouched down at the chain-link fence surrounding the shop yard. Atop the fence, the concertina wire glittered coldly, hungry for the softness of flesh.

With a leap, he bounded to the top of the fence, placing a

booted foot in a small section of unprotected fence top, and launched himself over the wire. A cloud of dust billowed out from his feet when he touched down on the other side, but his impact made scarcely a sound. He paused, listening to the night. Nothing out of the ordinary.

The inside yard made for easy maneuvering with so many cars parked close together and loads of sheet metal, frames and rims stacked in columns or dumped in haphazard piles. There were pallets with dozens of 55-gallon drums, rust speckling their rims, but when Karl had unscrewed the bungs he'd found they were empty. Near one garage rose an uneven pyramid of five-gallon pails that had once held some kind of ketone or thinner.

The back wall of the yard was built of cinderblock and not chain-link. Vehicles were parked inside a secondary fence whose rolling gate had a locking mechanism protected by hardened steel plates. He noted an Acura, two Audis and a dirty yellow Hummer, among others. These were parked too far from the shop to be damaged by any fire he set, and he didn't have time to deal with them.

He moved to the generator near the side of the shop. Here they stored two ten-gallon cans of gasoline. He'd discovered them last night, and it was always better to use tools on site rather than bring his own. One can was full, one was half-full. He set them below the ledge of a window so caked with grime that direct sunlight probably couldn't penetrate.

He snapped the lock on a window in the front office area and slipped inside. He used a small bit of his power to dampen the sound of the breaking lock, even though it likely couldn't be heard with the hip-hop thumping away in the back of the shop. One of the men—a Latino, by the accent—was rapping away in time with the rapid-fire words. From the shadows of the darkened office he could see into the garage area. Cigarette smoke curled beneath the overhead lamps and the hanging trouble lights. The smells of sweat, engine oil and anti-freeze hung thick in the air, while in the office area, the stink of cigarettes had long since mated itself to the worn brown carpet.

An orange trapezoid of light fell on the floor from an open office door to his left. From inside, Karl could hear the *scritch scritch* of a pen across paper.

He paused at the threshold, just out of sight. Listening.

One heartbeat. Breathing, somewhat emphysemic. He merged with the shadows of the hall and looked past the threshold.

Joseph Katz tossed a sheet of paper into his out box and then turned the page in a ledger. His skin was yellowed, like the nicotine-stained walls, and sagged from his face as if weary of clenching tight to his skull. His eyes were tired hound-dog eyes.

Karl leapt so quickly that Joseph Katz's mind wouldn't have registered more than a blur of movement. Karl wrenched him out of his creaking chair and pinned him against the wall by his neck.

Terror played in the man's eyes. He stared at Karl and his throat convulsed as he fought to pull in air to scream. But the action was futile. Karl was crushing his windpipe.

The smell of the blood in the man's veins made Karl's fangs tingle. He struck like a rattler, fangs sinking deep, the taste of blood so savory upon his tongue. He used his powers to fog Katz's mind and soothe his pain to nothing. It was the least he could do.

When he was done he set the body down gently. He pulled out his knife and paused, staring at the corpse, so pale now, a human-shaped cicada shell. The twin holes where he'd stolen the man's life seemed to stare back like mocking eyes. He knelt, crushing the knife hilt in his hand, and cut up the area of Joseph Katz's neck where his fangs had punctured. Damn the advent of Crime Scene Units.

Another soul to pray for.

The cans of gasoline sat below the window ledge where he'd left them. He drenched Katz's body, then moved on to the file cabinets, and from there he ran a gasoline trail to the area in the shop where paint was stored. He flipped open a book of matches, lit the whole matchbook and tossed it at the pool of gasoline. The heat wrapped itself around him as he turned to go, his ears full of the greedy roar of the fire.

He walked out through the garage. The three men—all young, stripped down to dirty white muscle shirts and grease-stained jeans—eyed him with surprise and suspicion as he walked past. He dulled their aggression and heightened the shadow of fear, making them hesitate, confused. He held the button for the bay door and waited until it rattled all the way up.

"There's a fire, gentlemen." He nodded back toward the

office door. The fire's roar could now be heard over the music. "I'd haul ass if I were you."

"Who the fuck are *you*?" demanded the young Latino—the rapper in training.

Karl didn't answer. He stepped out the door and vanished from the light, just as the paint cans began to explode.

Chapter Four:
Crosshairs on a Mule

Maria sipped her wine. Chateau Margaux, 1995. The color was almost black, but the taste was smooth and vibrant. She'd just slipped below the froth of suds in the tub, and the water jets pulsed against her skin. A single maroon candle burned on a gold plate near her feet, with rose petals strewn about the rim. Beyond the penthouse windows, Boston reclined in a glittering spread of lights, the ring of lights atop the Prudential Center glowing like a halo over downtown.

She laid her head back and closed her eyes.

Another long day.

An image of Karl Vance floated into her mind. That cool Northern European gaze. Eyes that would be frightening on the other side of a gun sight. Dangerous. She liked that.

Of course, the prick hadn't returned any of her messages so far, which made her want to punch him in one of those cool Northern European eyes. Bastard.

Maybe he'd lost his phone. Maybe he was dead. Not likely, given his reputation, and besides, that wasn't a possibility she really wanted to consider. She had to reserve judgment until she had the facts. If she were ever going to lead, she had to learn to keep her head. Especially when dealing with the egos of dangerous men.

Normally Daddy didn't let her play with the dangerous toys, but since her brother had been killed, her father had been a little more permissive. John Passerini had accused her of blackmailing her way in, but that was hardly true. Daddy had agreed only when she'd shown him what she could do with money, and right away he'd set her to work on the books—hide the money from the feds, create dummy corporations, incorporate, dissolve, merge, buy, sell, shelter, launder, and always—always—turn a profit.

It was a hell of a thing getting a leg up only because her brother Paul slammed his car into a concrete pylon. Asshole. She still missed him, even after all this time. Now there was no trueborn Ricardi male to head the family after her father.

She was only a girl.

Never mind that she had plans to make Boston rival New York for syndicate incomes. Never-fucking-mind that. She was only a girl. Good for screwing and raising kids. Little else. Except maybe clearing the table and serving Sambuca. Well, fuck them.

Her cell phone rang. "Witch" by Cold for her ring tone this time. A surge of adrenaline shot through her like some endocrine lightning bolt. She snatched the phone up and flipped it open.

"It's done," that deep, almost lazy, voice said from the other end. It sent a thrill of desire through her that started at the bottom of her spine and rode its way up.

"Took long enough." It was a fight to keep the excitement out of her voice.

She let the silence spin out until she couldn't stand it anymore. "Look, I'm glad it's done. Good work. Why didn't you return my calls?"

"I'm returning them now," he said. "You sounded as if you wanted updates. There's no better update than success."

"Do me a favor and answer next time, so I don't think you're dead in a trunk somewhere, okay?" She really just wanted to get up and dance on the edge of the tub. Imagine the look on the capos' faces when she brought in word of her success. Leverage against John Passerini and anyone else who thought her involvement a worthless eccentricity of her father's—priceless.

"Anyway," she continued. "Excellent work, but we can't stand around slapping each other's backs all day. There's a lot more to do, and we're on a tight schedule."

"No rest for the wicked." Now he sounded amused.

"I want you to meet me here." She found herself speaking before she'd even realized it, as if her body had reached up and wrenched control of her tongue away from her mind. "You know where I live?"

There was another very long pause.

"No," he said finally. "Tell me."

She quickly gave him the address. After she hung up, she called the front desk to let the doorman know that someone would be coming by to see her. Then she lay back in her bath to enjoy a few last minutes of peace.

He arrived sooner than she expected—she'd barely dressed herself when his knock sounded at the door. The smell of soap and perfume scented the air. She hoped he liked it.

You'd better know what you're doing.

Of course she did.

She considered lighting a few strategically placed candles and then decided that was three steps way too overboard. No need to come across as desperate.

When she checked the door's peephole she found Karl Vance standing outside in a perfectly cut, dark Caraceni suit and pale yellow silk tie, hands in his pockets, and staring right back at her, as though he were aware of her presence behind the door. That rattled her a bit. She couldn't exactly say why.

She let him in and told him to make himself comfortable on the couches, but instead of sitting, he followed her to the bar area where she poured them each a glass of wine. He moved with the grace of some predatory animal, wolf or panther maybe, and his feet made no whisper on the carpet—a strange thing for her to notice, but notice it she did.

"So what are these ideas you're so eager to share?" he asked, sipping the wine and then nodding as if he approved of the taste.

"All we ever talk about is business."

A ghost of a smile graced his lips. "I thought that's why you asked me here."

"It was. But now that you're here, I want to discuss something more interesting." She smiled at him over the rim of her glass. "So tell me about yourself, Mr. Vance."

"Is this a belated job interview?"

"Let's just say it's professional courtesy."

That intense blue-eyed gaze fixed on her. She thought

about all the people whose last sight had been those eyes and she had to suppress a shudder. And damned if she wasn't getting turned on.

"What do you want to know?" he asked softly.

"Everything. I learn by listening, and if there's one thing a good leader needs, it's the ability to listen."

"And the ability to judge the truth of what she hears."

"Who wants truth? I'll settle for clever flattery."

He smiled, took another sip from his glass and moved over to one of the windows. The shades were open to the glittering city below, and he glanced back at her. "A beautiful view. I always love looking down on a night-covered city."

"See? That's what I mean. That's the kind of thing you can tell me about."

"If I weren't mistaken, I'd think that inviting me here to discuss 'business' was just a cover." He turned from the window and walked toward her. Had she commented on how gracefully he moved before? Oh, right. Several times.

She lifted her chin toward him. "And what if it was just a cover?"

He leaned in very close. She could feel the hunger in his gaze, searing across her skin like a striking match. "Then I'd have to ask why a cover was needed at all."

His lips touched hers, softly, almost teasingly. She tilted her head up farther and pressed closer to him. His lips and his skin were surprisingly cool to the touch, nearly cold, but she didn't draw away. The kiss became more insistent, deeper. Desire, the same desire that had been an ember when she'd hung up the phone, now burned with new heat, and her skin felt shockingly warm against his, like fire meeting ice.

Her cell phone rang.

She pulled away from him. "Son of a bitch." Breaking contact with Karl cleared her head a bit, and she was none too sure if that was what she wanted.

"Ignore it," Karl suggested.

"It could be business." She stopped and corrected herself. "It had *better* be business at this time of night."

She flipped open her phone. "This better be good."

"Oh, it's good, you spoiled little bitch."

Roberto Pulani, her half-brother. Beautiful.

"Well, I guess being a bastard doesn't help with your manners," Maria said and hurried from the room. She could feel Karl's gaze on her back, and it was too piercing for comfort. "What do you want?"

"I hear *Daddy's* letting you play in the sandbox with the boys."

"Seems to be on everyone's mind lately. So what?"

"As if you'd earned the honor."

One thing she could say about Roberto Pulani—he wasn't two faced. He hated her and had no reservations about showing it. It had gotten him into no end of trouble with their father, but did that make Roberto behave? Hardly.

"What? I didn't make you enough money on that Wendell thing? Or is your dick just that much shorter than mine?"

Pulani laughed. It sounded as if someone had taken steel wool to a silver plate. "Fuck you, sis. But since you're playing now, I think there's something you should know."

"And that would be?"

"One of Barzetti's dealers ended today with two new holes that God never gave him."

"I'm crying inside, I swear," she said. "His loss of revenue will be sorely missed."

"I'll send his family your sympathies. He's only been a loyal associate for fifteen years, but what the fuck would you care about that, right?"

"Dealers are maggots. They flip the minute things get iffy."

"My mistake for thinking you'd care about anything besides yourself," Roberto said. "Make that yourself and your new toy. I won't even talk about how that's wasted money, cuz he doesn't even fucking earn for us, for God's sake, since I know he's good. I will say Vance's wasted on your little piddly-shit diversions. You should stick to partying and blowing Dad's money."

"Do you have something to say, Rob, or did you just call to be an asshole?"

"Yeah, I got something to say. I called to tell you to hang it up. Your little power play's not gonna impress anybody. And as for your little toy," menace growled in his words, "I'd have a real fucking problem if I'm still waiting to be upped and they bring in some motherfucker who isn't even Italian. So you just tell him to watch whose pool he pisses in."

She snapped the phone shut with unsteady hands. Typical that he could get her fur standing up. He'd been doing so since they were young.

"Who was that?" Karl asked, watching her from the doorway. For a moment she'd forgotten he was there.

"Roberto Pulani. My bastard half-brother. His whore mother should've drowned him when he was a puppy." She pulled open the fridge door with enough force to knock over all the mustard and salad dressing bottles in the door. Dammit. "Why my father tolerates him is a mystery to me."

"I've heard of Pulani. His mother was really a whore?"

She shrugged. Why was there never anything good to eat when you needed it? Like tiramisu, for example. She could go for about twenty pounds of the stuff right about now. "His mother was a stripper. He has a complex about it. Also has an incredible complex about not having Ricardi on the end of his name. Tried to have it changed to Ricardi when he was sixteen but Father crushed that hope real quick."

Karl touched her shoulder. Warmth spread through her from that touch, like the feeling of sliding between flannel sheets on a cold New England night. Strange that his touch could bring such a tactile image to her mind. It calmed her and soothed her, but it didn't bring back the desire that had burned in her earlier or the joy she'd felt at learning of her success against Katz. Roberto had pretty much killed both.

She grabbed a beer out of the fridge—screw the wine—and stepped away from Karl. He didn't pursue. Lucky her. Hit man Karl Vance was a gentleman down to his socks.

He glanced out the window, almost as if he were watching for something, and he walked out of the kitchen back into the large central living room.

"I'd better go," he said. "Do you have another job for me?"

Back to business then. "I do. The Lucattis have a mule named Francisco Cabrera. I need him dead."

He quirked that half smile at her. "No offense, but a mule? A little low down the food chain for what you're paying me."

"Actually, I'll be the one to estimate the value of our targets, thank you. And for your information, he's moved millions in Columbian marching powder for the Lucattis. Never been caught. No criminal record. As cold under stress as a four-day-old corpse. He's an utterly reliable source of income." She took

49

a long swig of the beer, and then picked up a photo and a sticky note from her desk and handed them to Karl. "Cabrera's address."

Karl watched her, his face without expression. "How do you know this is the right address?"

"I picked one at random out of the phone book."

Karl gave her the barest trace of a smile.

"He has to be done quickly," she continued, "before he heads across the border again. Remember, my goal is to disrupt income streams, not kill figureheads or do any macho grandstanding bullshit. This is business."

Karl peered closely at the grainy photo before slipping it and the address into his pocket. "Business then. I'll get it done quickly."

"Give me a day and time."

Irritation flashed across his face before fading again into his usual unreadable expression. She knew she was pushing it. Risky to push a man used to working as his own boss, but she had to establish some kind of control. Maybe if she'd slept with him, the request would have come off sounding softer and easier to swallow. Maybe not. Vance was hard to read. And she certainly couldn't try to seduce him now.

"I'll go tomorrow night and if things look good, I'll do it then. I can't give you a time."

"Can't or won't?"

He looked at her as if she were a spoiled little child. She had to fight to keep meeting his gaze.

"Can't."

"Fine," she said. "I'll look to hear from you tomorrow night then. Call me when it's done—no matter what time." No doubt he thought her controlling—a micromanager who couldn't delegate responsibility.

It was actually much simpler. She wanted to watch him work.

Karl Vance came in through the balcony slider. Xiesha was there to greet him with a thick, clean towel and a bowl filled with cold water. Part of him wanted solitude after the long night, but he merely smiled at Xiesha and said nothing. The coffin brought solitude enough.

He washed his hands and splashed water on his face. It would be a hell of a funny thing if someday she brought him holy water for this ritual.

But after seventy-five years, you had to trust a bit. Besides, she could kill him at any time during daylight hours if she desired. And why the hell were his thoughts taking these twisted turns anyway? Why was betrayal on his mind?

"Did you meet with your little mafia princess?" Xiesha asked.

"Don't remind me."

That brought a smile to her beautiful face. She had her hair up in a bun tonight, pinned with decorative chopsticks. Blue kimono this time, with bright pink cherry blossoms spiraling around it. There were times when he almost forgot she wasn't human. Of course, the fact that she gave off absolutely no heat image to his sight, nor scent of blood (nor any scent at all, other than her Sandalwood perfume) was always pretty telling.

"So you are no longer attracted to her?"

"Who said anything about attraction?"

Again the smile. "The stress patterns in your voice whenever you speak of her. They show it clearly."

"Stress patterns? Perhaps I regret agreeing to work for her."

She ignored that. "I think I approve of a distraction for you. We've spent too many years either hunting or fleeing Delgado, to the exclusion of everything else."

Karl tossed the towel aside and sat in the leather chair. "Delgado will eventually make a mistake."

"I hope so. The last mistake was ours."

"The Mancinos were out of their league," he said. "The Ricardis are stronger. And this time, I'll make certain I get to Delgado before he gets to me."

"And that's why you're siding up with the little mafia princess? She will point us toward Delgado?"

"We hurt the Lucattis enough and they'll send him out."

"Good. Then you can show him who is truly worthy to inherit Cade's title. It will be you. You killed Cade."

An image surfaced in his mind. Master Cade pinned to church ground with a silver stake through each hand, that blue fire eating away at him as the sky in the east slowly grew lighter and lighter. Cade shrieking curses at him—for betraying him, for fighting him, for killing him—between screams of agony.

Delgado hadn't felt any gratitude for the freedom brought by the death of their master. That stirred another memory—Karl's friend, John Avalon, dying beneath the blade of Alejandro Delgado. John's scream as Delgado severed his head, his wail as his body began to disintegrate, stripping away like sand from the top of a dune when the wind blew. A sight that never left him, and sounds that never grew completely quiet.

"If I spoke inappropriately," Xiesha said, "then I beg pardon."

"You know I never sought the title of Master."

"I know you hate the sound of it. I also understand that a true master needs no brood of sirelings to lay claim to the name."

"No more on that," Karl said. "Nothing's changed."

Xiesha bowed. "As you wish. I have other ill news."

"What now?"

"The Highcrest account is frozen. I tried to access it this morning and received notification."

The FBI and probably Interpol or the EU banking commission again. They had cost him millions in account seizures, and it was difficult to contest, considering he wasn't technically alive. He gave Xiesha a wry smile that she probably didn't understand. They didn't empty the accounts, they only froze access, which made the money just as unattainable. Ryan Highcrest was the false name on the account. It wasn't a large account at least, but things had been tight recently. Prior to this war, the Ricardis had been using their own talent to complete jobs, so cash had been scarce, and he had to pay rent on two places in Boston and another in Cambridge—bolt holes and safe houses in case this apartment was ever compromised.

"Amusing that the war on terror is costing me so much money." Maybe he should have Maria Ricardi set him up something less vulnerable to seizure.

"I'm glad you find it amusing."

"I don't. But it has that certain ironic tang to it that I have to admire."

"I see," she said, but he knew she probably didn't. Sometimes she had trouble with more subtle human concepts like irony or *schadenfreude*.

"Anything else, Xiesha?" He was already turning his mind to this hit on the mule. The question really was—how much trust did he have in Maria's plan?

"Nothing else. May the rest of your night give peace." Xiesha bowed slightly again and withdrew down the hall to her room. He heard the door latch shut and quiet descended like sudden snowfall. Outside his window, Boston glimmered in its night finery.

How long until Delgado showed himself? How much did Maria know about Delgado? Her father knew enough to prod Karl into joining the Ricardis, certainly, but did either of them realize what a threat Delgado was to their family? And why had she been so eager for Karl to give her a specific time for killing Cabrera?

Too many questions.

He heard the baby in the apartment next door wake and begin to wail, piercing the silence, and he found himself grateful instead of annoyed. He sat and listened to the mother soothe the child and wondered about the man Maria had fingered for him to kill.

Frank Cavallo was an asshole. He'd been that way since Maria was a kid. He ran the crew that boasted such fine specimens of humanity as her half-brother Roberto Pulani and Mickey "The Snail" Toloza. The Snail. Who came up with those stupid-ass nicknames anyway?

"We stirred up some trouble in the North End," Frank Cavallo said from behind a thick cloud of cigarette smoke. "In Stefano Lucatti's pissing ground."

Fat and ugly and an asshole. It had to be hard to overcome those particular deficiencies.

"What kind of trouble?" her father asked. The lines on his face seemed deeper today—his skin paler, shadows under his eyes. She knew why. They had made some great strides in the opening rounds of this turf war, but the Lucattis had come back strong. A made Ricardi man—Danny "Sleepy" Orsini—had disappeared when making collection rounds. The Jade Orient, a Ricardi massage parlor complete with happy endings, had been burned to the ground. A couple dealers had turned up dead. Costly.

She knew her father was thinking about the lost revenue.

War was never good for business. A family had to earn to keep afloat. Killing wasn't earning, but it could open up new earning opportunities. It could also bring a ton of heat rebounding on your operation—heat from law enforcement, heat from rivals.

"Broke up some games," Frank said. "We trashed four of those Joker Poker machines in bars paying back to Little Jack Cirelli. Muscled in on some opportunities. A boy of mine put one of the Lucattis, some nephew of Marco's, in the hospital."

"Nice job, Einstein," Maria quipped. "He wasn't even connected. With people like you on our side, we're certain to win."

Frank's face darkened with anger. He opened his mouth to reply, but her father spoke first.

"Enough, Maria." He turned back to Frank. "She right about that kid?"

Frank shrugged.

Her father frowned. "Try and get your shit correct before moving from now on. I don't need bad press, and I don't need civilians in the hospital. Understand me?"

"Of course, Alberto. It won't happen again." Frank attempted a lame puppy dog look that made Maria want to waltz over there and slap his fat face. Frank didn't have the balls God gave a gumball machine. It was one of the reasons his crew was so out of control. Might be time for a leadership change over there soon. After things settled down. She'd mention it to her father.

The rest of the gathered captains said nothing. It had been a tense meal—Chinese food in their own private party room at Kim's Palace—and she hadn't tasted a bit of her Szechuan shrimp. She'd also had to control her hand, which seemed to want to find her wineglass every three minutes. She was here at her father's request, at a meeting of capos that she was usually only allowed to attend when they specifically discussed money.

There were five captains in attendance. Frank Cavallo, of course. Resident big mouth prick with a crew that was always sliding out of line. Would it be cruel to wish most of them would get whacked in this little Lucatti-Ricardi fracas?

John Passerini, Ricardi family underboss. He'd nodded to her at first, but had said little since then. He was very well dressed, second only to her father, in a gray-blue Hugo Boss suit, his face guarded, his eyes unreadable. Leonardo Antonelli, young, handsome, and the newest and poorest of the Ricardi captains. Sam Fratianno, a guy who looked like a fat-cat banker with too many diamond rings for his bulging fingers. And finally, Alfonso Grimaldi, seventy-six years old with a bald, spotted head and dentures that were always yellow. Nearly knocked her over with his breath every time he kissed her cheeks. Alfonso had the largest active crew—made up almost entirely of his offspring, sons and bastard sons and grandsons. He had something like thirty of them in all.

Alberto Ricardi took a bite of his lo mein, then he tapped his fork against his plate. "What else?"

"We shut down one of their chop shops." Maria fought to keep a satisfied smile off her face.

Flat stares greeted her statement. Frank Cavallo's was hostile. Old man Alfonso managed to look slightly disapproving of the fact she had even spoken, which was a break from his usual lecherous glances at her tits. John had mastered the poker face, and young Leonardo and Sam the Banker did their best to look unimpressed. Bastards.

"I heard you killed the Jew that ran the place," Frank said. "Might have been better to bring him over to our point of view." He shoved more white rice into his face and grinned at her, showing teeth covered in rice, like tiny maggots in the mouth of a corpse. Suddenly she wasn't so hungry.

"He wasn't going to switch," she said. "I weighed the alternatives and this was the best way. Should free up some opportunities for Leonardo, if he moves on it."

At least Leonardo had the grace to change from unimpressed to interested. Of course, since he was always hurting for money, he'd probably look interested if she suggested rolling drunks for loose change.

"But you're so good at the money." Alfonso reached over and patted her hand with one clawed, spotted hand of his own. "Why get involved in all this..." he gestured vaguely, "...all this unpleasantness?"

She glanced at John Passerini. He watched her with shark eyes and a slight smile. Seems he'd found another mouthpiece. Bastard.

Frank chewed at her, gnashing those white rice maggots. "Yeah. The Boss should find you a husband. You need a man to quench some of that fire."

Her father turned and stared at Frank, and Frank shriveled under his gaze. But that didn't make her feel any better. She didn't need Daddy sticking up for her in front of these men. She wanted to earn the respect, demand the respect that she required.

"Anyone else have a problem with my involvement here?" she asked, hating the fact that none of them would dare answer as long as her father was present. Of course, none of them said anything. John watched her with those dark eyes. She met his gaze evenly until she felt it was safe to look away without losing face. "No? Good. Then when I bring you news of Francisco Cabrera's death, you can all eat your hearts out."

"The mule?" John asked. "How do you plan to do that?"

"Don't forget she has that hit man," Frank said. "Vance. Now there's a fat waste of money."

Alfonso Grimaldi wiped his mouth. "Due respect, Alberto, due respect as always, but I often wondered why we even use that boy. It's not like we don't have plenty of hungry boys of our own who'd be happy to clip a few Lucattis for you. Why waste all that money? I know he doesn't come cheap."

"I don't think you need to worry about what I'm dropping money on," her father said. "I'm certain I'm making myself perfectly clear."

Nods and shrugs all around. But Maria knew that wouldn't be the last of it.

"As for earning," her father continued, and that had everyone's attention instantly, "I know times are tough all over, and costs go way up during these uncertain days. That's why I'm dropping my cut of earnings down two percent during this war."

Frank Cavallo was the first to lift his glass and the others quickly followed suit. Two points off the cut was generous, even by her father's standards. She'd known it was coming, since he'd mentioned it to her first. It created all kinds of headaches for her, with incomes cut by over seventy-five percent, but she knew her father was more than willing to take short-term losses for long-term gains. When they had controlling interest in Boston, incomes would soar. For now, this cut would decrease pressures on the capos and let them focus on the fight.

Controlling interest in Boston. The thought made her all shivery.

Of course it would take time, blood and a whole hell of a lot of money to pull off. But she had Vance. Speaking of whom... She checked her cell phone, though she suspected it was still too early. He said he'd move tonight. She had to be out to Cabrera's address as soon as this meeting ended. She didn't want to miss the festivities.

The smile felt right on her face. Others noticed it, but none commented, though John Passerini watched her for a moment. He was too cunning by half. How many men had he watched die on his way to the top? If she wanted to join this power circle, she'd have to do what they did, experience what they'd experienced, so she could understand and use it to strengthen her position. She had to become harder. Who feared an accountant? Worse, who feared a female accountant?

Tonight she would watch Karl Vance at his work, and next time, she might just pull the trigger herself.

Chapter Five:
Revelation

The best laid plans and all that shit.

Maria made it to Francisco Cabrera's house an hour later than she'd intended. Fifteen years and fifteen billion and the Big Dig still sucked. A few years ago, a ceiling panel in the Ted Williams Tunnel had fallen and killed some poor woman. Beautiful fucking engineering. An hour late and it would be just her luck that Karl had already finished his work. She had the Bushnell night vision scope and a Fluke infrared camera she'd borrowed from one of their connected construction firms that used it in home heat-efficiency appraisals. About a hundred dollars worth of snacks and energy drinks sat piled on the passenger seat. All that, and with her luck she was probably late.

But for once she was happy to be wrong. With the infrared camera she scanned the house and picked out the heat signature and shape of a male through the kitchen window. He stood out as a human-shape in bright reds and traces of yellows, with his glasses showing up a cool blue in the imager. Behind him, the oven blazed in brilliant colors. Dinner for Mr. Cabrera.

He moved away from the kitchen window and she lost him for a bit. She waited, drumming on the steering wheel with her fingers. His neighborhood was affluent enough, nice, but not too over the top, and he lived on a corner lot on a quiet street. The wall between her and the house was built of unmortared stone but only came up about three and a half feet, so she could easily see over it. None of the birch trees blocked her view of the windows. Another lucky break.

She knew he lived alone. He didn't even employ bodyguards. Low profile, that was his game. But that bookie of his, Vatson, had given him up just the same. Which went to show you, you could always be had. Even that prick Saddam Hussein had eventually turned up in a rat hole and ended up doing the rope dance.

Of course, that meant that she could be found, too, even with all the precautions her father had taken. Not a comforting thought.

She watched for an hour, changing the batteries in the scope once when the power display warned her it was low. Nothing yet. Cabrera parked himself on the couch in his den in full view of her scope and grabbed his remote control. The sun had long since set, but Cabrera didn't close any of his blinds. Flickering light from the television suffused the den, which was otherwise dark.

It didn't take long for her car windows to start fogging over. She cracked them open, but it grew cold inside very fast. She considered starting the engine of the BMW she'd rented under a stolen credit card and fake ID just to run the heater for a bit, but then decided it was a stupid risk. Next time she'd remember to bring gloves. And a thermal blanket. And a 40,000 BTU heater, for God's sake.

Another hour. Nothing more thrilling than watching a middle-aged man asleep on the couch while the television threw its flickering light around the room.

She opened a can of AMP and a power bar, and then chased it all down with a cold Dunkin' Donuts caramel latte coffee. Her mother was probably in Heaven somewhere hiding her face in shame.

By one o'clock in the morning she was completely wired—in fact, she felt like her skull was shrinking while her brain expanded, thrumming away on overdrive.

Maybe Karl had already killed him. Maybe he was that fast, that good, that he'd done it when she was unwrapping the energy bar or something. And there went her chance of watching a man die—at least for tonight. She was still the little protected princess with clean hands. Figured.

She looked through the scope again. No, there was Cabrera sleeping on the couch. Or at least she thought he was sleeping.

Maybe he was dead. She couldn't see blood, but maybe she should check with the infrared camera and see if his body was cooler than it had been.

Movement. A glimpse of a black shape that merged with shadows and was gone, just as she'd taken her eye away from the night vision scope. She grabbed the infrared camera and the world swam in surreal swaths of bright oranges, reds, yellows and greens and blues. From her angle, she could see the heat image of Cabrera and the bright hotspot of the television through the window, but nothing else. She set the camera down and lifted the night vision scope again. Nothing.

The television went off. The room's vibrant green image dimmed slightly. Her heart jagged in her chest. It was probably nothing. Cabrera must have woken up and turned it off. She looked at his face, but didn't see the shiny, silver coin look of human pupils in light amplification, so he had to still be asleep.

Karl Vance appeared in her scope, standing right next to Cabrera. She was so startled she jerked the scope, drawing in a ragged breath, and it took her a second to center it again.

Vance stood there staring down at his target. Her gaze flickered to his hands, looking for his gun, but they were empty. Cabrera didn't even move. Karl's eyes glowed strangely in the ghostly green of the scope. Not the normal cat's eye flash, but almost as if his eyes shone with their own inner light. The hairs on the back of her neck lifted.

She saw Karl's lips move, and then Cabrera jerked awake. He started to stand, and panic twisted his face. Vance grabbed him by the neck, fingers under his jaw, and with one hand turned his head to the side. At first she thought Karl was trying to break the man's neck barehanded, but instead he only exposed the unprotected flesh of Cabrera's neck.

In an instant, the world became a surreal green nightmare. "Oh my God," she whispered.

Teeth—no, fangs, they were fucking fangs. Blood. Just like a fucking vampire.

Impossible.

Cabrera sagged, the will to fight draining with his blood, now held aloft only by Karl's one hand. Karl had to be amazingly strong to hold a grown man up with one arm as he locked his teeth into the man's throat. Jacked out of his mind on PCP—had to be.

Had to be.

Her heart slammed so hard against her rib cage it made her hands tremble and the vision in the scope shake with every thump.

Karl turned his head and looked right at her.

Before her numb hands could drop the night vision scope and fumble for her keys, before her mind could even begin to swallow what she had just seen, another man seemed to fold out of the deepest shadows in the room.

Karl spun away from her and faced him. The newcomer was dressed in a white suit, dark shirt and white tie, all glowing with that ghostly green night vision tint. God help her, she zoomed in on his face. His features were handsome to the point of eerie beauty—high cheekbones, dark hair, a short Van Dyke beard. Like Karl, his eyes seemed to burn with their own light, separate from the light amplification.

When they attacked each other they moved so fast she only saw green and white blurs. The window looking into the den exploded outward in a rain of glass and fragments of latticework. Vance had his hands around the newcomer's throat and they appeared to almost fly across the yard. She lost them for a moment as she frantically backed the zoom out to give her a wider field of view.

She found them again just as Vance rammed the other man into the trunk of a birch tree. The trunk buckled as if it had been hit by a fucking rocket-propelled grenade and long splinters of wood cut through the air like shrapnel. The cracking explosion of the impact echoed off the eaves and walls of the surrounding houses until it seemed to fill the neighborhood. Every leaf and branch shuddered violently and the whole tree began a slow topple forward, groaning and cracking as it fell.

Karl and the newcomer slashed at each other with nails that looked more like claws. She saw cuts open on both of them, saw the pale flesh separate, but no blood sprayed from the wounds. Zooming in on the face of the other was near impossible with the speed of the fight, but she did catch one close-up glimpse of his—its—face. Twisted and inhuman, lips pulled back from long fangs, all that eerie beauty she'd seen at first was now hateful and monstrous.

She knew she should run, but her hands refused to lower

the scope. She felt hollow—her will unfocused and drifting, a corpse floating along at the whim of the tide.

Vance ducked a slash and kicked out savagely, sending the newcomer flying backward. Vance's opponent kept his feet, crouched and leapt away, springing to the roof of the house. Vance followed an instant later and they turned to face each other from twenty feet away.

Vampires. It was insane. And still that strange lethargy gripped her—that need to watch for just a couple more seconds.

The other vampire smiled—an evil smile that seemed to make the air inside the car drop ten degrees. Then he turned and looked right into the lens of her night vision scope.

Hungry. That smile was hungry.

Now was the time to flee. Start the car. Escape. Don't go back to the apartment—just head north, call her father when she was somewhere safe. Sooner or later one of those two monsters would win.

She tossed the scope to the seat beside her and grabbed her keys, stabbed them into the ignition and the car roared to life. It leapt away from the curb with a shriek of tires, and she threw a frantic glance out her window at the roof of the house.

It was empty.

Something blurred across the lawn directly toward her. The other vampire. Its eyes glowed red through the darkness.

She floored the accelerator. The engine growled, and she went skidding around the corner of the T intersection onto Cabrera's main street, tires squealing. She saw lights going on in houses up and down the street, people opening doors and looking out windows. No doubt the cops were already on their way.

Something landed on the roof of her car. She screamed and jerked the wheel, sending the car's rear end fishtailing. Her car kissed the side of a parked SUV and her side mirror spun off through the air, shedding fragments of plastic.

She fought the car until it was back under control, and then she pushed it up to seventy, flying through the residential neighborhood, running stop signs without regard. She tore past one car whose driver was wise enough to pull to the side of the road when he saw her coming. But street after street only looked the same—a blur of large houses and parked cars. Where the hell was the main road? Why did this residential labyrinth seem to go on forever?

Claws punched through the roof overhead with a thunk and a tearing squeal of metal. A scream jumped from her lips. Her hand darted for the glove compartment where she'd hidden her Glock 9mm. The car drifted to the right, in the direction of her lean, but she straightened it out just before sideswiping a parked car.

Laughter sounded above her. Strange, inhuman laughter, like computer simulated speech, empty and completely devoid of humanity.

The Glock was in her hand. She pointed it toward the holes in the roof and pulled the trigger. Nothing happened. Safety on. No chambered round.

She nearly hit a minivan backing out of a driveway. No time to swerve, she roared past and missed its rear bumper by only inches. The blare of a horn chased her down the dark street.

Something landed on the hood of her car. Vance. She slammed on the brakes and the tires screamed in protest. He looked at her, his eyes red, burning with their own light. Vance seized the edge of the hood, below the wiper blades, and braced himself as the car slid to a stop.

She pulled back the slide on the Glock and flipped off the safety with shaking hands. Caffeine and fear didn't mix well. She'd never shot at anything other than a target, but she raised the pistol all the same. Vance looked at her, that piercing gaze icing her from inside out, and her hand stilled.

"Drive," he said, perfectly clearly, perfectly calmly. Then he looked up again to the thing that crouched on the roof above her.

"What fun, Karl." The other vampire's voice held the slightest hint of a Spanish accent. "We can share her if you're still hungry. Or you can let me dine alone, since you already fed on my unfortunate associate."

Maria turned the gun upward and unloaded the entire clip into the roof, spreading her shots to cover as much of the area as possible. The gunshots were deafening in the enclosed car, making her flinch with each pull of the trigger. After the last shot, her ears rang, deadening all other sound.

All but that strange inhuman laughter.

"This one's feisty, no? She smells like the man you work for. I find that interesting."

"That's irrelevant," Vance said. "All these petty squabbles are irrelevant. We have business. I'm glad to finally see you again."

"I'm certain you are."

"Shall we settle this, Alejandro?" Vance continued, then he spoke more softly and Maria couldn't make out his words over the ringing in her ears. She heard Alejandro's reply, however, and it seethed with hatred.

"No, I think not. Not yet. I want you to suffer more *acutely* before I kill you. Suffer as our Master suffered, when you betrayed and murdered him. Suffer as I have suffered when some black-handed Judas, the least of our brotherhood, destroyed our father of night."

Vance snarled, as dark and full of malice as any demon she could imagine. He launched himself off the hood of the car toward the creature on her roof, so fast she barely saw him.

She floored the accelerator and the tires squealed for a moment before the car caught traction and sped off. She took the next turn at forty miles an hour, tires losing grip with the road, back end sliding free, but somehow she saved it, pulled the turn off without crashing head-on into the Cumberland Farms store on the corner.

Finally, a main road appeared ahead. She turned onto it against a red without stopping, cutting off a Honda and earning another horn blare. When she finally saw the 93 onramp it was more beautiful than the Florence Cathedral.

Her hands started to shake again shortly after she entered the freeway, weaving through traffic as she raced north. She could see the muscles in her arms trembling and she clamped her hands down on the steering wheel until the shaking went away.

One part of her mind thought the whole thing surreal, a dream, something that couldn't possibly be true and happening to her. She must have made some mistake, seen something wrong. The other part, the rational part, concerned only with saving her ass, didn't really care whether Vance was a vampire or just believed he was. The result was the same. She had to get away from him and that other freak before she died like Cabrera.

She started shaking again, and she clamped her jaw shut tight to stop her teeth from chattering. It didn't help that the roof had a bunch of holes and tears in it from the earlier festivities. She cranked the heat in the car to the highest setting with one angry flick of her fingers.

There was no way she was going home now. Vance knew where she lived now, thanks to that night she'd been horny. She shuddered, trying not to think about him. She'd go to her friend Carrie's apartment in Brighton for a while. Until this thing with Vance—whatever it was—cooled down.

Then she remembered her laptop. Son of a bitch! It had all her father's accounting on it. If she fled now and the cops seized it...well, there was no way she could disappear without that information unless she wanted to find her family up to its neck in a shitload of RICO charges with no rubber booties in sight.

She'd keep it quick. In and out in less than fifteen minutes.

The elevator at her building seemed to take an eternity to arrive, then an eternity to get to her floor. She was out before the doors had even finished opening. Her heart beat faster the closer she came to her apartment, until her hands were trembling again and she missed the keyhole twice.

The lights were off inside. She flipped on the entry hall light and hurried into her living room, turning on every light as she went. She held the Glock in her hand, though the gun was empty. The first thing she wanted was the extra box of 9mm ammunition she kept in the spare bedroom closet.

Movement. Something seen out of the corner of her eye. She spun toward it, raising the pistol.

The balcony sliding glass door stood open, and a twelve-inch gap of darkness seemed to peer in at her, as if gloating at the breach in her brightly lit world. A cold breeze poured in and rustled the leaves of her ferns and spider plants. She didn't dare to breathe.

She strained to hear past the rustling of the vertical blinds moving with the cold air. The heating system hummed softly to itself and that was all.

There was no possible way Vance could have beaten her here at the speeds she was traveling, but she also knew there was no way in hell she'd left the balcony doors open in the middle of November.

So something had been here, or was still here. And she had to get that laptop.

She slid along the wall toward her desk, where the silver-gray laptop lay shut next to her Tiffany lamp. Five running steps and she grabbed the laptop, yanked the power cord out and turned back toward the door.

Karl Vance stood behind her.

She stumbled backward and might have fallen if he hadn't reached out, quicker than any rattlesnake, and caught her arm.

"How did you get here so goddamn fast?" she whispered. Too many impossible things tonight. It felt as if she had leaked all her strength out through a thousand cracks in the world she'd known just a few hours ago.

"*Denn die Todten reiten schnell.*" His lips curved in a gentle smile.

"What?"

"A line from Bram Stoker."

She pushed away from him. "I'm an accountant—not President of the Bram Stoker Fan Club, you asshole."

"You don't have anything to fear from me."

"Not like Cabrera, right?"

He tilted his head and looked at her. "You sent me to kill him. You didn't say how."

"You drank his blood, you fucking sicko. Every time I shut my eyes, I see your teeth in his neck."

"You chose to watch."

Her face grew hot. She had been some kind of *Faces of Death* voyeur, hadn't she? And look what she'd gotten for her curiosity. She flung the pistol on the couch. It was empty anyway, and even if it weren't, what good was it against someone like him?

"So why are you here then?" she asked. "Cleaning up the rest of your mess? I'm sure you won't hesitate to kill me too." She began to shiver again. Damn it was cold.

He still wore his work blacks, but one sleeve was partially torn off and there was a gaping hole in his pant leg. Long cuts traveled up his arm where the sleeve was torn, and she could see where the flesh was opened to muscle, but only a small amount of thick blood, almost black in color, seeped from the wound.

She felt like she might be sick.

He followed her gaze to his wound. "I heal quickly, but supernatural wounds don't heal as fast."

"Fascinating. I'll die easier now."

He smiled tightly. "We have to talk."

"I don't like men who talk too much. So why don't you take the hint and get the hell out of here."

"What you saw tonight—"

"I saw a man killed by some kind of human leech. So what? No big thing. There are giant albino alligators in New York sewers too." She started to laugh, but his face was so guarded that her laughter died.

"Oh, I get it," she said. "It's not funny."

"Not particularly."

"Then talk, damn you. Get it over with."

He was silent a moment. "Your father changed things when he brought me in. I'm not usually this close to people."

"You took the job, if I remember. And just for your information, there seem to be a few things you left off your resume."

"I must feed." His face was very still, his eyes somber. "But I can choose the victim. I don't kill innocents anymore."

She didn't know what to say to that, so she kept her mouth shut.

"I didn't want to see your father end up like Salvatore Mancino and all the rest," he said. "You're all in danger now."

"Who was that other vampire?"

"Alejandro Delgado."

"The Spaniard. The one who sent you that message. You weren't going to accept until you heard his name."

"I couldn't refuse after learning he'd returned to Boston. I've been waiting a long time to find him."

"It doesn't seem as if he likes you much either. Tell me I'm fucking crazy."

"We are sworn to destroy each other."

"I see. So it's a Republican-Democrat kind of thing."

"Amusing."

"It's what I do," she said. "Laugh in the face of certain death. Ha. Ha."

A silence fell between them as they stared at one another. She looked away first, and hated him, and hated herself, for it. His eyes...

"So Delgado is why the Mancinos went down so hard?" she

asked finally. She pulled out the leather executive chair she had at her desk and sank into it. She set the laptop back down, then put her face in her hands, massaged her eyes. There wasn't even fear anymore, just a kind of numb exhaustion.

"The Lucattis hit hard one day, before I knew Delgado was with them. He told them something—enough for them to spike the caskets at two of my sleeping spots with silver and seal the rooms with holy water and crosses. Delgado killed Salvatore Mancino himself, and Lucatti soldiers hunted down most of the Mancino capos one after another. There was nothing left to do but escape."

"So you're a coward," she said, part of her mind knowing she was well past insane to continually provoke him.

"There is little in this world as vulnerable as a sleeping vampire during the daylight. It was only by chance that I wasn't asleep where they'd come looking."

"So why does he want to kill you?"

Vance shook his head, but would say nothing else.

"I don't suppose you killed him tonight?" she asked. When he didn't answer, she pushed onward. "How did you get away? You run away again?"

Anger darkened his face. "I'm growing tired of your baiting. You complicated things by showing up where you didn't belong. I threw Delgado from your car's roof, but he escaped. I feared that he might be headed here, after you."

"How would he know where I live?"

Karl's mouth tightened almost imperceptibly. "Maybe he'd pick an address at random out of the phone book. There are ways."

"But you got here first, didn't you? I guess the prize goes to you."

A long pause. "I was concerned about you."

"That's bullshit. You came here looking for *him.*" She leaned back in the executive chair and looked at the phone. She couldn't even call the cops. How sad was that?

He said nothing. It was eerie how still he could be when he wished. How often did the human eye take for granted the barely perceptible rise and fall of the chest as a person breathed? On Karl, even that was missing. His chest only moved when he drew in breath to talk.

"I'd like to ask some questions," he finally said.

"Fuck you. You work for me."

He smiled, but there was nothing nice about it. "Why were you there tonight?"

"You work for *me*. Don't make me say it again."

His smile widened—became predatory...almost... anticipatory? And that sent waves of cold washing down her skin from head to foot.

"You're trying my patience. You should remember you have far more to lose than I."

Damn him. "I was curious."

"About what? About me?"

"I wanted to watch someone die."

He thought about it a moment. "Fair enough. Some urges are not pretty."

She laughed, and the hairs on the back of her neck raised at the sound of it. "Like the urge to bite people?"

The smile danced in his eyes but never made it to his lips. He turned away from her and crossed her living room toward the balcony. For a second her heart lifted and she almost made a break for the door, but she'd seen how fast he could move. Karl slid the balcony door shut and latched it.

"Why'd you leave that open?" she asked. "I knew someone was here as soon as I saw it."

"With all your attention focused on the door, it was easy to come up behind you. Chasing you down the hallways might have attracted attention."

She looked at him, frowning. "Shit. I want some wine. I want my damn hands to stop shaking."

She walked into the kitchen and flipped on the light. Her feet slapped lightly on the travertine floors. Karl followed her in, but she was very aware that his feet made no sound. She'd noticed that before, what seemed like a long time ago now.

A small wine rack sat on the counter. She traced her fingers over the necks of the bottles until she found the one she wanted and grabbed it. When she tried to open it with the corkscrew she almost impaled her hand.

Karl moved in close to her and took the bottle and corkscrew. She flinched at his touch and almost dropped the bottle, but his quick hands caught it with ease. He opened the cabinets until he found wineglasses and set two on the granite countertop. He smelled slightly of blood, just a hint, and it made her dizzy. She clutched the counter for support.

There's a vampire pouring a '99 Casanova Di Neri in my kitchen.

What a fucking day.

The wine, when it came, tasted like heaven. She clutched the glass in both hands and let the wine's bouquet envelop her face.

"You need to pack some things and move to a safe house for awhile," Karl said. "This place isn't secure anymore."

She could only stare at him. "Really?"

"Do you have a place to go?"

"Yeah, I have a place. I'll get my stuff and get out of here. But you don't get to know where I'm going."

"Is this the end of our business together?"

She hesitated. He likely wasn't going to kill her if he wanted her at a safe house, but her weariness sapped all relief from her. A curious heaviness sat on her, making a drink from a hundred-dollar bottle of wine an effort to swallow. Everything whirled in her mind until it became a jumbled mess. It was all too much to digest tonight, after all the terror.

But one thing remained—she still wanted to crush the Lucattis. If Alejandro Delgado was a threat, then Karl Vance was her answer.

Vampires. God. It had been the stuff of movie and legend this morning, and now look.

"You have my cell number," she said. "Call me in a couple days. I need to think."

"Very well." Karl turned and walked out of her kitchen.

She didn't hear him leave so much as feel his presence disappear. It took her ten minutes to gather everything she needed into a Louis Vuitton duffel bag—computer, 9mm and ammo, toiletries, clothes, her gold crucifix necklace from her Confirmation—and flee to her car. What the hell had she unleashed? And what in God's name would she do now?

Chapter Six:
Thorns

Boston, one of the oldest cities in the States, was still little more than a wide-eyed child compared to London. Karl loved Boston, but there were times, like tonight, that he longed for those fog-shrouded London avenues of his vampire youth. What he didn't yearn for were the years spent in slavery to Master Cade. Debased and dishonored—forced to do the most horrific things...

No, he wouldn't think of it tonight. The night was black enough without him adding to it.

Karl leaned against the cold wire of a chain-link fence and waited. He had circled through the area twice, searching for signs of either Delgado or his sirelings, or of a Lucatti trap.

Or maybe even a Ricardi trap. Maria was the first normal human to know exactly what he was in over a hundred years. He'd be willing to wager she would keep her mouth shut, but who knew? Back someone into a corner and anything could happen.

But the area around this run-down convenience store held only the usual motley assortment of human predators and people just trying to live. Junkies and pushers and the like. A burglar he'd passed testing for unlocked windows on a fire escape. The homeless like lost herd animals going here and there but never truly arriving.

He smelled Little Ricky before he saw him, heard the flat slap of his boots on the macadam long before his hooded head peeked around the corner of the store. Karl could smell the threads of fear on Little Ricky, and smiled at the exaggerated gangster stance Little Ricky took to disguise that fear.

"Little" Ricky was of average height and tending toward heavyset. His blond hair had been ratted into dreadlocks, and his goatee was a scraggly smear across his chin. He wore a black hoodie, with the hood up, out of which his dreads spilled like dirty vines.

"Hello, Little Ricky," Karl said softly.

Little Ricky jumped and then glared at him. "I hate when you fucking do that."

"I hate to stand in the cold. So what?"

Little Ricky moved closer, shoving his hands inside the joined pockets of his hoodie. Karl could smell the faint scent of gun oil. Probably something small and cheap. Not that it mattered.

"What? Not happy to see me? I pay enough to deserve better customer service." Karl tossed him an envelope filled with cash. Ricky pulled a hand free of the hoodie in time to catch it and stuff it back into his pocket.

Little Ricky flashed a smile. One front tooth was missing. "You pay for the straight dope, not for verbal blow jobs."

"Eloquently said. Now, what do you have for me?"

"Nothing much on that Delgado guy. Vic said he heard from some Southie whore that Delgado was a mean motherfucker who was all wrapped up with the Lucattis, but that's all I got on him."

Karl kept his face noncommittal, despite his disappointment. He really hadn't expected much. Delgado hadn't lived for so long by being stupid and careless. But still, sometimes the strangest things leaked out.

"What about the Lucattis?"

"That's easier. Most of them are laying low. I keep hearing rumors they're gonna hit back soon. Hit back hard." He shrugged. "But it's all just talk until it happens."

"Specifics?" Karl asked.

"There's a— Hey, man, what the fuck?"

A man jumped down from the roof onto the closed dumpster, landing with a loud clang. Karl turned toward him, one hand slipping inside his jacket to grab the butt of his SIG-Sauer. He could feel the burn of holy objects, and he squinted at the brilliant flash of crosses. Little Ricky yanked out a snub-nosed revolver from his hoodie pocket—a dirty little gun that looked more like a toy in Ricky's large hand.

Another shadow, moving fast, ran around the corner of the store toward them. Little Ricky spun and fled along the chain-link fence, into the adjacent weed-choked lot and off down the street. Karl spared him a quick look and then turned back to the two men facing him. The two men didn't even glance after Little Ricky.

These men were human, but were certainly no Lucattis. They held swords and wore a strange mix of Kevlar body armor against projectiles and silver-plated chain mail against slashing vampire claws. Their armor was black and silver and a deep cobalt blue, with silver crosses imbedded in a dozen places. They wore heavy Kevlar guards around their necks, and a thick necklace of silver with a crucifix that burned in his eyes with its blue holy brilliance. Large revolvers sat in holsters at their sides, but it was swords they bore against him. The blades gleamed in the meager streetlight, a ghostly radiance like slivers of the moon—broadswords of silver-plated steel, etched with crosses.

He could see nothing of the men's faces except their eyes, gleaming out of hardened armor facemasks beneath Kevlar helmets. Their heraldry was easily seen. A thorny black rose bloomed on a gold field upon each shoulder and over their hearts.

Knights of the Thorn.

"May I help you?" Karl asked, fighting with all his long-focused willpower to avoid backing up in the face of all that silver and all those crosses.

"You can help me by dying quietly," the closest knight said. His voice was scratched and raspy, and he advanced toward Karl, sword raised.

Now Karl could sense the tingle of spellwork—some human conjure that had hidden them from his vampire senses until they were close. Had Little Ricky been in on it? Probably not. He'd seemed just as startled as Karl had been.

"I have a pardon from the High Lord Chattingham for my service to the Order of Thorn."

"Vampires are killing innocents here." The knight on the dumpster had a deep voice that hummed with a kind of hypnotic energy, like a hellfire preacher. He leapt off the dumpster and landed in a crouch, then slowly stood and began to advance as well.

"But not I."

"Masters of lies," the hellfire knight said. "Every vampire's tongue is twisted. We'll suffer none of them to live."

The two knights circled away from each other, so Karl could no longer face them both at the same time. He took a step backward.

They attacked in unison without another word. Their heavy boots thudded on the asphalt as they sprinted toward him with their swords lifted. Karl left the SIG-Sauer holstered. It wouldn't breach their armor anyway.

He backed up again, hesitated, caught between wanting to convince them of his innocence and wanting to flee all that silver and holy light. He couldn't kill Thorn Knights without starting a war he would certainly lose. A surge of fear and pain washed over him like an invisible wave as the knights and their holy symbols and the silver drew close. They weakened him, made him slower.

And then it was too late to talk.

The first knight swept his blade down in a wicked arc, but Karl managed to throw himself aside. The blade was back up in an instant and thrusting at his chest, but he spun away from it. Barely.

The next attack came from behind, and Karl ducked his head low under the sword, feeling the wind of its cutting blade on his skin. The blade sparked as it glanced off the dumpster with a hideous metal screech. The holy aura around the knights and the poisonous miasma of the silver slowed him, seemed to crush down upon him like a weight, seemed to tangle him in heavy chains and destroy his agility. It wouldn't be long before one of those swords connected.

He slipped another thrust and dodged aside. Clear alley opened before him and he darted toward it. There was no pride at stake. If he stayed, they would destroy him.

His gaze by chance fell upon one of the crosses on their armor and he staggered, half-blinded by those painful dagger-rays of light. A sword blade cut so close to him that he felt the tug as it sliced open his coat.

He stumbled again, found his balance, and ran, but the drag of the silver and the crosses made him sluggish. It felt as if he were trying to run through water. In the far darkness of his mind, panic opened its eyes.

Behind him, the unmistakable steel on leather sound of a pistol drawn from a holster. The next instant, the click of a hammer cocked back.

His only chance was to throw himself aside at the last minute—an instant before the gunshot—

"Stand down!" a woman yelled, her voice cracking in the air like the gunshot he'd dreaded. "Put that away, you fool!"

Karl sprinted onward for twenty more feet before slowing and turning back. Claws out. Ready to flee again in an instant or throw himself out of the line of fire. He had to sort out this misunderstanding if he could. Being hunted by the Order of the Thorn was the last thing he needed.

The two knights stood unmoving. The one with his pistol drawn slowly slipped it back into his holster. The other still had his sword free, but he looked back over his shoulder at another knight who walked up from behind.

Where she had come from, he had no idea, but she'd been concealed from his senses just as the two other knights. She wore armor but no helmet or mask, and her long hair lay upon her shoulders. Her storm cloud gray eyes were sharp, intelligent, and the air of command bristled from her like the thorns on the rose insignia she wore. She kept her sword sheathed as she approached, but she watched Karl closely with those dark eyes.

"Your attack is unjust," he called to her.

"Only the sword is justice for a vampire," the hellfire knight said.

The woman glared at him. "Be silent. You've done enough."

"You reprimand me in front of that?" The knight swung a hand toward Karl in disdain.

"I'll reprimand and add more if you don't be *silent*." Her steel gauntlet groaned as her fist clenched.

The second knight spoke, his gritty voice little more than a whisper. "My lady, we have bodies. We have people dead from blood loss and puncture wounds. And we have a vampire right here in front of us."

"I'm not the only vampire in this city," Karl said, before she could answer.

"I know. Do you still abide by the terms set down by the Order?"

"Of course."

"Then be at peace," she said. The hellfire knight laughed derisively. The other knight said nothing, but his eyes glittered behind his facemask, and they never once left Karl.

For a long moment nobody spoke and nobody moved. A car drove past on the distant street, but they were too deep in the shadows to worry about being seen.

"I am Lady Kimberly MacKenzie of the Order of Thorn."

Karl said nothing.

There was enough distance between them that he could flee if they attacked again. But those pistols were likely loaded with silver-jacketed bullets, and that made things much more dicey.

"We think that the vampire called Alejandro Delgado is in this city," Lady MacKenzie said. "One of Cade's ancient brood."

"There's a master vampire in Boston." The decision to lie was instantaneous. "But I haven't heard a name yet, only a rumor that she arrived with some Colombian drug kingpin or other."

"She?"

Karl nodded.

"See?" The hellfire knight waved a dismissive hand at Karl. "He betrays even his own filthy kind."

Lady MacKenzie spun and backhanded the knight in the face with her steel-shrouded fist, knocking his facemask askew and sending him staggering. Karl smelled the sharp scent of blood. The man stayed on his feet, but just barely.

"Don't disgrace me," she said, very softly.

The knight bowed his head. "Yes, m'lady."

Lady MacKenzie turned back to Karl, her eyes sharp. "The Order is sending a company to put an end to this. It will be like the Silent Purge. Are you familiar with that?"

"A little." The Order had once slaughtered two entire werewolf clans that had taken up residence among the citizenry of Belgium. No werewolf had even managed a howl while the hammer came down, and thus the name. Even today it stood out as a single example of the Order's utmost ruthlessness. Not a single member of those clans survived today.

"With that in mind, I suggest you don't violate the terms of your pardon. Even I will not aid you if you're caught up in this."

"Understood." Few things were more difficult than a lecture by a human not even a quarter of his age, but he swallowed his ire. He could nurse his pride later, after he'd had a chance to think about what all of this would mean to his hunt for Delgado.

"Good," Lady MacKenzie said and bowed. "I bid you farewell. Hopefully our paths will not cross again."

She turned and strode away from him. Her two knights followed her, but the hellfire knight sent a hateful glance back at Karl. Marking him, no doubt. Karl kept his face neutral.

Only when they turned the corner and were out of sight did he allow himself to turn away and retreat.

The Order of the Thorn in Boston.

Sooner or later they would find out that he had lied.

Chapter Seven:
Sit Down

"So you killed the mule," Frank Cavallo said. "Great big fucking deal. We lost another two pushers in the downtown projects, a pimp working Dewey street, and worst of all"—he glanced at her father—"another of our own. Christopher Grimaldi."

Maria gritted her teeth to silence a particularly venomous comment.

Christopher Grimaldi was one of Alfonso Grimaldi's grandsons and a soldier in his crew. He'd been found in a dumpster with two .22 caliber holes in his head. Alfonso wasn't at this meeting, claiming the need to be with his family, something her father had been kind enough to grant, though it went against the code. The Grimaldi crew had closed ranks since Christopher's death, and the money wasn't coming in because they weren't on the street earning. That was a far bigger blow to the Ricardis than the death of one of their soldiers.

"We knew we'd take losses," John Passerini said. "Everyone at this table knew."

"That being said," Frank continued, "I don't think we really knew how much this was going to hurt our wallets. I know I didn't."

"Did you think the Lucattis would just roll over and die when we made our move?" Maria asked, not bothering to keep the scorn from her voice.

Frank glared at her. "No, but I remember certain promises. Promises that if we hit them where they earned, we'd win quickly."

"Nobody said 'quickly', Frank." *What an unbelievable prick.*

"It doesn't matter now," Leonardo Antonelli said. "We're in it until the end. It's either the Lucattis or us."

Her father had said little so far, and he gave nothing away now. He kept his face indifferent, almost bored, whenever his capos argued.

"That's not completely true." Frank gave her father a glance. "Antonio Lucatti talked to me yesterday."

All eyes fell on Cavallo and did not move. Smoke drifted across the single overhead lamp like gray clouds against the sun.

"What did he have to say?" her father finally asked. His voice was soft, which meant one of two things. Either he didn't care, or he was extremely displeased.

"The Lucattis want a sit down. They're prepared to negotiate an end to this mutually costly war."

"See?" Maria leaned forward. "We're hurting them. They wouldn't make gestures like this if they were untouched."

"Look, Boss," Frank said, "we're hurting here. They mentioned on the lowdown they'd be willing to concede some territory and some protection opportunities to us. No retaliations. I think we should at least talk to them."

Long silence.

"Let's hear what they have to say," her father said.

The meeting took place at two p.m. on a Tuesday inside the basement of the Catwalk Glitz, a new nightclub near the Theater District. Her father sent underboss John Passerini to negotiate. The Lucattis sent Antonio "Patient Anthony" Lucatti. Maria wasn't invited to attend.

Karl Vance's cell phone rang ten minutes after the sun set. "Yes?"

"We have to act fast." Maria's voice sounded tense. "I'm getting bits and pieces here and there, but it sounds like we might not be allowed to play for very much longer. I want to meet. You up yet?"

"If I'm talking, then I'm up."

"Fine. Same place I dropped you off. Find me at the tunnel,

near the ruins. One hour." She hung up.

He closed the phone slowly. He dressed for work, lifted his freshly cleaned SIG and slid a magazine inside.

Someone knocked softly on the bedroom door. Xiesha. She bowed.

"Will you be feeding tonight, master?"

"I doubt it. Just business." He smiled. She said nothing and withdrew. Like any good servant, she knew when to keep her mouth shut.

They were to meet at Franklin Park in Jamaica Plain well outside of downtown Boston. She'd chosen the Overlook ruins as their meeting place, near the stone remains of a building that had burned in the forties.

The night was moonless, but the high floodlights of White Stadium in the distance haloed the barren branches of the oak trees. Karl circled past drifts of brown leaves collecting around the roots of trees and rocks, careful to step only where his light footstep would make no sound. He paused beneath the denuded branches of a Hemlock tree, listening to traffic on Seaver and Washington streets, the slosh of a bottle, the crinkle of paper and the delayed step of a homeless man limping along one of the paths, the *thup-thup* of a helicopter north over Roxbury.

Karl cut a wide circle through the park, using every heightened sense to search out federal agents hiding with parabolic microphones, Lucatti henchmen or Delgado's vampire sirelings. So far nothing. He slipped past two lovers embracing near a broken stone wall, lost in the touch of one another. They were human, and had neither the smell of gun oil nor the sub-audible crackle of hidden earpieces to warrant a closer look. He found a park ranger talking to an elderly couple about how Curt Schilling was six times the pitcher that Randy Johnson was and that the Yankees were screwed, deep pockets or not. The elderly couple had a dog—a Cairn Terrier—who seemed to sense him as he slid through the shadows behind them. The Terrier began to whine, and the woman bent to comfort it. He hurried onward before the dog began to bark.

When he saw Maria, she was bundled into a heavy winter coat, standing near the stone arch built of moss-stained boulders. He moved silently behind her, approaching through the darkness of the tunnel-like arch, through the smell of decaying leaves, old stone and the faint, lingering odor of urine. She kept turning and scanning around her, searching for him or any other person who might be approaching.

He moved within five feet of her. She hadn't sensed him yet.

"Maria," he said, letting the name pour off his tongue.

She flinched and whirled to face him, her lips pulled back from her teeth. "You bastard—"

"I'm pleased to see you too."

"Don't ever sneak up on me again. I'm not impressed by your pointless vampire bullshit. Understand?"

"Perfectly." He behaved himself and didn't even say it with a smile.

"Good. Look, I'm sorry, but I'm still a little weirded out by you. No offense."

"None taken." He noticed that she didn't move closer to him, as she often had before she'd found out the truth. That was normal too, but he missed her closeness. "So what do you wish done now?"

"I want you to kill Stefano Lucatti."

"I see. Not a big request—just whack the head of the Lucatti family." He sighed. "Can't do it."

"What? Why not?"

"If it were that easy, don't you think I'd have done it long ago?"

"That's not what I asked."

"Delgado works for them," Karl said. "He's told Stefano how to guard against the undead."

Anger burned in her eyes. "So why haven't you bothered to tell us how to guard against Delgado?"

"Delgado sells his services as a vampire. I sell my services as a hit man." He smiled bitterly. "And what Ricardi would believe me if I started teaching your crews to use silver against evil? They think every problem can be solved using a larger caliber hand gun."

"I fucking believe."

"That's because you saw something you were never meant to see."

She rubbed a hand across her face. "So Stefano Lucatti knows..."

"Stefano does, but few, if any, of his people take any precautions. Delgado may have a deal with Stefano to keep details to himself. And besides, Stefano Lucatti has a priest in the family. A cousin, I believe. Plentiful access to holy water."

"A priest." She laughed. "I'm sure he's a real Mother Teresa if he comes from the Lucattis."

"His holiness can be questioned, but the symbols retain their power."

"Fine. Be specific. What will stop you?"

He hesitated.

"I'm already wearing a cross." She opened her jacket. Piercing blue-white light burned off the crucifix around her neck. He winced and looked away.

"You brought me here to insult me?" he asked quietly, fighting to hold down his sudden anger. Reminded of everything he'd lost.

She slipped the necklace into the neck of her sweater. "No. I'm sorry. I just had to know whether the myths were true."

"Many of them have some element of truth. Legends evolve for a reason. My kind has been around for long, long years."

She smirked. "'Stolen many a man's soul and faith', that it? Nice, but I'm notoriously short on sympathy when there's something I want. And I want to know your strengths and weaknesses. Specifics. Mind control? You bulletproof? Shrivel in the sun like a grape? That kind of shit."

He shook his head, watching her breath steam in the cold. Watching her clouds of breath trailing away, and from his lips, nothing.

"I'm not here to show you what it is to be a vampire. Believe me when I say the powers come with a crushing price."

"Those powers can't be much if you can't even kill an old man."

"This isn't the movies. I can't kill Stefano Lucatti in his home if he has it protected. If he were set up somehow, then perhaps. But that's hardly easy—the man didn't get where he is by being incautious."

"I knew there'd be a catch." She folded her arms across her chest. "I have another idea. You can make other people vampires, right?"

"Didn't you hear me? That's not a fate you want."

She shook her head impatiently. "No, not me. Other people."

"What exactly do you have in mind?"

"I want to terminate his prostitution income. I want all his honeypots to work for us."

"Through me."

"Exactly." She smiled, as if he couldn't help but agree with her plan.

"No."

"I'm sorry?" Her eyes narrowed.

"You heard what I said. My answer is no."

She blinked, and then her face got that angry obstinate look that must have driven her parents mad. "If you don't want Ricardi money, then fine. We'll end this partnership."

"If you insist on this course of action, then end it by all means. I won't change my answer."

"But why?"

"Just envision Boston aswarm in vampire streetwalkers, preying on johns. Beautiful bloody idea."

"But—"

"Was there anything else?" he asked.

She hissed out a stream of air, turning her face away from him. "I'm sure you'll end up useful for something. I just have to think of what. I'll call you."

He watched her retreating back, and then followed her from a distance along the paths, camouflaged in shadows to make certain she made it safely to her car.

Vampire whores. God save us.

Chapter Eight: Choices

Maria Ricardi stood with her father on the back deck of his big bungalow in Martha's Vineyard. The air smelled of the ocean, salt and seaweed. Her father held a glass of brandy in one hand, and the sunlight occasionally refracted through it, creating amber shadows upon the decking. She had wine, a Pinot grigio. The sun was out, but the air was cold. Ice ringed the pond in the backyard, and the bare branches of the trees were stark against the brilliance of the blue sky. Drifts of vibrant red and yellow leaves lay scattered below the trees. She remembered jumping in leaf piles as a kid. Getting wet, not caring. The only thing she'd worried about was rolling on a snail hiding under a leaf.

"I know you don't like it," her father said.

"I think we're letting everything slip through our hands, just when we're ready to grab it."

"This truce will let both families start earning again. And we'll be in a far better position than before."

"They give up all their protection rackets in Dorchester and Charlestown," she said, "hand over a few blocks in Roxbury to our pimps and dealers, and give a two hundred large death payment for Christopher Grimaldi. Of course they still hold eighty percent of the Westside—let's not forget that. And we both know they aren't going to forget this war—or forget Frankie Lost, Leon Penny-Ante, or any of the other Lucattis we offed."

"I'm aware of that."

"They'll move against us again," she said. "When they've had some time to stop the bleeding."

"I don't agree. New York isn't happy about things."

"I suppose the Commission is making noise?" She fought to keep her frustration out of her voice and failed.

"Yes."

"Well, fuck 'em. Fuck the five families and fuck the Lucattis. There's no reason we can't compete directly with New York."

His jaw clenched. "Shut your mouth. Now you're just talking like a know-nothing half-assed wiseguy. Where's the strategy I need from you?"

"Alfonso is your *consigliere*. Ask him."

"He thinks this is best. We come out more powerful." Her father shook his head. "A long war, and maybe we're so weak afterwards that anyone can come in and roll us up. Maybe the feds get something on us. Maybe somebody turns."

"If you believed that, then why start the war at all?"

"We proved our point. We bloodied their nose. They aren't going to want to tangle with us again."

"Bloodied their nose? I say cut off their heads and have the whole pie to ourselves."

He took his time answering. She could hear the absurd, mournful honking of geese off on the horizon. Her father's face was deeply lined and shadows seeped into the crevices. When had he grown so old?

"When the Mancinos and Lucattis were running things, we only had a sliver of the pie. Now we have half. Too much, too fast, and maybe someone realizes just how powerful we've become. Sometimes being a good leader is knowing when not to fight."

"Spare me the fucking platitudes. The Lucattis came to the table because we're hurting them. Give them a chance to recover and we may be the ones who end up like the Mancinos."

Her father's eyes tightened in anger. "No chance. The Mancinos had people inside who went over to the Lucattis before that bloodshed began. They were ripe for the picking— disorganized and unfocused. We're nothing like them."

"Except that we both have Lucattis for enemies."

Her father didn't say anything, just stared out at the pond and the stands of barren trees that covered his twelve acres of property. There were more geese on the horizon, their imperfect

V jagged against the sky.

"I don't understand why you're changing your mind when we're this close."

"And I'm not required to explain things to my people, much less my daughter. It's over. I'm accepting the truce at the sit down and we'll get back to the business of being a business."

"What about Vance?"

He turned to look at her, his eyes piercing. "What about him? We won't need him anymore. Pay him and cut him loose. He knows to keep his mouth shut."

"So what do I get? I go back to the books and that's it?"

"Did you think you would get more?" he asked. "I let you play because you had some good ideas and I knew that Vance was good enough to keep you safe. And I'll admit, I think you and Vance were the reason the Lucattis were so eager to come to the table. We may have won this war because of your efforts, but nobody's ever going to acknowledge it. You knew that going in."

"Oh. Right. My mistake."

"I look the other way on a lot of things, and I let you have far more sway than I should, because I love you. But don't push this with me." He looked out over the pond and took a long pull of his brandy. "If your mother could see this, it'd kill her all over again."

"I only want what's best for the family."

"Then you'll go back to working the books and making sure those motherfucking forensic accountants can't string us up by the balls. This isn't an army, it's a business. We're here to make money. We make money, everybody's happy. We don't make money, people start thinking about changes in leadership."

He left those words dangling there, frosting the air.

"If I were your son, things would be different."

"Of course they would," her father said.

There were times when Karl missed the deadening effect of alcohol upon his thoughts. He could've used that effect whenever the memories threatened to drown him like some dark, churning sea rising against a levee. Such as now, sitting there with a book in his hand and seeing none of the words because his mind watched instead the tide of memory.

Maria's talk of turning prostitutes had brought it all back again. The first innocent he'd ever killed. Her face was one of the few that stood out in his memory as if under some stark surgical light.

Master Cade had lounged in a high-backed chair made of ebony, a golden cup in his hand, swirling it slowly. Karl could smell the blood in it. No amount of illusion could make Master Cade beautiful, and while all other of his sirelings spent a good deal of power making themselves seem so, Cade never even tried. Hairless—without even eyebrows. His eyes glowed a strange soft violet, with silver circles around his iris, as bright as newly minted coins. His lips were red, though his skin was albino pale. He was a large man, tall and thickly built, bordering on obesity, and his features were blunt and heavy, as though his face had been bludgeoned out of clay.

"It's time to stop nursing you, my puppy," Cade said.

His voice was warm and resonant. Compelling. Karl felt the need to obey it, as if there were a hand upon his brain, ready to clamp down into a crushing fist should he defy the will of his Master.

Another vampire stood behind Cade. Alejandro Delgado, the vampire with the strangely beautiful Spanish face and empty eyes. He'd been the one who first dragged Karl shaking before the Master, with soil from his grave still clinging to him, reeking of his own death and loathing the smell. Disoriented, starving for something he couldn't identify. He'd hated Delgado ever since.

"Look," Delgado said. "Our puppy is afraid of being weaned."

Cade laughed. Hatred, bright and furnace-hot burned in Karl's mind.

"No, no, my puppy," came Cade's amused thought. Behind the amusement loomed a cold malevolence. *"I'll suffer no insolence from you."*

Sudden blistering pain swept through Karl, as though his insides were enveloped in fire. He screamed and convulsed, rolling on the stone floor to smother invisible flames.

Abruptly, the pain vanished. He was left panting on the floor. Cade laughed. Delgado smirked.

"Tell John to bring in the meal I've prepared," Cade said, and Delgado withdrew.

Karl slowly stood. The stone beneath his bare feet felt cold. The walls of the room were built of massive blocks. Rusting iron sconces lined the walls, rust staining the stone like trailing tears, but all the candles were unlit. A rotting tapestry sagged on one wall, its threads dangling as if it had been disemboweled. Across from it a faded banner hung, splattered with ancient gore.

"You don't yet realize the honor I bestowed upon you, puppy," Cade told him. "But you will. In time."

Karl said nothing. His hands itched to drive a sword through Cade's heart, but he immediately crushed the thought. If Cade sensed it, there would be more pain. Much more pain. He'd learned that. His lips spoke the word *Master* readily enough now, bitter as it was on his tongue.

"What predator on this earth can match mankind for ruthless intelligence?" Cade sipped at his cup. Licked his red lips. "Only we. My Mistress is darkness. Shadows are my children. I remain constant while the world decays. Do you understand what it is to be eternal? It is to laugh in the face of God. What creature wouldn't want that?"

"Blasphemy." Karl spat upon the stones.

Cade clenched one hand into a fist and Karl dropped to his knees, holding his head and fighting not to shriek.

"Blasphemy?" Cade said. "Aye. It is indeed. But who can blame a vampire, when his communion is sacrilege? More profitable to curse the oak tree for losing its leaves than to lay blame on the vampire for preying upon mortals."

Delgado came back through the stone archway, his eyes on Karl, a small smile gracing his lips. Behind him came John Avalon, another of Cade's sirelings. He carried a young girl in his arms. She could not have seen sixteen summers. Her face was smeared with grime and soot, and her clothes were little better than rags. Karl could smell her unwashed skin and hair from across the room. Her eyes were wide and terrified, though she made no sound. Tears had carved twin tracks through the soot on her cheeks.

Karl could smell something else. Blood. His fangs began to tingle.

The vampire John set her down gently in the center of the room, and the girl huddled there on her knees, her head bowed. John glanced at Karl. The pity in his eyes made Karl close his own.

"Don't hesitate, puppy," Cade said. "Or I may have that succulent little treat myself."

Karl felt a great emptiness inside him, as if he were a cracked cup, and all that he poured in seeped back out again. But the girl had something that would fill that cup for a moment, one blissful moment, and he longed for it. He could feel her heat, smell her blood...oh, her *blood*...

"Take a step closer," Cade's voice came into his mind.

Cords stood out on his neck as he fought that command, but it did no good. His eyes opened and he took a step forward. Cade's smile widened. Delgado watched him with those flat, dark eyes, contempt etched across his face. John was nowhere to be found.

When Karl closed within a few feet of the girl, she seemed to sense him, because she turned toward him and her breathing quickened, rushing in and out over her teeth. She smelled of fear—stank of it—and it was stronger than anything but the scent of her blood. He hated that fear smell, knowing he was part of the cause, but a part of him reveled in it. A part that had never before existed until Cade.

"Take her, puppy," Cade urged. "Don't fight what you are."

And God help him, he sank his fangs into her soot-covered flesh, tasting the soot, tasting the blood, feeling her struggles begin to weaken. As he fed, the vampire part of him pushed what was still Karl Vance into a little box deep in his mind, and instinct held reign.

When that inner monster was satisfied, Karl regained control, and looked on what he had done.

Her lifeless body lay cradled in his arms, and the taste of her blood still lingered in his mouth. Karl laid her down as softly as an infant, then stumbled and half-fell as he tried to back away from her. Damned. He was damned.

He tore at his mouth with his claws, ripping, cutting, slicing open his lips and gums. His claws clacked against his teeth. His own vampire blood seeped thick and black onto the stone.

Cade laughed.

"You bastard!" Karl screamed, and leapt at Cade, claws outstretched to gouge out his eyes.

Cade hit him so hard he smashed into the stone wall at the

opposite side of the room. The dark world spun around him and pain throbbed in his head. He tried to stand again, but didn't have the strength. He sagged to the floor, the stone cold beneath his face.

Boots approaching. Even, unhurried steps. He blinked, tasting blood. Always tasting blood.

Cade leaned over him and whispered, "A vampire has no use for morality. No use for honor or mercy or pity. We inspire horror—we do not feel it. Remorse is as strange to us as the stars. We are above these limiting human concepts. You would do well to remember that."

Karl didn't hear him leave, but he could sense that he was now alone with the body of the young girl. His weeping echoed from the walls.

It had been that moment that he'd known no matter what else he had to endure, someday he would kill Cade.

And how he'd made Cade suffer when Karl had finally driven those silver spikes into his wrists, pinning him to holy ground, burning his own undead flesh and not caring, because the sun was rising fast, and he wanted Cade to greet it with eyes wide open.

Karl couldn't hide his mood from Xiesha. She knew him too well.

"Can I help in any way?" she asked, after having kept her silence for a long while.

No need to tell her of his slouch down memory lane. She was used to it.

"No," he said. "The Lucattis and the Ricardis are going to sit down and stop the little war Alberto started. It seems New York is less than pleased with what's been going on."

"I see." She paused. "Anyone vocal?"

"Two of the five families have made their displeasure widely known. They fear media coverage. And nobody's happy about the loss of income." A part of him felt like driving a fist through the wall. A part of him just felt tired. "That's what it always comes down to. Money."

"These families and syndicates remind me of the..." she gestured smoothly with one pale hand, "...guilds, perhaps is the word, from where I come."

"You've mentioned that before."

"In five hundred years of existence it's hard not repeat yourself once or twice."

She managed to win a smirk from him with that one, but his amusement didn't last. He could feel his power coiling in the center of himself. He hadn't fed as often in thirty years as he had during this war. And this dark feeding frenzy would leave him at peak power to face the end of his personal war. Alejandro Delgado was out there somewhere. Waiting. And that made him feel a level of tension and excitement—no, *anticipation*—that he hadn't experienced in hundreds and hundreds of years. Life could grow remarkably banal over long stretches of time, but now he felt a build up, a movement toward crescendo and it made him feel almost alive.

And then word of this truce.

"You could always break the truce," Xiesha suggested. "It will foster the instability that we thrive in."

That would be risky, but certainly something to carefully consider. If the war continued then the Ricardis would retain him, and the Lucattis would keep their pet Spaniard. And that meant he would have another chance at Delgado.

His cell phone rang. "Vance," he answered.

"It's over."

He could hear the anger and frustration in Maria's voice. He knew this was what she had feared.

"I see."

"They had the sit down today," she said. "John accepted the offer. We're done."

"I'm sorry to hear that. I know that's not what you wanted."

"Well, nobody really gave a fuck about what I wanted. It's for the good of the family. I shouldn't even be saying anything. Me and my big mouth."

"I can keep confidences." Out of the corner of his eyes he saw Xiesha grin.

"A dead man tells no tales," Xiesha whispered, too quietly for any but Karl to overhear. It was a wonder he put up with her.

"You know, I don't know why I believe you, but I do," Maria said. "Not that it matters anymore. Back to the business of money for everybody. I'd like to say it was sweet, but it really wasn't."

"I'd like to say the Lucattis are finished, but they really aren't."

"Yeah. *Touché.* You get your money anyway. I'll transfer the rest tonight." She took a breath. "I guess this is goodbye then."

He was silent a moment. "Goodbye then."

He listened to the dial tone and stared out his darkened window at the Boston night. Xiesha withdrew, and it was suddenly very quiet.

Chapter Nine:
Loss

"Where can I reach you?" Leonardo Antonelli asked. Her father's youngest captain had been leaving message after message on Maria's voicemail. You'd have thought she was his pusher or something.

"Look," Maria said, "I have to keep my head down for a little while. I don't want to be reached. When I want to contact someone, I will."

It was bad enough that everybody knew she was hiding. At least no one except Vance knew the real reason why. She hated the loss of face, and dropping off the radar in the capo meetings made her grind her teeth in frustration, but the memory of what had happened to Cabrera the mule made her accept the sacrifices.

"I don't get why you're laying low now that things have settled down," he said. "What's the point? It's over."

"I know it's over. I have my reasons, and I'm not going to tell them to you, so don't waste my time asking."

"It's just fucking annoying, that's all. I need some cleaning done and you're nowhere to be found."

"I'll have it done by the end of the week." If his crew earned like they should, he wouldn't be so desperate for her to immediately launder the money he was bringing in with his Friday night games. With him, it was always a crisis. She had other problems.

"Thanks, babe."

The line went dead. And that was what she got for her troubles. A *thanks, babe*, like she was a fucking *goomah*. Well, that and a five percent cut for laundering the money, but still.

She hadn't seen Vance in two weeks. She hadn't gone back to her apartment yet either, instead hiding out at a friend's place in Brighton. What if Vance suddenly decided to clean up loose ends? Her knowledge had to be dangerous to him. Or what if that other vampire—Delgado—uncovered where she lived? Her apartment was under a false name, and only her father and a few select others knew where it was, but it was best to keep her head down until she knew how things would play out.

Her cell rang again, playing The Clash's "London Calling". "Yeah?"

"Guess who, sweetcheeks."

"What do you want, Roberto?"

"Where's the love?" her half-brother asked. He dropped the mocking tone and got to business. "I need to meet with you. Father's orders."

"Absolutely not." She glanced at her bureau with her Glock 9mm lying on the top next to her overnight bag and a tube of lipstick.

"I know something spooked you. Tell you what, I don't even care what it was. Maybe you just don't have the stomach for running with the big dogs. It don't matter. This isn't about that."

"Then what do you want?"

"Like you've never heard of RICO? Like I'm going to say something specific over a phone line? Not even. I just want to say we have one more chore for our mutual friend. You know the one I'm talking about?"

Karl Vance, of course. What did he want with Vance? Vance belonged to her.

Or he *had* belonged to her, before the truce. So did this mean there would be one last target? Something using an outside gun—even less traceable than importing ghost soldiers from Sicilian *borgatas*? If so, it had to be something big, like a strike at the Lucatti underboss or *consigliere*, or maybe even the boss himself, Stefano Lucatti.

"I know which mutual friend you're talking about. I want to talk to Father first."

Roberto laughed. "Fine. Good luck. He's removed himself to Florida for the moment, with the feds all over the place lookin' to make any charge stick and the Globe goin' on about Chicago-style gangland war in the streets of Boston, so good fucking luck reaching him. An innocent man had better keep his head down to not get hit with some of the flying shit."

That last was no doubt for the wiretaps, if any agents were listening in. Unlikely, since everybody used prepaids or switched cells as often as they could.

"I don't believe you," she said. "Why would he have you call me?"

"Because I hate your guts, that's why. He wanted to rub my nose in it. Look, Daddy's keeping things in the blood on this one. It's that important. He wants me to meet with you, and for you to speak to our mutual friend."

This was the first she'd heard of her father leaving Boston, but it made sense. With all the heat the war had generated it was safer to stay clear of the fallout zones until things settled down. Still, she was irritated and a little hurt that he hadn't trusted her enough to tell her. And why would he think that she'd trust Roberto?

"No," she answered. "I'm not telling you where I'm at."

Roberto gave a dramatic sigh. She could almost see him rolling his eyes and flinging a hand at the obstinate foolishness of women.

"Fine. I'll let Daddy know you wouldn't play ball. I'm sure that'll make him really happy. Maybe I'll just take care of things myself. Who needs a fuckin' barbarian working for us anyway? You know that some people been talking? Seems our friend traces his roots back to the Visigoths."

"And I'm related to Cleopatra. It never got me free gas at Sunoco, did it?"

"What the fuck are you talking about?" Roberto said. "I'm being serious. The Visigoths sacked Rome. Watch the History channel sometime. You might learn something."

"Yes. I can see why the Goths sacking Rome means that our friend is untrustworthy. I'm grateful for the enlightenment."

"I don't need this shit. You don't want to meet? Fine. I'll pass word back up the pipe."

But what if he were telling the truth?

"Wait," she said. "Don't hang up."

There was a long pause.

"Yeah, I'm waiting…"

"Fine, I'll meet you. But not here. There's a little coffee shop off Chatham. Meet me there at four."

"I can't make four. Seven instead. That works better for me."

It would be dark by then.

"You there?" Roberto asked. "I said, let's do seven."

"All right. Seven."

Her half-brother hung up without a goodbye. She walked to the Glock 9mm and stared at it for a moment before slipping it into a holster and putting it on, so that the gun was hidden at the small of her back.

She glanced at the clock. Almost four hours to go until the meeting. She considered calling Vance, but this was family business. She'd see what it was all about before involving him further.

She only hoped this would be worth her time.

Roberto Pulani was on time for once in his life, which Maria found somewhat strange. Things must be more important than she'd thought. It certainly lent weight to his claim that her father was authorizing this. Roberto was a lot of ugly things, but he had always hesitated to cross their father directly.

She sat at a table in the corner of the little coffee shop, preferring to sit across from Roberto. He had a cup of espresso in front of him and he blew on it, sending wisps of steam across the table. He glanced up and leered at her.

"Your tits are looking good, sis."

"Fuck you," she said, already wanting to be gone. "So what's this big secret you had to drag me down here for?"

"First things first. Were you tailed?"

"Yeah, by the entire Presidential motorcade."

He snorted. "And how the fuck would you know if you were followed?" He peered around the mostly empty shop as if he believed that every customer was an FBI agent.

"Give me a break, Rob. My IQ is a good fifty points higher than yours. I think I can spot the feds."

"Someday someone's going to rip out that sarcastic tongue of yours."

The weight of the 9mm was a comfort. "Can we skip the

usual I hate-you, you-hate-me bullshit and get to the point?"

"Fine. *Daddy* wants one last thing done. He wants Vance to off Marco Lucatti."

Marco Lucatti was a son of the Lucatti boss and likely heir to the Lucatti *borgata*. It had to be a long-range move, because while Marco ran a good-sized crew, his death wouldn't immediately cripple the Lucattis.

"How do you suggest he do that? All the Lucattis have been keeping a very low profile."

"Simple," Robert said, and smirked. "Marco just served out a ten-year sentence for moving heroin. What's the first thing a man needs when he gets out of the joint?"

"I don't know. Tampons for his bleeding asshole?"

"Fucking cute. The answer is, he needs a woman."

"A woman. Well he's had three months to have his fill of them. Your point?"

"He favors this one hairdresser chick, and we know where she lives." He slid a napkin across the table to her. On the back an address was scrawled in her brother's handwriting.

"That easy, huh?"

"Of course. Women have been getting men killed since the beginning of forever."

"Profound. Really. Where'd you get this idea, anyway? The Godfather?"

He got that sulky look she hated even more than his usual insolent and angry expressions. What did her father see in him?

"Look, if you're not interested, forget about it. You were the one all hot and bothered to get involved."

"True," she said, "but the thing is—I don't trust you. I think you're too stupid to come up with anything on your own, and this is probably some scheme of Cavallo's to get me on the outs with my father. I have Marco whacked, all of a sudden the truce is in question. New York's already ruled, so we really don't need the Commission siding against us. Sounds like bait to me. But this is all probably over your head, so I don't know why I'm wasting my time explaining it."

His eyes were cold and furious. He gripped a plastic coffee stirrer as if he wanted to leap across the table and stab her with it. Her heart started to beat harder, and a drop of sweat trailed down from beneath her right arm, so cold it almost made her shiver. Suddenly, her pistol seemed a poor defense against her muscular half-brother, with his unibrow and his expensive but ill-fitting clothes. She wanted something else. Something bigger. A cruise missile maybe.

"Well, that's that." He stood. "Don't cry to Daddy that I didn't try."

"I'll do what he orders," she said, standing as well. They faced each other from a couple of feet away. She saw that they were drawing a few glances, and that was dismaying. "Only I want the word to come from him, not you."

Roberto Pulani pushed past her. "See you around, sis." He laughed, and the door chimed as he pulled it open.

She stood there for a moment, breathing in the mixed scents of a dozen kinds of coffee beans. Her coffee sat untouched on the table. She sat back down and finished it, and then left through a side door. Why had he left laughing?

The night air was cold, and the cloud ceiling was low and gray, threatening early snow. Her half-brother's Cadillac was gone. A slow survey of the lot showed her nothing out of the ordinary. Still, she watched the shadows for several minutes, her hand near her automatic. Finally, she hurried to her car, dropped into the leather seat and gunned the engine, tires chirping as she left the parking lot.

Maria took a convoluted route home, checking and rechecking for tails. She doubted the FBI was on her, but she didn't trust Roberto as far as she could kick him, and the Lucattis were still a potential threat, truce or no. *Cosa Nostra* history was rife with failed truces. Talk to the Colombo family about that. That *borgata* had been hemorrhaging from violent internal power struggles for as long as she could remember. Truces only lasted until the clips could be reloaded.

Maria pulled into the driveway of the three-decker house in Brighton. The top floor was for rent, the middle floor was dark— a nurse who worked night shift—and the bottom floor belonged to an out-of-town friend from college who was totally unconnected to the mafia. Carrie had agreed to let her hide out there for a few weeks, until the shit storm subsided.

She opened the Mercedes door and stepped onto the pavement, sighing out breath that steamed around her face. Cold and getting colder. She hated the cold. Her father had better be enjoying his time in Florida. God knew she'd love to be someplace where the sun was still warm.

She shut the car door and was about to turn up the brick path to the house when something under the car grabbed her ankle.

Karl Vance stood just outside the ring of light from the overhead streetlamps and watched a Lucatti enforcer named Guiseppe "Mutton" Avellino. Mutton Avellino spoke into a pay phone near the men's restroom at a 7-11 gas station, his shoulders hunched and his face tense. Karl could smell the stench from the restroom mixing with the pungent odor of gasoline. He could hear Mutton's conversation with another man, but Mutton was smart enough not to use names. They were talking about the truce, and how Mutton was expected to start kicking back upstream again, now that things were settling down. Mutton said he had a guy in Quincy who owed him big for last year's Super Bowl bets and he'd be paying him a visit shortly.

For two nights straight Karl had been stalking Mutton Avellino, learning his patterns. Tonight he'd move to feed, just as soon as the man left the light.

He ran his tongue across his fangs and waited.

Maria stared down at the hand locked around her ankle, her heart beating hard and fast. Her ankle ached where the cold, white fingers dug into her, claws pricking though her jeans. A face peered out from beneath the Mercedes—red eyes and long fangs gleaming in the porch light. The other vampire. The Spaniard.

His hand was grimy with dirt from the undercarriage, his silk suit rumpled and stained. But his grip was like an iron shackle and his skin was glacier-cold. She yanked free her Glock and shot that hand four times, *pop-pop-pop-pop*. The muzzle flash was a bright flare, and the brass shell casings tumbled to the cracked driveway with a musical ringing. She didn't care if she shot off her own foot, but she was lucky, and the fourth shot weakened his hold enough for her to wrench her leg free. A hiss of frustration escaped him. She remembered her crucifix necklace, and then remembered she'd left it by the sink when she'd taken it off to shower. She sprinted for the door, praying there was some truth to the legend that vampires couldn't enter houses uninvited.

"Did I startle you?" a smooth, dark voice said behind her, with that hint of a Spanish accent.

She whirled, raising the pistol, but he snatched it out of her hand before she could pull the trigger. His hand crushed the gun's trigger guard and grip, and bits of metal and plastic clinked to the cement. He tossed the ruined weapon aside.

The vampire stood half illuminated in the light from the porch and adjusted his silk tie, which had come askew.

"Maria Ricardi." He gave her an elegant bow. "We haven't been formally introduced, though we've met before. I'm sure you remember. I saw you watching, naughty girl."

She said nothing, not daring to move. Her heart was beating so hard she found it difficult to think. Lights had come on in one of the adjacent three-decker homes and she saw a curtain twitch. Delgado flicked a hand and the porch light went dark, drowning them in sudden shadows.

She drew in breath to scream, but Delgado raised a finger. "Shh," he whispered.

The breath leaked from her lips with a gentle sigh.

Someone had to have heard the gunshots. The cops had to be coming. If only she could last until then. Delgado waited, unmoving. She matched him, as still as if she stood before a cobra. A neighbor opened the door of a gray, weather-beaten three-decker and stuck his head out. Middle-aged, balding, gray-streaked mustache. He glanced up and down the street and then slowly shut the door.

Firecrackers. A 9mm could sound just like kids screwing around with—

The lights in the houses went off one by one. She saw another set of blinds move and then go still. The watcher had abandoned his post.

Delgado smiled. "That's better." He took a step toward her, cat quiet and sinuous as an eel. Maria took a matching step backward.

"We have a mutual friend," Delgado continued. "Karl Vance. I believe you know him." His hand shot out and gripped her neck, turning her head from side to side as he examined her flesh. "But it doesn't look as if he's bothered to taste you. Why is that, *querida mia*? Are you a bit too sour for his tongue?

I know for certain he likes them young."

She said nothing, straining to hear sirens. Anything.

"Still so quiet, *querida*. And you strike me as a woman who loves to hear her own voice. My name is Alejandro Delgado. We shall know each other very well before this night is done."

She was off and running before she even realized it, sprinting as hard as she could for the open night. She managed only ten steps before he grabbed her by the arm and pulled her close. His red eyes blazed in his white face and she could smell his breath, reeking of blood and crypts.

"No, no, no," he whispered. "That won't do, at all." He handed her a cell phone. "Now I want you to make a little call." His smile was all fangs.

Karl slipped through the shadows, close enough that he could smell Guiseppe Avellino's sweat. It was stale and heavy, with traces of garlic lingering in his pores. It was fortunate the tale about garlic repulsing vampires was only a myth. Mutton wore a heavy winter coat that smelled faintly of mothballs, and a cigarette hung from the side of his mouth.

An instant before Karl moved for the kill, his cell phone vibrated in his pocket.

He faded back into the darkness. Mutton started his Mustang, revved the engine twice and then pulled away from the gas station.

Damn it. The light of the cell's screen turned Karl's hand a ghostly pale blue. "Yes?"

Crying on the other end. Sobbing. *Maria.*

He didn't expect the surge of feelings that rushed through him. It felt as if someone were scraping the inside of his gut with shards of glass.

"Calm down," he said, the weight of command in his voice. "What's wrong?"

"He's here," she whispered. "He's *here*."

Delgado. So many emotions roared through him like a whirlwind, none of them good, ripping pieces of him free and hurling them into the darkness. "Put him on."

"He doesn't want to talk to you. He wants you to talk to me."

"What does he want?" Years of existence kept his voice

calm, disconnected.

"He wants you to come here." She seemed to pull herself together a bit, her sobbing breaking off into sniffles. She gave him the address and he memorized it. "Please hurry," she added, a whisper more terrible than the sobs for the grain of hope it still held.

"I'll be there soon." In the background Karl could hear Delgado's laughter, colder than the emptiness unfolding inside him.

It took him an hour to get there, moving as fast as he could. No matter how much he'd wanted to run to her immediately, first he'd needed a weapon from the apartment. Something suitable for a Master as ancient as Delgado.

He stood outside the three-decker house and watched it. The house was completely dark inside and all the blinds were shut. Maria's car sat parked in the cracked driveway. Brass shell casings lay scattered on the asphalt.

Too long. I took too long.

He could smell Delgado, the scent of the dead, roses and decay—slight, barely detectable, even to him, but still there.

A hundred night sounds assaulted his ears. The *plink* of a slowly dripping faucet. A small animal rustling in the ivy. Traffic three blocks over. More sounds, too many to name. Distracting, as he filtered through them, searching for one coming from inside the house, or one that would indicate that an ambush had been laid.

No sound came from behind those dark windows, though he listened for a long time.

He prayed silently, standing on the frost-covered lawn. *God help her, please.* But as always, he couldn't tell if anyone listened.

Karl walked up the brick path leading to the front door. When he reached the door, he drew out the knife he kept in a sealed lead box in his apartment. He'd never handled it directly, careful to only touch the grip with gloved hands, which was painful enough. The knife was over two hundred years old, with a blade of pure silver, heavily tarnished, and a cross etched in the metal. A priest, long dead, had blessed it, and it glowed a shimmering blue-white to his eyes. The hilt was rosewood, carved with Greek writing. He'd known what it meant, once upon a time, but he'd forgotten.

He gritted his teeth and kept his fingers tight around the hilt, though it burned his hand through his glove. The blade had been created to destroy malign creatures—vampires, werewolves, the evil fae, and on and on. A knight of the Order of the Thorn had given it to him in payment for a job. A hit. He'd kept it all these years, waiting for the chance to plunge it into the heart of Alejandro Delgado.

The smell of Maria's perfume lingered around the door to the bottom floor apartment. The door itself was unlocked. It swung inward at his push, and the first thing he smelled was blood.

Inside was a maze of shadowed pseudo-shaker furniture and shabby chic décor. Picture frames lined the shelves and mismatched pillows were piled on the chintz couch. He moved silently across the wood floors, following the scent of blood and the first faint sounds he could hear coming from deeper in the house. Almost absurd sounds. A slurp—the sound of throat muscles swallowing.

He found them in the kitchen on the patterned linoleum. Maria was sprawled across Delgado's lap, her head turned up as Delgado dripped vampire blood from a deep cut in his arm into her open mouth. Black blood smeared Maria's lips and ran in rivulets down her cheek and neck. Two puncture holes marred her neck, her skin moonlight pale. She drank Delgado's blood greedily, her eyes unfocused.

Delgado looked up when Karl entered. He smiled. "Welcome, friend. I was just finishing."

Rage opened its red eye within Karl. He took two running steps and leapt at Delgado, knife slashing through the air in a wicked arc. Delgado threw Maria off him and jumped to his feet, but not quickly enough. Karl's knife caught him at his left wrist, the deadly sharp silver blade slicing through the vampire's flesh. Delgado shrieked, holding his severed stump aloft as if accusing Karl with the sight of it. The skin around the cut smoldered. Dark blood seeped from the stump. On the floor, the severed hand clenched shut and then trembled as it opened again, already dissolving into nothingness.

"You insolent dog!" Delgado screamed. "You bring one of their weapons against me?" He staggered away, his eyes wild with pain, rage and something beautiful—fear. "I swear before the Morning Star you'll suffer for this."

"Cade said the same thing when I staked him out in the sun," Karl said.

His hand hurt from where he held the knife, but it was nothing compared to what Delgado must be enduring. Delgado's hand would never regenerate, cauterized, so to speak, with a holy silver blade. But that didn't matter, because Karl would never give it time to heal. Delgado would die tonight. For killing John Avalon. For a thousand faceless victims. For turning Maria.

For Maria, most of all.

Karl struck again, but Delgado spun and fled through the house. Karl followed right on his heels, slashing with the knife and barely missing.

"Help me," Maria whispered.

Karl slowed, glancing backward, checked by the defeat in her voice. Delgado leaped a sofa and sprinted for the open door. Karl tore himself away from her and went after Delgado, hating himself for leaving her, but hating Delgado more. He reached the door in time to see Delgado leap to the top of Maria's car, and then bound off into the night.

"Help me, Karl," Maria whispered again. Her voice floated through the house to him. "Please..."

He turned back, still smelling Delgado's scent in the air, his arm still tingling from the blow he'd struck. Ashamed that he'd turned his back on her at all.

He stepped into the kitchen. The vampire light shone weakly in her eyes, that spectral red glow so like the coals of a dying fire. He could smell the scent of vampire inside her skin, at odds with her expensive, floral perfume.

Maria would die tonight. There was nothing he could do to stop it, no way for him to save her. She would die tonight and rise again tomorrow after sunset, a slave to Alejandro Delgado.

Karl stood over her, staring down into her pleading eyes. There was fear in those eyes, desperation on her face. His grip on the knife was crushing, and it seared him in turn.

"He did this to me," she said, her voice weak. "Said it would make you suffer...no matter what you chose to do. I'm sorry..."

"Don't talk," he whispered. One stroke of the blade was all it would take. It would be mercy.

"I...don't want this... I thought I did, but I don't."

"I know."

"Kill him for me?" That pleading request. John Avalon, and now Maria.

"Yes."

"I..." but she didn't finish. He watched as she died, and the last of her humanity left her face. He stood there, staring down at her and the twin puncture wounds in her neck. No sound of breath in a night that screamed its sudden silence.

The knife hung heavy in his hand. Burning him.

A kindness. How many times had he wished someone had done the same for him, before he'd become so corrupted?

Her face. So young.

She no longer belonged to anyone but Alejandro Delgado. Surely, it would be mercy.

He closed his eyes.

Chapter Ten:
Night Falls

"[W]hich way shall I fly
Infinite wrath, and infinite despair?
Which way I fly is Hell; myself am Hell..."
—Milton, *Paradise Lost*

The dreams were the worst. Maria sprinted through empty courtrooms and abandoned buildings where shadows bred, feeling the weight of a hundred pairs of eyes watching her run. Whispers, soft and malevolent, drifted down halls and corridors. When she turned to look, she could see nothing. Just shadow.

Something pursued her across those empty places. A darker menace, always just beyond her sight, always just behind her, around a corner. It seemed to draw her, to slow her footsteps.

This thing, this terror that pursued her called her name, over and over, *"Maria. Maria Ricardi. You are mine."*

Images drifted through her mind. Disconnected. Hauntingly real.

Images. A cracked wineglass, the wine seeping out onto a white tablecloth. A field of dandelions nodding in the breeze and casting thin shadows. The sun setting behind jagged mountains, bleeding the meadow red. Her dead brother Paul, standing beneath a barren maple tree, beside a huge pile of fallen leaves. The leaves shifted and churned as if something were trying to crawl out. Her brother stared at her with those dark eyes so full of sorrow it felt like her heart would drown. He opened his mouth and said something, but no sound came out.

His teeth were very white, his lips very pale. A moment later he opened his mouth again, but instead of words, blood poured out, pattering onto the leaves.

Again, someone whispered, *"You are mine."*

Recognition flooded her with fear. Delgado. His voice was compelling, commanding every ounce of attention. Those red eyes, searing her mind.

She fled toward the dream darkness, but another scene fell into place around her like a net.

Her father, smoking a cigarette and leaning against the stained brick of an alley wall. A memory full of vivid detail. He'd stared at her with those sharp, appraising eyes. Angry. Indignant.

"No," he'd said. "Never."

She had stood before him. Young—what had she been? Seventeen? Eighteen? How her hands had wanted to shake, and how hard she'd fought to keep them still.

She'd said something—she couldn't remember what. But every word of his reply had pierced her through.

"My son is dead. There's no place for you."

"I'm better than he was." Her voice—the quaver belying the arrogance.

Her father had slapped her. The view of the alley with its puddles of engine oil and litter spun wildly. Her cheek burned as if branded.

"I said no, goddammit. Women don't have a place here. Don't ask again."

Her hand lifted to touch her cheek.

"You will kill him, Maria," Delgado said. His tone made it seem inevitable.

She shook the memory apart, and it shattered like a mirror into a thousand shards, each bearing the image of her father into the darkness around her.

"You will kill them all," Delgado continued. *"You will rise to command your family. And you will take your place in service to me. Kill your father and take everything that should have been yours…"*

"Never!" she shrieked back into that darkness.

Laughter. *"You are mine."*

She woke with a scream on her tongue, but without the

breath to give it voice.

There was no heat, but there was thirst. Her throat felt as if it had been scraped raw with a rusted piece of metal. There was no light, but darkness she had in abundance. She could smell soil—dark, rich earth—and something that reminded her of her mother's funeral.

She felt...strange. Enhanced somehow. The smells were richer and more vibrant than anything she'd smelled before. She could see nothing, but her nerve endings sent back a thousand signals amplified far beyond anything she'd ever experienced. She lay half-submerged in something cool and damp—the soil that she could smell. Something was wrong, though—her body felt...silent. That made no sense, but that's the only way she could think to describe it.

Voices distracted her. Very soft. Far away. A woman's voice.

"She belongs to him, Master. Bringing her here..."

"She's my responsibility." A man this time. The voice was familiar, but she couldn't immediately place it. The words were tinted with something she didn't quite understand, a kind of power that pulled her attention to it, resonant like a church bell and impossible to ignore.

"She will tell him where we are. Even if she doesn't want to. She won't be able to deny him."

"Let him come."

"He won't come himself. He will use her against you. That's what I would do."

"Possibly."

She recognized the voice. Karl Vance. There was silence for a while, and Maria stared into the darkness, terror building within her. Something was wrong with her breathing. She *wasn't* breathing. Her heart should have been pounding away, but she could feel nothing.

And why was it so fucking *dark*?

"I know why you want this," the woman's voice said. She too sounded strange, her voice more resonant, but somehow less natural, as if her words weren't shaped by human tongue. "You want to teach her. You want to raise her to be like you."

They were talking about her. Those words drove a stiletto of ice into the center of her thoughts.

"She'll kill innocents unless she's guided carefully," Karl

said. "She'll damn herself like I did."

"She's his slave. And dangerous. I wish you would reconsider."

"I've made my choice."

There were a few more minutes of silence, in which she should've felt the physical effects of fear—adrenaline, increased heart rate—yet she felt nothing but an intensifying of the feeling in her mind, as if the picture of her terror came into sharper and sharper focus.

The total darkness suddenly disappeared as light streamed in—a violent flash that made her flinch, displacing the soil she was half buried in. Karl's face appeared over her, staring down with his mouth set in a grim line as she rapidly blinked. His face was a more welcome sight than she ever would've admitted a day ago.

He reached a hand down to her, and after a pause, she grabbed it and allowed him to pull her to a sitting position. Soil showered down from her, and she brushed it away. She could see that she was in a dimly lit room, inside a steel box filled with dirt.

Another glance told her this was Karl's room. A massive four-poster bed loomed in the center, with thick carved teak head and foot boards, but the comforters and pillows looked as if they'd never been used. The steel coffin sat at the foot of the bed. The room's windows were sealed up with heavy black draperies. On one wall a battered old tapestry hung from the broken haft of a pike. The tapestry was woven of deep red and gold thread, and showed mounted horsemen hunting a fox beneath a setting sun. Along the opposite wall stood two exquisite armoires, dark wood, beautifully carved.

She tried to speak. Couldn't. Her mouth gaped open, but no sound poured out. She began to panic, her hand reaching to her throat, clawing at it.

"Breathe in first," Karl told her quickly. "You can't speak until you draw in air."

She did so, drawing a great gasping breath. The muscles in her chest felt strange—she'd never been so conscious of how they worked before.

"Karl," she said, and then stopped, wondering at her voice. It was fuller than it had been, richer in timbre. "My voice is different."

He gave her a small smile, but it was not a happy smile. "You'll find a lot of things are different now."

"Why?" She touched her throat again and all the memories came flooding back. Delgado. What he'd done to her in the kitchen of her friend's house. The shock of that first bite—pain and pleasure interwoven. The dark, rich taste of his blood as he dripped it onto her tongue. How powerless she'd felt, weaker than a kitten, more helpless than a child, and how she'd hated that, wanted to claw his eyes out but was unable to summon the strength. Her fingers searched for Delgado's bite wounds but could find no trace of them. No scarring. Nothing. The thought of his name sent a surge of power shuddering through her, making her dizzy, making her stomach feel as though someone had just twisted it up and wrung it out. She clutched the sides of the steel box for support.

"Don't think of him," Karl said. "It will only make things worse."

"Can you read my mind?" Funny how the thought didn't seem so far-fetched now.

"No. But I've been through all this before."

She stood slowly, and the dizziness passed. Now she could feel the strength pouring through her limbs like hot oil, all the way down to her fingers and toes. She seemed to weigh nothing at all, and suddenly realized that if she wanted to spring to that opposite wall and climb it, she could. If she wanted to do handsprings and back flips, she could. She'd never felt this in touch with her body before. And not the slightest desire for a cigarette.

But that silence...

No rush of blood through the veins, no beat of heart, no gurgle of stomach, no steady rasp of breath. Nothing.

"I'm dead, aren't I?" she said, needing the confirmation. The disconnected, eerily calm feeling was back. Her laughter was shaky. "There's a question you don't ask every day."

Karl nodded. "Delgado."

Delgado.

Again that spike of reaction, a head rush that had her rubbing her temples and trying to shake away the sudden fog. Why did that happen every time she thought of him?

"And now I'm—" she couldn't say the word that was hovering over her tongue, "—like you."

"Not yet," Karl said.

She didn't have time to ask what he meant. An exotic-looking woman entered the room and bowed. Her face was exquisite—glowing with a serene and statuesque beauty Maria immediately envied. She wore a red kimono with black Chinese dragons cavorting down the sides. Now why had Karl never mentioned her before? Maria turned to look at him.

His smile was amused. "She's my bodyguard." He glanced at Xiesha. "Xiesha, I'd like you to meet Maria Ricardi. Maria meet Xiesha."

"An honor," Xiesha said. Maria recognized her voice as the one who'd been speaking with Karl while she'd been inside the box. "He saved my life years ago, and now I ensure he is safe during the daylight."

"An honor to meet you," Maria replied, not really meaning it, the phrase feeling awkward in her mouth.

Xiesha bowed to her again, then turned to Karl. "I'll be scrying if you require me." Karl nodded and she withdrew, leaving them alone.

Maria folded her arms together across her chest to keep herself from shaking. These shifts from calm to terror were wrenching her into knots.

"Somebody said I was a slave." For all the power and strength she now had, perhaps she had nothing after all.

"Delgado turned you. You're his sireling."

"What does that mean?" she asked. His face was set and grim, and maybe that told her more than she wanted to know.

"He's your Master," Karl said. "You're his slave."

"I don't know what Mickey Mouse channel you've been watching, but I'm nobody's slave."

"You're bound to him. When he calls, you'll go. When he commands, you'll obey."

"I don't believe you," she said. Delgado couldn't force her to kill her father. Never.

"You can't deny him." His expression had turned unreadable, but his eyes were angry. Angry at her? Or angry at Delgado?

"How do you know?" she demanded. "Who commands *you*?"

"I killed my Master a long time ago. The death of a Master

vampire frees his slaves."

"Then I'll kill Delgado." But even as the words left her lips, the futility of what she'd said seemed to strike her across the face. If Karl had hunted Delgado for hundreds of years and hadn't killed him yet, what hope did she have?

Karl touched her shoulder, pale hand on pale skin. "You're too young yet. Too inexperienced to resist him. That kind of power takes time to build."

She laughed bitterly. "Sounds like something my father would say."

Karl only looked at her.

She walked away from him, put one hand on the smooth wood of the bed and leaned against it, head down.

"So what do I do? You can't be telling me to give up, cuz like hell I will. There must be something I can do. Fight. Run. Something."

"I can destroy Delgado."

"God knows you've been so successful so far."

Karl said nothing, his face very still.

"Can't you bite me?" she asked when the silence grew too long. "Can't you make me *your* slave?" She moved close to him, touching his cheek, how cool the skin was. The detached part of her was amused at what she was doing. The rest of her was disgusted.

His face remained unreadable. "It's impossible. You belong to him."

The finality of his words clanged in her head like a bell. No options.

"I need to sit down," she said, almost dropping on the edge of the steel box Karl called his bed.

A vampire.

Fearing the sunlight...what if she forgot? What if she were out late one night and was caught away from her refuge and the sun came up? She'd seen her last dawn two weeks ago. If she'd have realized it would be the last, she would've taken a picture or something.

"Does my father know?"

"He knows nothing yet."

"Thank God for that."

"And he won't. You have to put that life behind you," Karl

said. "There'll be too many questions."

"Like hell I will. I put everything into that family. I won't abandon him now."

"What makes you think you'll have a choice?"

"There's always a choice. I don't care what anyone says—there's always a choice."

He touched her face. "No, Maria. Slaves make no choices."

"No!" She slapped his hand away. "Maybe I'll kill Delgado for you. I can feel the power in my body. I won't accept that I'm helpless."

"He'll come for you. Tonight, probably." He seemed as if he would say more, but kept his silence instead.

"What happens then?" she asked. "Do you let him have me?"

Her father. Oh God. Could Delgado make her kill her father? She slowly bit down on her tongue with one of her fangs, tasting only the barest trickle of blood—blood that tasted more like dirt than anything else. The power she'd always dreamed of, at the price of betraying everything she believed in.

"No," Karl said. "If he's foolish enough to come himself, I'll destroy him. I have a weapon that he's learned to fear." He clenched his right hand. When he opened his fist, she saw that strange characters were seared into his white flesh.

"What happened?" She took his hand. His skin was soft and cool, but the characters stood out in angry red.

"I touched a holy item and paid the price."

"So I guess Sunday Mass is out for me?" she said bitterly. "Not that I was in the habit of going. A bit hypocritical to attend Mass when you're cleaning money for the mafia."

"The power and symbols of faith can destroy us."

"I guess I'll take myself off the Pope's e-mail list then."

"Don't mock."

"It's how I deal with things."

Karl opened his mouth to say something, anger in his eyes, and she knew that the argument she'd been provoking would be a wild one. But then Karl paused, his head cocked like a wolf listening for a rabbit in the underbrush. His eyes narrowed, and she took a step away from him without thinking.

Xiesha strode back in the room. She carried a Beretta 12-gauge pump action shotgun, and the look on her face spoke volumes.

"Someone's here," Xiesha said. "Not human."

Karl went first, his strides confident, almost unhurried. Xiesha followed, flowing away like water running downhill. That left Maria to bring up the rear, and despite her newfound grace, she felt like an awkward colt. Part of it was not being able to identify whatever it was that had alerted the others.

"How do you know?" she whispered to Xiesha, hurrying to catch up.

"One of the outside windows was probed."

She'd always believed strength would eliminate her fear. Certainly she had strength in abundance now, yet it was all she could do to keep her voice even. "You have an alarm system?"

Xiesha shook her head. "*I* am the alarm system. I have wards on every entrance."

"Can they hear us?" Maria cocked her head to listen. Water in the pipes. A dozen random conversations. Footsteps. Televisions. What had tipped Karl off?

"No. I built the wards so that sound waves may enter the barrier but are absorbed if they move outward."

"What for?" Maria asked.

"Let them through the wards when they push," Karl said to Xiesha as he moved toward the closet in the living room, "and seal the wards behind them. We'll destroy them here."

"That's how come," Xiesha said to her, tapping one finger on the slide of her shotgun.

Maria turned to Vance and could see the dim ember of red in his eyes. How could he seem so calm? She felt as if her skin were three sizes too small, and any quick movement would burst her open.

Karl pulled open the closet door. It swung open with a smooth silence.

Maria didn't know what she expected but it definitely wasn't a closet full of tools, weapons, ammunition and strange objects, some of which she could sense had great power. There were a couple of hanging swords, an axe, a horizontal rack of assault rifles and shotguns with one empty slot—for Xiesha's shotgun, she guessed. A half dozen pistols, automatics and revolvers, sat on a gray metal shelf next to stacks of clips and ammo boxes. A crossbow and silver-tipped arrows. Necklaces with strange glimmering symbols dangled from hooks, thrumming with power. A golden pair of shears hung on a steel chain, seeming to chime with a distant music. Strange things, dozens, too many to take in at a glance.

Karl took down a gray leather box, pulled on a pair of black gloves, and raised the lid. He lifted out a dagger, and Maria shrank back from the blue-white light that gleamed from the blade. The light hurt her eyes, like a nail scratching at her exposed iris, and she raised a hand to shield her vision.

"What the hell is that?"

"Hell has nothing to do with this," Karl answered. "I cut off Delgado's hand with this when he killed you. It knows his blood now."

Xiesha came up beside Karl. "How many are out there?" She began to load a canvas ammo strap that slipped over the shotgun's butt. The strange looking slugs resembled pointed silver cylinders encased in red plastic shells. The sight of the silver made Maria shiver.

"Three," Karl said. "Two males and a female. Delgado's not with them."

That was both relief and disappointment. She didn't have time to sort out which of the two she felt more. Outside the window, the night pressed its face against the glass, and she felt exposed and vulnerable to its dark eyes.

"What weapon do I get?" She glanced at the blades and guns in the closet. There must be more of them that would be effective against vampires. The crossbow looked good. She'd never fired one before, but if people in the Dark Ages could do it, then so could she.

"You get to stay out of the way."

"And you get to kiss my ass," she replied. "I don't need to sit here cowering in a corner like a child."

He turned and looked at her, awash in that eerie blue light from the blade. "Yes," he said, "you do."

Maria ground her teeth to control her reply. Some things never fucking changed. "If I don't do something the fear will kill me. And I'm sick and tired of being afraid."

"One at the front door." Xiesha flattened herself against the wall, covering the doorway with the shotgun. "He is probing the wards. Be ready."

Maria's nails grew and hardened into claws in anticipation. She stared at them in surprise, pale hooks that would've been more at home on a jungle cat. She turned to Karl, but his absolute stillness and concentration silenced her. He now stood in the middle of the darkened room, his head down, listening for sounds she couldn't discern from the myriad noises of the building.

Karl lifted his head and looked at the sliding doors leading to the apartment's balcony. "Here they come."

A flash of purple-black light burst at the sliding door, not at the front door as expected. Maria heard Xiesha spit some strange word that burned the air like a curse, and a sound like breaking pottery exploded around them. At the sliding door, something that looked to Maria's enhanced senses like a chain built of black-light shattered into ethereal links that evaporated as the ward broke apart. The glass door began to slide open.

She could see nothing out on the balcony except furniture and plants.

A man-shape leaped to the balcony rail, then sprang through the open gap into the apartment. He wore a bright orange jumpsuit and his feet were bare. Long claws curved from his fingers and his eyes glowed an angry red. His head was completely bald, and his shoulders were massive, bestial. Broken handcuff bracelets circled his wrists.

The shotgun bellowed. The vampire's head exploded outward in a spray of flesh, brain and bone. He shrieked as his body unraveled, smoking and dissolving into a thousand black specks, like black sand thrown into the air. Grey-black ash drifted to the wood floors like snowflakes. Maria shuddered, still hearing the scream, though the vampire had vanished—a scream that faded to nothing, as if the creature were being pulled down to Hell.

"One," Xiesha said, working the slide on the shotgun. Maria glanced at her, and the exotic-looking creature gave her an angelic smile.

"No more shooting until the sound wards are back up." Karl's voice stayed even, almost unconcerned. His head was tilted downward in concentration again. The knife in his hand glowed with the blue-white light that hurt Maria's eyes until she looked away again.

Her ears throbbed from the shotgun blast, and she

understood the reason for the wards. She immediately understood something else as well—if gunfire was a normal enough occurrence that they'd have measures in place to protect them from the fallout, then Vance wasn't so unlike her own family after all. She wondered who else had heard the gunfire, and how many cops were on their way. The night was a cacophony of noises to her enhanced hearing, but she still couldn't tell which sounds were made by the vampires. It was all just a jumble of noise to her, and her ringing ears didn't help.

"We want the girl," a female voice called. Maria could feel the power in that voice. The sound of it pulled at her like a demand. She found herself starting toward the balcony doors before getting control of herself and stepping back.

"Tell Delgado to come get her himself," Karl said. "We can discuss it over dinner."

"The Master isn't in the mood to discuss anything with you, Betrayer. The old codes apply here. She belongs to him."

"She was taken against her will. No code applies."

"I think you're wrong about that, Traitor. She wanted it oh so badly."

"Run and tell your Master that she's under my protection. He knows where I am."

"I don't think that's an option." The voice's tone hardened, cracking like a lash. "Maria Ricardi. Come to me."

Maria found herself halfway to the balcony again before she even realized it. Her legs seemed to move of their own volition. The desire to obey that voice overrode all thought.

"Maria," Karl said. "Stop."

She halted. The fog that had swept over her mind vanished.

"The front door ward." Xiesha swung the barrel of her shotgun in that direction.

This time there was no flash of black and purple light, but instead a sensation of a curtain being lifted and suspended overhead. There was silence for a long moment. The door splintered around its reinforced hinges and deadbolts with an angry crack, but held fast.

A woman dropped onto the balcony from above, crouching outside the open sliding door. She was wrapped in some strange black leather outfit embedded with steel rings. A black choker circled her neck with a small ivory carving of a wolf's head at her throat, and raven black hair poured down over her shoulders. She bared her fangs in a hissing challenge to Karl. Xiesha swung the shotgun around, but Karl lifted a hand, stilling her.

Maria glanced toward the closet. Now. While everyone was distracted. She edged toward the weapons.

The woman stood, seeming to unfold from her crouch like a cobra rising from its coils. She crossed the threshold, her red eyes never leaving Karl. She glanced down at the knife he held, and she paused, her full lips twisting in hate.

"The Master has named you truly, Betrayer," she said.

Maria reached the closet. There were so many weapons that the sheer choice was overwhelming. There was one, however, that immediately caught her eye, because it shone with a black miasma beside the more ordinary weaponry. It was something she hadn't seen with her first glance into the closet—a flintlock pistol, its barrel carved with runes and symbols she didn't recognize, but which gave off the shimmer that had attracted her eye. A single raven feather hung from the pistol's handle. She seized it, feeling a surge of power tingling up her arm. The wood felt disgustingly warm, and she had the sudden feeling that the pistol was aware of her in some horrible way. She let go of it with a moan, and the pistol thumped to the floor. She wiped her hand on her clothes.

The front door crashed open with the sound of splintering wood and twisting metal. Maria turned toward the sound, but Xiesha was already advancing with the shotgun. Another massive figure stepped through the ruins of the door, red eyes in a square-jawed face with huge, hunching shoulders. His eyes moved over Xiesha and locked on Maria. A slow smile spread across his face, revealing huge fangs.

The female vampire leapt at Karl, slashing with her claws, her face twisted from beautiful to monstrous. Karl struck back with the knife, and the leather-clad vampire barely avoided it. She crouched on top of the table and hissed at him.

The massive vampire in the doorway laughed, a sound like breaking rocks. He took another step toward Xiesha, who tracked him with the shotgun.

"You think that toy's going to bother me, bitch?" he asked.

"Drop the barrier, Xie." Karl's voice was still calm, almost uncaring. Maria envied it.

Xiesha whispered words in a language Maria didn't understand—something liquid sounding that twisted with power. Maria felt the ward Xiesha had temporarily lifted fall back into place across the door behind the vampire.

The huge vampire laughed. "A little late, honey chile."

Xiesha fired, but the vampire must have been watching for the movement of her trigger finger. He threw himself to the side, and the shotgun slug impacted Xiesha's invisible barrier. A strange sound like the moaning wind filled the air, and the slug clinked to the wood floor.

The vampire moved toward her again, taking his time, grinning shark-like and malevolent. Xiesha never moved. She continued to hold the shotgun on him as the distance between them shortened.

Maria snatched up the crossbow she'd been eyeing earlier. She reached for a silver-tipped quarrel, but her hands were so unsteady she fumbled it. The silver tip skated across her skin, searing her. The pain was so sudden and so vibrantly real that she bit her fangs into her cheek to still a scream and almost dropped the crossbow. God she was handling this beautifully.

The huge vampire closed in on Xiesha. On the other side of the room, Karl and the female vampire clashed again at close range, their attacks so fast even Maria's vampire eyes barely caught them. A leather couch exploded into ribbons and stuffing as they fought their way around it.

The vampire at the door stumbled, a flash of red light filled the air, and his legs burst into flame. He threw back his head and howled in pain and rage.

Xiesha smiled. She pulled the trigger and the shotgun kicked. The vampire flew backward, a huge hole in his chest. His body shook, as if a violent seizure convulsed every muscle, and then his flesh fragmented into those dark motes and burned off into a flurry of ash. His last scream echoed from the walls and faded.

Maria spun back to the fight between Karl and the female vampire. The last vampire had paused at the death scream of her comrade, out of range of Karl's knife. She stood near one of the windows, her lithe form outlined by the moonlight. Her red eyes flitted around the room as Karl and Xiesha advanced on her.

"You watched your brothers die tonight, Maria," she said.

"And you did nothing."

Maria felt the power of the vampire's gaze focused on her.

"I am Minsku. Your sister through our Master. He wants you. Come with me."

Maria fought against the sudden urge to obey. "I'm no one's slave."

Minsku's laughter invaded her head. *"We are all slaves to something."* She began to feed Maria images, and Maria couldn't stop them from coming. Sprinting across rooftops in moonlight, leaping from roof to roof while the city slept below. The sensation of drinking blood, how it ran in a hot and rich flood down the throat. The dying light in a man's eyes as Minsku drained him.

That last image repulsed Maria, filled her with loathing, gave her something to push back against. But Minsku sensed her horror and laughed, taking another tack and sending fresh images. Delgado. His voice. His command. His hands on her breasts, sliding down her waist. His tongue on her skin. His teeth on her neck.

Maria staggered, weakness flowing through her. She held her head and shook it slightly, fighting to clear it, to find some way to break this link between them.

"Enough."

It was Karl's voice. Minsku turned to him and snarled like a beast, fangs bared, hate flaring in those red eyes.

"Go tell Delgado that she belongs to me," Karl said. "If he wants her, tell him to come himself and not send feeble lackeys to botch the job."

Minsku gave him a cold smile. "Don't think this is over, Betrayer. Next time I'll taste your ashes on my tongue."

Minsku whirled and sprinted for the balcony door, a blur of movement. She leapt onto the balcony rail, turned and pierced Maria with a look so intimate and knowing that Maria had to glance away. Minsku laughed and then leapt off the edge of the balcony and vanished.

"We should have killed her," Xiesha said.

"Delgado might do that for us, when he finds out they failed." Vance looked at Maria. "How are you?"

"Peachy," she replied. "I love being mindfucked by monsters who can get into my head any time they want."

Karl glanced at the crossbow in her hands and then down to the flintlock pistol. "Don't touch that again. It's extremely dangerous."

She fully intended to obey him. The gun had felt odd in her hand. Curiously...alive. Yet another strange thing in this new disturbing world she'd woken up in.

"Xiesha, grab some tools," Karl said. "Let's get that door back in its frame. The balcony ward is gone. What about the front door?"

"I lifted it for him to slip through and dropped it behind him. Most of the sound of the first shot was directed out the balcony."

"Still, we have to work fast." Karl opened the gray leather case and set the knife back inside. Maria was glad to see it disappear. "Can you weave some kind of illusion to conceal the damage to the door?"

Xiesha nodded. "I can do it quickly."

"And put that broken ward back up as soon as you can," Karl continued. "We'll have to lay low until any police are gone."

"What if he comes again?" Maria asked.

Karl shook his head. "Not tonight, I think. We hurt him. But you have much to learn before they come again."

She leaned against the remains of the couch. He was right. She'd been nothing more than a liability the entire fight. She was tired, though the weariness lingered only in her mind.

The night beyond the open balcony doors was dark and full of a million city sounds that drifted in with the cold air. She moved to the doors and slid them shut, then snapped the pathetic little lock into place, a pointless ritual that somehow she couldn't leave undone. How long until Delgado came for her? And how long until she ended up on the other end of Xiesha's shotgun—or the silver edge of Karl's knife?

Chapter Eleven:
Virgin Killer

Karl Vance had always been good at waiting.

For two weeks there was no sign of Delgado. Karl kept the silver dagger in a sheath by his side, bearing the discomfort without comment. His right hand still ached from where he'd held it, and the wounds in his flesh wouldn't heal.

Long years taught a creature patience. One year rolled into the next like waves crashing, reaching, and then withdrawing in a hiss of sea foam. Maria hadn't existed long enough to truly learn patience. Karl couldn't blame her for it.

She came to him on the balcony one night as the last of twilight faded and darkness settled. The clouds hung gray and low, threatening snow. The air held a bitter chill.

He'd always loved the balcony—it had been one of the key reasons for his choice to live here. It was walled on either side so he couldn't see his neighbors, decorated with sculpture and filled with Xiesha's plants, overflowing their urns and pots, so that in the spring it turned into a riotous jungle. Now cold weather had turned it into a brown tundra, but the abstract sculpture retained its eerie shadow play on nights when the moon shone. He'd been watching the traffic on the street below and thinking about Elizabeth Alvey, a girl he'd loved when he'd still been human.

Strange to remember her. He hadn't thought of her in a very long time.

The door slid open behind him, but he didn't turn.

"I want to call my father," Maria said.

He'd been waiting for this, though it had taken longer than

he'd expected. "You may call him at any time, if you must. I'd use a pay phone and follow all your usual precautions."

Her face betrayed surprise. "I didn't think you'd let me."

"I'm not your master."

She took a step and then hesitated. A breeze lifted her hair and blew it across the bottom of her face, so that all he could see were her eyes. "It's just that I thought you'd say no. That maybe calling wasn't a good idea."

"It's not a good idea," he said.

"Why not?"

"The daughter he knew is dead. He won't love you for what you are."

"My father—"

"We kill them, Maria. They have race memories of us. You've seen the movies, read the books. They remember—even if they don't believe. The only thing shielding us is their strong belief in the rational—in the world seen through the lens of science. But in their hearts, they fear."

"How would they even know? You walk among people all the time. You worked for us. I ate dinner with you, for God's sake, and I never even suspected what you were."

"It takes decades to gain the skill to deceive like that. If you were to go among them now, there's no telling what might happen. You might be consumed with bloodlust and attack them."

She drew back against the balcony rail, one hand clutching it. "You make me sound like a monster."

"You are."

"Then you're saying I should never speak to him again?" Her hand tightened on the railing, bending the ironwork. He placed his own hand over hers, but there was no heat between their flesh.

"Better he think you gone forever, than you suffer his loathing." He drew away. "But I'm only one voice. You're free to do what you feel is best."

She began to say something and then stopped, leaning her weight on the railing. She frowned, staring down at the traffic on the street far below. He watched her, seeing how pale she was, dreading this moment.

"I don't feel the same as I did when I first woke up," she

said, her voice little more than a whisper. "When I woke, I felt more *conscious* than ever. Colors were brighter, sounds a hundred times clearer, and the scents—overwhelming. Now I just feel hung over, and nothing is as clear as it was before."

It always came to this in the end. "You need blood."

Maria didn't answer, but he could feel the tension in her. She was terrible at masking her emotions, and he could see the war between her instinctual hunger and her fear, her bloodlust and her revulsion. This was damnation he couldn't save her from, though he would've given nearly anything to do so. Fresh human blood. There was no substitute.

"Come." He touched her shoulder. "Let's get it over with. This will be hard enough."

She looked at him with those wide brown eyes, and he was filled with so many regrets that he didn't trust himself to speak.

She was hungry. And she was young. But soon she would be neither.

Karl waited with Maria atop a high-rise building. They stood there in the wind near a huge thrumming A/C unit on the tarpaper rooftop. The floodlights near the stairwell were burned out, so they had the roof and the darkness to themselves.

Would Delgado come? It seemed likely. This was the first time they'd been far from the shielding of Xiesha's wards. Though perhaps Delgado was holed up in his coffin, too weak from his wound to do anything. Karl had brought the knife, just in case.

Maria said nothing the entire time they waited. She seemed lost in her own thoughts. No doubt she could feel Delgado out there somewhere, perhaps even speaking to her in her mind.

But as time passed and there was no sign of Delgado or his sirelings, Karl decided to move further into the city, keeping all his senses at their peak, wary lest they stumble into a trap.

They raced through the streets, darting between shadows, leaping rooftops and tightrope-walking power and cable lines from building to building.

"How does this happen?" Maria asked as they crossed another rooftop. The strain cracked in her voice like shattering ice. "How do I...?"

He stopped and faced her, but he did not touch her. There was no comfort to be had. For either of them. "First, there are rules, and you must learn them quickly. They're as much for your protection as they are for the rest of the world."

"Tell me."

"Never kill an innocent," he said. "There is never an excuse. Better to starve."

Maria's pale hand came up and touched her throat, then fell away again. She said nothing.

"We kill wiseguys. We kill mob wannabes and hangers on. We kill dealers and enforcers, bookies and hit men. It's never pretty, but they're all fair game because of the lives they choose, preying on others. The first time you feed on an innocent will be the day we part ways. After that, if I come across you again, I'll destroy you."

"Do we have to kill when we...feed?" she asked quietly.

"You can survive on fresh blood alone. However, you'll find you won't be able to stop, once you start." She would understand that soon enough. The bloodlust was like battle frenzy—it was difficult to think when feeding, especially at first. "But the main reason is that we cannot leave witnesses. We only survive because they don't believe. If every person starts to guard against us, we'll starve soon enough."

She nodded, watching him with those dark eyes. The vampire glow in those eyes was mostly hidden, but it had grown stronger as she'd talked about the killing.

"If you kill too many people, you'll stir up the police and the feds," he said. "You'll also draw the attention of an organization that you don't want to ever encounter—the Order of the Thorn. There's no saving you from them. It's safest to hunt people connected to the mob since they're always disappearing anyway."

She looked away from him. "How often...?"

"You can survive on one feeding per month, two months at most. More and you build your power, but at the risk of discovery. Less and your powers start to fade. You've never fed, and that's why you feel so drained after only a couple of weeks."

Her face was drawn, but the glow in her eyes was brighter. "Let's just get it over with."

"Patience. I have a target for tonight."

They completed the rest of the journey in silence, and despite his words and her assent, he had to keep her on a short leash. Already she'd let her eye roam to two civilians who'd passed close enough to smell the blood in their veins and feel their body heat. Both times he'd gripped her wrist, and the contact was enough to bring her back to herself and keep the predator inside under control. But the experience had shaken her. He could see it in her eyes, feel it in the tremble of her hand.

They finally arrived outside the Blue Northie Social Club, a hang out for Lucatti captain Dino Rotolo, and took up positions on a fire escape in the alley. Frost had already begun to form on the rails and the metal grates. Steam poured up from the gutters and the manhole covers, spectral in the light of the street lamps.

From the fire escape they could see the club's back door, where three men stood beneath a floodlight. Each man had a beer bottle in his hand. Broken glass glittered all around a large recycle bin. As Karl watched, one of them hooked his bottle at the bin and missed by a good foot and a half. The bottle shattered on the cement, the sound echoing up and down the alley.

"Nice fucking shot, Sal," one of them said, and blew cigarette smoke at the man who'd thrown the bottle. "NBA for you next."

"Suck it. Have a few beers and see how you shoot. I'm goin' in for a piss. It's wicked fuckin' cold."

One of the men pulled open the back door, filling the night with a blast of music and the smells of alcohol and cigarette smoke. All three went back inside, letting the door slam behind them.

"What now?" she whispered.

"We wait," Karl whispered back. He knew waiting would be a torment to her. This close to warm blood she'd be aching for the release of a feeding. "Perrazio will be out soon. He'll leave through the back, since there's an unmarked car on the main street and he knows it. Two FBI agents taking pictures and writing down license numbers."

"How do you know all this?"

"Why do you think your father employs me?"

"So who is he?" She stared unblinking at the back door. The soft yellow light from the far streetlamp outlined her features, flawless now that he'd taught her the art of illusion. Part of the vampire allure that made it easier to approach and control victims.

"Vito 'Mint' Perrazio. A lower level Lucatti associate."

She snorted. "Mint? What, is he a counterfeiter or something?"

"Bad breath. He chews breath mints nonstop. Apparently they don't help."

She looked at him skeptically.

"They gossip like old women out here," he said.

It was another two and a half hours before Vito pushed open the back door to the club, shouted some cheerfully obscene goodbyes and shut the door behind him. He stopped, cupped his hand around a cigarette and lit it, taking a long drag, and then let his head fall back as he blew the smoke up toward the stars. He wore dark trousers and Italian shoes. A leather bomber jacket was his only defense against the cold.

"Do it." Karl kept his voice so low only she could hear. "Like I showed you. Make it fast."

She hesitated. Her knuckles were white as she gripped the iron rail. He watched her, and he could almost feel the war within her.

"You must feed, Maria," Karl said in her ear. "Finish it and we'll go home."

But still, she didn't move. Vito began to walk toward the street at the end of the alley.

"I can't," she whispered.

Vito was only thirty feet from the street entrance and moving quickly.

Karl leaped over the fire escape rail and landed nimbly on the cement twenty feet below, making no sound. Vito never saw him coming. Karl seized him, and Vito uttered a surprised curse. He crushed Vito in a bear hug, pinning his arms so he couldn't fight and clamping a hand over his mouth. Vito began to struggle, but Karl hauled him back into the shadows, smelling the strong reek of peppermint.

Maria stood on the fire escape railing staring down at him, a silhouette with red eyes.

She wasn't going to be able to do it. He could see she either wasn't hungry enough or wasn't desperate enough to overcome the part of her that was still human.

But she surprised him, dropping down like a spider to land

in a crouch. She stood and moved with a deliberate stride toward Vito. Vito hurled himself against Karl, wrenching back and forth, frantic to be free. Karl stilled him with little effort, but the difference in strength never made him proud. It always made him feel like he was holding a puppy's head under water.

Maria stopped in front of Vito, staring at him with glowing eyes.

Vito thrashed again but Karl forced his head still. Maria leaned in closer, moving with sinuous grace, as if she were going to kiss Vito, staring deep into his eyes. Vito had frozen in Karl's grip, his heart slamming against his rib cage, like a rabbit in the shadow of a hawk.

She grabbed him by his jacket, opening her mouth slowly, her fangs long and gleaming. Vito tried to bolt again just before she bit him, but he was no match for the strength of two vampires. When Maria sank her fangs home, Karl released Vito into her grip and moved back.

He glanced at the floodlight above the rear entrance of the Blue Northie Social Club and caused the light to flicker and go out, filling the alley with darkness. That girl he'd killed—his first, the one Cade had forced him to murder—he'd never known her name. Her face...her eyes... Those eyes never stopped watching him. Through memories, through the centuries.

He turned back to Maria. She had done as he'd taught her. He could feel her fledgling power dampening Vito's will to fight back as she drove her fangs deeper into his neck. Dampening his pain too, intermixing it with pleasure to calm that will-to-live panic that flooded through every victim. Maria's eyes burned a deep red like spots of wildfire in a dark field. Her eyes flicked up to him from her prey, and he saw the vampire in them clearly enough, but very little of the Maria he knew.

No one else came out of the club's back door while she fed, and no one crossed the mouth of the alley. The feeding itself took only minutes. When she was done she stood and wiped the blood from her lips with the back of her hand. Then she licked her hand clean of blood while he watched and said nothing, his hatred for Delgado coiling ever tighter inside.

She seemed to come back to herself all at once. "What..." She stared at her hand with horror painted across her face. "What am I doing?"

He handed her a knife—not the knife he'd used on Delgado. "Now cut away your evidence. Make it look like a stabbing. Quickly. Like I showed you."

She stared at the knife, uncomprehending. The red glow had faded from her eyes.

"I can't..."

He seized her and yanked her close, so that his face was inches from hers. He could smell the blood on her breath. "This isn't a game. Get a hold of yourself and do what I say."

She tried to pull away from him. After a second he let her go. When he'd held her, he could feel every muscle in her body trembling. Even her teeth were chattering as she shivered—though the cold would no longer matter to her.

"I can't..."

"We can't let him be found like this."

She raised a tentative hand to her mouth. Touched her lips. Her voice was little more than a whisper. "I can feel the corruption inside. Oh, God..."

There was no time to ease her through this, and he hated himself for having been so cruelly blunt. He never should've made an issue about finishing. This was the least he could do for her. He turned to the corpse and completed the work himself.

She watched him in silence.

When he was done he took her hand and led her to the fire escape. She climbed readily enough, seeming eager to be away. He followed her, wishing he had words of comfort to give. Knowing there were none.

The wind started as they retreated across the rooftops and crossed two streets by running along power lines. He tossed the chunk of Vito's marked flesh into a dumpster behind a Thai restaurant for the rats. That seemed to hit Maria hardest, and she hid her face in her hands like a small child.

It was only when he told her it was done that she uncovered her face. But she wouldn't look him in the eyes. The wind seemed crueler than he remembered in years.

The sleet started just as they arrived home. The wind drove the sleet into Karl's exposed skin like a million frozen needles. He ignored it. Maria paused, turned her face upward with her eyes closed, letting the freezing rain pierce her.

He touched her shoulder and she trembled, shook her head as if to clear it, and then walked inside without a word. They had said nothing to one another on the way back across the city. The silence had made the wind seem even colder.

Karl drew the blinds and drapes, shutting out the city. Xiesha watched him from the kitchen, but she too had stayed quiet since they'd entered reeking of death. He could hear the squawking of the police scanner in the other room. A body had been found in the North End. Coroner and Crime Scene Units were en route.

Maria headed toward her room and shut the door.

He could feel the sun lurking just below the horizon. A heavy weariness always weighed him down as that sun crept upward, as if he were on a balance ever-tilting in one direction or the other. Xiesha had gotten him another steel coffin, and now he moved toward it, yearning for the lightless emptiness of his daylight sleep.

He passed Maria's room and paused. The sound of weeping drifted through the door. Quiet, almost silent weeping. But bitter.

Bitter.

He raised a hand to knock, but stopped before his fist touched the wood. There were no words to ease the last change. From victim to killer, covered in bloodstains that never faded.

He walked down the hall and shut his own door behind him.

Chapter Twelve:
The Call

The waiting frayed Maria's nerves until it took mental effort not to pace like some pathetic zoo animal. She never would've guessed how much work it could be to keep quiet when part of her wanted nothing more than to scream and break things. But instead, she sat in a leather armchair, her leg thrown carelessly over the side, and stared out at the city lights beyond the window. So much of her time now was spent looking out windows, as if she were some princess in a glass tower. Waiting.

Delgado was out there, somewhere. Sometimes his presence was very close. Once she'd thought she'd seen him on the roof of the Motori high-rise across from Vance's apartment. He was gone before she was sure, but the sense of his presence had been very strong. It had felt like he was calling to her, and his call was only muted by Xiesha's wards.

A week and a half since she had killed that man.

Don't think of it. Yet, everything from the taste of the blood to the feel of the wind stayed as sharp in her memory as the edge on Karl's knife.

There were dreams that Karl insisted weren't dreams, but visions. "Vampires don't dream," he'd said. "Your Master is sending you visions across the connection you share with him. There is nothing to be done about it."

Dreams of hunting. Dreams of sex. Dreams of feeding.

The one that terrified her most was the vision where she sat at the head of a table in the darkness, her captains gathered all around her, cigarette smoke curling in the air like serpents. Her father's body lay upon the table. His eyes held the glassy blankness of a child's doll. His head was turned to the side, his throat torn out, while blood dripped, dripped, dripped from the wound.

Her captains held wineglasses filled with her father's blood. They raised their glasses to toast her, their eyes shining with that hungry red glow. Before she could say anything, a pair of pale, smooth hands fell upon her shoulders from behind. Someone leaned down, whispered in her ear and sent a shiver of mixed pleasure and fear arcing down her spine.

"Well done, *querida*," Delgado said, and kissed her throat.

She hadn't told Karl about Delgado's promises. Most of the time she avoided him, and Xiesha as well, needing the silence but feeling more ghost now than anything, drifting through the apartment while Karl hunted her Master.

Vito Perrazio's blood had tasted so good, so hot on her tongue, and her reaction had been almost sexual in its intensity. She'd felt her power building as she drained him, felt herself brimming with energy when the life had flickered out of his eyes. She hated that she'd loved it so much.

She understood Karl Vance a bit more now. His reasons and his refusals were all much clearer. It was too late to matter, but she understood.

Karl walked up behind her armchair as she faced out at the city lights. She glanced at Karl's reflection in the glass. Another myth—that vampires cast no reflection. Things were so different than she'd expected.

"I thought you'd be hunting him," she said.

"I wanted to see you."

She didn't reply.

"I know things have been difficult." He knelt down beside her. Seemed to want to touch her, and didn't.

"I doubt I'm anything special."

"Talk to me, Maria. I can help."

But she didn't. Not at first. She only stared out the window, watching the lights of a distant plane and wondering where those people were bound. Who waited for them at the end of their journey? Lovers? Husbands? Wives? Children? Were they missed? Were they happy to return home?

And why did it matter?

"My half-brother betrayed me," she finally said, when it was clear Karl wanted something more from her. She could hardly whine about the airplane, now could she?

Karl walked around the armchair and squatted down in front of her, so she had to look into his eyes. "How?"

"I was in hiding, at a friend's house—a college friend who was on a trip out of the country. Roberto lured me out, saying he had a request from my father for one last job. Using you against the Lucattis—he said we'd go after Marco.

"I agreed to meet with him. Hell, maybe I just wanted to get in the game again, I don't know. I've been thinking about it since I...woke up again. Did I tell you Delgado was hiding beneath my car? Yeah. Clinging on the bottom like a fucking spider. I drove him right back to my safe house, easy as you please."

"Anyone can be betrayed."

"I can feel the silence of this body. So quiet. Not even breath."

"You're young—new," he said. "It takes adjustment—"

"They took much more from me than my life."

He leaned back on his heels, his hands on his thighs. She could see him struggling to find the words to say, and that touched her. But not enough.

"I can't go on like this, Karl. I can't exist like this."

He rubbed a hand across his mouth and watched her with eyes that suddenly held something like fear.

"You get numb—"

"I don't want to get numb! I don't want to never *feel* anything. For my heart to match this corpse I'm trapped inside."

"It's always difficult to kill. I tried to tell you that."

"I know you did..." She'd be damned if she'd let him see her cry. No one ever got to see her cry again.

Karl was quiet for a long while. When he spoke again, his tone was gentle. "Your half-brother may know a way to contact Delgado."

"It's always about Delgado, isn't it? You're like an unattended baggage announcement at the airport. Every fucking three minutes."

"It's all about Delgado for both of us now."

"What's the point? Even if you kill Delgado, I'm still

this...abomination. *There's* a fucking word for you. I never get to be normal again."

"Normal is gone."

"Gone forever," she agreed. "And now I live forever."

He gave a slight shake of his head. "I don't know how to say what you need to hear..."

"I'm sorry," she said, and she even meant it. "Histrionics were never my forte."

Karl reached out and opened her clenched fists, running a pale finger across the cuts her claws had made. "Your whole world has burned to ashes and been reborn into something darker than you ever dreamed."

She withdrew her hand from his, but gently. "I wanted to kill Roberto so badly. I wanted him to suffer. I wanted to carve him up with these claws and pour battery acid all over him and watch him *smoke*. I wanted to laugh while he screamed. A thousand things, I wanted...but I don't want that anymore. It changed to something else."

"Changed to what?"

"When I killed that man. That man, Perrazio. Something broke inside. I don't think it can be fixed."

"No...it can't be fixed."

She smiled. "That's what I like about you, Karl. You don't mince words."

"I want to lie," he said. "But I can't. Not to you."

"Lying wouldn't help me, anyway." She took his hand, lifted it to her lips, kissed the cool skin. "Thank you for everything, Karl. I wish there was some way to repay you."

She stood slowly, and Karl stood as well. He seemed to want to say something, but she turned and left before he could.

When the sun rose, the visions returned.

Maria walked naked through a desert of blazing white sand, so bright that she could see only by squinting. The sun was monstrous above her, ten times its usual size, glaring hatefully down and scorching the earth to dust. The heat shimmer turned the world to a blurry nightmare. Her throat felt as if every drop of moisture had been wrung out of it leaving only a throbbing pain behind. Her head pulsed with agony as the bright light seemed to claw its way past her squinting eyes to dig at her brain. Her feet had been burned so badly that every step was like treading on fire. And still she labored on, because she knew that behind her, just over the curve of the horizon, Delgado followed. Relentless. With blood staining one hand red, and shadows staining the other a spectral black.

The desert changed to post-apocalyptic ruins. The sand gave over to cracked pavement. The sun did not disappear, but at least the jagged teeth of broken skyscrapers hid it when she stumbled into their shadows.

Ruins gave way to ocean. Churning seas of gray water. She walked atop the water. The salty water was warm and did nothing to cool her. And still the sun beat down. And beyond the crest of the farthest waves, Delgado followed.

"Come to me," Delgado said. His voice seemed to float above the waves. *"Come to me and I'll make these nightmares stop. It is because you're severed from me that you suffer,* querida.*"*

She dove into the gray water to escape him. Breathing the water in. Feeling the burn of it in her lungs. Trying to drown herself and escape. But she knew she could not die that way.

His laughter followed her into the darkness, and before merciful oblivion, she heard him say:

"It is because you're apart from me that you suffer, my love."

God help her, the first thing she did when that damning sun finally sank out of sight and she shoved open the coffin was to go to the balcony door. She stood absolutely still in front of it. Her hand lying upon the cold latch. Feeling the thrumming magic of Xiesha's ward. Wondering if she could escape to Delgado before Karl caught her.

A shudder twisted through her with such force she felt as if it would shake her apart. The desperate desire to go to Delgado faded. Its departure left her shaking on the threshold, with the newly born night sprawling just beyond.

What in God's name was she doing? Was she going mad? She clenched her fists, feeling the tips of her claws biting into her flesh. After awhile, her hands stopped shaking.

She didn't tell Karl.

She was too ashamed to admit that she'd become a slave after all.

Two days later it rained over Boston, low gray clouds spitting down on the rooftops. A gusting wind seemed to drive the rain horizontal and mock those who thought to hide beneath umbrellas. The rain stopped by nightfall, but the clouds fled and the temperature dropped below freezing, sheeting the streets with ice. Steam poured from the gutters and manhole covers as if the city breathed through a thousand slits.

The phone call came much later than Karl expected. He'd been waiting for it since Maria had lost her cell phone the night she died.

"Where is my daughter?"

Beneath the anger, Karl could hear the worry like river water under a layer of winter ice.

"She's dead," Karl said.

There was a long silence on the other end of the line. Karl stood on his balcony and scanned the rooftops of the buildings around him, tuning his senses to find any trace of Delgado or his sirelings. Karl had killed one three days ago atop the Motori high rise and had let his ashes drift into the wind, hoping Delgado would taste his slave's death.

"How did she die?" Alberto finally asked, voice flat, defeated.

"Lucattis ambushed her."

"How can that be?" Alberto nearly screamed. "She went into hiding. *I* didn't even know where she was."

"She was set up."

"How the fuck could you let that happen? I put her with you for protection."

"You had me doing jobs for her. I was never a bodyguard. And she fled me as much as anyone. I had no idea where she was either."

"Then how the fuck do you know she's dead?"

"Alejandro Delgado told me. Remember that name? He was the bait you dangled to entice me into your war."

"Goddamn him. And you, you worthless piece of shit. Is this how you repay me? You let them kill my daughter and then you don't even have the balls to tell me? You wait until I call you?"

"No one could reach you." Half true. He hadn't even tried.

"You should've told one of my people," Alberto screamed. "I trusted you to keep her safe, you motherfucker." Then quieter,

"Oh *God...*"

"If you wanted her safe, you should never have brought her into this."

"Fuck you, you worthless bastard. I should've used one of my own. What was I thinking entrusting my daughter to some *forestiero*. My God."

"I'm sorry for your loss, Alberto."

"Fuck that. Where's her body?"

"There's no corpse for you to find. Delgado took care of that."

"What proof do I have that the Lucattis killed her?"

"You don't have any proof except for what I've said about Delgado."

"I think someone's trying to start the war up again. Could be you, you greedy son of a bitch."

"It was your war. I was doing you a favor."

"A favor." There was a long pause. "I want to talk to you. Face to face. Meet me at The Glass Slipper at nine."

"I don't think a meeting would be wise."

"You refusing me? You say you're innocent and yet you don't have the balls to look me in the eyes."

"I don't think you want to see what's in my eyes."

"What the fuck are you talking about? That almost sounds like a threat, but nobody could be that stupid. You be at that fucking strip joint at nine or we're going to have a very serious problem. You fucking hear me?" A laugh, as harsh as sandpaper on a mirror. "A fucking *favor*."

The line went dead.

Alberto would try and have him whacked if Karl were foolish enough to meet him. He really didn't want to kill a bunch of Ricardis, so it was better for everyone if that meeting never happened. He sighed.

"Was that my father?" Maria asked from behind him.

He turned to her, a hand on the balcony rail, a cold wind pushing up along the walls. She wore silk pajamas borrowed from Xiesha. Her dark eyes were intent upon his own, and her hair streamed out unbound around her face. She seemed smaller somehow, large eyes in a face suddenly childlike.

"Yes, it was your father."

"You told him I was dead."

"You are."

"What gave you the right to do that?" Sudden anger vibrated in her voice like a tuning fork striking a steel girder.

"Someone had to tell him. He had a right to know."

"I didn't want him to know," she said. "Somebody should have some hope."

"You knew you could never go back. Not now. Not even after Delgado is destroyed."

Maria laughed, a sharp and brittle sound. "Destroyed? When will that ever happen? You spend all your time brooding on revenge. Just fucking *finish* it. You can't tell me you two have been fighting for two hundred years and there hasn't been any end to it." She pointed a finger at him, her nail curved like a knife. "Let me explain something to you that you seemed to have missed in all those books of yours. When a thought comes into my mind I either do it, or I forget it. Understand? What, you need him around to measure yourself against or something? You might be evil, but you're not as evil as *him.* That it?"

"You were determined to bloody your hands. Now they are. Is it what you'd hoped it would be?"

"Do you ever answer a fucking question?"

"Delgado murdered my friend." Karl ran his finger along the railing Maria had twisted out of shape. He settled his fingers around the metal and bent it back to true. When he looked up again he found her staring at him. Her hair blew unheeded across the lower part of her face, her eyes as intense as a tiger watching prey through river reeds.

He went on. "He murdered the friend who taught me that one could be cast in the mold of evil and still retain some modicum of honor. And you think me hesitant to kill Delgado? As if I were playing a bloody *game?*"

She flinched back and looked away.

"I answered your question," he said, "now answer mine."

Maria shook her head, and then turned her palms upward, looking at them. She gave him a little smile.

"It doesn't matter if it's what I hoped for or not," she replied. "I sold every part of my soul to earn a place in that family. To earn a fucking ounce of respect for my pound of flesh. I thought I wanted it more than anything."

"Your hope was misplaced."

"You don't know jack shit about it. Now I'm just like everybody else. Red hands. And you keeping me holed up here like I'm some prize. What am I? First in your little harem? Oh yeah, forgot about that slinky little minx you already have locked up here. I must be *second* in your little harem—building it fast, aren't you?"

"Are you through?"

"Oh, did I *offend* you?"

He thought he saw the glitter of a tear, but her face contorted in fury and she swiped at her cheek so hard she scratched her skin.

"So what are you going to do?" she demanded. "Throw me out? Ship me off to Delgado with your compliments?"

A cut. He'd long since forgotten he had the ability to bleed. "Never."

"Never what? You'd never let Delgado have me—but only because he wants me and you hate him. You have something he wants, and I'm just a tool to get what you want."

He spoke slowly, stressing each word. "I won't leave you."

She spun away and leapt to the top of the balcony rail. She flung her arms out and stood there, a cross on the iron. The wind snapped at her pajamas, making the cranes and lotus flowers dance.

Maria laughed. "My dead brother, Paul, said that to me once." She leaned her head back, her eyes closed, the stars around her face. "But he lied."

Karl said nothing.

She turned back to him. "If I fell, would I die?"

He shook his head no.

"That's amazing," she said, and looked down at the traffic far below. "So tiny down there."

Faint drifts of sound wafted up to them. Engines, and tires on icy pavement. Voices and stereos.

She turned and jumped down from the rail onto the balcony. He wanted to hold her, but she seemed too brittle.

"So my father wants to meet you..." she said after a while. She wouldn't look at him.

"He's not interested in hearing what I have to say."

"He'll be interested in what *I* have to say."

Karl frowned. "You want to tell him about your half-brother? I thought you didn't want to kill Roberto."

"Everybody has to pay sometime." She touched her lips, her eyes sad, thoughtful. "But I didn't mean tell him about Roberto."

He watched her. Waiting.

"Something will have to be done about him." Her eyes flicked to his face and then danced away. "Roberto, I mean. What he did to me, he could do to my father. It wouldn't be vengeance. He has to be stopped."

"You?" he asked, knowing the answer.

"I don't know if I could, even after everything."

"I'll do it then."

She came close to him, looked up at him for a moment, and then leaned her forehead on his chest. He put his arms around her and felt her tremble. His betrothed, Elizabeth Alvey, had kept a kitten that had trembled like this whenever the thunderstorms had come rolling through. She'd always tried to distract it from the thunder by dangling one of the ribbons from her hair, trying to make the kitten leap and swipe—but he could never remember it working.

Maria finally pushed away from him gently. "No," she whispered. "Don't do it."

She didn't look at him or raise her head, but instead turned and fled in a swirl of bright silk.

Chapter Thirteen:
Brother Dearest

Maria was reading Proust when she felt eyes watching her. She looked up to see her half-brother, Roberto Pulani, standing atop the Motori high rise, his eyes burning holes into her through the window of Karl's penthouse.

For a moment she couldn't move. Every muscle within her seemed to turn to wet clay.

Roberto stood on the ledge, the toes of his leather shoes hanging off into space. He wore a dark suit and a long winter overcoat. The wind blew his coattails out in front of him like the wings of some great black bat.

She vaulted out of the leather armchair, flinging her book aside as she sprinted for the balcony. The book thumped as it hit the carpet.

Karl was out searching for Delgado. Xiesha was in her own room. Though Maria couldn't feel her Master close by, who knew if she could trust that feeling? But for the moment, it felt as if there were only her and Roberto left in a vast, empty city.

Her half-brother stood unmoving, even as the wind made his jacket and clothes writhe around him.

The balcony slider was locked and warded. Maria let her hand drift toward the handle. There was no way to get out without alerting Xiesha, but she hardly considered that in the wash of gray shock that surged through her at the sight of her half-brother.

She flipped the lock, pulled out the bar and jerked the door open. A shiver of power trailed along her skin and the hairs on her arms stood erect as she pushed through the ward. She ran to the end of the balcony and gripped the rail with both hands.

Roberto's laughter drifted to her with the wind. Even from here she could see the red pinprick glow of his eyes, those demon coals pushed into that hated face.

"Sister." His voice rang as clearly in her mind as if he'd spoken in her ear. *"Come with me. Master Delgado wants to see you again, you lucky slut."*

"How...?" she sent back, but the question died unasked. She could feel the connection between them, repulsively intimate, the same she had felt with Minsku. Her mind reeled from the shock of seeing him now exactly the same as her. The sight of him *offended* her, made her feel the same kind of revulsion she'd feel if cockroaches were crawling all over her body, and she hated him all the more. *"Why would he give immortality to an asshole like you?"*

His head tilted as he regarded her. Again, laughter drifted to her across the hundred or so feet of emptiness that separated them.

"That's not very nice," he chided. *"As if I didn't deserve this prize."*

"Is he here?"

"He's hunting Vance," Roberto said in her mind. *"They sent me to see if a little brotherly love can bring you out of that little spider hole you cower in."*

"Go back and tell him never." The telepathic thought thrummed with all the rage, frustration and loathing that had lived in her quiet heart since she'd reawakened.

He hesitated for a second, and then he stepped back off the ledge and vanished from sight. She kept staring upward, scanning for him.

A long minute passed.

"I don't think that's what he wants to hear," came Roberto's sudden thought.

He leapt from the roof of the Motori high rise, launching himself across the gap. He kept himself still, arms tight against his body, legs drawn up, an inhuman missile that sailed across the river of traffic far below.

She stumbled away from the rail, backing up until she hit the wall. Roberto landed in a crouch just inside of the railing. He stood slowly and adjusted his tie. She had only seen him in a suit once before—at her brother Paul's funeral. The fact that he wore one now only enraged her further. His face held the undead pallor, his eyes glowed that predatory red. The grin he gave her was a jagged trap of fangs, as if he sensed her loathing.

She returned the grin, showing a little fang of her own. "So was this the promised payment for betraying me, you motherfucking little prick?"

He waggled his tongue at her from between his fangs, and then laughed at the disgust on her face. "A little extra gravy. They paid me, but the Master sent our new brothers and sisters to collect me for something special."

"Couldn't collect you himself, could he? I bet he was too busy bleeding. How's his hand? I hear it was about as crispy as a tater tot in a jet engine after the sun got through with it."

"I'd watch that mouth, sis. Our new Master is nothing like Father. He's what Father *should've* been."

"You bastard."

"Yeah," Roberto said and laughed, "and that's the fucking point, ain't it?"

"How much did they pay you to give me up?"

"That again?" He shrugged. "I got twenty large for it."

"Twenty thousand to sell out your own blood. You come pretty fucking cheap, Robbie."

He grinned and leaned back against the rail. "I came so cheap because I was a true believer in the cause. I only thought the Lucattis wanted you dead cuz you and that Judas bloodsucker you're fucking put such a hurt on them. But then I was brought before *him*, and I looked into his burning eyes and I *knew*. Knew that I deserved so much more than I had."

"And does Father know?"

"He knows I'm dead. They left my body to be found. Weren't those some trippy fuckin' visions, though?" He laughed harshly. "I woke after sunset, in the morgue—I shit you not, sis. The fucking *morgue*. A bit disoriented, but then one of my new sisters arrived to collect me. And my new sisters are a lot more friendly than you ever were."

"And look at you now. In the same shit hole as me."

"Not even close. The Master says you're fighting. I love what I am, baby doll."

"And you think you can take me back to him against my will?"

He shrugged again. "Oh, I know I can, sis."

She felt her claws sliding out of her fingers. "He wants me to kill Daddy. You know that?"

"Then kill him." He took a step toward her, graceful as a cougar stalking his prey.

"And he wants me to run the family in Father's place. You know *that*?"

Roberto stopped. His eyes narrowed to slits. "You lie."

It was her turn to laugh and she did, relishing it, throwing back her head and laughing into the wind. "Looks like you're on the short end yet again. What do you say about that?"

"Only that you're a no good cunt who never should've been let in the family." His lips peeled back from his fangs. "Not even as an associate. You never got straightened out, and that's the one thing that kept me smiling. I'm only sorry the Lucattis didn't put a coupla .22s in the back of your skull instead of our Master wasting his gift on you."

"Nice fucking speech." She rose to her full height, every nerve ending humming with power, her hatred cold inside her, dense as a dwarf star.

He bared his fangs completely, throwing wide his arms as his claws gleamed like light on onyx. Hardly any part of his face was recognizable as Roberto now. The figure that crouched before her seemed all fiery eyes and long face, with those wickedly sharp teeth thrusting out of the black hole of his mouth.

Behind her, a shotgun roared.

Roberto twisted aside and an urn exploded into a thousand shards. Soil sprayed everywhere, showering over the ledge, pattering to the balcony floor. The shotgun slide racked behind Maria, and she glanced back to see Xiesha standing in the open sliding doorway, tracking Roberto as he fled toward the railing.

"Bitch!" he yelled and vaulted over the side, plunging off the balcony into the night.

Maria ran to the railing with Xiesha right on her heels. She heard the groan of twisting metal somewhere below. When she looked over, she caught a glimpse of Roberto dragging himself off the misshapen wreckage of another balcony railing forty feet down. Then he pulled himself out of sight, hidden by the ledge of the balcony immediately above him.

Xiesha took Maria by the arm and drew her back from the edge. Maria didn't resist. The barrel of Xiesha's shotgun sent out curls of smoke that the wind snatched and whipped away. The wind grew more insistent, sharpening its icy edge on every flat surface. It moaned as it pushed through the balustrades and slid between the barren pots. The pieces of the shattered urn looked like shards of teeth—fangs, even—lying in disarray amidst black ashes. Maria closed her eyes and tried to remember the summer sun.

"Why are you outside without me?" Xiesha asked. Her tone was calm, but Maria flinched as if slapped.

"I saw Roberto—"

"And you had to confront him."

Maria paused at the edge of the ward, looking back to where her half-brother had thrown himself off into the night. "Shouldn't we go after him?"

"He's gone. You might be able to track him, but he might be acting as a lure. Scrying is too slow to check, and I'm unwilling to take any chances without Master Vance."

Part of her was glad it was over, but another part of her cursed Xiesha's interruption. How would she have done against Roberto? She thought about the strange weapons in Karl's weapon closet. Maybe she should ask to carry one.

Finally she pushed back through the ward, frowning at that gossamer chain of energy that enveloped her for a moment, as if she'd walked through a spider web. Xiesha locked and barred the slider behind her.

Maria looked back to her. "Why did it take you so long to come?"

"I was scrying. I caught Delgado with his defenses down, the first time ever, just as I felt you pass through the ward. I was still trying to pinpoint him, and then I heard you talking to another vampire. Delgado's intentions then became clear."

"He was distracting you..."

Xiesha nodded. Her eyes were solemn.

Maria continued. "What did you see?"

"Of Delgado? Nothing much. Dark water. Everywhere. The glow of lights reflected upon water black as a Stygian tide."

"The docks?" Maria asked.

"Perhaps. I saw no landmarks."

"Well...thank you."

"I know you feel restless and trapped, but you must stay inside the wards. If Delgado comes for you himself and catches you outside the wards, away from Karl, then your Master will control you completely, every action and thought. The wards protect you from that. Karl protects you from that. You are fortunate Roberto was more interested in arguing than in doing what he was sent to do."

Maria nodded, not trusting herself to answer.

"I'll stand watch at the windows." Xiesha slid another slug into the shotgun to replace the one she'd fired. "I think it might be best if you stayed away from them for a while."

In a glass cage, she thought, *and now I can't even go near the glass.* But she nodded and headed to her room, while Xiesha walked to the phone and lifted the receiver. Calling Karl.

Her new body brimmed with energy and stamina, but exhaustion fuzzed her thoughts, her mind suddenly too tired to think. She wished the sun were closer to rising, so at least she could find solace in the empty bliss of vampire sleep. When there were no visions, that was...

Sunrise.

She could watch at least one more sunrise, if she chose. A last sunrise that would sear her with an unquenchable fire. It might be the final one ever, but wouldn't that make it the most glorious? If only she could be guaranteed her destruction would lead to an eternal heaven of non-existence, non-thought and non-pain.

Dangerous thoughts. She turned her mind aside and willed them away. Yet, the image of the sun, that blazing disk just peeking its way over a horizon bleeding in purples, pinks and reds, stayed with her.

The docks.

Delgado was near the waterfront. Karl could sense him—a strong, dark presence—a flash of anti-light from some backward lighthouse that absorbed light instead of giving it off. All his fears about Maria vanished. Every part of him attuned itself to the feel of Delgado, stripped of the magic concealment that a vampire wore like a cloak.

Karl crawled down the side of the tenement and hurried to

the street. A minute of watching from the shadows and he saw what he wanted—a large delivery truck headed east. When it passed by, he leapt from concealment onto the rear bumper, and from there vaulted himself onto the roof. This was the easiest way to travel great distances rapidly throughout the city. He had to burn power to keep himself concealed from sight—a kind of blind spot that human eyes would slip around if they happened to glance down from a window.

He was well on his way when his cell phone began to vibrate.

"Delgado's luring you," Xiesha said when he answered. "We were attacked."

"Maria?"

"Fine. Her half-brother has been turned. Delgado sent him to retrieve her. I sent him off."

"I'm on my way."

He ran along traffic back toward his apartment, leaping from car to car when traffic stopped, riding when it was faster to do so. He might have been seen for a moment here or there, a shadowed blur in the darkness, but he automatically kept the magic tight around him, cloaking him in that sense of the non-important, the every day. His mind remained focused on Maria.

He ran harder. The buildings blurred past. The lights were streaks of color passing alongside him.

Traffic ahead was too dense, and too many people were about. He launched himself onto the roof of a Dunkin' Donuts, ran across the landscape of vents and ductwork and then began his trek west again, keeping to rooftops and alleys. Keeping to the dark.

Karl saw the impact damage to the lower balcony as he climbed up the side of the high rise. He didn't stop to investigate.

Xiesha met him at his own balcony. She still held the shotgun in her hands. A glance showed him the shattered remains of a planting urn and the dark mound of potting soil. He could smell vampire—someone other than Maria. The scent lingered even in the wind, strongest by the railings.

"Where is she?"

"Safe," Xiesha replied. "In her room. Reading, I believe."

How things changed. She hadn't been much for books when he'd first taken her in. Hours of boredom with late-night television could turn anyone into an avid reader.

"What happened?"

"Delgado tried to distract us by revealing his location, just as Maria was lured through the wards by her half-brother."

"Damn it. I told her to stay inside. Doesn't she—?"

"She's young, Master."

"Reckless, you mean."

Xiesha tilted her head and considered him. "There was a time when you described yourself as such to me. Many times, in fact. The most recently when you spoke of killing that werewolf for the Order."

"That was simply desperation."

She smiled slightly. "Delgado has his link to her. He knows what strings he can pull."

And that was the worst of it. Delgado knew her much more intimately than he. What hope did he have against that?

"Still," he said, "this can't go on. We've been lucky so far, but relying on luck is not acceptable."

If Delgado had come for her tonight instead of playing the role of bait, then Karl would have come home to an empty house. Distance was their friend—if Delgado got close enough and found Maria outside the shielding effect of the wards, he could compel her, and free will would be a distant dream to her.

"What happened to that lower balcony?" he asked after a moment.

"Roberto landed awkwardly when he threw himself from our railing." She nodded at the urn. "I missed."

Karl slid open the door and passed through the ward into his apartment, and Xiesha followed him. The smell of gunpowder lingered. He washed his hands and face in the crystal basin, taking his time. He paused to stare out the balcony windows, imagining the confrontation that had taken place there.

Finally, there were no more excuses to put it off. He walked down the hall to her room. The door was shut. Instead of faux wood paneling, it seemed to him more like the stone sealing the entrance to a tomb. A crypt door through which he didn't dare to pass.

He watched his own hand form a fist and knock lightly. For a long time there came no answer. Then, just as he was about to leave:

"Come in."

Maria sat upon the floor with a circle of books laid out around her, as if she were a sorcerer performing a magic rite. One book lay open in her lap and she bent over it. She glanced up as he entered, and ventured a smile tinged with chagrin.

"I blew it again," she said.

He crouched down and lifted a book. Camus, *The Myth of Sisyphus*. He glanced over several others by Goethe. Deep reading. He set them down carefully in the places she had ascribed them in her circle.

"We had a visitor."

"*I* didn't invite him. But we girls won't throw parties when you're gone anymore, Dad."

He couldn't help his smile. "I hear your brother has joined our ranks."

"I can't think of anyone less deserving of immortality. He's too stupid to ever realize the cost—and that stupidity allows him to be happy. It's a crazy fucking world, isn't it?"

"I'm not surprised Delgado turned him." Karl picked up another book, absently turning it over in his hands, running his fingers along the leather. "I would've done the same."

"No, you wouldn't have."

He looked at her, one eyebrow raised.

She shook her head. "You wouldn't have taken a man like him. I don't care how expedient it would've been—how much it might've hurt Delgado's cause—you wouldn't have done it."

He set the book down. It gave him an excuse to break eye contact with her.

"I hope you're as confident that you can deny your Master when he calls, Maria. Going outside of the wards without me—"

"Was a mistake, okay? I admit it. Stupid thing to do. Bad girl, no chocolate. But he made a play for me. That fucking cock-less, piece of shit, no-account bastard brother of mine. Came *here*. Strutted around like a fucking rooster. And suddenly I wanted to make him pay."

"He's like us."

"He's nothing like us. He's enjoying it."

Karl was silent. Considering her.

"That's where the line is," she pushed on. "I may be forced to get off on...on feeding when I have to...because of what I am. But I don't have to love it or trip on it at any other time. It's fucking sick and I hate it and I hate what I am, but I'm not as bad as Roberto or Delgado—and I never will be."

He kept his face carefully blank, but his heart, that silent vampire heart inside him, lifted as some of the weight upon it fell away. He had saved her...

So far.

"What now?" he asked. Sometimes he didn't trust even himself to say the right thing.

"You've been really good to me, Karl. Thank you. Thank you more than I can even say. You didn't have to do all this." She swept a hand around her. "Take me in. Protect me."

His smile was bitter. "I only did it because Delgado wants you, remember?"

Her face turned rueful. "I was angry."

He stood. Disgusted with himself for the cheap shot.

"I know," he said. "I'm sorry I said it."

She shook her head as if it didn't matter. "Tonight..." She fell silent and looked away. After a long moment she began again, speaking slowly, as if the words were fishhooks caught in her throat, coughed up one at a time. "I can't go on like this. This waiting. This constant demoralizing fear. When's he going to show and finally pull me in? Will I even recognize myself after he's done with me? I can't do it anymore."

There it was again. He felt the fear building inside him at her words, and it had been a very long time since he had feared anything.

"You must have patience," he said. "Xiesha and I both sensed his location tonight—"

"That was a ploy to distract her so that Roberto could have a go at me. That's all."

He wondered if Xiesha had told Maria her suspicions or if Maria had merely worked it out on her own. "You're right, but it's more than we had this evening."

"And I want to go out—to help you hunt. Hunt vampires, I mean. This inability to do anything is driving me insane."

"You don't understand. You won't have a choice if he shows

up when we're out there. You'll obey anything he commands."

Then Karl would have to destroy her. How dark the night would be then.

"It doesn't matter," she said. "Even if he takes me, I can always choose to face the sun. That's my out. But this waiting... It's like I've been thrown into the ocean with an anchor around my neck. The surface light is long gone. I keep sinking and sinking into the black."

He was silent for a very long time.

"No," he said.

Shock. It stilled her face as if she'd plunged through thin ice. It had hurt him to say it, but it would hurt him more to lose her.

"Fuck you." It came out as a whisper, the rage so immense it sucked the oxygen right out of the words.

"I'm sorry."

"*Fuck you!*" She screamed it this time. "You don't have a fucking choice about it! I'm outta here. I'll find my own hole to sleep in—take my own chances. You bastard. Keeping me here like I was your fucking slave—"

"Then go."

She gaped at him. The silence stretched. If his heart had not been dead within him, he knew it would've been slamming away at his rib cage. A prisoner, trying to pound its way free.

"Go..." she said softly. He saw something in her eyes fall and break. Something that made no audible sound, but the crystal shatter of it resounded between them like a thunderclap.

She stood and walked toward the door. Slowly, almost like a sleepwalker, a shell-shocked soldier.

Last chance to keep her.

Delgado. He had to keep focused on Delgado, didn't he? What had she been but a bother from the beginning? None of the wiseguys he killed meant anything. To hell with the Lucattis—they were only a means to an end, a way to get at Delgado. It was Delgado. God damn him. Damn him forever.

Maria opened the door and stepped into the hall. He watched her back, the curves of her body, that dark length of hair.

"Wait," he said.

She paused, but didn't look back.

"We'll go together. Whatever comes, will come."

"Thank you," she said and closed the door behind her.

Chapter Fourteen:
For Good or For Ill

Karl didn't immediately keep his promise to take Maria on the hunt for Delgado. She still needed training, and in the meantime, the war intervened.

Roberto Pulani's death and the subsequent disappearance of his body from the morgue made front-page news. Karl read the article twice. Pulani's body had been found in his SUV near his girlfriend's apartment three days ago. A sheet of paper had been impaled on an ice pick and driven into Pulani's eye socket. It read: *BUENOS DIAS AMIGO* in block letters. The next night Pulani's corpse had gone missing from the morgue where it had been awaiting an autopsy.

The gruesome death of a mafia soldier had reporters speculating on whether this would restart the Lucatti-Ricardi gangland war. Editorials demanded that the police and DA's Office snuff out the spark before the inferno reignited.

Less than a week later, a Lucatti soldier named Vinnie "Nails" Carpisio and two Lucatti associates—an enforcer and a bookie—were found in a dumpster behind a pet store, each with two holes in his head. A pimp in South Boston was shot twice with a 12-gauge shotgun as he walked out of a 7-11 with a burrito at two in the morning. He was rumored to have ties to organized crime, but it was unclear which family received his protection money.

When Karl told Maria about the chaos her brother's death had caused, she didn't even turn to look at him.

"I didn't want that war to end, anyway," she said, and walked away.

With Maria hiding in his penthouse and himself on the outs with Alberto Ricardi, Karl had to risk leaving the apartment again to search for his street contacts. He needed info, needed the details of the war and the word on the street that wouldn't appear in the papers. With luck, he might be able to trace Roberto Pulani back to Delgado.

Little Ricky was nowhere to be found. Another contact, a male prostitute named Jimmy Low, told him word was there'd be no more truces, no matter what those assholes in New York wanted. There were only a few things that could decimate a crime gang. Everybody dies, everybody runs, or everybody goes to jail. Jimmy Low was putting his money on choice A.

Another contact, a kid called Mixer, had disappeared from the streets entirely. Karl's last contact—an Irish kid who ran numbers and crap games—refused to talk to him at all. Apparently, Karl had earned his way onto Alberto Ricardi's shit list after refusing to show up at that meeting.

The next night Alberto Ricardi called again, just as Karl settled himself on his damaged couch with the Boston Globe. He snatched up his cell when it vibrated, wondering if Maria would overhear the conversation, or if she were locked too deep in concentration to notice. He could sense her in her room practicing concealing herself with her vampire powers. She'd been working at it with a single-minded determination that he admired, and she was getting better.

"Did you have anything to do with my son's death?" Alberto's voice was calm, cold even.

"Does that look like my style?"

There was a long pause before Alberto spoke again. "He had an ice pick in his eye and a mangled throat—but no blood. Sounds like your MO, you sick fucker."

"Did you ask yourself why would I go after a Ricardi? There's no gain and much to lose."

"Maybe you got a better deal working for the competition. My daughter's missing, after all."

"We already discussed that," Karl said. "Alejandro Delgado killed her."

"That fucking Spaniard. But the funny thing is, I don't have a body to bury. In fact, two bodies are missing. And I had a little dialogue with a Lucatti soldier we got our hands on. Seems he knew nothing about any animosity against Maria."

".Just because a low-level soldier didn't know about it, doesn't mean it isn't true."

More silence. Karl could hear the man's breath whistling off the phone's receiver. In the background, he could hear a voice calling out departure times. Seemed the senior Ricardi was either leaving town or just arriving back.

"You didn't come when I asked," Alberto said. "I've killed made men for less than that. You have some brass balls, I'll fucking give you that."

"I told you a meeting wouldn't be wise. You hold me responsible for your daughter. Very well. You're wrong, but I can understand why a father would want someone to punish. You think I'm easier to get to than Delgado. You're wrong again."

"Seems I'm wrong a lot of the fucking time."

Karl didn't reply.

Rage flashed bright and hot in Alberto's voice. "When we meet again, you'll be begging for your worthless life."

"I assume this means I can't use you as a business reference," Karl said. Alberto began to blister the air with curses, and Karl hung up.

He started toward Maria's room, but an article headline on the front page of the Globe caught his eye. *Mutilated Body Found in Harbor.* He snatched up the paper and scanned it. This was the third body discovered down at the docks in less than a month. The police had assumed it was part of the gang war, but the docks were where he'd sensed Delgado the other night—the night when Delgado had been trying to lure Xiesha's attention away so Roberto could make a play for Maria.

The docks. They might only be the feeding ground for some of Delgado's sirelings, but if Delgado could be lured out...

He went to tell Maria. Tomorrow night he would keep his promise to her. For good or for ill.

Chapter Fifteen:
Hunt

No moon in the sky, only stars. Cold too. Karl crouched beside a line of parked cars and focused on searching for vampires. Maria crouched next to him. She'd grown quite good at concealing her presence from humans and other vampires, but she'd never be able to hide from her Master.

The silver knife was a weight on his hip that seemed to radiate its poisonous miasma even through the sheath. It had tasted Delgado's blood once, and he was eager to let it feed again. He had the SIG-Sauer in the shoulder holster on the outside of his black turtleneck. The silencer was attached, the long cylinder lying alongside his ribs through the open bottom of the holster. The SIG was loaded with silver-sheathed, lead-core bullets. Another clip of silvered bullets sat in the left pocket of his black cargo pants. A third, filled with brass-core, Teflon coated bullets, sat in the right pocket. Those were for the Thorn knights. Just in case.

"Anything?" Maria whispered, so faintly only a vampire very close could've heard. She held his recurve crossbow cradled in her gloved hands. A silver-tipped quarrel with an ash shaft was nestled in the cocked crossbow, and more bolts sat in a quick-detach quiver. She'd been a fast study when he'd shown her how to load, cock and fire it. There still remained the dice roll on the possibility that the quarrel might end up stuck in Karl's own unbeating heart before the night was over. It wasn't something he wanted to dwell on, but he'd made promises, and he was willing to accept the risk if it lured Delgado to him.

"Nothing yet," he answered, trying not to think about the

silver so near him, in hands that he almost trusted. But she had needed a weapon. She wasn't skilled enough yet to destroy another vampire with fangs and claws.

They had staked out the shipping docks since an hour after sunset. More research had revealed that three bodies had been found there recently, with two more dumped in the harbor, all with suspicious throat injuries and blood loss. Something was feeding down here. Delgado's sirelings, most likely. Too sloppy for Delgado. But if Maria were there, it might just bring him down in person.

They stalked past the warehouses, keeping to shadows. A thin layer of frost covered the pavement. A freight truck had driven past a few minutes ago, but since then they had seen no one.

Closer to the water there was more activity. The whine of forklifts and the scrape of forks on pavement and skids was much louder, intermixed with the drifting sound of dockworker voices. They skirted these brightly lit pockets of activity, keeping to the shadows at the perimeters.

A short time later he sensed something near a huge warehouse flanked by high stacks of shipping containers. He signaled to Maria, not daring even a whisper. Together they crept closer.

The security lighting was out and the loading dock was flooded with shadow. Roberto Pulani stood next to a two-story support pillar, one of half a dozen holding up the overhang. Steel-gray bay doors marched in a line along the red-brown building, all of them shut tight. The scarred loading bumpers and the black and yellow hazard tape looked worn and hard-used. Roberto watched the back and forth trips of the forklifts in the distance as they unloaded cargo containers. His head turned to track a particular forklift driver.

Maria raised the crossbow to her shoulder and brought the scope to her eye, but Karl put his hand on her arm. He could feel Roberto's presence but there was something else—

Roberto turned and looked right at them. A smile carved his face and his eyes glowed with evil humor.

"You're trespassing, sis," he said.

Maria shot the quarrel at him. It sliced the air with a hungry hiss, but Roberto flung himself aside and the quarrel vanished into the darkness. Roberto launched himself toward them.

"Shit. Shit. Shit," Maria whispered, yanking back the string—something that would've required the crank without her vampire strength—and fumbling with another shaft. Karl stepped in front of her, slid the dagger free and dropped into a fighting crouch.

A blur of motion in the corner of his eye. Karl arched back as claws cut the air where his throat had been an instant before.

A stunningly beautiful vampire with long red hair screeched laughter and slashed at his eyes. He slipped beneath her claws and drove the silver blade into the center of her chest. Her eyes widened as hunter-joy shattered into agony. She drew in air to shriek but never got the chance. She disintegrated around the unborn scream, leaving him standing in a swirl of ash.

Karl turned back to Roberto. Maria had the crossbow reloaded, but Roberto dodged behind shipping containers when she tried to sight in on him. Karl started after Roberto, but out of nowhere a ghostly white wolf sideswiped him, knocking him off balance, freezing his skin where it touched. The wolf's translucent body shimmered with a strange, internal light. Its eyes were the blue of sapphires, almost electric in their intensity. Clouds of ice crystals had formed around its teeth and muzzle, and it left paw prints of frost on the ground.

A spirit wolf. A familiar of one of the vampires here. He'd not seen one since John Avalon had been murdered.

It turned far outside of his strike range and circled back, snarling silently. He switched the knife to his other hand and drew the pistol with the silver-encased rounds.

The spirit wolf sprinted away. He fired twice, the *twup twup* of the silencer almost smothered by the noise of the far off forklifts. The wolf disappeared behind the bulk of a semitrailer.

Motion caught Karl's attention. It was Roberto again, running out from behind cover and now almost on top of them, fangs bared and claws cutting air as his arms pumped. Karl spun toward him, raising the pistol, turning the blade, but as Roberto got closer, he suddenly lurched. An ash shaft appeared in his throat. His eyes widened in pain and fear as both hands clutched at the quarrel.

"Bastard..." Maria said, a curse as soft as a sigh.

Roberto began to unthread. His lips worked but no sound got past the quarrel in his throat, and a moment later he was nothing but a flurry of ashes like gray snow.

Maria set her foot in the crossbow and yanked the string back again to set another bolt. The spirit wolf streaked past the semitrailer, sprinting toward the red and gray rows of shipping containers. Karl lifted the pistol again, but new movement caught his attention. At the top of the stacked shipping containers stood Minsku, the vampire who'd first come to claim Maria. The spirit wolf leapt twenty feet up and landed at her feet. Karl shifted the gun sights to her.

"Enough," called a voice from the end of the shipping dock. Karl heard Maria's shocked draw of air.

Delgado.

And behind him, his undead army.

Karl stood at the far end of the dock, Maria to his right and a little behind him. Facing him were thirteen vampires and Alejandro Delgado. Fourteen pairs of angry red eyes. Fourteen pairs of fangs.

"Shit," Maria said.

Delgado wore a dark greatcoat over his suit. His leather shoes gleamed. He held a spear in his right hand, its silver tip pointed toward the sky. Around the base of the spear blade, where the silver met the wood, hung a string of yellowed fangs. They rattled in the breeze coming off the water.

"Goodbye, Karl Vance." Delgado smiled, his eyes glowing. "Thank you for bringing her to me."

He heard the click as Maria drew back the bolt and set a quarrel.

"Maria," Delgado continued. "Kill him."

Karl spun toward her. The crossbow rose to meet him, the silver quarrel tip colder than death. Maria's eyes were just as cold. Empty. She belonged to Delgado, and he had claimed her.

But Karl was faster. The butt of his pistol struck her on the temple and she jerked back. The quarrel hissed free of its restraint, and he felt the push of air as it missed him by millimeters. Maria's eyes rolled up in her head. He caught her awkwardly before she crumpled to the cement, then sheathed the silver knife to avoid touching her with it and threw her over his shoulder. He touched her forehead, using his power to send her deep into unconsciousness.

"I want his black blood," Delgado shouted.

Karl, still holding Maria, turned the SIG back at Delgado and opened fire.

Delgado darted aside as the vampires surged forward. One round clipped the blade of Delgado's spear, deforming the silver, before Delgado disappeared from sight.

Karl didn't try to track him. He shifted his aim to the closest of the sirelings, an angry-looking young Asian man. The pistol hissed three times and the vampire tumbled toward the cement dock, covering his eyes and wailing as he disintegrated.

The others came on, barely pausing. Karl ran. With one arm he steadied Maria's limp body on his shoulder, with the other he clutched the pistol. He ran with every bit of speed he could muster, but still they stayed with him.

A car rounded the street corner as he sprinted for the security gate leading to the dock area. He had a glimpse of a terrified security guard as he leapt onto the car's hood and then bounded off again. The security patrol car screeched to a halt as the wave of vampires broke over it, smashing the overhead emergency lights and rocking the car on its springs.

Karl sprinted down the middle of one of the access roads. Dogs everywhere began to howl. He cut through an empty lot, down an alley and back out again. Across a street with fast moving traffic. Again, he had to vault a car that would've run him down. The car slammed on its brakes and the two vehicles behind it also slid to a stop. Horns blared as he vanished into a service alley. A quick glance behind showed him the surge of vampires still following, breaking over and around the cars like a tidal wave, their red eyes glowing with the lust of the hunt, eerie in the darkness.

He ran on, as fast as he could with Maria weighing on him. If he could make it home, with Xiesha's help and all his weapons, he might be able to fend off a concentrated attack. Might.

If they dragged him down before that, his chances were far slimmer.

If Maria awoke still under Delgado's control, things would end badly.

He leaped to the top of a dumpster and ran along the narrow ledge of a retaining wall, careful to keep Maria balanced on his shoulder. "Gonna get you, Traitor," a voice said behind him. Not loudly, and not close behind, but loud enough for his enhanced hearing. "Gonna smoke you."

Another female vampire laughed—a throaty sound filled with anticipation.

"You're gonna die screaming," said another voice.

"Run, coward, run, run, run, *run!*"

Karl ejected the clip one-handed and heard it clatter to the pavement. He nearly fell when he jammed his hand into one cargo pocket to pull out his last clip of silver-plated rounds while trying to keep Maria's inert form from sliding off his shoulder. He staggered, lost ground—could hear them a little bit closer behind him. He took two quick turns, down a street for a moment and back into an alley. The clip made a satisfying click when he slapped it home. A round still sat in the chamber.

The alley ended, opening onto another street. He flew out of the alley entrance, running as hard as he could.

The MBTA bus that hit him was speeding, and he felt every last bit of those extra five miles per hour as his left arm shattered, his collarbone broke in three places, his pelvis was reduced to fragments. A tremendous metallic crunch filled the night air, almost as if someone had taken a bite from a soda can and amplified it a thousand times. Maria was flung like a rag doll off into oncoming traffic. The SIG clattered off to his right and he turned his head to try and catch sight of it in the crazy tumbling mess the world had suddenly turned into.

Karl rolled to a stop, the cold, rough street pressed against his face. Bits of metal and one twisted windshield wiper fell around him. The bus's airbrakes hissed and the bus veered off to the left, barely missing Maria and an oncoming car before coming to a stop against a row of parked cars. The shriek of more tires and the smell of burning rubber filled his nose.

The pistol.

Karl pushed himself up, ignoring the flare of pain. Already he could feel his bones realigning, the breaks sealing over, arteries mending and the massive bruising from leeched blood being reabsorbed into restored tissue.

The pistol lay a mere six feet off, near a no parking sign.

A glance at the alley showed vampires coming on like a tidal surge.

Fuck.

He looked to Maria. She remained unmoving, but the

impact wouldn't have hurt her permanently.

"Hey, man!" someone yelled. "Holy shit! You all right?"

Vampire laughter from the alley. Very close.

Karl threw himself at the pistol. The first vampire left the shadow of the alley.

Karl's fingers closed around the grip of the SIG-Sauer. He hit the asphalt and rolled, twisting back to face them, the pistol's silencer up and aimed and rock steady. Not even the waver of a heartbeat.

The first vampire caught three rounds. One in the forehead, one in the eye and one in the heart. For a moment its momentum carried it forward even as it began to dissolve from the bullet holes on outward. Another vampire was directly on its heels, pushing through the swirl of black motes and ash.

Karl's first shot missed. His second caught the vampire high in the chest, close to the shoulder, spinning the vampire around so that it stumbled and fell. It screamed, but didn't disintegrate—instead rolling on the filthy pavement and tearing at the silver wound with its claws. Four more vampires were staggered in a rough line behind and came full on out of the alleyway.

People began to scream. There was a chorus of car door slams as people ducked back inside their vehicles. He caught a glimpse of the bus driver out of the corner of his eye, limping away as fast as he could.

Five rounds left.

One shot hit a male vampire in the throat, the next hit him in the center of his chest and he burned into smoke.

Less than forty feet between him and the next onrushing vampire. A female vampire—pale blonde and ghost-like. He shot her in the face and dropped the sight to her chest and followed up with a round to the unbeating heart.

The two vampires remaining in the front line turned and pushed back into the other six, causing chaos as the charge faltered and broke. They screamed at him as they pressed back, trying to hide behind one another. One of them ran up along the wall like some kind of black spider. The vampire Karl had shot high in the chest dragged himself across the pavement toward the illusory safety of the alley, lips skinned back, peering back at Karl with terror in his eyes.

One bullet left.

He shot the crawling vampire through the eye. Sometimes mercy and murder were very closely entwined.

He stood slowly, a curl of cordite rising up from the muzzle of the silencer. Sirens. Not much time.

He jammed the pistol back into his shoulder holster and ran to Maria. She still lay unconscious on her side near a street grate. Her eyelids began to flutter, but he touched her forehead again, concentrating on keeping her asleep until he could get her behind the wards.

He gathered her up in his arms and began to run, dodging aside from a few panicked drivers and fleeing people.

A few moments later he heard the pursuit start up again behind him. The vampires no longer bothered to yell mocking words. There was only silence and the very faint pad of their running steps.

He jumped to the side of a building and ran up its brick facade, clutching Maria so she didn't fall. It had been perhaps a dozen years since he had moved this fast, practically flying along the rooftops. His pursuers fell farther and farther behind, their newfound wariness slowing them.

He was shielding with almost all of his power. Another glance behind showed empty streets. He didn't slow. The night was filled with what sounded like a thousand sirens.

They had lost sight of him, and shielded as he was, without a visual they wouldn't be able to track him. Their voices called out behind him in the distance, searching, calling to one another and guessing at his location. He kept sprinting. In time he could no longer hear them, only the dogs, howling in the distance.

But he had a long way to go until the safety of home. And Delgado knew where he lived.

Chapter Sixteen:
A Bitter Hell

Maria awoke in darkness, leaving the comfort of unconsciousness with reluctance, fearing the thoughts, pain, memories that might return to her. For a moment her mind reeled, disoriented by the dark and the touch of metal and dirt against her skin. Then she realized she was in a coffin. But whose coffin? One of Karl's, or one of Delgado's?

The first thing she saw when she shoved open the lid and sat up was the stack of books she'd borrowed from Karl's library. Her room, thank God. A glance down showed her she still wore the clothes she'd had on earlier, except now she was barefoot. Her room had no windows, but she sensed it was night. How long had she been out?

She got her feet under her and crouched, both hands on the cold metal of the coffin's side. The last thing she remembered clearly was killing Roberto...and then Delgado had said something and it had been as if someone had pushed her into a far corner of her own mind and locked her there. The need to obey had overridden every thought. She'd watched her own hands load the crossbow, but it had been like viewing something on a movie screen.

Oh, God. Had she tried to shoot Karl...? Delgado had said something and then everything had gone black.

She stepped out of the coffin and touched the side of her head. No pain. She padded to the door and tried the handle. Unlocked. Somehow, that surprised her. At least Karl hadn't resorted to locking her in her room, despite how badly she'd failed him.

The apartment was very quiet. When she walked into the living area, she saw Karl sitting in the leather recliner, watching her approach. His hands were empty, and there was no sign of that silver knife or his pistol. Or the crossbow he'd loaned her, for that matter.

"How are you doing?" The concern in his voice was another surprise. How could he sound so calm, even after she'd tried to kill him?

She didn't know what to do with her hands. "I don't feel any different, so Delgado must still be alive."

Karl nodded. "I missed, and then I had to run. It was a near thing. We almost didn't make it back. You've been unconscious for two nights."

Two nights... "I didn't want to wake up and find myself with Delgado."

He nodded. There was so much sympathy in his eyes that she had to look away.

"I'm sorry," she said.

"Don't be. It's not necessary."

"It's necessary for me. I insisted on coming."

Karl leaned forward. "You didn't expect his control of you to be so sudden and complete, did you?"

"I was sure I could fight him." How bitter the reality had turned out to be. A lesson that would haunt her.

"I felt that way too," he said. "With Cade."

"I could have killed you. Shot you in the back with your own weapon."

"Yes."

"Then why did you let me come?" she asked.

"I didn't want you to leave."

She stared at him. No words came to her.

"Don't mistake me for a prince." Karl's smile had a bitter twist. "I suspected that Delgado would come for you. I just didn't think he'd risk creating so many sirelings. I wagered I could kill him quickly, before he compelled you, and I lost."

There was a long pause. She walked away from him, over to the windows. "I remember shooting Roberto..."

"Regrets?"

"I did the world a favor." She was surprised at the vehemence in her own voice. "I should get a medal."

His smile made her feel a little better. Not much, but a little.

Silence opened up between them. A hundred thoughts fluttered through her mind and were gone, leaving only one lingering question. A question that seemed to have even more resonance, now that she had killed again.

"How many people have you killed?" she finally asked. She leaned her forehead against the glass and closed her eyes. She knew it was an obnoxious thing to ask him, perhaps even a dangerous thing to ask, but she asked anyway.

He stayed quiet for a long time. "Too many to remember."

"God. I can't even imagine."

"No, not yet." His voice seemed almost shattered, an undercurrent of pain so deep she had no real way to truly understand it.

"I'll be like that someday," she said, not opening her eyes. "A few hundred years from now. That's what you mean. Someday, I'll understand exactly."

He said nothing.

"You said it was a curse, and I didn't believe you." She had been such an idiot. Naïve, my God—naïve beyond imagination. How had this started? She wanted to watch Karl work, wanted to see someone die—at her command even. How sexy and powerful that had seemed at the time. What a fool.

"We have nothing." Karl's voice was hollow, empty.

"What do you mean?" She could hear the tremor in her own voice.

"We pay a terrible price for power, for existence. Do we create? Never. Do we heal? Only ourselves. Do we love?" He paused, staring at her. The smile he gave was the most cynical she'd ever seen in her life. Weary and sad and bitter.

"Sunlight," he continued after a moment, standing and moving beside her. He touched the glass. "You know I often think of it? My memories of it are vague now—true memories, not scenes taken from movies. I remember it as liquid gold suffusing everything. Warm. So very warm."

"Yet you go on." How often had she been thinking of the sun lately?

"I fear what comes after. When your list of sins is so long you've forgotten the faces of those you've slaughtered, a particularly bitter hell awaits you."

"And hope?"

He smiled at her, just barely, but it was enough. "I hope for some things. And I have the patience to wait for them."

"Well, I don't," she said and kissed him.

Chapter Seventeen:
Heat

Her lips were soft, but not warm like Karl remembered—like he expected—though he should've known better. It didn't matter. He could feel himself stirring at her touch.

Xiesha cleared her throat behind them, and they broke their embrace slowly. He turned to look at Xiesha, an eyebrow raised.

"There are men outside the door," she said, her eyes far off as if she were seeing through the wall.

Karl refocused his attention to the hall outside his apartment and cursed. He'd been too intent on Maria, losing himself in the sensation of her like a fool. Now he detected three distinct, rapid heartbeats. He could hear the rustle of their clothes as they shifted, the sound of their breath slipping in and out of their mouths.

At first they knocked—a sharp *rap rap rap*. Next, the doorbell chimed. Karl waited. How persistent would they be?

The door shook with a deep boom when someone kicked it, but it stayed closed. Getting past the reinforced deadbolt would take quite a bit of determination. Another kick, harder this time, the boom of impact even louder as the door rattled in its frame. It seemed they were determined. Karl heard someone work the slide of an automatic pistol. A Lucatti hit team, sent because Delgado's vampires had failed? Or a Ricardi hit team, sent because of Maria and her half-brother?

"They're going to draw attention," Xiesha said. "If someone calls the police, there will be problems."

"They aren't going to go away on their own," Maria added

quickly.

The door juddered from another booming kick and the wood splintered around the steel plate of the deadbolt.

Damn it.

"Let them in and raise the wards," he said, "since they're so eager to die. No sound escapes this time. Finish it quick and clean."

Xiesha hurried to the door, flipped the locks and pulled it open, careful to stay hidden behind it so the three men could enter unimpeded. One of them, a huge muscular man in a tracksuit and gold chain, had been attempting another kick when the door swung open, and he stumbled across the threshold, cursing. He clutched a snub-nosed Smith & Wesson with a shrouded hammer in one massive hand. His eyes flicked around the dark room, seeking a target.

The other two men pushed inside after him. Both had guns out and raised—the one on the left whose face was pitted by acne scars held his 9mm sideways, gangsta-style. The skinny one on the right had one of those long-barreled, six shot .44 or .445 Magnum arm cannons that could give an elephant second thoughts.

Karl sensed the wards drop behind them as they charged in—a latticework of cold purple-black light slamming down like a portcullis. The men couldn't see it, but they must have sensed something, because Muscles glanced back and hesitated, as if suddenly unsure.

Xiesha flung the door closed with a bang, and Acne-scars spun toward her, swinging his automatic to bear.

Xiesha's hand shot out and grabbed his wrist. Her eyes blazed blue for a second and Karl felt her powers flare to life. Acne-scars dropped the pistol and began to shriek as he burst into spectral white flames.

Muscles, cursing nonstop, turned toward the flames. He threw one hand over his face against the heat and raised his snub-nosed revolver with the other. He fired at Xiesha, pulling the trigger over and over.

Acne-scars jerked as two bullets tore into his back. A third bullet would've clipped Xiesha in the shoulder, but it struck some invisible barrier around her and exploded into blue sparks.

Xiesha dropped Acne-scars and his charred body crumpled

to the ground, burned flesh crinkling like plastic wrap. A strange smell like ozone and ethanol filled the air. The ghostly white fire vanished the moment she released him.

"You bitch!" the third one, the Hand-cannon guy, screamed. He drew down on her, his face twisted with rage. Karl leapt forward out of the shadows, right in front of the 8-inch barrel as the gun went off with a roar. The bullet slammed into his chest and blew a gaping hole in his back, scattering his vampire blood and bone. But even as his flesh exploded outward it was already pulling itself back together, rethreading into his being. The bullet wasn't silvered, and no amount of lead could hurt him, no matter where he was shot.

Karl smiled.

Hand-cannon opened his mouth, his eyes filling with fear. Karl seized him and pulled him close, then drove his fangs into the man's throat. The man's neck muscles twitched against Karl's mouth. He stank of sweat and stale cologne, but the taste of blood was sublime.

Karl's eyes flicked to Muscles, standing there, snub-nosed revolver still raised, watching Karl with horror sewn across his face. Then Muscles darted for the door, his gold chain flopping, his lips pulled back from his teeth in a simian smile. He yanked at the doorknob, little whimpers shivering in his throat. Karl could hear the man's heart thundering along like hooves at Suffolk Downs.

Maria got to him first. He was so much taller than she was that she had to seize his head and force it down so she could bite his neck. The pistol tumbled from his fingers and thumped to the carpet. The only sound he could hear was the swallowing of blood as they both drank their fill.

A short while later, someone knocked on the door. Karl pulled his fangs free and set the dead body down. For the second time tonight he'd been too distracted to notice someone approach the apartment. Unforgivably sloppy.

Xiesha hurried to the peephole and peered through. "A security guard. Someone must have heard the banging on the door and called him."

"What about the gunshots?" Maria swiped a hand across her face, smearing the blood from her lips. When she looked down at the back of her hand, she grew very still, staring at the blood with that mix of revulsion and desire that he knew so well. But there was less revulsion than the last time she had fed, and that was another thing he knew far too well.

"The wards were in place," Xiesha replied. "Nobody heard gunshots."

The knock came again, more insistent.

"Answer it," Karl said. "You're the only one who's halfway presentable. Maria, help me get these bodies out of here."

They dragged the bodies out of sight and threw an afghan over them. They tossed a towel over the few bloodstains on the carpet from Acne-scar's gunshot wounds. The air reeked of blood and gunpowder and that ozone-ethanol scent, but not charred flesh, strangely enough, though Acne-scars now more accurately resembled a charcoal briquette.

Xiesha had waited until they cleared away the bodies. Karl glanced at her, expecting the knocking to turn to pounding at any moment. "Talk to him outside."

Xiesha looked at Maria. "As if I'd just started doing this yesterday."

He frowned at Xiesha until she turned away and opened the door.

The young man was college age, with a blond Vandyke beard. Handsome in a captain-of-the-football team way. He smiled and tipped his hat to Xiesha. It was a curiously old-school gesture that should have looked contrived but somehow didn't.

Xiesha stepped across the threshold. Karl sensed that electric sizzle as she passed the wards—but the security guard sensed nothing. She left the door halfway open, so that Karl and Maria could watch from the shadows of the room.

"Sorry to bother you, ma'am," the security guard said. His name badge read Randall. "A client on this floor was concerned about some noise. She said it sounded like something was wrong."

"I heard some thumping." Xiesha smiled, and the security guard automatically smiled back. "Perhaps someone was playing their music too loud?"

"Might be, ma'am. Not to worry you, but we saw three guests enter on one of our outside cameras." He handed her a picture that still smelled of printer ink. "Have you seen any of these gentlemen?"

Xiesha looked over the photo. She tilted it slightly so that

Karl and Maria could see it from inside. A grainy video surveillance shot of their three dead friends at one of the side entrances with a swipe card reader.

"I'm sorry. I don't know any of those men. Are they still here?"

"That's what we're trying to find out," Randall said. "They came out on this floor. Are you sure you didn't hear anything?"

There were no security cameras on any of the room floors, just the lobby, elevators and ground floor entrances. Security would've lost track of the men as soon as they had left the elevator. They could still avert suspicion if Xie played this perfectly.

"No, I'm sorry. I was just in the shower." She paused, letting that image settle in his mind. "But how would they have gotten past you?"

Randall cleared his throat. "They came in a side entrance only for tenants using a swipe card. It's probably nothing, but we like to look into these things." He set his hands on his belt, with its clips for mace and a walkie-talkie.

"I'll let you know if I see or hear anything else, Officer Randall. Thank you." She smiled again, this one her most dazzling yet.

"Oh, one last thing." His eyes had cooled a few degrees.

"Yes?"

He indicated the door with a lift of his chin. "There are shoe prints on your door."

Xiesha laughed. "Oh my husband did that. Carrying in my shopping bags and too lazy to set them down." She shook her head. "Pushing the door open with his foot. Now I have to clean it."

Randall nodded. "I'm sure housekeeping will take care of it. Thank you for your time."

Xiesha came back inside, closed the door and locked it. "Going to be interesting disposing of the bodies with everyone all stirred up."

"We'll take care of the bodies, Xie," Karl said, "if you'll clean up all traces here."

He cast around for any sense of Delgado or his sirelings that might be concealed nearby, waiting to learn what had happened. Or perhaps waiting to press another attack. But he could sense nothing. Not even a twitch. He moved to one of the windows and pushed aside the shades and then the blinds, but he felt nothing out there, either.

"I recognize this guy," Maria said, staring down at Muscles. "Antonio Sarto, a Lucatti soldier, certainly not one of his best. But I don't recognize these other two. Probably just wannabes."

"There's only one reason to send incompetent people. Delgado wants to flush us out."

She nodded. "A big fight with lots of noise. Delgado basically sent these clowns to their deaths. Why would Stefano Lucatti agree to something like this?"

Karl gave a little shrug. "If Delgado's using low-level soldiers, it's likely something off the record." He glanced down at Antonio Sarto. "A side job. Perhaps something Delgado is paying for himself."

"So what do we do now?"

"I think we throw these idiots in the bathtub and help Xie clean the blood spatter. Things are too hot tonight. I don't want to do anything Delgado expects."

"Won't they start to smell?"

"Eventually," he said.

"Ugh. Then we might as well get started."

They finished cleaning an hour before dawn. A forensics team would find trace evidence of the killings if they worked over the apartment, but there was little he could do about the effectiveness of luminol. At least the place was clean enough to pass a quick check by security.

Xiesha crossed the room, taking the blue tote full of cleansers, scrubbing pads and paper towels back to the kitchen. The sight of Xiesha in her silk dress carrying around cleaning supplies smacked of the surreal.

He followed her to the bathroom and looked again at the bodies in their sheets, piled in the tub. He tried to capture any sense of Delgado nearby, but again he sensed nothing. There was something odd about the bodies though... Some very faint sense of void...almost as if...

"We should consider moving, Master," Xiesha said from the doorway.

"Hmm?" He glanced at her. "Yes. I want to leave for the

house in Cambridge as soon as the sun sets tonight. See if you can rent a truck on short notice and pack all the essentials. Leave the silver dagger and the SIG unpacked, and your 12-gauge. Load the rest."

"Should I select a weapon for Maria?"

He thought about it for a moment, then, finally, "No."

"You have no more silver rounds for the pistol. And I have fewer than ten for the shotgun."

He frowned at her. "I'm aware of our shortages."

She nodded. "I'll handle the arrangements today. We'll move as soon as you rise tonight."

He gave the burned corpse one last glance, and then walked back to the living room. Maria came up to him as he entered.

"There's something strange about all of this." She shook her head slowly. "I'm not certain what, but something feels wrong."

"We move after sunset. I have another house. If we stay here, our luck will run out eventually one way or another. It might be harder for Delgado to watch us outside of the city."

"How will we get rid of three bodies?"

"Someone in your line of work has to ask?" he said, and she scowled at him. Standard practice was to cut off their heads and hands. Dump the body in one location, hide the head and hands someplace else. Body dumps in water were an old favorite.

Maria turned away. "You know, I never realized how much work it would be covering everything up. I take it you've done it before?"

"Yes."

"I say we dump them on Stefano Lucatti's front yard. Let him deal with it. Send a message."

"Too risky."

"But it may cause strife between Delgado and Don Lucatti," she said. "Wouldn't that be worth a bit of risk?"

Karl had to admit it would be. And it had that Machiavellian flavor that made him smile. Besides, it wasn't as if he had to worry about mafia patronage with how things had fallen out between him and the Ricardis.

"Then we'll dump the bodies tomorrow night," he agreed,

"before we move."

"Beautiful." She smiled and headed for the kitchen. Karl followed her into the empty kitchen with its long stretches of bare marble countertop. Even Xiesha's scrying bowl was gone. The only thing that was stocked was a wine rack, and that was mostly affectation.

Maria put her hands on her hips. "The cockroaches are starving in here, you know."

"Good."

"So what does Xiesha eat, anyway?" She opened a cabinet. "Baking soda?"

"She doesn't eat."

"No wonder she can keep that figure. Is she even alive?" Maria cocked her head and laughed. "You know, there's something very disturbing about asking a question like that and not thinking anything of it. But then again, there's something rather disturbing about not being alive yourself while you're asking it."

Karl smiled. "She's not completely on this plane of existence."

Maria snorted. "And I thought *my* life was complicated. So how did you meet her?"

"Why all the questions?"

"Because I'm jealous. Because she was here first and she's known you so long. Because she's so beautiful she'd make supermodels grind their teeth. Do you sleep with her?"

"No."

"Like I believe that."

He shrugged. "Believe what you want."

Maria frowned. "Well, there's *something* there. What's the story between you? Why does she do the *I Dream of Jeanie* thing?"

"She's paying off a debt. By her choice, not mine. When she feels the debt is paid, she'll leave. Perhaps. We've never discussed it."

"What debt?"

"I saved her from the Order of the Thorn a long time ago."

"Them again." She folded her arms and looked down at the tiles. "I really don't think I like them."

"She was a refugee, fleeing her home. They condemned her

as a threat when she arrived."

"Sounds like judge, jury and executioner all rolled into one nice neat little package." She brushed her hair back from her face and stared at the racks of wine. "Some things never change, I guess."

"They're in Boston already. Stay far from them. If they were to learn about you..."

"I'll keep it in mind," she said, but her tone...it was as if she only half believed what he said.

He took her arm. "Listen to me. Don't let them know you exist. You're full of your new powers now, think you can take on anything. You can't. Believe me."

"Okay, Karl. Get a grip, will you? I think Delgado's the bigger migraine right now."

The sudden urge to slap that annoyed look off her face came over him, and he kissed her instead.

For a moment she was stunned, her lips yielding to his, but then she kissed him back, wrapping herself against him. She licked at his lips, flickered her tongue over his fangs.

Her nipples were stiff against the dress she wore, and his sensitive skin could feel them against his chest. His hand slipped inside the top of the dress, pulling it down, massaging a thumb over her nipple. She growled deep in her throat and kissed him harder, rocking him back on his heels. With one yank she ripped away his shirt, sliding her hand across his skin.

Karl picked her up, so suddenly that she uttered a tiny shriek of surprise. He carried her into his room. When he laid her in his coffin, she laughed. He grinned and pulled her dress off her, and she leaned back, her long dark hair spread out around her. She opened her mouth to say something, but he kissed the words back into her throat.

He remembered the first time he'd seen her, in the restaurant next to her father. He remembered her standing in her apartment with the city lights at her back, a glass of wine in her hand and a smile on her face. And even in all this cold passion—for there was no heat, even now—he found it within himself to hate what had happened, and his part in it. He kissed her again. Their kisses and their caresses helped push all thought from his mind except for the feel of her against his skin.

Maria closed her eyes when he entered her, tilting her head back, exposing her neck. He kissed along her throat as he thrust deep within her, moving slowly at first, then faster as their passion built.

She drove her fangs into his neck, screaming in pleasure when she came. He let her bite, knowing she couldn't help it, and when he followed her into bliss, he drove his own fangs into her soft white skin. They cycled blood through each other, drinking, sharing, until finally she released him, and he did the same. They lay back in each other's arms, mingled scents, mingled blood.

He lay still, enjoying the softness of her skin against him, the taste of her in his mouth. Suddenly, she sat up and turned to him, a dawning fear in her eyes.

"Why did Delgado send those hit men at night?" She grabbed his shoulder and he could feel her trembling. "Why not send them during daylight? Why at *night?*"

His mind shuttered through possible reasons faster than shuffled cards. Nothing made sense. He'd assumed Delgado had been trying to destroy their sanctity here—compromise their defenses and bring in human authorities to drive them out. Delgado obviously hadn't told the men what they'd be going up against, since they hadn't even brought holy objects along with them for defense. It also might have been some internal political thing for the Lucatti family that they'd never know about, forcing Karl to kill those men. There wasn't enough information to do anything but guess.

But it was disturbing.

"We need to check the bodies," Maria continued. "Something's wrong—"

But at that moment Karl felt the sun break over the horizon.

His strength began to pour out of him and float away with the night. His limbs grew heavier until it took every bit of his willpower just to move them a little. As the sun crept higher, every passing second brought the darkness of sleep closer, made it that much harder to deny.

He fought against it, even managed to lift a hand to the lid of his casket, but in the end, the darkness lost to day. The paralysis of sleep swept over him, and in his mind, the darkness reigned.

Chapter Eighteen:
Escape

Maria sat up as soon as the sun vanished below the horizon and released her from the paralysis of vampire sleep. Her sleep had been visionless, for once, and so deep that she'd heard nothing happening in the real world. But her fear was as real as it had been before the dawn.

Karl was on his feet next to her. He stepped out of the coffin and began pulling on his clothes. His face was grim and his motions hurried. She followed suit, yanking her dress over her head.

A low boom shook the walls. They both paused for a second, and then ran for the door.

They found Xiesha in the living room. The leather sofa was upended and lying against the wall. The bottom of the sofa smoked, but Maria could see no flames. There was a hole in the wall leading to the kitchen, and she could see right past the studs to the sink. Debris lay strewn about the carpeting— broken end tables, books, drywall.

Xiesha stood in the middle of the room, one hand raised and held palm out toward a shape standing in the doorway to the kitchen.

It took Maria one long moment to accept what she was seeing. The burned corpse of Acne-scars from yesterday— withered and charred almost to the bone—shuddered as it tried to advance against whatever force Xiesha was using against it. White pinpricks of light glowed deep in its empty eye sockets.

Karl stepped in front of Maria. His voice was amazingly calm. So calm it soothed her own confused panic.

"What the hell are you playing with, Xie?"

Xiesha's fine features were rigid with her efforts to hold the charred corpse motionless. It made her seem almost feral, wolf-like. "He's trying to pull something through the Seam."

Xiesha hissed out breath and clenched her raised hand into a fist. The corpse's right arm disintegrated at the elbow. The thing didn't seem to notice.

"Delgado." Karl's voice was so soft it was almost a whisper.

"Who else?" Xiesha said. "He's using my residual magic in that corpse to locate the wormhole."

"How?"

"I don't know!"

"That's what he wanted," Maria said. "A Trojan horse." She could feel the beginnings of panic and it was a strange feeling. No physical sensation at all, but just a fluttering of thoughts in her mind like frenzied bats all flapping in and out of a cave.

Karl put a hand on her shoulder, but he didn't look away from the corpse. "Where are the weapons, Xie?"

"Packed," she answered, her voice strained. "Your knife and pistol are on the table."

Karl glanced at the table but didn't move for the leather case. "They won't do any good against this thing."

Xiesha's voice had always been calm, almost serene, but now Maria heard a note of cold panic when Xie spoke again. "I need you to keep it busy while I seal the crack he's opening. There's a Thresher on the other side. They know I'm here."

"What—?" Maria began, her mind whirling. Karl cut her off.

"Maria, when I count to three, Xie's going to release it and it's going to go straight for her. We have to stop it. Are you ready?"

"I'm ready." Her nails grew and hardened into claws without conscious thought. The panic that had almost gripped her died down to a whisper when Karl spoke, but when Delgado's name slipped through her mind again, the panic rose once more to beat against her thoughts. She fought to get control of herself.

"One. Two. *Three*."

The burned corpse leapt forward with startling agility. She could see its teeth, white against the charred red and black of its seared muscle, and she knew there was no way it could move that fast with so much damage to its tissue.

Karl was quicker. His fist impacted on the side of its head just as it gathered itself to spring at Xiesha. The corpse flew through the air and slammed into the opposite wall.

It didn't even turn toward Karl. Those empty sockets with the two pinpricks of light stayed locked on Xiesha. It staggered to its feet again and took another step toward her.

Maria slipped behind it and slashed at it with her claws, ripping gaping holes in the charred remains. Her lips pulled back from her teeth in revulsion as her claws sent chunks of the thing flying in every direction, spattering on the walls, the carpet, her face.

She didn't even slow it. Karl jumped in its way, seized its remaining arm and hurled it across the room into an ornate china cabinet. Maria heard bones break amidst the crash of shattering china, but the corpse rolled back to its feet, reeking of charred flesh and that strange ethanol-ozone stench. Its burned skin and muscle hung in tatters from its back where her claws had shredded it. The white-light pinpricks glowed in its eye sockets. It made hungry little clicks by snapping its teeth together as it moved for Xiesha again.

Maria glanced at Xiesha, hoping she was finished. Xiesha's hands folded and unfolded, forming complex patterns, almost as if she had an invisible cat's cradle, and her lips moved rapidly, but she made no sound. Strain had turned her beautiful face harsh and fierce.

Maria ran around Karl and leapt at the walking corpse as it took another bounding step. She drove it into the wall hard enough to crater the drywall. The sweet chemical stink of it filled her nostrils, so strong she almost gagged.

The corpse clicked its teeth at Maria and reached for her eyes with its burned fingers. She ducked beneath the hand and grabbed its left leg. The flesh sloughed off in her fingers and she gave a cry of disgust. She ripped the leg clean away with a huge tearing wrench, hearing every sinew and bone pop. Then she swung the leg around and hammered the corpse in the head with it, slamming the thing into the floor. The corpse hit the ground so hard half its face shattered. It turned its head, tendons in its neck creaking, and *looked* at her for the first time.

"Good," Karl said, so near he was talking in her ear,

startling her because she'd never sensed him get so close. "You got its attention. Now help me pull it apart."

They set to it with ruthless efficiency, ripping the thing limb from limb until it was little more than twitching pieces. Its skull still clicked and snapped, until Karl crushed its lower face with a stomp of his heel.

Maria backed up and turned to Xiesha. She stood at the mouth of the hallway, her motions coming faster and faster, her hands blurring through complex patterns. Now Maria could hear her words—a strange liquid tongue that flowed through her mind like mercury and was gone.

"Xie?" There was hesitation in Karl's voice, and Maria guessed he feared breaking her concentration.

"The break in the Seam will not shut." Strain made Xiesha's voice waver. "The Thresher's fighting me."

A keening wail filled the air, like metal crushed in a compactor. Light poured down the hall, a strange light that flickered and danced along the walls, like sunlight on a swimming pool.

Karl ran toward the hall, Maria a step behind him. Halfway down, a jagged rip opened in the middle of the air, stretching from carpet to ceiling. Bright, blue-white light flooded out through the rip.

As she watched, the keening grew louder and the rip split wider. She shielded her eyes, barely able to make out a figure just beyond the crack. Vaguely humanoid, featureless except for one huge red and pupil-less eye in the center of its head that was curved like the lens of a telescope. A half-dozen smaller eyes were clustered around the central one, all of them glowing softly, almost vampire-like.

Bitter cold poured out and frost spread across the walls and carpet. The Thresher pressed forward, moving slowly, seeming to fight against an unseen counterforce. Its large body was armored with irregular plates of some metal that shimmered like an oil slick in sunlight, so that its outline appeared jagged and angular. It gripped some strange snaking metal thing in one metal-shrouded limb, something like a steel whip that seemed to move of its own accord, wavering back and forth like the head of a cobra. The landscape beyond the rip—a cold white-blue wasteland—swirled with blue-tinged vapor. A sun, dimmed by the churning vapors, burned blue and huge, filling much of the sky. Maria's eardrums ached as if there were great pressure on them. "God..." she whispered.

Karl kept his eyes on the thing that pushed through the crack, its leg, as massive as a phone pole, thumped down on the carpet. "Can you slow it, Xie?"

"Trying." Xiesha's hands had stilled, folded together in a way that looked physically impossible to Maria. The tension in her body made her appear as though she were about to try shoving a piano through a concrete wall. "Drive it back!"

Karl spun and ran toward the gray leather lead-lined case that sat closed on the glass coffee table next to his pistol. He leapt over the sofa and landed on the table in a crouch. He swept up the case and a second later the knife was in his bare hand. A spasm of agony distorted his face, and blue fire burned around his clenched fist. The blade shimmered with a holy blue glow that pierced and ripped like someone using a hypodermic needle to etch initials on her eyeball.

A pulse of light filled the hall like a flashbulb. The Thresher pushed fully through the crack. It held its snakelike whip out before it, thrashing in the air. The cone-shaped drill tip suddenly unfolded like a flower into a hundred jagged teeth that spun like a blender.

"Put it back inside!" Xiesha yelled. "Get it back in so I can close it!"

Karl sprang past her, zigzagging down the hall, and even now her enhanced vision had trouble tracking him. Mostly she only saw the afterimage of his burning fist.

The Thresher slashed its whip at him, the tip snapping closed into the drill and spinning with a whine that made Maria want to shiver.

Karl blocked it with his forearm and then grabbed it with his free hand. He wrenched the whip toward him, jerking the Thresher off balance. The Thresher made a deep chiming sound, almost like a tolling church bell. Karl drew back the knife and stabbed it dead center in its red eye-lens. There was a loud crack as the blade shattered through the eye. Blue fluid bubbled out around the blade, and a cloud of white smoke poured off its face.

Karl wrenched the knife free with a snarl. He kicked the Thresher dead center in its massive chest, knocking it backward into the rift. It toppled with a spray of blue fluid, churning the vapor around it.

Xie shouted a guttural word that made Maria flinch. The rip sealed upward from the bottom, like a zipper pulled closed. The blue-white light vanished and left only darkness. The following silence was very deep.

"Shit," Maria whispered. She ran a finger along the frost on the wall and stared at the tip. Her hand was shaking.

Karl pried his fingers free of the knife and dropped it. The blade stuck in the floor, wisps of smoke curling from the hilt.

"Your hand," Maria said, taking his wrist. She touched the fingers of his closed fist and Karl opened it slowly. His palm had been seared black with the pattern of the hilt design. It looked as if the hilt had eaten into his flesh.

"It will heal, eventually." He drew his hand away.

Maria walked to the place where the tear had been and walked around in a circle, searching for any trace, but she found no sign of any rip in the fabric of reality. Only a couple of spatters of that blue fluid that had sprayed from the thing's eye.

"What the fuck *was* that?" she asked.

"Thresher." Xiesha leaned against the wall with one arm out to support her, her head hanging down and strands of her hair undone and in her face. "Waiting for me to try and go home."

"Looked like he was done waiting."

Karl turned to Xiesha. "Can they open another rift?"

Maria saw something new in Xiesha's eyes. Fear.

"I don't know," she answered. "I had to drop the wards to close that rift. If they were able to track me through the brane..."

"Brane?" Maria looked at Xiesha as if she were mad.

"A spacetime dimension. A gauge-gravity duality that—"

"Never mind."

Karl turned his hand over and stared at the wound. "How did Delgado reanimate that corpse? That's not something I've ever seen a vampire do. Not like that."

Xiesha shook her head. "He could have used the remnants of my power to trace back to the string. A wormhole finder, in effect, through spacetime foam."

"What?" Maria said. "Like tracing phone calls?"

A tired smile. "Essentially."

"I don't know how to do that." Karl glanced at Xiesha. "How could he do something like that?"

"I think the more important question," Xiesha said, "is how did he know to even try?"

Karl didn't answer, so Maria did instead. "You think we have a leak."

"Who would tell him?" Xiesha stared at Maria. "Unless it were you."

"Fuck you. I'm no rat."

"Maybe not consciously," Xiesha said. "But he owns you." She cut a look at Karl. "I told you it was wrong to let her live."

"*Enough.*" Karl's voice cracked with anger. Only his eyes seemed haunted. "She doesn't know enough about who and what you are to give him anything, even if she wanted to."

"I think—"

"I know what you think." Karl rubbed a hand across his face. "Be silent and consider this for a second. Use Occam's razor—*all things being equal, the simplest theory tends to be correct.* So either Delgado really is some dimension-bending sorcerer, or there's a simpler answer."

"Maybe you led that thing back to you when you burned that guy," Maria said.

"Is that possible, Xie?"

"Many things are possible... That corpse was acting as a sort of beacon. But I've never seen it happen before."

"We can untangle it later," Karl said. "Right now we have to get out of here. We've overstayed our welcome."

"Time to go to the mattresses. I thought we were already doing that, but whatever." Maria laughed, thinking she sounded half-mad, like some cackling swamp hag. "Of course, we're leaving behind a bunch of corpses. Two of which have curious bite marks and no blood. And the third is scattered around the place in snack-size portions."

"Stop your jesting," Xiesha said. "This is your fault."

"*Enough.*" Karl glared at Xiesha until she looked away. "We're wasting time. Is the truck loaded?"

"Fully loaded and in the parking garage. We may leave at any time."

"Excellent. Thank you. If the wards were down when that rift opened, we probably alerted every person and creature with the least bit of supernatural sensitivity in a hundred-mile radius."

"So what do we do?" Maria asked.

"We run," was all he said.

They took the loading elevator down to the parking garage. No one talked. Karl stared at their warped reflections in the metal-plated door—all hunter's eyes and distorted mouths. Carnival funhouse portraits.

The floors counted down with a rhythmic ding as they passed. The ride seemed to stretch on forever, down and down. Karl would've been only mildly surprised if the doors had finally hissed open on a wave of heat and living darkness, where souls writhed in empty agony as a leering prince with a cherub's face looked on in satisfaction.

Or something like that.

He wondered if Xiesha had been right. He refused to believe Maria had purposely given Delgado the information he needed to set that trap, but could he have gotten it out of her unknowingly? Or was there another, simpler solution? He looked at her smeared reflection in the imperfect steel of the door. She was busy watching the numbers count down and didn't notice.

The elevator hissed as it descended. The SIG 9mm felt slightly unbalanced with the silencer attached, and it felt stranger still in his left hand. No silver-clad bullets left, and no time to have any made. He'd loaded it with the Teflon-coated rounds, in case the Order of Thorn changed its mind.

The silver dagger was in his right hand, painful even through his glove. It had done its job against Delgado the last time, but now he found himself wishing it were a sword instead. Something with more range. The freight elevator doors might just open up on Delgado and his remaining brood standing silent on the hoods of the BMWs and Audis, their skin deathly pale in the fluorescent light. Now wouldn't that make for an interesting going-away party?

The elevator dinged a final time as it settled to a stop. The doors opened on the brightly lit parking garage, its hash-marked concrete and yellow-black striped barriers a much tamer milieu than he'd expected. The twenty-four foot moving truck Xiesha had rented sat in the loading zone, its sliding door shut and padlocked. Karl paused, preventing the elevator door from closing with one booted foot. He raised the 9mm and kept the knife mid-chest level, ready to thrust or slash in an instant. His right hand still throbbed from touching the silver dagger barehanded, and he could feel his skin tightening up, seeming to shrink around his bones.

He stepped out of the freight elevator and listened, scanning the rows of cars and SUVs. Their windshields reflected back the overhead lights. He could hear water running through the water main and the sound of sporadic traffic out on the street. One fluorescent light buzzed and flickered far off to the right, near a glass-encased fire extinguisher.

No Delgado.

"Let's go," he said.

They set off toward the rental truck walking three abreast. Xiesha had dressed in a cobalt blue suit and a long black coat better suited to an executive lunch. Her hair was still in a bun held with black and imitation-ivory chopsticks. She carried a Beretta 12-gauge close to her body, mostly hidden by the length of the coat. Maria wore brown slacks under a long, dark winter coat of her own. She had no weapon except her claws and fangs, but if that upset her, she didn't show it. Karl wore a set of his work blacks, fatigues, jump boots, a black T-shirt, shoulder holster and knife sheath on his left hip. No coat for him. He didn't want it getting in the way if he had to use the knife.

"Check everything," he said. "No surprises."

Running was no surprise though. Here he was, fleeing one of his safe places again. This was just like with the Mancinos. Exist long enough, and déjà vu was an old friend, as intimate as a shadow.

Xiesha circled the truck from the right, shotgun up and at her shoulder. He moved in from the other side, tracking left to right with the 9mm. Maria stayed close to him, her gaze darting around the garage.

The cab was empty. They quickly checked the rest of the truck, from engine to axles and even unlocked the back. No sign of sabotage or unwanted guests.

So how had Delgado set that trap for them with the corpse? He'd never seen the kind of magic he'd seen tonight. Xiesha had said that Delgado had exploited her magic somehow, and that made a certain amount of sense, because neither of the two men Karl and Maria had killed had stirred from the bathtub where they'd stashed the bodies. Only the body she'd burned had come crawling out after the sun had gone down.

Even the dead didn't stay dead. He had to love the irony.

"Xie's driving." Karl opened the passenger door for Maria. "Why don't you ride shotgun with her. I'll ride on the top of the truck."

"No," Maria said. "I'll ride up top with you."

Karl frowned. "Ride in the cab with Xie. I don't want to lose you if Delgado shows up."

"If Delgado shows up, I won't be able to resist him, whether I'm on the roof or in the fucking cab." She raised her chin and stood her ground. "I'm riding on the damn rooftop with you so I can at least feel the night."

He stared at her for a moment.

"Please," she said softly.

"Very well." A spasm of pain twitched through his burned hand, but he ignored it.

The air felt tainted with evil premonition, as if he had already lost her.

Both Maria and Karl lay flat on their stomachs atop the moving truck as Xiesha pulled out into traffic. They held onto the riveted seam between the roof's overlapping metal plates, something only a vampire could hope to pull off. The cold air cut against Karl's face, while the vibration of the engine thrummed through the frame of the large truck up into his forearms.

He was using power to divert attention from them as they merged with heavier traffic. When they stopped to make the turn to head south toward Cambridge Street, he sensed them. Three vampires. Their shielding couldn't hide them from Karl at this distance. He stared off in the direction his vampire senses told him the vampires would appear. A moment later he spotted them running across a rooftop in hard pursuit. Xiesha must have seen them too. The truck roared off, shunted southeast on Merrimac with the vampires in pursuit.

"We've got company." He pushed up to a crouch and pointed. It would be all knife and claw work.

Maria rose to a crouch, mirroring him, her eyes locking on the vampires. Her face was calm, but he could smell the fear on her, ripe and rich, like roses in decay.

Delgado's vampires leapt along the roofs and the sides of the buildings on their left, across the Boston Globe building. They flicked in and out between light and shadow, disappearing behind A/C units and venting, visible for a moment and gone the next. When parking lots stretched between buildings, they hurled themselves off the roof, landing without a stumble, and continued to sprint alongside, no more than shadowed blurs. Cross traffic slowed them not at all. They leapt from car roof to car roof without pause.

Bloody-handed hell. Nothing was ever easy. "Get ready," he said.

With one hand he slipped the dagger free. A glance over the side of the truck showed only light traffic. Xiesha kept their speed steady, despite the pursuit, heading roughly east-northeast, past Haymarket Station and toward the North End. They were making good progress, but the vampires easily kept pace.

Then he sensed two more vampires, raising the total to five. One was Minsku, the raven-haired beauty with the spirit wolf. The last was Delgado.

"He's *here*," Maria said. Her voice was near panic. "What do we do?"

"Nothing. We wait." He couldn't risk tearing off after Delgado and leaving her unprotected. Delgado had the initiative, damn him. All they could do was hunker down and defend.

They turned down a side street empty of traffic. Dark storefronts and three-story tenement houses lined the avenue. Cars were parked bumper to bumper along the curb in a long snaking line. Karl shifted his weight from boot to boot. His blade gleamed each time a streetlight flashed overhead.

A figure appeared in the headlights, flooded to ghost-white against the darkness. A male dressed in jeans and a T-shirt despite the cold, his eyes glowing red and his bared fangs bright against his red lips.

Xiesha gunned the engine. The instant before the grill of the truck impacted with the vampire's chest, he dropped from sight and the truck roared over him.

Karl walked to the back of the truck and crouched near the edge. Below him, the ground sped past in an unceasing blur. A moment later the vampire's head peeked out from beneath the bumper. He pulled himself out and crept up the side of the truck toward Karl with grotesque, almost spider-like deliberation.

"You're pretty," the vampire called. "But I bet you taste like salt." A high-pitched laugh bubbled out of his mouth. He reached the metal edge of the roof and settled his long fingers over the lip, ready to pull himself up.

Karl slashed at the vampire's hands, forcing him to let go and drop to the bumper to save his fingers. The vampire teetered on the edge of balance for a second, but grabbed the side of the truck before he fell. He glared up at Karl and hissed. Karl hesitated, unsure if he should risk descending, but he sensed a stronger presence approaching from behind. Scrambling back, he glanced over his shoulder and saw Minsku perched on an arching streetlight ahead of them.

Maria still knelt near the front of the truck, but she was looking back toward him, at the vampire who was pouring up over the edge.

"Maria," Karl yelled. "Look out!"

The truck's front end passed under the streetlight. Minsku dropped to the roof of the truck, just behind the cab. Maria turned and half-stood, but Minsku kicked her in the chest, sending her sliding toward the roof's edge. Maria drove her claws into the roof and Karl heard rivets pop as the metal peeled back.

The climbing vampire leapt, and Karl spun back to face him. The vampire's claws were out, his face hideously changed into a mask of stretched skin, pale red eyes in sockets that were more like wounds, and long fangs.

Karl caught him by the front of his jeans with his free hand and hurled him toward Minsku. Minsku dodged, but not fast enough, and his legs clipped her, knocking her off-balance. He tumbled over the edge just as Maria rose and rammed her shoulder into Minsku's stomach. Minsku flailed backward, windmilling for balance, and disappeared over the side. There was a screech of tearing metal, and then silence.

Xiesha took a wild left turn. Karl felt the truck lean alarmingly to the right and heard the thuds of cargo banging

189

around before the truck rocked back to level on tired springs. The truck's engine roared as Xiesha buried the accelerator and tore down a side street full of worn-down houses.

Maria stepped to the edge of the roof and peered down.

"Get back—" Karl shouted.

Minsku launched herself back onto the roof from the side of the truck where her claws had ripped into its metal, stopping her fall.

Two more vampires hurtled out of the darkness and landed lightly on the roof. One of them, a blond man well over six feet tall, was dressed in a tuxedo. Dribbles of red stained the white of his open shirtfront like a scattering of roses on snow. The second wore nothing but a pair of running shorts, his lean muscles bunching as he sprinted toward Karl.

Xiesha roared around another turn, swinging out into the oncoming lane as the whole truck tipped to the left, its tires squealing in protest, before slamming back down. A car horn blared, and more tires screamed.

Karl glanced to the street. They were back on a main road—Hanover Street, from there they could get on 93 north. Xiesha missed the turnoff, nearly driving a Corolla off the road, and the truck charged into the darkness beneath the overpass.

Tuxedo, Shorts and Minsku attacked Karl, all at once. He leapt backward from their slashing claws, hearing Maria cry out a warning. Tuxedo tried to tear out his throat with his fangs, and Karl slammed his knife hilt-deep into Tuxedo's throat. Tuxedo's mouth flared open but no sound escaped as he began to disintegrate into black specks and ash.

Minsku raked Karl's chest with her claws, shredding shirt and skin. He turned toward her, but Shorts was in the way, slicing with his claws and snapping with his fangs. Karl blocked a blow and slashed his blade across Shorts' eyes. Shorts wailed—a scream of purest agony that reverberated in the dark folds of concrete overhead. Karl kicked him backward off the end of the truck.

Movement above him caught his attention. He glanced up to see Delgado sprinting overhead, upside down, along the concrete supports of the overpass. Just as they came out from beneath it, Delgado tucked into a ball and flipped down to the roof, smashing huge dents in the metal when he landed. He lifted his arms to Maria, as if to accept her embrace, but his left arm ended in a blackened stump.

"I've been waiting for you, *querida,*" Delgado said. "Come."

Maria jerked as though he'd struck her. The tendons in her arms and neck stuck out as she fought his will, while her feet moved her step by step toward him.

Karl launched himself at Delgado, screaming wordless rage, but Minsku got in his way. She dodged two of his slashes, but a third opened up her arm to the bone. She fell back, clutching the arm and cursing him.

Maria was a hairsbreadth from Delgado, her eyes burning pure hatred while tears of defeat scored her cheeks. Her Master had come to claim what was his, and it tore Karl's heart out to see it.

Delgado laughed. Karl raised the blade, but Delgado swept Maria into his arms and leapt onto a passing semi headed in the opposite direction.

Karl spun to follow but Minsku attacked him again. Delgado leapt onto another car, with Maria cradled in his arms, and then to another before Karl lost him.

Minsku grinned and danced around him, slashing at him as if this were some sort of sparring match. Karl screamed again, frustration and rage twisted inside him. He took two of her glancing cuts before his nails grew and hardened into claws, splitting open his leather gloves.

He feinted with the knife, and when she flinched away, he shoved his other hand like a blade though her chest. Her eyes flared wide in pain and she drew in a hitching breath. He seized her spine in his fist and crushed it, feeling the vertebrae snap. Then his head darted forward and he drove his fangs into her throat and tore it open. He drank for a moment, using her dark vampire blood to quickly heal his wounds, and then hurled her from the roof. She hit a guardrail, wrenching it out of shape before tumbling from sight.

His only regret about her was that there was still plenty of time before dawn for her to pull herself together and take shelter to heal. His regrets about Maria, though, were endless. He'd failed her. Delgado would never let her go.

He ran to the front of the truck, sheathing the knife, and crawled down along the door. Xiesha reached over and opened it for him and he climbed inside.

"Did we lose them?" Xiesha asked, her voice tight and

clipped. "Where's Maria?"

He sagged in the seat, his forehead on the cold glass beside him. "Delgado took her."

Xiesha pulled the truck to the side of the road. "Which way?"

"Back about seven, eight hundred feet from a damaged guardrail."

"Can you track him?"

"I don't know."

They found the guardrail, but no sign of Minsku. Or Maria. An hour slipped past as he searched, then another, while the relentless turn of the earth toward the sun drained his hope.

No sign of Maria, no sign of Delgado.

He found Shorts, though, or what remained of him. He was drained down to a twitching, emaciated thing, muscles atrophied to nothing, every bone clearly visible. Blind, but still aware. He had two holes in his neck, probably Minsku's, Karl guessed, from where she'd have fed on him to replenish her blood and heal from the wounds Karl had inflicted. Shorts opened his mouth and meaningless sounds tumbled out. Karl had taken his sight with a slash of his knife, but Minsku had taken his tongue.

Karl thought about leaving him for the sun, but at the last moment, he turned and cut his throat with the silver blade.

Xiesha stared at him expectantly when he climbed back into the truck. The cab stank of stale cigarettes and ancient spilled coffee. Dark stains marred the seats. Crushed Cheetos were ground into the floor mats. He felt just as filthy.

"Nothing," he said.

She looked away, out at the stream of headlights and taillights. The truck engine turned over and rumbled to life, and she guided the truck back into traffic without a word.

Karl turned to stare out the window at the buildings and shops they passed. Almost six hundred thousand people in Boston, and Karl had never felt so alone.

Chapter Nineteen: Traitors

Maria stood naked before Delgado, shoulders back, staring him in the eye. They were in his room in a pseudo-French Baroque estate in Newton, about five or six miles from Boston as the crow flew. He'd smiled when he told her that he'd killed the old couple from New Orleans who'd owned it. She hadn't thought she could hate him more than she did, but she found it in her heart to do so whenever she looked at the pictures of the old man and woman and their flock of kids and grandkids hung all over the house.

The room's single candle flame flickered, making the shadows of the high-backed chairs and massive, ornately carved four-poster bed jump along the walls as though they were alive. Heavy velvet curtains were drawn back to show the stars beyond the floor-to-ceiling windows. She wished she could throw herself from the window and escape his eyes, but there was no hope of that. Pseudo-Louis XIV furniture, complete with almost grotesque detailing, ebony veneer and lavishly engraved brass and pewter stylings overfilled the room, giving it a suffocating feel, as if one were drowning in gilt opulence.

Delgado circled her. Not touching, just looking. She could feel his red gaze trailing across her skin, like a brand searing its way across every inch. She kept her chin raised. When he circled behind her she busied herself by staring out at the night. The room smelled of sachets and old lady and dust. Delgado smelled of death.

"Beautiful," Delgado said from behind. He set his cold hand and stump on her shoulders and she shivered. From disgust, not cold. He laughed softly and brought his lips close to her ear. "I knew I was right to give you the gift of eternal night. My former Master often explained how such gifts were not to be wasted, but conferred upon only the worthy few. You, *querida mia*, are so worthy."

"What about the vampires you lost tonight?" Maria asked, turning to look him in the eye. He was close enough to kiss, his haunting Mediterranean beauty all angles and dark slashes framing those dangerous eyes. "They were your best, and Karl chewed through them like a fat man through a cannoli." She smiled. "To coin a phrase."

Delgado's own smile flickered for a moment when she spoke Karl's name, then it returned full force, gleaming with charm and seduction. She almost felt she wanted to like him, but she knew it was just another part of his power—a glamour that terminated any time he left the room or was distracted.

"Do not grieve on their account. To die obeying a Master's will is a servant's greatest joy." He shrugged. "And there are always more. Always another human lusting for power and life eternal."

Bastard. That fucking smile. She held his gaze. Kept her chin high by will alone. Refused to look away.

Delgado slid his hand along her thigh. She could feel him in her mind, a shadow that couldn't be ignored or denied. Her body responded to him, and she cursed it for a traitor. How could she forget that just a second ago his presence had made her skin want to crawl off her bones and slither down a gutter?

"Don't fight me, querida,*"* Delgado said in her mind. *"I will have what I want. I always have what I want."*

He moved his hand higher.

Her nails hardened and pushed through her skin until her claws curved from her fingertips. Her hand blurred up to slash at his eyes.

Her hand made it halfway before a crushing wave of pain enveloped her and dropped her to her knees. She howled in agony, every muscle trembling, her head thrown back and the cords standing out in her neck like steel cables.

Delgado smiled down at her. The pain abruptly stopped, leaving her hunched over and panting. He put his hand on her hair.

"A first lesson," he said. "It will probably not be the last, littlc sireling. But you will learn who is your Master."

She tried to stand, couldn't find the strength.

Delgado touched her throat with one long finger. "Karl Vance cannot help you. Next time you see him, you'll kill him for me. And how I'll laugh..."

Anger. Focus on the anger. It gave her enough strength to stand again. The look she fixed on him strove for contemptuous disdain. Little good that did against a creature who could feel the fear and despair inside her, beneath the outward mask.

"Come, *querida*," Delgado said, a knowing smile on his lips. "You'll sleep with me this day, since you have no resting place of your own. It will be safer, as my sirelings can be jealous of my attentions, and that could be unfortunate for you."

He pulled her to him, crushing her body against his, and kissed her, nicking her lips with his fangs. There was new hunger in his eyes. He slid his one hand down her body, circling one of her nipples gently with a dark claw.

"There are other things I wish to show you. Ways in which we might come to enjoy one another...more completely."

She leaned in close, a small smile on her lips and hate in her eyes. "Karl was first. Once again, you come in second."

Rage warped his features. The sunburst of pain returned, burning through her body until all she could do was curl herself in a ball and shriek, praying that he would kill her and stop the agony.

All at once the pain shut off, leaving her trembling on the floor. He forced her to her feet and led her to his coffin. She swore she wouldn't cry, but she broke that oath, too, before he was done with her.

The church of St. Rosa stood silent and empty. Karl kept his eyes away from the cross, but he could feel it burning away above him with the holy light that made him feel tainted. Made him feel evil, no matter what atonement he offered.

He stood behind the church, near the small, enclosed cemetery, now an historic landmark, just beyond the blue shimmer of the borders of the holy ground. The pain reminded him of frostbite—something he'd endured as a soldier, when breath had still steamed out of his mouth, before the blood and the darkness. Yet he refused to back up a single pace.

The windows of the rectory were dark, the ivy on its walls

rustled when a breeze found its way through. The gravestones were covered in moss—some of the inscriptions worn away by weather and age, others still readable. The most striking was the weeping cherubim, hands folded, head bowed, leaning over the grave of a child.

One hour and thirty-nine minutes until dawn.

The passage of time hung like an iron chain around his neck, pulling him down link by link. He could stand on this spot and burn when the sun rose. It would be weak and disgusting, no fitting end for a warrior and murderer, but he could do it if he wished.

No. What fool would rush to eternal justice? Embrace destruction? Never. The weariness he felt now was no worse than he'd endured before. The woods were lovely, dark and deep, but he had promises to keep, and things to kill before he slept.

God, You have turned Your face away from me always, and everything I thought a blessing turned to bitter ashes on my tongue. But she's a blessing I hadn't hoped to find. Since we are cursed, let us be cursed together, with the comfort of each other alone to sustain us. Amen.

Silence. Radio messages into the void. What was the point?

"You're not like the others, Karl Vance," a woman said close behind him.

He spun, cursing his carelessness, allowing himself to become distracted in his despair. Now he could hear her heartbeat, smell her blood. How had he missed it?

Lady Kimberly MacKenzie, the Thorn knight. Up close he could see the gray at her temples streaking through her long brown hair. A silver cross on a chain dangled around her neck, which burned with the same blinding white light. He scowled and glanced away, but not before seeing the blue-tinged ghost image around her neck where a priest had circled her throat with holy water. There were more silver crosses at her wrists on bracelets, and he sensed two more around her thighs beneath her body armor, so that it took an act of will and a defiance of pain to look at her.

She also wore the same Kevlar and boron-carbide plate that the military used. On her left hip she bore a long sword, the shimmer of blessings and holy imagery turning the sheath an ethereal blue. On her other hip she wore a large caliber pistol in a holster. The grip of the pistol had an intricate silver tracery of crosses. He cast out his senses in search of other knights, but she seemed to be alone.

A knight of the Order of the Thorn.

As if things weren't bad enough.

She raised her hands, showing him they were empty. "I'm not here to kill you, Karl Vance."

"Lady Kimberly MacKenzie. I would say it was a pleasure to see you again, if your ornaments weren't causing such discomfort."

"We all have to take precautions. I apologize that it's even necessary."

He looked off at one of the streetlights beyond the graveyard. A trio of dogs barked in curious counterpoint. He could smell the grass, burned by frost, smell the dumpster, smell wood smoke, very faint, drifting from somewhere. Smelled blood rushing through veins very close at hand.

"You lied to me," she said. "I'd like to know why."

"Do I need a lawyer then? Find the vampire responsible for all the deaths and destroy him. You don't need me."

"He's a Master."

"Then charge overtime."

She ignored that. "I think you know the details."

It had always been disturbing how well informed they were. They posed as reporters and police with equal skill, with impeccable documents and credentials, hacked databases, scanned confidential reports, data-mined with the best of the CIA's analysts all searching for rogue supernatural creatures that posed a threat to humanity.

"Our agreement was clemency in return for a job. We both did our part. There was no agreement that I would act as one of your informers for the rest of my life."

"That's true. But we know you have information we need, and I'd rather not have this turn unpleasant." She took a step closer, making Karl turn his head from her acidic, blue-white aura. "We also know you're after something, something important. And you can't pursue it sitting in a cell, or with a silver blade through the heart."

"Is that an offer to help?"

"It's an offer to talk like civilized people."

"The Master you're looking for is Alejandro Delgado."

She nodded. "We thought as much. He's of Cade. Like you. Lying makes you appear guilty."

"Tell your superiors not to be concerned. I'll kill him before you can find him. He stole something of mine."

She watched him for a long moment. He looked up at the few stars that could be seen in Boston's light-polluted sky because it was easier than burning his eyes out on her silver crosses. "Could you...?" he said, waving her back.

She took a few steps backward, and the burn of her on his eyes cooled to a simmer. "We also detected a dimensional rift in the Beacon Hill area. Do you know anything of that?"

"No."

"I think you're lying again, and it disappoints me, Karl."

He turned to go.

"Why do you come here?" she asked before he'd taken more than two steps. "It must cause you a great deal of pain."

"There are things worse than physical pain."

"That's no answer."

"Do you pray?"

She nodded. "We all do. Faith is armor."

He laughed at that. "A hell of a lot of good that armor did against Cade's fangs when he sank them in my throat. I had faith then, and prayed, but no one heard. I pray now, but still no one hears. Next time you bend the knee, think of what it means to have the faith but be denied the love."

She considered him for a long moment. "I have information for you. We found one of our knights dead yesterday. Sir Brian Hanley."

"I'm sorry." But he wasn't. It just didn't seem important. Not with Maria gone and everything coming apart.

"Don't be. He was pinned to a tree, hung upside down, impaled with various tools—the straight end of a crowbar, an old-fashioned railroad spike, and so on. His hands had been cut off. They were set below his head, lying on his sword. We think Delgado murdered him."

The suppressed anger sparked in her voice like flint on steel. He watched her, waiting for more.

"It shames us to admit it," she continued, "but Brian Hanley was a traitor. He was working with Alejandro Delgado."

"Working, how?"

"Selling his talents for money. He was the one who brought the corpse back to life. The one killed by the spirit kyveryn you call Xiesha."

He strove to keep his face from showing emotion. Lady Kimberly was not fooled.

She smiled. "Oh yes, we've known for awhile how that creature Xiesha had come to reside with you."

"Go on."

"Hanley knew how to trace across the Seam. He wormholed through to her home and almost brought out something that I never want to see set foot on earth again. You were lucky or blessed enough that you could stop it."

Blessed...not a word he usually applied to himself, but he'd used it twice tonight already. And here it was again.

"How do you know this?"

"I shouldn't tell you," Lady Kimberly said, "but I will because I want your help. We bound Hanley's soul, called him back and asked him. Our oaths are binding, even beyond Hell. One may break faith, but the soul is forever chained with obligation." A shadow flickered across her eyes and was gone.

"Sounds like black magic."

"You don't know anything about it." Real venom in her voice.

He shrugged. "So how long had Hanley been working for Delgado?"

"Not long. Since we came to Boston. But he had a long list of crimes and betrayals, and Hanley sang them all to us before we sent his soul back to Hell."

"Weeping and gnashing of teeth, and all of that?"

She stared at him with a hollow gaze. "You can hear it, dim, but there, when you call a soul back from the Outer Darkness."

"So now I know. What now? I won't let you destroy Xiesha."

"No, she's safe from us."

"Why should I believe you?"

Her voice turned official—a jury foreman reciting a verdict. "Since she has yet to harm an innocent or act in any threatening manner toward greater society or the communities she lives in, the Order of the Thorn will turn a blind eye—*as long as she is with you.* I can't stress that last enough. She has been deemed non-malignant. But if things start coming across the Seams to get at her, I can't tell you what will happen, because I have no idea. Though I doubt it will be good for anyone."

"Non-malignant. Like a tumor."

"Consider our diverging points of view on the issue of supernatural beings. I think you'll understand where we're coming from, even if the language we use is not to your liking."

He had no answer for that.

"I thought you'd be pleased that we're agreeing to leave her alone if she behaves," Lady Kimberly said. A touch of resentment there? What did she want? Kowtows and bootlicking?

"I am pleased. Thank you." Another debt.

"Now tell me about Delgado."

"What's to tell?" he said. "He's in Boston. He's killing people. And when I catch him, I'll pin him to the roof of a church and let him watch the sun rise."

"You said he took something from you? Something valuable I'd guess...?"

"It becomes more precious to me every day it's gone."

"You don't want to tell me." Not a question.

"You don't want to know."

"I'd hoped you'd be more forthcoming."

"You seem to know more than I. That whole thing with the corpse... Are there other Knights working for him?"

"No."

"I knew you'd say that."

They shared a look. She smiled first, and then he smiled back, showing no teeth. Then the moment passed and it was all business again.

"May God bless you, Karl Vance," Lady Kimberly MacKenzie said, bowing. "Peace unto you."

He turned and walked away, using power to mask himself in shadow as soon as he was far enough from St. Rosa.

Peace. What a crock of shit.

The war between the Lucattis and the Ricardis had grown hot again. Karl read about slayings and truck hijackings and clubs burned down every other day in the *Boston Globe*. The press was screaming for the authorities to bring an end to it, and the DA issued indictments against Stefano Lucatti, Alberto Ricardi, John Passerini, Small Boy Michael Naldi, Orton Caruso and a dozen others. Of those indicted, only Caruso, a Lucatti capo, actually made it before a grand jury. It seemed the bosses and their captains had all gone to ground. Police raided social clubs and massage parlors and came down hard on bookies and enforcers, but the flood of violence continued.

Karl roamed the city like a ghost. He slipped along in darkness, listening, scenting the air, hunting.

No sign of Maria. No sign of Delgado.

It had started snowing that night, soft and wet, large flakes that stuck fast and turned cars into barrows and trees into winter sculpture. Far off, Karl heard an ambulance wail, but it was muted and indistinct beneath the hush of snowfall.

It had been a challenge convincing Little Ricky to meet with him again after the Order of Thorn had crashed their last meeting. Money had finally drawn him out. Karl carried seventeen hundred in a manila envelope in the interior pocket of his heavy black overcoat. Beneath the overcoat he wore a dark suit, Italian silk, tailored for style, not the cold. Karl didn't feel the cold. Dressing to make an impression. Nothing else.

He met Little Ricky in front of a three-story brick tenement with a rusting swing set, now a white abstract sculpture, sitting in the yard. All the windows were dark and there were no porch lights. The nearest light came from the yellow streetlamp twenty feet away. The snow drifted down softly, smothering sound.

A snowplow roared past as Karl stalked up on Little Ricky. Its blade scraped the street and buried the parked cars in drifts of snow. Little Ricky turned to watch the plow, the end of his cigarette glowing as he took a drag. Karl used the cover of the plow's rumble and scrape to move up next to him.

Little Ricky glanced back down the street and jumped when he saw Karl. He jerked, fumbling his cigarette, which tumbled into the snow and went out with a hiss.

"Jesus! Give a guy a fucking heart attack, why don't you?" Little Ricky said. He'd put on weight since Karl had last seen him, and he'd shaved his goatee. His dreadlocks peeked out of the fur-lined hood of his green parka.

"You should be used to it by now, Ricky. It happens every

time we meet."

"No shit. You gotta stop that shit, it's rude. Just fuckin' obnoxious. And it's *Little* Ricky. I hate the name Ricky, plain like that. We gonna be interrupted by those crazy motherfuckers again?"

"I don't think so."

"Good. Fucking beeoootiful. Now, you got my slice?"

Karl tossed him the manila envelope. Little Ricky bobbled it but caught it before it fell in the snow. With a whispered "Sonuvabitch" he tore open the top and shook out the money into his hand. Karl waited while he counted it, scanning the streets and rooftops, listening for a sound that might indicate Delgado was close.

"All there, like I thought." Little Ricky stuffed the money into the pocket of his cargo pants. "You're one creepy-ass dude, but you always have the money. No short shrift like those fuckin' cops. I tell ya, you'd think you could trust a cop, but they're the worst. Ever have your car impounded?"

"Back to the point," Karl said. "Have you considered my question?"

Little Ricky shifted and glanced away. Karl could smell a change in him, uneasiness that bordered on fear. He lit another cigarette, taking his time about it.

"I hate the fuckin' snow."

"I can take back my money if you don't have anything for me."

Little Ricky's hand flew to his pocket, clutching there as if afraid Karl had already pick-pocketed it away. "I have something for you. I'm just workin' up to my routine."

"Hurry up. I'm busy."

"Money to earn and people to kill. Not that I know about killing people, you understand, but that money-earning bit I understand perfectly. Anyway, I been askin' around about this Spaniard of yours. His name don't make anybody happy. Just like yours, *mi amigo*." He turned a piercing gaze Karl's way, more intelligent than his usual diarrhea grammar would indicate. "He ain't loved, even by the people he works for. If he was a made man, you understand this info would be harder to come by. But people love to talk, that's what makes the world go round. Well, that and sex, but who's countin'?"

Karl said nothing.

"Well, that, sex and money. I stand corrected." A quick glance at Karl. "Anyway, info on this Delgado dude's sketchy. Worked for the Lucattis for seven, eight years. Just showed up one day in the Boss's bedroom, bold as a stripper with F cup titties. Well, that's the rumor anyway. This is coming down the grapevine, and things tend to get a little distorted, if you catch my drift." Little Ricky laughed, a little too long and a little too loud.

From behind him, Karl heard a heartbeat and smelled sweat and gun oil. Twenty feet behind him and closing slowly. The snow had worked in the man's favor, dampening sound and smells. Now, Karl's vampire gaze could even see the hit man's silhouette against the streetlight in the reflection of Little Ricky's eye. The man took another soft step, quiet for a human.

Karl smiled at Little Ricky. Little Ricky's heart pounded away like a piston in a racecar, and Karl could smell the stink of fear evaporating from his pores. Little Ricky too, then. A shame.

"I'm surprised you had the balls to set me up, Ricky," Karl whispered.

"I don't fucking know what—"

Karl spun around as the hit man raised his pistol. He'd closed within ten feet, and Karl could see his eyes beneath the shadow of his hat. Snow fell all around them, and the city seemed very quiet.

Karl stared into his eyes, meeting his gaze, and bending every part of his power on dominating the man's mind. The hit man's finger tightened on the trigger, then stopped. It was a mind Karl had encountered before, and that gave him an extra edge.

"Hello, Bobby," Karl said. "How's Alberto Ricardi? I take it he's still upset."

Bobby De Rege's throat muscles convulsed as he fought against Karl's control. His gun hand wavered, but Karl wouldn't let him pull the trigger.

"Where's your back-up shooter, Bobby? Just point, please."

Slowly, Bobby De Rege's left arm lifted and pointed up the street, though Karl could feel the massive strain as he struggled against the command.

The headlights of a Monte Carlo suddenly flashed on high beams. The light reflected off a million snowflakes and scattered around the car, likely blinding the driver far more than Karl. The engine gunned, and the heavy car spun its tires as it pulled away from the curb less than a block up the street. Its back end slid around, almost nailing a parked minivan, before its tires found purchase again.

Karl stood very still, snow falling all around him. Bobby stayed in place, his eyes locked on Karl. Little Ricky ran, loping through the snow, flailing through a drift and panting like a winded dog.

Karl let him go. He needed his concentration for what he was doing. There would be time for Little Ricky later.

The Monte Carlo rolled in close, skidding as the driver braked. The passenger side window went down and a shotgun barrel thrust its way out. The shotgun bellowed, the muzzle flashing like lightning. The first shot clipped Bobby, who was standing rooted between Karl and the car.

Bobby never even screamed.

A fine mist of blood sprayed into the air, staining falling snowflakes and the powder alike, black in the light from the streetlamp. Bobby toppled into the snow, still gripping his pistol, still unable to fire it. Steam poured from his buckshot-riddled back.

Someone in the car screamed, *"Fuck!"*

The shotgun slide racked and the gun fired again. Some of the buckshot clipped him in the shoulder, and he made a show of being knocked off balance, staggering. The slide racked and the gun fired once more, barrel flashing and smoking. This shot was better aimed and hit him squarely in the chest, knocking him down. Karl could feel the buckshot tearing into him, but he could also feel his flesh knitting itself back together just as fast. He turned as he fell, hiding the healing wound from them.

Time to play possum. Alberto would have his vengeance, and once he believed Karl was dead, Karl would be free to hunt Delgado without the continual nuisance of Ricardi's thugs.

He lay unmoving in the snow, near the rust-flecked swing set, hearing the snow crunch as he settled into it, keeping his eyes open and staring.

The doors of the Monte Carlo opened, one of the hinges *screeking*, and two men stepped out. He didn't recognize their voices, and he couldn't look at them while he played possum.

"Fuckin-A, I got him," one said. "Shit! That barrel's hot."

"Get Bobby in the fucking car, you nimrod. You fucking shot him too, Wild Bill. I don't even want to think what Cleaver's gonna say."

The snow crunched around him. A dark figure shone a flashlight down at him.

"We fuckin' whacked him good," the first voice said. "Guess his reputation was all bullshit."

"Get over here! The motherfuckin' lights are comin' on. You wanna be here holding your dick when the cops show up, be my guest."

Footsteps hurrying away. Car doors slammed, and he heard the tires spin again as the driver gave the engine too much gas too quickly. Fools.

The street slipped back into its snow-quiet when the car rounded a corner and the sound of its large engine faded. Karl pushed up, wiping the snow from his face. Lights were going on and curtains and blinds were twitching. People were looking out to see what had happened.

He stood up, brushing the snow off his arms, legs and back. The suit and overcoat were ruined, riddled with holes from the shot, and that was an irritation. Two grand at least to replace them, and the money factory had gone offline since Delgado had turned Maria.

A door cracked open. Karl turned and retreated, merging into the shadows.

Little Ricky had quite a head start, but the snow betrayed him. It wasn't falling fast enough to fill his footprints as Karl tracked him, and Karl could run much faster.

Little Ricky had stopped in a parking lot, doubled over, panting and holding his stomach. His head whipped around like a rabbit edging out of its burrow. Karl moved in close, unseen.

"Hello, Ricky," Karl said.

Little Ricky screamed and flailed backward, knocking into a parking berm and toppling into the snow. He lay there gasping, his breath streaming out into the cold air, staring at Karl with an almost resigned terror.

"I didn't know anyth—"

"I could start breaking your bones, Ricky." Karl leaned his head back and stared into the dark flakes drifting down. "I could do any number of really evil things to you, so that you'd tell me everything I want to know and more. But I think I'm going to ask nicely first, before I have to get ugly. Because, you know what, Ricky? I'm really tired of having to get ugly."

He leaned toward Little Ricky. Ricky scooted back a couple of feet on his ass, digging a shallow trench in the snow and probably getting a decent amount down his pants.

"I'm even going to say please. So. *Please.*"

Little Ricky began to cry. Karl watched him, wondering how cold it had to be to freeze tears.

"Everything," Little Ricky said between sobs. "I'll tell it all. Fuckin' hell. Every little bit and more. Just don't hurt me. They made me do it. They fuckin' made me—"

"I know, Ricky." Karl nodded, his face solemn. "And it's okay. I'm a very forgiving man. Are you religious, Ricky?"

Little Ricky stared at him, uncomprehending.

"It doesn't matter," Karl said. "I want you to tell me who tried to set me up."

"The big man. The boss. Fucking Alberto Ricardi. He's paying for Lucattis, but he's throwing seven hundred large after you. Seven-fucking-hundred thousand. B-Town's crawling with people who'd give you up for a fraction of that."

"Maybe I'll have to speak with Alberto. Straighten things out."

Little Ricky's eyes flicked around everywhere but into Karl's own. "Best of luck, man. I really hope things work out for you. Really, really."

"What's the matter, Little Rick? You don't like to look at me now?"

"You fuckin' scare me, man. I heard that shotgun."

"You're not stupid, Little Ricky. Your choice of careers could use some work, but you're not stupid. So, has the big man given out the reason he wants me clipped?"

"He didn't give reasons. But I heard his hot little daughter disappeared." Little Ricky's mouth clamped shut on whatever else he was about to say.

"Delgado killed her."

"That why you're so hot for him?"

"Something like that."

"Man, it's like a soap opera. Everybody's got some shit goin' down. Can't tell the good guys from the bad guys half the time."

"There are no good guys, Little Ricky. Perhaps I should take back that comment about you not being stupid after all."

"Well, shit, I know there's no good guys. I was only sayin', like a figure of speech. Look, man, can I stand up? This snow is fuckin' freezin'."

"Little Ricky, I should kill you."

Ricky stared at him in open-mouthed shock for a moment, then his face crumpled and he began to sob in great shaking convulsions. Karl held up a hand for quiet, but it was awhile before Ricky could pull himself together enough for Karl to make himself heard.

"I said I *should* kill you. Every rule of the game dictates that you die. First, you sold me out. Second, you know I'm still alive, while the hit men who shot at me think I'm dead."

Little Ricky glanced down at Karl's clothes, eyes wild. Karl's overcoat and suit jacket had been torn up by buckshot in two places, riddled with holes while small pieces of it hung like dangling leaves, ready to fall away at any time. Little Ricky stared, but he kept his mouth shut.

Karl went on. "Furthermore, you talk too much. Your mouth opens and your guts spill out. A wrong word from you might make people wonder—might make that seven hundred thousand bounty come back. I don't need that kind of distraction right now. I'm trying to get back something that was stolen from me. Something very important."

"I know about that, man." He clutched at the air in front of Karl's coat, as if he wanted to hold onto it as he groveled, but wasn't sure if that would make Karl change his mind about killing him. It was amusing and depressing at the same time, and it made Karl feel like a mugger who assaulted old ladies.

Ricky continued, "I know all about that cuz someone jacked my bike when I was a kid. Brand new BMX Diamondback. Fuckin' badass snake on it. Those bastards. My mom saved for a year for it." He began to cry again.

Karl sighed. "I paid you good money tonight—"

"I'll give it back!" Little Ricky yanked the money out of his pocket and thrust it at Karl. "Take it!"

"—and I'm hoping you have a little more for me to go on than just telling me that people don't like me and people don't like Delgado. Because if you do your job well, that might go a long way toward making me believe I made the right decision when I didn't put a hole in your head."

Little Ricky's eyes danced around, never settling on anything for more than a second. Karl could smell the desperation on the man, and suddenly he just wanted to go home. But without Maria, things seemed so damn quiet, and he hated that now.

"I don't have anything on Delgado. I tried, man, I really did. People are afraid of him. He's connected, for one. And he's a freak for another. Don't fuck with freaks, that's what I say." When Karl frowned, Little Ricky began to talk faster than ever. "All I have is a name. Turned up once when I was talkin' to a bunch of Teamsters guys. The Serb at the Seismic. That's all. I know it ain't much—"

"Seismic, the club? That one?"

"Think so. Yeah. Could be."

Karl reached down with that vampire speed, seized the front of Little Ricky's coat and hauled him to his feet. Ricky cringed back, crying out, but when Karl only dusted off some clinging snow, a tentative, unbelieving smile formed on Ricky's lips. It was the look of a man who had fallen down in front of a semi, only to have the truck's wheels miss him by an inch.

"I want you to keep quiet about this, Ricky. I'm going to spare you because I like your haircut. Don't make me regret it."

Karl let go of Little Ricky's coat and walked away. He could hear Ricky breathing hard behind him, his heart thundering along like the hooves of a panicked gazelle.

Karl walked the empty streets, head down, listening but not heeding much.

Maria.

What had Delgado done to her in the weeks since Karl had lost her? He thought about Cade, and how his Master had forced him to feed on that girl. He thought about monsters, what made them, what destroyed them. He thought about the Order of the Thorn, here in Boston and hunting.

And around him, the snow fell.

Chapter Twenty:
Seismic

The club had once been a warehouse on Lansdowne Street near Fenway and was now competing with the better-known Avalon. Cars were double parked outside the entrance and one bouncer was engaged in an animated and profane argument with a limo driver about how long the limousine could remain blocking the front entrance. Bouncer: Move that fuckin caah now. Driver: Five more minutes, asshole.

Karl glanced at the display screen flashing the club's name, showing changing graphics of earthquakes, real footage of the surface of a bridge wobbling like a sine wave, and shots of lithe, curvaceous dancers real time from within the club.

Inside, the sound of the music was deafening. The bass kicked like the recoil of a shotgun. The dance floor was packed—couples writhing together to the heavy beat. The DJ held one headphone to his ear while his free hand spun turntables and adjusted what to Karl looked like more knobs, sliders and controls than lived in a jet cockpit.

Two girls danced atop cylinders that rose ten feet into the air. The cylinders were filled with something that looked like bubbling magma—a lava lamp for the seismic catastrophe theme.

He scanned the room. Sinuous bodies on the dance floor, all swaying motion and sweat. Dark booths lining the walls. A second floor built of diamond plate and iron grating. Swirling lights playing havoc with his vampire sight.

The bar ran along the north side of the building. It had *Richter Scale* spelled out in red and purple neon lights.

Recessed lighting illuminated the bottles along the mirrored back wall. Three bartenders served drinks in rapid economical motions, setting drinks on the translucent bar with tubes of neon snaking through it like electrical wire. Waitresses swooped by to pick up drink orders and dove back into the crowd while balancing loaded drink trays over their heads.

Karl slid onto a stool and motioned one of the bartenders over. Shaved head, devil-goatee, ink-sleeves and more tattoos all the way up his neck. The look he gave Karl was full of studied boredom. He lifted his eyebrows in silent question.

"I want to see the Serb," Karl shouted.

The bartender shook his head and shrugged, pointing to his ear as if he couldn't hear what Vance had said.

"The Serb," he repeated, louder. "I need to see him." He slid five one hundred dollar bills across the bar. The bartender stared at them for a moment, then leaned toward Karl.

"I don't know any Serb. I don't know what the hell you're talking about. Now if you don't want a drink, get the fuck away from the bar."

Karl swept up his money and pushed back into the crowd. The smell of sex and sweat and oh-so-much warm blood was making him unsteady. He felt torn in two between the desire and the loathing of that desire. He brushed against sweating bodies. Women gave him the eye, and many tried to dance with him, grinding against him, pressing tempting flesh, flashing warm skin and pulsing carotids. He slipped from them with a regretful smile in a failing burst of light. The club went dark during one song, and mist drifted down from misters hidden in the ceiling, as blue wide-angle laser lights swept up and down the dance floor. The DJ transitioned from one heavy dance track to an almost hypnotic one, pulsing bass and dreamlike loops. The bodies on the dance floor writhed like mating snakes.

He asked a bouncer and got nothing more than a glare in response, and the waitress he asked stared longingly at the money but didn't know anyone called the Serb.

Another circuit produced nothing more. The music jumped back to House Techno, so loud it made his teeth ache.

Nobody knew any Serb. Little Ricky had been pulling desperate things out of the air. He should've guessed. He might as well leave them to the mindless joy of dancing, before all the warm blood beneath smooth, firm skin made him do something he'd regret.

He turned to go and saw the vampire.

Master Delgado summoned Maria to the fountain on the back patio. The cobblestone patio was a beachhead against a swell of frosted grass. From here she could see the old lady's garden. A row of dead tomato plants lay uprooted and cast aside, and two irregularly shaped mounds filled the beds where they had been planted. Dogs had been sniffing around the graves. She ran a hand across her cool face and looked back to Master Delgado.

He sat on the edge of the still fountain, one leg crossed over the other. He wore a black Caraceni suit and leather shoes with a shine so deep she could see the moonlight gleaming on the toes. The end of his stump was seared black where he'd lost his hand. Near him on the river-stone fountain edge sat a wineglass filled with blood. The smell of it had her fangs tingling. Delgado noticed her interest and smiled.

"You've fed once at least since I created you," Delgado said. "Did you enjoy it?"

She kept silent.

For once he didn't immediately bring her to heel with pain. "Come, come. Don't be that way. If you enjoyed it, I won't tell."

"No," she said. "Yes..."

"Your enjoyment will grow. The first is like losing one's virginity."

"I don't think so."

Delgado laughed.

"Have I told how much your beloved Karl enjoyed his first?" He dipped a finger in the fountain and watched water droplets *plink plink* back into the basin, rippling across the moon-silvered surface. "Our master had a young girl brought in especially for him. How he savored her..."

She placed the heels of her palms against her eyes.

"Upsetting?" Delgado asked. "There's much you don't know about Karl Vance. Amusing, since you hold him in such high regard."

She didn't want to hear. She really didn't want to hear.

Master Delgado grinned. "He came to my Master seeking eternal life, and when Master Cade granted it, Vance plotted against him at every turn. Eventually, Vance murdered him."

"I heard a different version."

Master Delgado watched her, trailing his clawed finger in the fountain, lifting his hand and letting the drops plink down.

"Indeed," he said at last. "Let us leave that for the moment. Instead, let me remove some of the noble illusions you hold of him. He's some mongrel of Goth ancestry. Some Germanic northerner, whose parents by some unlucky turn ended up in England. That's where Master Cade found him—a loyal Dragoon of no exceptional rank, between wars and courting some merchant's daughter."

She shook her head. Glanced at the mounds of dirt in the garden. Smelled the blood in the glass, and fought to keep from rushing to it and downing it all.

"Of course that matters little to you," Master Delgado said, "as you were raised in America, where such things barely hold significance. A pity. Let me give you more enlightenment that might have more bearing on your present state of being." A grin, with fangs. Water dripping from the tip of his claw.

"He's a fool. Praying to some faceless God who doesn't heed. A God who *can't* listen to him because he is debased, degraded, debauched and depraved." Laughter. "Fearing for a soul he no longer has. Don't waste pity on a weakling. Mock him instead."

Maria looked away. Stared at the crescent moon. Wished she were alone.

"Do you pray, *querida*? Answer me."

"Not anymore."

"Good girl. Smart girl."

"Why do you say that?" She didn't truly care. She only spoke because she knew he would hurt her if she dared keep her silence again.

"Vance goes about in terror of divine judgment. That's why you see him on the knees, chewing God's ear to bless the worthless souls he sends to the afterlife. Such as it is."

"You mock him."

"Of course I mock him," Delgado said. "He's worthy of mockery."

"Maybe he's right."

"Master Cade tried his best to torment the God out of him,

but like a good believer every blow only deepened his stubborn refusal to give up what was now beyond him. That, dear, is the definition of hopeless. Sad, no?"

"It's not funny."

"And yet I keep laughing."

"Why do you hate him? He set you free."

"Perhaps freedom is the most horrible curse."

She didn't know how to answer that. It was so at odds with everything, so strange and foreign to her that he might as well have contended the moon was really the eye of a demon, slowly blinking, watching in pale approval the depravity of humankind.

"You think he's committed to you?" Master Delgado smirked at her. "So naïve, my *querida*. You belong to me and me alone."

How she would've loved to defy him. She felt his presence in her mind, waiting to chastise, and she held her tongue.

"That's better," he said. "Give up this delusion of choice you cling to. Your future is blood and power, darkness and immortality. Grow used to it. Vance can't save you from it. He is as incompetent and cowardly as he is stubborn and ignorant."

"And yet he was good enough to kill Cade."

Pain arced through her like electrical current. She dropped to all fours, fighting the urge to scream.

"Never refer to my Master by name again, slave." Master Delgado lashed the pain up and down her body, forcing the muscles of her throat and jaw and chest rigid so she could not scream. "Vance betrayed him. Murdered him when the Master was warring against another. His betrayal cost us London. We few who were left were forced to scatter."

The pain cut off all at once. She touched her jaw with a trembling hand. "You didn't kill him."

He stared at her for a long time, one finger tracing concentric circles on the riverstone fountain edge. His stump lay along his thigh. The sight of it always gave her a perverse, hateful pleasure, knowing Karl had hurt him. She waited for another explosion of pain, but it didn't come.

"Not yet, but I destroyed his traitor friend John Avalon." His tone was gentle, confiding. "Thus, we've been set against each other for hundreds and hundreds of years. Your scorn is born of ignorance. Vampire travel over great distance is limited and dangerous, especially in the summer's long days. Human affairs interfere—wars, plagues, famine, revolution, mass migration. It is more difficult than you guess to find a vampire who doesn't wish to be found."

Except a slave had that invisible chain around the throat. A chain that Karl and Xiesha had kept from choking her until Master Delgado had finally yanked it tight. But if Karl were to find her somehow...

Master Delgado stood and walked to her. He held the glass of blood loosely in his hand. Blood from the owners of this house, collected and stored in their freezer.

"You are lost," he said. "Sundered from everything you want. Let go of that last hope. Vance won't save you. You'll kill him for me, or he will kill you. Either way I'll put lie to this *love* you prattle on about in your head."

"Never." She expected pain. She got mocking laughter instead.

"Oh, you shall. Everyone loses faith, my hungry little *pajaro*."

Not everyone. Karl hadn't. She wouldn't either.

But Delgado only smiled and handed her the cup of blood.

She tried to refuse. She really did.

The vampire was upstairs in one of the balcony booths that looked down on the dance floor. A short beard covered the bottom of his face and close-cut, thinning hair covered the top of his head. His illusion-face made him seem a young thirty, with more hair than in reality. To Karl his face was long and pale, cheeks sunken, eyes glowing the red of fire embers. He nuzzled and whispered in the ear of a pretty red-haired girl with a dress cut down to the middle of her flat stomach. She giggled at something he said, though there was far too much noise for Karl to overhear.

Karl moved closer, pushing through the dancers, wallflowers and barflies. He slipped beneath the iron grating of the balcony, near a wall lit only by the ghostly green of an exit sign.

He'd have bet ten to one that was the Serb. And there he was lining up dinner and entertainment for the night. No wonder nobody wanted to talk about him.

Another song came on, one with a dark, animalistic groove, simultaneously melancholy and savage.

A smile spread across the vampire's face and he stood, tossing a handful of bills on the glass table and helping the redhead to her feet. She was a little unsteady, and she took his arm as they walked along the balcony and across the main catwalk that crossed over the dance floor. The vampire nodded to a bouncer who stood at the entrance to a passage leading somewhere Karl couldn't see from this angle.

He hurried up one of the spiraling iron scrollwork stairwells. Many of the booths up here were occupied, but most of the people took little notice of him. He did all he could to foster that unconcern, using his own power to turn aside interest and dull speculation.

That bouncer presented a problem. Karl didn't want to hurt him, but he had to get to that girl before the Serb killed her. His eyes scanned the crowd, the catwalk and balconies—and then he glanced up and smiled.

The lights dropped again and the blue lasers began to sweep the dance floor below him. He took the opportunity to climb the club's wall, running up the side until he walked upside down along the ceiling, some forty feet or so above the dance floor, threading his way through the lights, vent ducts, speakers and sprinkler systems. He crossed the dance floor directly above the catwalk the other vampire had taken, walking upside down along a narrow gray sprinkler pipe. It wasn't likely that someone glancing up would see him, but he again used his powers to cloak himself in shadow—easy enough in the darkness between the spinning and shifting lights. He kept the working subtle. Too much and the Serb would sense him.

He passed just above the bouncer at the entrance to an L-shaped hallway. Neon tubes circled the ceiling in the hallway, red and bright blue. Karl passed out of sight and dropped to the carpet without making a sound that could be heard over the bass. Only one of the doors in the hall had light shining below the crack. He pressed an ear to it, feeling the pulse of the bass in the wood. He pulled on his black leather gloves as he listened.

At first he heard nothing. Then he heard giggling. The redhead.

He stepped back and drew the SIG-Sauer from the holster

beneath his left arm and drew the silver knife from the sheath beneath his right in one quick motion.

God, let me not be too late.

He kicked in the door on one thump of the bass drum, timing it perfectly. He stepped into the room with pistol and knife raised as splinters of wood fell to the floor.

The redhead lay in the vampire's arms, staring up sleepily into his burning eyes. His mouth was open, fangs out, gleaming with spittle, and he leaned toward her.

The vampire's head snapped up, baring fangs like a wolf. His eyes flared wider, pupils dilating, and Karl saw recognition flash in his gaze, mixed with rage and lust and fear.

"Sorry to interrupt," Karl said and shot him in the head.

The vampire's head jerked. A hole appeared in his forehead, and bone, brains and blood splattered out the back of his skull. But even as his brains sprayed outward, they suddenly slowed and reversed direction, and the bone, blood and brains pulled themselves back together, as if captured and rewound on video.

The woman screamed and tumbled off his lap onto the floor, her trance-state shattered. Karl took three more quick steps into the room. A rapid glance confirmed it was an office, empty except for the three of them, with a digital aquarium glowing on a computer screen in the corner. A huge window filled the wall beyond the big teak desk. He had a feeling he'd be leaving that way.

The vampire stood slowly, his nails hooking into claws. The girl, seeing that Karl blocked the doorway, fell to all fours and scrambled for the cover of the desk and disappeared behind it. He could hear her panting breath in the lull between the bass.

"How dare you?" The vampire ran one long-fingered, pale hand through his disheveled hair, smoothing it back into place after the gunshot. "I'll have you screaming for that."

"Promises, promises." Karl slipped the 9mm back into its holster and shifted the knife to his right hand. The vampire saw the knife and his eyes narrowed. His lips curled into a sneer, one fang visible, and he hissed.

"The Master told me about you." The vampire backed up a step until his heels touched the couch. "He has such things in store for you."

"You're the Serb." Statement, not a question.

The vampire laughed. "Branko Petric is my name.

Remember it. It'll be the last thing you scream, Traitor."

"You're new to the fangs, aren't you?" Karl stepped closer. No sounds of alarm from down the hall, where the music thumped on. "I can smell the green on you."

"Fuck you."

Karl only smiled. "Where is Alejandro Delgado?"

"Why do you want him, Judas? You going to pray for his soul?"

"He stole something, and I want it back."

"The Master is busy with his newest addition, a fiery little dago bitch," Branko Petric said. "He'll deal with you in good time, don't worry, Traitor."

Every time this green little maggot spat the word *traitor*, Karl wanted to smash those new fangs down his throat. And the slur against Maria had rage sizzling and burning inside him like a firedrake sliding through his skin.

Karl stepped forward, holding the knife lightly in one gloved hand.

The redheaded woman leapt in front of him, holding a small pewter cross and a St. Michael pin toward Karl—something she must have found in or on the desk, some free charity gift, since she couldn't have been wearing it when Branko had been ready to feed. He halted and drew back from the piercing blue-white glow of the cross, more appalled at her foolishness than anything. It had to be one of the bravest and most unrepentantly stupid things he'd ever seen.

Branko flinched, crying out in pain, though the redhead brandished the holy items at Karl and not at him. He threw up a hand to shield his eyes, and then he laughed.

"Excellent, Tina." Branko slid past her, edging along one wall toward the door. "Touch him with that cross and he'll be destroyed, and we can finish."

"He was going to give me eternal life!" Her voice was high-pitched and strained. "I'll never get old, and you can't keep it from me!"

There were so many things he could've said to her. How silent the moon on its long paths across the night sky, over and over again, as you killed over and over again, walking your own path down into darkness. And she wanted that.

She moved toward him, holy objects outstretched to touch

him. He backed away, out of her range.

The Serb made a break for the door. Tina kept Karl back, her hands shaking violently, but she kept inching closer.

"You're making a horrible mistake," Karl said.

She screamed something, but it fell on a bass beat and was lost. She lunged forward and slashed at him with the cross. He ducked aside. She yelled again and ran at him, but she was too slow. He dodged past her and out the door after the Serb, slamming the door behind him. Sobs came from behind the wood, but she didn't chase.

The bouncer was waiting for him, cracking knuckles and looking arrogant. Karl caught the man's punch in his hand and crushed down, cracking bones. The man screamed and fell to his knees. Karl darted past him, scanning the dance floor for Branko.

Screams rang out. Karl spun in that direction. Branko shoved his way through the crowd, and the people who saw him with his masks and illusions cast aside scrambled out of his way.

Karl launched himself over the catwalk rail and landed nimbly on the dance floor, startling dancers and earning screams of his own. Someone saw his knife and screamed louder. People began to flee for the exits, even as others pushed to see what was going on. Karl caught a glance of the bartender he'd spoken to earlier with a cordless phone to his ear, staring directly at him.

Police would ruin things quite nicely. Not much time.

He sprinted after Branko, who crashed through an exit door into the night. The alarms blared and then stopped, and the club was filled again with the pulse of the bass and the melody of screams. Karl banged out through the door a moment later, and the door hissed shut on the noise.

Branko leapt onto a dumpster and from there onto the back wall of the alley behind the club. Karl chased him across a street, bounding across the hood of a passing car and catching a glimpse of the startled driver's face. Branko reached the far side of the street and climbed up the side of a tenement house.

Karl followed. He was close, twenty feet and gaining. Branko sprinted across the sloped shingles and leapt to another tenement. From there he fled across the rooftops, glancing back every few seconds with fear in his eyes as Karl matched his every move.

So much for Branko's threats. He didn't seem very eager to make his name the last thing Karl screamed.

Branko glanced back, saw Karl less than six feet behind and tried to change directions, heading off toward a forest of ventilation ductwork. The direction change cost him time.

Karl seized the back of Branko's silk shirt and spun him around, hurling him into one of the heavy iron legs of a rust-speckled water tower. The metal shrieked and bent. The entire tower leaned over them as the leg buckled, but held.

Branko snarled and slashed with his claws at Karl's face. Karl dodged back out of range, then closed again in an instant, slicing with his silver blade. His strokes were precise. He opened cuts on the vampire's forearms and across his palms. Branko wailed in pain, pressing back against the damaged water tower. The cuts weren't deep, but the pain from a silver wound was impossible to ignore.

"Mercy, mercy, brother." Branko dropped to his knees, hugged himself and shook, seeming unable to stop the trembling.

"'Brother' now, and not 'traitor'?"

The Serb opened his mouth, but seemed unable to think of anything to say. Karl gave a bitter smile.

"I'll give you mercy, *brother,*" Karl continued, "if you tell me want I want to know."

"He'll kill me. He'll kill me if I tell."

"I'll kill you if you don't. And I'm closer."

Branko licked his lips, tongue poking out between his fangs. His skin was extremely pale, and dark circles ringed his eyes, as if some rapidly spreading cancer were hollowing him out as Karl watched. Things weren't as pretty when the illusions disappeared.

"What will you do to me if I tell you?" Branko whispered.

"I'll give you that mercy you begged for. More than you were going to give to that girl back there."

"She wanted it. She begged me."

Karl leaned in very close, close enough to smell the stench of the grave on Branko's breath. "You don't even know how turn a person. You don't have the power, and you don't have the knowledge, and if you lie to me again, I'll start to cut you. I know you lack imagination, Branko, because I can see the smug stupidity in your eyes—but picture this with me, if you can. Imagine Branko Petric crawling desperately for shelter from the rising sun, with no hands and no feet, on the top of the highest building in Boston. Imagine that, and then try and distort the truth again."

Branko closed his eyes. The fear stink was so heavy on him that Karl could feel the darkest part of himself—the caged and hidden part—gloating and reveling in the scent. He crushed down on that dark pleasure as ruthlessly as he would carve up Branko if Branko refused him.

"I'll tell you," Branko said finally. "Anything. Just, no more..."

"Where is Delgado?"

The Serb gave him an address in Newton. "That's where we've been crashing during the day."

"How many slaves does he have now?"

Branko shook his head. "I don't know exactly."

"Try counting. Use your fingers if you have to."

"Fifteen at one point," Branko said. "You killed some. He was so pissed, like you wouldn't even believe. A few disappeared recently—we figured it was you again, but they were out hunting alone, and we weren't sure. The Master didn't say one way or the other what happened." He put a hand on the bent pole of the water tower, running his fingers over the huge dent seeming fascinated by it. "The Master might have made more since then. I don't know."

"Does he know you're talking with me?" Karl asked, and new fear flashed in Branko's eyes. He tilted his head, as if listening to faint music, and then his eyes lost their faraway look.

"No. He's busy with the others."

"Maria. Where is she?"

"With him. She doesn't leave his side. Ever."

If someone had shoved a sharpened crucifix into his eye, it couldn't have hurt more than hearing those words. When he found her, would she still be the same girl who'd almost refused her first feeding? Or would she be some gluttonous monster like Delgado, reveling in the bloodshed?

And what would he do then?

He was silent for so long that Branko began to fidget, glancing around at the dark buildings surrounding them. Karl stared down at him, knife gripped in his hand, feeling the burn of the silver through the glove on his already-seared palm and tightening his grip.

It would be mercy to drive the knife into Branko Petric's heart and end the curse, but he'd given his word. And though Branko didn't realize it yet, Karl was doing him no kindness by letting him continue to exist.

Karl turned his back on Branko and walked away, leaving him clutching his wounds beneath the water tower, with its single light at the very top like an angry red eye blinking its monotonous warning. He slipped the knife back into its sheath, and then clenched and stretched his hand to work out the lingering pain. Snow still remained in the shadows where the winter sun couldn't reach during the day, and the air was corpse-cold against his skin.

Maria...

The Serb had given up an address. There were only three hours until dawn, not enough time to get to her tonight. She had to hold on a little longer.

But if Branko should talk...

Karl could go back and silence him. Ensure Delgado had no idea he was coming.

But he'd given his word.

He stood on the edge of the building, staring down four stories below him. The wind pushed at his face, chillingly cold, but that cold meant nothing to him. He could hear Branko's faint footsteps on the gravel of the rooftop as he edged away from Karl.

Not too late to wrap up loose ends. Even now.

Karl's hand moved toward the knife hilt.

No.

His hand fell back to his side. All he'd kept through these long years was his word, even when his honor was lost. And there was a practical enough reason—if the Serb betrayed him, he'd have to tell Delgado that he'd given up Delgado's sleeping spot, and that would mean destruction for Branko. No, Branko had to keep his mouth shut, but there was always the possibility that Delgado would glimpse his thoughts. And with less than three hours before dawn, Delgado might not be able to risk moving to another of his sleeping spots even if he did discover Branko's betrayal.

There was nothing to do about it now. He'd made his decision. The dice were cast.

He leapt from the building and caught the rain gutter of the opposite tenement house and climbed down to the concrete.

How Cade had screamed and wept when Karl had driven the silver spikes into his wrists and legs. How that silver had burned Karl's hands, even through the thick leather gloves. The scars had lasted for a hundred years. He'd felt the sun rising, inching upward, ready to shine its deadly rays down upon them both.

Little Ricky's terrified face swam into his mind.

You fucking scare me, man.

Of course he did.

He scared himself.

Maria Ricardi suffered.

She'd had no concept of the kind of dominance Alejandro Delgado would wield over her. She was laid bare before him. He'd invaded her thoughts—more invasive and humiliating than any physical rape. Images came to her, occasionally, powerful enough to take her out of the now and put her in some past vision of Delgado's, and they were all horrible things of blood and hunting and killing.

How had she ever wanted to watch someone die? She'd been such a child, ignorant and naive, and what a fool she'd been to try and lose that innocence. Karl had known. He'd tried to tell her, but she wouldn't believe.

All her life she'd never been content to simply *think* about something—to be satisfied with imagining what it might be like. No, she had to get her fucking hands dirty.

And now to pay the piper.

She stood behind Delgado, holding a golden cup filled with cooled blood. This was another of her Master's little torments—to keep her hungry and have her hold his cup until he desired a sip. The last time she had tasted blood was the night at the fountain. Once she'd dared a drink when he'd looked away—she couldn't help herself. Of course, he'd known. Later he had made her scream for her insolence. It was as if he had some shadow hand resting lightly on her brain, and when he wished it, he clamped that hand down into a fist, making her scream and weep. As much as she hated giving him the pleasure of her tears, she was powerless to stop it.

"*Querida*," Delgado said. "You're brooding."

No ability to hide her moods or emotions. Under the microscope of some evil god. She knew he found her humiliation the most amusing of all.

"I'm sorry, Master," she replied, softly.

Delgado nodded and turned his attention back to Minsku, who stood before his ebony chair with its carvings of ravens and vultures. Minsku wore her black leathers with the steel rings. The choker with the white wolf's head circled her throat, and her raven hair was twisted into a braid and hung over her shoulder. Her spirit wolf was nowhere to be seen, probably off being dusted for ghost fleas.

Delgado glanced at her, a mixture of impatience and amusement on his face, apparently catching some of her last thought. Maria had supplanted Minsku in Delgado's coffin, and she knew that Minsku would happily kill her, if the chance arose. She wasn't powerful enough to fight a vampire like Minsku, much less Delgado. Nothing like a good helping of humble pie to eat away at her like acid on her marrow.

Minsku stood in the middle of the marble floor, shaded in yellow candlelight. Candelabras lined the southern wall. Master Delgado loathed electric lights, and the mansion was filled with candles. The rest of Master Delgado's sirelings gathered along the room's north wall, lounging on low cushions or leaning against the stucco. They were far from the candlelight, and seemed mostly a wall of dark shapes and slowly blinking red eyes.

"I've found no trace of Nathan," Minsku said. "From what I've gathered, he went out to hunt and never returned. That's three in a week."

"I know better than you how many that makes." Master Delgado's voice was cold, but Maria could feel the great heat of his anger, blazing away like a furnace. "They are destroyed. All three. I am their Master, and I *know*. I want to know if the Traitor killed them."

Not Vance, the Order of the Thorn, Maria thought.

"*Yes, my sweet,*" came Master Delgado's cold thought. His

words felt like icicles in her mind. *"I'm surprised you know of the Thorn. I see Vance wasn't lax in his teaching. Only weak."*

Maria clamped down on all her thoughts, making her mind as blank as possible. This close to him, without Karl or Xiesha around, he seemed to be able to read every strong thought of hers. If she filled her mind with chatter—the same phrase repeated over and over again as a wall behind which her true thoughts could take shelter—then he grew angry and closed that shadow fist on her mind, making her writhe in agony. Blanking her mind was the only way to keep him from knowing everything without enraging him. Too bad she'd never gotten into meditation.

Minsku sank to one knee. "We might want to consider the possibility that we have other enemies here, Master. Human enemies. The Order of the Thorn, perhaps."

"Maria and I were just discussing that," Master Delgado said, and laughed at the hatred in Minsku's eyes when she glanced at Maria. "It is ill news for all of night's disciples."

"Perhaps we should consider leaving Boston, Master."

"Not before I've finished with the Traitor. Afterwards...New York again, perhaps. I've always been fond of that city."

She knew Delgado wanted New York so he could stay in contact with the Lucattis, where his power had been growing. The other Lucatti captains and soldiers feared him, though they didn't seem to know the true reasons behind the fear. As far as she could gather, only Stefano Lucatti, boss of the Lucatti *borgatta*, knew what Master Delgado really was. But Master Delgado had taken over several rackets that now brought in money for him—many of them from Jimmy de Carlo, though he used human enforcers to collect and supervise during the daylight hours. She knew Master Delgado wasn't on the books with the Lucattis, but still he was taking privileges reserved for made men, and his power was growing. Fleeing to New York would be a setback for him, but not a defeat.

Maria didn't want any of them to get to New York. She wanted the Order of the Thorn to destroy them all. Or Karl. Better for Karl to do the honors.

Blank. She had to keep her mind blank. This time, Master Delgado didn't seem to notice.

Master Delgado stood and let his gaze travel around the room. "From today on, we must be careful. No more indiscriminate hunting. Bring your prey here. There must be no bodies for the police or the Order to find—not until it's too late for them to bother us."

There was a rustling of dissatisfaction among the vampires lounging along the wall.

"Peace, my children," Master Delgado said. "Remember what we are. We are like Cain. Wanderers in the dust. Every hand against us. Listen, children, it is no great surprise, for we are the greatest hunters—the kings of evening, the princes of the night."

A silence fell among the vampires as every eye turned to him and stared, unblinking.

"The night I was taken, my Master told me of his dreams, and I wrote them upon my heart. He would have us ascend to rule the darkness unchallenged. For an endless span of years we might command those lesser beings, slaying as we will, sparing as we chose. We will be gods ourselves, stalking amidst the starlight, drinking of life and fearing no death. For what is God but undying? And we share that, my children, so why should we serve? We are equals, should we but reach out our hand and seize what destiny lies before us.

"I have not wept since my Master died. Ghosts have mourned more than I since the hour I put all sorrow aside and swore vengeance upon the Traitor. I swear upon the Citadel of Nightfall that I will weep again for joy when we enter into our own and sit in dominion over the earth, given to us to do with as we will."

Master Delgado took the cup from Maria's hand and raised it to his lips, staring out at the room with those eyes like embers.

"I drink in salute to our future. Years may wear man down, but for us death springs eternal. Now go, my children. There is not much time before dawn."

The others left the room, all except Minsku, who took her place behind Master Delgado at his left shoulder. Master Delgado didn't remain seated, however. He stood and faced Maria.

"I have a special job for you, *querida*," he said. She hated how soft and knowing was the tone of his voice. She hated it because she feared it. He always sounded like that just before he hurt her. "You'll be my beautiful assassin, my answer to Karl

Vance. It's time you killed Alberto Ricardi for me. Your sweet father."

No.

He laughed. "Don't worry, sweetling. You'll be just like the Traitor then, won't you? And since you love each other so, it will be my little gift to you both."

She fell to her knees, claws scraping on the marble as she clenched her hands shut, while Minsku grinned at her, and Master Delgado laughed that cruel, cold laughter.

Chapter Twenty-One:
Search and Destroy

Karl set off the next night only moments after the first stars of evening opened their eyes. Xiesha had wanted to come as well, but he denied her. With the Order of the Thorn about in the city, he wouldn't risk her safety, no matter what they had promised. He'd already lost one woman he'd cared for, his fiancé in England, all those long years ago. And now Maria was a wild card. He wouldn't gamble with a third.

Xiesha had bowed and said nothing, retreating to her rooms. Her silent rebuke had almost been enough to make him reconsider. Almost.

He arrived at the Warren estate in Newton a little before ten o'clock. The trip from Cambridge had taken longer than he'd wanted, most of the time wasted in his approach to the house. Utmost care had to be taken. Delgado would have lookouts and perhaps snares. Rushing in might mean disaster.

But he'd found no lookouts or traps. Still, the sense of something wrong increased with every step.

He should have killed Branko.

The house's façade was baroque in detail, painted a pale cream. Small *trompe-l'oeil* paintings on the walls gave the illusion of ivy cascading down from two upper-story windows. Lavish decorative details framed the eaves and windows. Fat *putto* smiled serene baby smiles as they frolicked beneath the curved cornices.

He stood in the shadows of two great elm trees across the street and watched.

Nothing. No movement. He could hear nothing except for

the usual clutter of city sounds. Traffic. A distant siren. A helicopter to the east. Dogs barking a mile or so off. Human voices. The scrape of bare branches against the sides of houses.

Karl slipped through the shadows beneath the trees, approaching from the west. The moon shone full and bright in the sky, giving the earth an eerie, silver sheen.

The farthest perimeter wall from the house had been swallowed in ivy, real, not painted, but it was partly shadowed from the moon by the barren branches of two oak trees. He leapt to an overhanging branch and crossed the wall—the ivy would've made climbing the wall itself far too noisy. The yard was winter desolate, the only green from ivy and a few evergreen shrubs.

No movement from the house. He probed with his senses. There was something...a feeling of unnatural cold and evil.

He vaulted onto the upper deck, landing between an intricately carved stone bench and clay pots filled with dying plants. One of the windows had its maroon drapes pushed aside. The room inside was dark, except for a brilliant patch of white-silver moonlight. Too many pieces of Louis XIV style furniture made it seem cramped and busy. The room's door was shut.

Another scan of the shadows of the yard. That sense of cold malice lingered in the house. It was so strong it masked everything else, the way a cheap perfume could drown a small room. Maria might be standing in the hall guarded by a dozen other undead, but with that evil miasma suffusing everything, he couldn't tell.

A skylight had been set into the sharp slope of the roof above the kitchen. He ripped the curved window out of the frame, and the gearing gave a ratcheting, mechanical scream.

He could hear nothing from inside except the hum of the refrigerator and the gentle rumble of the furnace. He dropped down onto the patterned ceramic tiles, landing in a crouch with his dagger out.

Stainless steel appliances. More frescoes, grapes and vines along the walls, a scene of some French countryside, and above, around the skylight, an illusory sky and clouds.

Something growled, but the sound was strange, half coming in his ears, half in his mind, sounding deep and threatening, like a large chainsaw idling. He glanced at the door leading into the kitchen from the dining room. A wolf stepped into the archway. Its lips were pulled back from its teeth in a vicious snarl, and its eyes were a blue the color of glacier ice. At first Karl thought its pelt was white, but he was mistaken—the whole wolf shimmered in a kind of spectral translucence.

It was the spirit wolf he'd seen near the docks when Delgado's horde had ambushed them. It sent out waves of malevolence that pushed against his mind, flooding his senses. Karl froze, watching.

The wolf leapt at him as quickly as any vampire. Its teeth tore into his forearm with a malignant coldness that seeped into his flesh like a poison. Karl grabbed at its pelt with his free hand, but his fingers passed right through.

He switched the knife from his right to left hand, fighting the wolf as it worried at his arm. The wolf released its grip and dropped to the linoleum before he could drive the knife into its throat. Its claws clicked and tapped as it turned back to him. The wolf's breath steamed out of its mouth, and there was frost around its muzzle.

Karl leapt backward to put some space between him and those teeth. He heard the humming and the rattle of chain an instant before he saw the blur of something dark swinging at his neck. He ducked and rolled as a blade attached to a long iron chain sliced into the cabinets overhead with a *thunk*. The wolf went for his throat, and he turned aside just in time. The wolf's teeth tore into his shoulder instead, shredding his shirt and sending that biting cold deep into his muscles.

He slashed with the silver knife, but he was off balance and the blade only glanced along the spirit wolf's side. The wolf gave a great howl of pain and scurried away from him, shivering.

"You're in my playground now," a woman said, thrumming with an almost sexual promise. Minsku. She stood in the opposite doorway, and the spirit wolf circled around her legs, glaring back at him. The wound in its side was a depthless black, like a crack into the abyss. That pulse of evil coming from the wolf had hidden Minsku from his senses.

"I'll have fun before you die," Minsku said.

He stood from his crouch slowly, feeling the throbbing ache in his left arm, the deeper pain in his shoulder, and the burn of the silver on his scarred palm. "Where's Maria?"

"Not asking for Delgado first, love?" Minsku laughed. She

arched her back, stretching, displaying for him her lithe body covered in leather, while the white wolf's head on her choker seemed to glow with cold light of its own. Did the wound he'd given her on the roof of the moving truck still pain her? If so she showed no hint of it. It had been a serious wound, and though she'd drained her brother vampire to help heal it, only an extremely powerful vampire would be so fully recovered from a supernatural wound in so short a time.

"You've got it bad," she continued. "I doubt you'll like what the Master is doing to her. No, you won't like that one bit."

She wrenched free the blade half-buried in the cabinet. Her weapon was deceptively simple—a six-foot length of chain with weighted, curved blades on either end. The blades were sheathed in silver, so that they gleamed in the white square of moonlight pouring in through one of the kitchen's windows.

"Where is she?"

"She's gone, Romeo," Minsku said, and turned away from him. The spirit wolf followed at her heels. "Come. I have something to show you at the Master's request."

He followed at a good distance. A spark of fear had flared to life within him. Fear—something he hadn't felt in an age, but that had returned to him with Maria. His feelings for her made him as weak as they made him strong—a dichotomy both wonderful and terrible.

The spirit wolf glanced back at him, growling that half-audible, half-telepathic growl whenever he lagged. Minsku never looked back. She moved through the rooms of the mansion as if she'd lived there her entire life. She led him into a gaming room, where a pool table sat in the center on an Oriental rug.

Branko Petric lay upon the pool table, spread-eagle, with what looked like a dozen broken cue sticks impaling his body, pinning him to the felt. Thick vampire blood had blackened the green and a smear of it lay across the lapis lazuli diamonds along the rails.

Minsku walked around to stand next to Branko's head, and the wolf followed. Karl stood just inside the room, staring at Branko's face. Branko's eyes were shut and he wasn't moving.

Should have killed him back on the roof.

"Don't think too badly of him for betraying you, Karl." Minsku ran a blood-red claw along Branko's cheek. "He couldn't help himself. Once the Master set eyes on him, he knew everything. This fool was an open book. And the Master never forgives. As you know."

She slapped Branko's cheek and Branko's red eyes fluttered open. He lifted his head and stared at Karl with hate and pleading mixed in his eyes. Someone had shoved the eight ball into Branko's mouth, breaking his fangs and jaw before they healed around it, wedging it inside. Branko lived only because they hadn't driven a cue stick through his unbeating heart.

Minsku laughed again. "Far wiser to have destroyed him when you had the chance, Traitor. No wonder the Master hates you. How a weakling like you ever killed the legendary Cade is a mystery to me."

She took a quick step back from the pool table, swung her chain in a looping arc and buried the blade in Branko's neck. Branko never even screamed. His eyes widened for a moment and every muscle went rigid. Then his body began to dissolve into smoke, an invisible fire consuming him, turning him into a thousand drifting black specks—ash that fell back to the felt as it vanished. The eight ball thumped to the felt and rolled until it bumped up against one of the broken pool cues embedded in the table's slate.

"That's done then." Minsku yanked free her blade and held the chain loosely in both hands as she came around the table. "You realize you lost Maria the moment you let that little rat live. So much for commitment. You know this is really about you and the Master. That little bitch is just a toy you're fighting over at the moment."

Karl didn't reply.

"Think about it," she said with a wicked smile. "If she were anything more than just another piece of ass for you, you wouldn't have betrayed her by letting Branko go. Words are shit—actions tell the story. And you've said all you need to say about your *love*. Vampire love—ha. Makes a fucking dark Hallmark card, don't you think?"

"Are you through?"

She laughed. "The Master said rub salt, so here I am, rubbing away."

The spirit wolf threw back its head and loosed a haunting howl that seemed to reverberate in the marrow of Karl's bones. Dozens of dogs in the surrounding neighborhoods took up the cry.

Minsku stepped toward him, swinging the chain with its blades in shallow arcs. Karl held the knife at his side and watched her slink toward him. The spirit wolf came around the other side of the table, flanking him.

"So the fearless Delgado couldn't be here to do the deed himself?" Karl asked, meeting her eyes. "He flees and leaves behind this little show for me"—he gestured at the pool table— "as if he's telling me something I don't know."

"It's simple. He's insulting you. You aren't worth his time."

"I'm sure he feels that way every time he looks at that stump on the end of his arm."

The hate in her eyes burned all the deeper.

Karl cocked his head and smiled sadly. "You think he'll take you back if you manage to destroy me? New blood is always the sweeter. I suppose pity is wasted on you."

Minsku screamed, lips skinned back from her fangs. The chain rattled as the blades hummed so fast they were only silver blurs like propellers. The spirit wolf howled again as it leapt atop the pool table and then sprang at him, jaws wide and fangs gleaming.

Karl raised the knife and met them head on.

To kill her father...

For some reason the conversation she'd had with him at his house in Martha's Vineyard kept coming back to her. They hadn't parted happily. She kept seeing him standing there with the sunlight refracting through his brandy snifter.

All of Master Delgado's sirelings were gathered at Like-Gnu-Cleaners, some carpet and upholstery cleaning shop her father had chosen at random, with its gaudy sign of a cartoon Gnu scrubbing itself in a clawfoot bathtub, grinning like it had just snorted half the cocaine in Back Bay. The vampires lined the roof, hid beneath cars, camouflaged themselves in the strip of trees and underbrush near the end of the parking lot, where the dumpster sat cockeyed—its wheels half on and half off the curb.

Her father was dead. Even if she didn't kill him with her own hands, he wouldn't escape this trap. She had killed him with her phone call.

How happy he'd been. God, she could feel the relief and

elation in his voice over the line as if it were something tangible—warmth that froze her heart when it should've been the greatest comfort. She'd told her father some lie about hiding from Karl, who had murdered Roberto, and he believed every word that she spoke softly into the phone, while she stared Delgado right in the eyes. His eyes shone a deep red as he drank in every ounce of her pain.

She hated Master Delgado so deeply that it wasn't even a real emotion to her anymore. It merely colored everything with reds and blacks.

Karl must feel this too. How could he have endured it for so many years?

The worst thing was that Master Delgado knew exactly how she felt, and it made him laugh.

Of course she had tried to refuse him again. Hours of exquisite agony finally broke her of that. She'd dialed her father's cell number with shaking hands, tears on her cheeks, but her voice, when she spoke, had been even, if not completely calm. Too calm and he'd think something was up. It was best that her voice have a taste of fear, a taste of pain and desperation, so that he'd believe her lies, and his fatherly feelings would kick in. He'd want to rush to protect her, Master Delgado had said with that evil smile on his lips. To protect his little girl.

Her father's Jaguar XJ pulled into the empty parking lot, its tires whispering on cracked pavement. She started to cry silently. The engine shut off and the headlights went dark. She could hear the ticking of the cooling engine, an erratic clock counting off the last seconds of her father's life.

Delgado put his lips to her ear. His touch made her shudder.

"Go to him, *querida.* I want you to do it. You haven't fed on warm blood since I tamed you, and I know you're hungry."

Hungry? She was weak with hunger. Her hands trembled for it. Her fangs ached.

"No," she said.

The pain hit her with the force of a train. She crumpled to all fours. He wouldn't let her scream, though. His power had clamped down on the muscles of her jaw and her vocal cords. All she could utter was a whimper.

A car door opened, very loud in the night's quiet. She

looked up to see her father and two other men step out of the Jag.

"Go, *querida mia,*" Delgado said. "And do not disappoint me."

So she went, wiping her tears and smearing them along her cheeks like war paint. He was facing away from her, so he didn't see her until she spoke.

"Daddy," she called softly.

He spun toward her. The joy and relief on his face made him seem a decade younger. "Maria."

"Daddy, I'm sorry."

She watched the joy disappear.

Karl jumped the banister and then ducked as Minsku's blade hissed overhead and slashed into the wall, raining plaster dust down. He turned to exploit her open guard and that damned spirit wolf lunged at him, nearly taking off his arm. Every time he had the upper hand or Minsku overextended or somehow made a mistake, that damn spirit wolf was there to prevent him from finishing it.

He sprinted up the curving stairwell, past alcoves with shadowy sculpture inside. He felt the wolf right behind him, its frosty breath on his back. Minsku was a step behind the wolf, whirling her chain to lash at him.

The hum of the chain stopped and he threw himself to the side over the banister. The silver blade kissed his shoulder, just the barest cut, before it stuck into the wall. Bright hot pain coiled up his arm as if a burning rope lashed tight around his muscles. He clamped his jaws shut to stifle a scream as he thumped down to the tile floor fifteen feet below.

The wolf followed him, leaping over the railing toward him with its claws out and jaws open and cold malice in its eyes.

He waited until the last possible moment and fell backward, shoving his dagger up into its throat as it overshot him. He gripped the knife with both hands and it tore down the length of the wolf from throat to belly. As the wolf opened, a blast of frigid arctic air blew out, frosting his hands and crystallizing the air into drifting snowflakes.

He rolled away and rose in a half-crouch, dagger held close in front of him. The spirit wolf staggered a couple of steps toward him, panting heavily, its breath steaming from its mouth, a blue-tinged tongue lolling across its teeth. Curls of mist like sublimating dry ice poured from its belly and rolled along the ground.

A sharp gasp of breath from the stairwell overhead made him glance at Minsku. She stared at the spirit wolf in undisguised anguish, the chain still gripped in her hands and the blade still in the wall. With a shriek she tore it free and vaulted over the banister.

The spirit wolf fell on its side. Ice spread across its body, freezing its ghostly flesh and encasing it as Karl watched, until it resembled nothing more than an ice sculpture. Then its edges began to shine and grow indistinct, melting into a watery blur as drops of water began to collect in a pool around it.

Minsku fell upon him. She held both ends of the chain and slashed with both blades, whirling them so fast they flashed in a silver blur. He retreated, cursing the fate that had matched him with a knife against her double-bladed weapon.

She drove him back into the foyer, with its high, atrium-like ceiling. He maneuvered until the French doors were to his right, held shut by only a thin lock that would break as soon as he threw his strength against it.

He faked making a dash for the doors and she followed, twisting her whole body into one vicious arcing swing of her blade. He caught the chain and yanked as hard as he could before she could try to pull it free. She stumbled toward him, off balance.

He drove the dagger into her belly, shoving her back until he slammed her up against the stucco, lifting her off the ground and pinning her to the wall. She grunted. Every muscle in her body seemed to clench as she hung rigid in his grip.

Her other hand swung up, slicing with the one blade she still had, aiming for his throat. He barely caught her arm in time, shoving it backward and burying her blade deep into the wall.

Minsku's head darted toward his neck, her fangs long and white. He let go of the dagger, leaving it buried in her flesh, seized her by the throat and rammed her head back.

"Where is Maria?" he asked.

"Burn, Traitor." She spat in his face.

"Tell me where she is and you may even survive."

Minsku laughed—frantic, desperate laughter that ended in

a scream. She shook her head from side to side, like a child dramatically refusing medicine. He looked into her eyes, his face betraying nothing.

"Is he worth dying for?" Karl asked.

"Yes."

"Where is Maria?" He turned the knife in her guts and she threw back her head and shrieked, her beautiful face made long and haggard.

"She won't be coming back here," she said after a long while. "None of them will."

"Where did he take her?"

Minsku shook her head again. It seemed to flop from side to side on her shoulders.

"May God forgive you," Karl said.

"There is no God," she replied, but he saw the fear. It shone in her eyes like the sun off of brand new copper pennies.

"I hope you're right." He wrenched free the dagger and drove it into her heart before she even had time to blink.

Her eyes widened and her scream sighed out over her teeth. Their faces were very close together, as if he were going to kiss her, and she stared into his eyes. Then her body began that strange dissolution until there was nothing left but ash.

He yanked the dagger out of the wall and slipped it back in its sheath. He wrapped his hand around the iron chain, listening as it rattled and clinked, and then he pulled her blades free from the wall. More for the collection.

He searched the house quickly but found nothing that would tell him where Delgado would take Maria next. The sun raced him. He could feel time running out, the night dwindling toward morning.

So close. So very close.

If you hadn't let Branko live, she would've been waiting here for you.

He wanted to drive his fist through a wall until the wall crumbled. Instead, he walked out onto the patio and looked up at the stars.

They dragged Maria back to their new home at the Lucatti mansion, but she hadn't the strength to lift her head, much less walk down into the cellars by herself. Instead, two brother vampires carried her by her arms, face down, her feet scraping and bouncing along. All she could see were the changing patterns of ground in front of her. Pavement, blacktop, sidewalk, cobblestones, marble tile, crossing a threshold profaned with pig's blood and a dozen other foul things, then Persian carpets, and finally wooden stairs leading down into the basement.

Her father was gone.

It seemed a strange thought. Disconnected and unreal. Grief would come later. She could feel it swimming around in her chest, cold-eyed and circling her heart like a shark. Yet, for now all she felt was a kind of dazed horror—a disgusted disbelief that her father had walked unharmed through the dangers of mob life only to die at the hands of monsters. Monsters led by her. The blurred sense of emptiness would not diminish.

Her mind swam into better focus as the pain diminished a bit. The Master must be busy with other things and not able to direct all his concentration at hurting her. How long would it take until he returned his attention to her torment?

The vampires carried her into a windowless room, dropped her and left. She hadn't the strength to crawl under the bed, so she simply lay there on the cool tile floor and let her mind drift. Dehumidifiers hummed, and she hummed back tunelessly. She could still feel the miasma of evil against her face—the profane spells that had smothered the blue-white blaze of holy water and left only a churning smoke of malevolence. They were spells the traitor Thorn Knight Hanley had taught to Master Delgado before Master Delgado had slaughtered him. She shuddered at the memory.

Since every entrance to the Lucatti mansion had been sealed up with holy water and silver crosses against Karl Vance, the only way Master Delgado could stay here was by profaning the seals, destroying the holy magic that kept evil out. The Master had worked the spells himself over the thresholds he wanted to use, with only Stefano Lucatti looking on. Where the traitor Thorn knight had learned such black arts she never found out, but it was knowledge that had thrilled her Master immensely, leaving him in a pleasant mood for days. But in the end, Master Delgado had killed the traitor knight anyway. She couldn't say she mourned. Deal with the devil and expect a few blisters.

The Master...

The Master was furious with her.

She smiled, but that hurt too, so she stopped.

Two things she had done against him, but so far he only knew the first.

She'd refused to feed on her father. Master Delgado had starved her of blood since he'd reclaimed her, except for a cup here and there, and still she'd found the strength to refuse. Score one for the princess.

Master Delgado had driven her to the ground with blistering pain—mind-shattering agony that still had her shuddering. Then he'd released the pain, and as horrible as it sounded, part of her had been so hungry for blood, any blood, that the temptation to feed had almost been irresistible.

Blood. She could smell it, even now.

Instead, a dozen of her Master's sirelings had swarmed her father and his bodyguards. She had listened to her father's screams and she had wept. Her weeping had seemed to enrage Master Delgado further, until he'd been dealing her so much pain she knew that if she were still human, she'd have already died. Her heart would've burst. But she had denied Master Delgado something he'd most wanted to see, and she thought it would've made Karl proud.

Karl.

Where was he? Was he searching for her? Or did he simply assume that she'd fallen in with her Master and his butcheries?

Would he save her?

Her second small triumph—she'd left Karl something in the Warren mansion, while Master Delgado was busy with another traitor—Branko Petric—amusing himself with the cue sticks. But she dare not even think of it again, lest her Master sense it.

She managed to lift her head and look around at her surroundings. A plain room. No windows. A bed and a bookshelf and a table. Little more than a cell, but there was no Master here, and that made it better than any five-star hotel. She lay there, aching. Where was the legendary healing power of the vampire?

Don't tell me they left it out of my contract. Always read the fine print.

Outside the room's door she could hear Master Delgado's other sirelings talking, but she scarcely paid attention until she heard the word *Lucatti*.

"I don't like fleeing him," one of them said. She recognized the cynical, sharp voice as belonging to a vampire named Adam. Corporate guy. Suits and GQ stylings. Enron eat your heart out.

"Why doesn't the Master face him?" Adam continued. "Why are we hiding here, with all these damned crosses? You can hardly move around without scorching off your face."

"Don't go upstairs then. Those wiseguys are jumpy enough." She thought that voice belonged to a vampire named Michael. Asian guy. Tall and thin with eyes like a dead jackal's. She thought he was ex-military but wasn't sure. "We won't be here long anyway. He left Minsku and her pet behind to take care of the Traitor."

Karl. They were speaking of Karl. She cocked her head, all lingering pain suddenly unimportant.

"Yeah. And did you see Minsku come limping back here after the Master caught his little Italian toy? Vance had fucked her up good. The Master had to give her some of *his* blood or she'd still be lying in her coffin. So what makes you think this time will be any different?"

Long pause. "Maybe he wants her to prove herself."

"Prove herself. You notice how thin the ranks have been getting lately?"

"What are you saying?" Michael asked.

"He should do it himself if he expects respect."

"If he hears you..."

"That new Italian bitch gets away with murder. She defied him tonight and what did he do?"

"Did you see her? He practically turned her inside out."

"But it didn't get him anything, did it? We still had to take down the old guy. I'm telling you, since he lost his hand, things have been different. Now we're hiding with humans—it's like living in a barn. You don't sleep with the animals."

"You saw what he did to Branko."

"Fuck the Serb," Adam said. "He deserved it. All I'm saying is, if I have to serve someone, they'd better be worth it. I don't want to serve any coward."

"Better watch your tongue. Minsku will kill the Traitor, and if she doesn't, there's a new opening for the Master's right hand. And if the Traitor comes here, we have a mansion full of vampires...not to mention the mob."

"A lot of fucking good *mafiosi* will do against him," Adam said. "I thought they were here for midnight snacking."

"The Lucattis and all their people are strictly hands off. Besides, all those Italians are waltzing around with silver crucifixes around their fat necks. You try some midnight snacking and you're likely to turn your tongue into a used match. And then the Master will be waiting for you."

"I still say the Master's afraid. Or else why would we have picked up and run when Branko sold us out? We had a mansion full of vampires then, too, and our own turf, without all these damn crucifixes and shit."

"You're a fool. You don't think others can hear you?"

"I don't care anymore. This isn't what I thought it was going to be."

The voices fell silent. She heard another door close, and water running through pipes overhead. The words of Adam and Michael spiraled in her mind, chasing each other down into blackness. She tried to think, but her mind was so tired, and her body hurt.

The sun was almost up, she could feel it. The darkness of vampire sleep awaited her—and it was a blessing that the pain did not follow her down into it.

Chapter Twenty-Two:
Regrets

The man you couldn't kill.
MR

Karl found these words written in red lipstick on the backside of one of the upstairs closet doors when he began a second, more systematic search through the Warren mansion. He touched the words gently. They were slashed across the white wood, above the louvered panels. She must have feared discovery.

Smart girl.

So what did it mean?

Not Delgado—he wasn't a man and he was already dead. Semantics, yes, but he didn't think Maria would waste her time taunting him.

Unless she was completely corrupted...

No, too obscure for a taunt. Too obscure for her—she seemed to prefer the direct route.

All right, so what did it mean? She might prefer a direct route, but she hadn't taken it here. She must have feared Delgado snatching knowledge of her message out of her mind, so she'd kept it ambiguous.

The man he couldn't kill.

The only man who fit that particular description was Boss Stefano Lucatti. She'd wanted him to kill Stefano, but he'd told her it was impossible. He'd already tried twice, stalking the man for months at a time, but it always came down to the same thing. The man believed in holy objects, and kept them close at all times. His mansion was nearly as protected as a church.

But if Maria were telling him that Delgado and his brood had gone to the Lucatti mansion, then things would've had to change. At least some of the supernatural wards had to be down, otherwise Delgado would not have been able to enter.

The Lucatti mansion. It was a lead he would gladly take. He searched again, but found nothing else except the bodies of the unfortunate old man and woman buried in shallow graves in the garden. He closed his eyes and leaned against the side of the house. Too tired to even curse, seeing them again in all the hundreds of pictures placed throughout the house, in ornate gilt frames so they didn't clash with the decor.

He went back inside, picked up the phone and dialed 911.

"911, what's your emergency?"

"Two good people have been murdered."

He gave the operator the address, told her where the bodies were. Hung up.

First time his voice had ever been recorded that he knew of. He hurried out the back door, across a cobblestone patio with a fountain, leapt the wall and began to sprint. Ignoring the pain of his wounds was something he had grown quite good at.

Four hours and thirteen minutes until dawn. Not much time to get back to St. Rosa's to pray for the murdered Warrens, so he had to move fast.

Sirens started to wail in the distance. He thought about the problem of the Lucatti mansion.

Holy wards or no, there had to be an effective means for him to force his way inside and face off against an army of vampires and *mafiosi*. But without silver-encased rounds for the SIG...

Then he had it. Unorthodox, yes, and risky as hell—half-insane even—but there was a chance. He smiled for the first time since finding the Warren mansion empty and Maria gone.

The news carried the death of Alberto Ricardi on every front page on the Eastern Seaboard and at the top of every newscast. Karl read the story twice. The articles said little about the manner in which he'd been killed, but it was described as sadistic and brutal—a mob hit where a point was being made.

Karl knew better. He stared out his window at the overgrown yard, his shoulder and arm aching from the wounds Minsku and the wolf had given him. The wolf wounds were deeper, but they already showed signs of slow healing. It would be a long while before the silver wound began to heal. He was lucky it was such a small cut. Xiesha had looked it over grimly and shrugged, shaking her head. There was nothing either of them could do about it.

The man you couldn't kill.

Tomorrow night he'd discover if she were right.

Chapter Twenty-Three:
Final Assault

—Milton, *Paradise Lost*

Karl and Xiesha stood in the yard with the burned remains of Katz Collision and Auto Body Repair. A few girders still stood, several charred car frames sat where the garages had been, and assorted burned wreckage was heaped and scattered everywhere. Yellow DO NOT CROSS tape had been wound around everything.

The yard, however, had not been damaged much. The stack of empty 55-gallon drums still rested against the fence. The row of cars waiting to be stripped still sat against the far cinderblock wall that lined the back end of the property and the gate was still locked, but every vehicle had a bright orange tire lock attached to the right driver-side wheel and a seizure notice on the windshield.

Karl walked over to the Hummer. It was a dull school bus yellow under the layer of black soot. Xiesha stared at it for one long moment and said, "The color leaves something to be desired."

Karl tore the steel plate off the gate lock and wrenched the gate off the track, shoving it out of the way. It gave an almost human groan and rattled and crashed backward before finally leaning drunkenly to the side. He bent down, examined the bright orange tire lock, and then twisted apart the clamp and tossed the destroyed car boot into the oil-stained gravel. They'd

244

agreed earlier that Xiesha would drive. Together they loaded the back of the Hummer with an empty 55-gallon drum and as many five-gallon pails that still had lids and spouts that they could find and would fit.

Karl climbed inside the Hummer and shut the door. The inside stank of chemicals—residue in the drums. Xiesha set her shotgun next to her and glanced at him.

"Ready?" she said.

"Let's go." The air felt charged, almost crushing in its intensity—destiny slowly clenching its fist around him. It was almost as if he stood on the spot where lightning was about to strike, and he could feel his hair lifting from his scalp and a shiver trembling up his spine. The air pulsed with conclusions—of terminus and violent ends. Things would be settled, one way or another.

Xiesha provided the spark for the engine, and the Hummer rumbled to life. They stopped to fill the drum and pails at a Citgo station a few miles down the road. The clerk glanced out the window at them and immediately went back to reading his magazine. It cost almost five hundred dollars to fill everything, including the Hummer. Xiesha stared at the amount on the pump and shook her head.

"The last time I filled an automobile, I believe I paid a dollar ten a gallon," she said. "I need to get out more."

"When did you ever have a car?"

"I stole one, remember?" She tightened the bung on the drum. "To learn how to drive."

He didn't remember, but it didn't really matter. They got back inside and drove away, windows rolled down to minimize the fumes, the drums covered with blankets in case some sharp-eyed police officer should pull up next to them.

The next half an hour passed in silence. He stared out the window and thought of Maria and he remembered Cade, all the torments, all the suffering. The neighborhoods grew more and more upscale as they headed into Concord—changing from large expensive houses to mansions with perfectly manicured lawns and properties surrounded by gates. Xiesha stopped two blocks from the Lucatti mansion on a long, wide street flanked by rows of ancient trees. Karl got out of the Hummer and climbed onto the roof. He held the SIG-Sauer in his hand, getting accustomed to how the silencer changed the weight distribution.

Stefano Lucatti's mansion was walled in by a seven foot, red stone barricade with ornamental spikes set into the top stones. The homeowner's association probably wouldn't let people erect razor wire in this neighborhood.

They pulled up to the gate and stopped. A *mafioso* in jeans and a heavy jacket sat at the window of the small guard booth, leaning back in his chair and reading *Hustler*. Karl could sense the silver crucifix pressed against the man's chest and could smell gun oil. The man stared at Xiesha for a moment over the top of his magazine and then slid back the window glass. He leaned forward, annoyance on his face, and then he saw Karl.

"Oh shit—" he said, grabbing for something.

Karl shot him in the forehead. He tumbled backward, careening off his cheap swivel chair and falling to the ground. Karl jumped down from the roof of the Hummer and went inside the booth.

Another soul for the list.

The smell of blood was distracting. The man's eyes were open, staring at the fluorescent light, where a moth threw itself against the bulb. Sitting next to a small television and a bunch of closed-circuit monitors was the Ingram Mac-10 he'd been reaching for.

Karl slapped the button and the heavy iron gates slowly and soundlessly swung open. Xiesha drove through and Karl walked after her, but he paused before passing across the gate boundary. Black stains marred the ground beneath the gate, and a hideous stench assaulted his nose. Blood—human mixed with pig and dog's blood. Excrement. Heartsbane and bile. Sulfur. Other foul things he didn't immediately recognize. The sense of strange black magic was very strong, humming painfully in his back teeth. The black magic that profaned the entrance, once sealed with holy water and sacred rites, sent a wave of nausea cramping through him. It took all his strength of will to cross over that disgusting smear of filth.

Xiesha slowed to a stop just inside the gate and he came up to her window.

"You smell that?" he asked.

"I felt the stain," Xiesha said. "But it's better than holy water and incense."

"He's here, then. Delgado must have profaned the holy

seals in order to come and go as he pleased."

"Do we still need the Hummer?"

He nodded. "We'll still use it even if they undid every barrier."

Karl walked around and opened the back of the Hummer. He unscrewed the cap to the 55-gallon drum air vent and bunghole. Then he did the same to all the five-gallon pails. The smell of gasoline grew even heavier as it started to pour into the back of the Hummer.

"Go!" he said to Xiesha and she floored the accelerator. He sprinted alongside her, keeping pace until she pushed it over forty and began to pull ahead of him.

The driveway ran perhaps four hundred feet in a straight line to the front of the Lucatti mansion, lined with trees with flood lamps at their bases, shining up into their barren branches. The Hummer roared down the drive ahead of him now, passing a parked BMW and two Escalades pulled off to the right.

It must have been doing seventy-five by the time Xiesha rammed it through the double front doors of the Lucatti mansion. The impact was shockingly loud in the post-midnight quiet. The mansion doors disintegrated into slivers of wood and glass and the framework buckled and collapsed as the Hummer shattered through, bounced and continued into the house, slamming into something else with a thundering crash.

Karl stopped short of the hole in the front of the house. Pieces of wood hung broken from the frame. As he watched, another piece tumbled down with a dry clatter. Dust rose in a cloud over everything, then he heard the Hummer's door open— wrenched off the frame and tossed aside—and he heard Xiesha's voice.

"Better run, rabbit," she said.

A twenty-something-year-old man in a T-shirt and jeans with a pistol shoved in his waistband came sprinting full bore out of the destroyed doorway. Terror sewed his features into an opened-mouthed mask of fear. He ran right past Karl and never reached for his gun, never even slowed, the steam of his breath trailing out behind him.

Smart man.

Xiesha appeared in the doorway, her shotgun held by the pump in her right hand.

"Light it up," he said. She smiled and walked out of the wreckage of the doorway toward him, then raised her hand. She snapped her fingers together, calling a spark between them. There was a matching spark inside the foyer, where the air was saturated with flammable gasoline vapor.

The explosion seemed to shake the ground. The front of the Lucatti manse blew out in a huge red-orange fireball, throwing fragments and shards of debris everywhere. Karl and Xiesha stood dangerously close, and he gritted his teeth against the shockwave that rammed against him. Xiesha didn't even seem to notice the detonation wave. The heat danced against Karl's skin, hot enough to burn, but he healed so fast he withstood that as well. He watched a small curio table topple end over end through the air above their heads, still burning, looking for all the world like some strange, otherworldly comet.

The police would arrive soon, and the fire department. He had a lot of work to do before then.

"Let's go," he said, pistol heavy in one hand, dagger burning in the other.

The explosion shook the mansion right through to its foundations. Maria slapped her hands over her ears and ducked down against the basement wall, certain the first and second floor would come crashing in on her. An image flittered through her mind of a colossal dragon seizing each end of the manse in massive claws, leaning down and shrieking a deafening roar through the front door, blistering paint from the walls and shattering every window. How well did vampires do buried in a hundred tons of rubble?

Master Delgado didn't flinch. He sat calmly at the carved oak table the Lucattis had brought down here for him and ran his glance across the sirelings who sat to his left and right. No two of Master Delgado's children were dressed even remotely the same—they wore everything from power suits to blue jeans. Maria wore a short red dress that hugged every curve, boots with heels, and her hair curled into a nest of long ringlets, all at her Master's insistence.

One of the female sirelings half-stood, staring up at the cellar's support beams, sharp fear-scent rolling off her skin. The others were just as restless. One of them, the Asian named Michael, stood guard near the door with Delgado's spear in his hands, the one with the silver blade and the string of yellowed fangs, and he peered up at the cellar doors as though he expected to see the devil himself come crashing through at any moment.

"Vance," Master Delgado said. He touched the stump of his left hand and such hatred flared in his eyes that all present leaned away, as if being too close would consume them like sunlight.

Karl. Maria ruthlessly crushed down the surge of joy within, praying Master Delgado didn't notice. If he did, he was likely to destroy her where she stood.

This part of the basement was large, lightless save for the meager flame of a single oil lamp. The air smelled stale, of mold and mildew and the faint odor of natural gas from the two large water heaters and the furnace at the far end. Boxes were stacked along the unfinished cement walls, and cracks spread across the cement floor like tributaries of a violent river. Not a place she wanted to be her last.

Gunshots boomed above. Not the pop of Karl's 9mm, but the primal roar of Xiesha's shotgun.

Think of nothing, think of nothing, think of nothing, think—

"Stop him," Master Delgado said to his sirelings. "Help your brothers and sisters who are already fighting him. Prove yourself worthy of serving me."

The sirelings rose as one and bounded away toward the angled cellar doors leading outside, jostling each other in their eagerness. Maria stood with them, but Master Delgado's voice in her mind stopped her.

"Not so fast, querida mia. Let the others delay him. I have something special planned."

Michael threw open the doors for the sirelings and stood back, and Maria watched her brothers and sisters leap out into the night. She felt no pity for what they were going to meet.

"Shall I go as well, Master?" Michael asked, tapping the spear butt on the cement floor so that the fangs rattled against one another in a way that sounded almost hungry.

"Stay here and guard our coffins," Master Delgado said. "I don't want to win this war only to find my coffin spiked with silver and holy water come dawn."

Michael bowed low and turned back to face the double cellar doors.

Master Delgado moved through the cellar into the finished part of the basement, near the stairs leading into the main house. She could hear fire crackling overhead and smell the acrid reek of smoke and synthetics burning, but Master Delgado seemed not to care. A narrow case, about a foot and a half long, sat on a rack of wire shelving. Master Delgado lifted it with his remaining hand, his thumb sliding along the dark leather as softly as a lover's caress. The case was embossed with gold letters, but they were in a language she didn't understand. The hinges creaked when he opened it. Inside lay a dagger on velvet. She drew away from it when he lifted it from the case.

"Yes." He smiled at her. "It's an unpleasant piece of workmanship, isn't it?"

The dagger blade was blacker than anything she'd ever seen. It almost seemed as if a slice had been cut out of reality, a gouge in the fabric of the universe into some starless void. Staring at it churned her stomach.

"A gift for Karl," Master Delgado said. "A blade to match that cursed silver shank he carries."

More gunshots from overhead. The roar of the fire was louder; the dragon was growing above them.

Master Delgado beckoned her closer. "Shall we go await our friend somewhere we won't be bothered? Let him weary himself on wiseguys and sirelings. Let him burn the Lucattis out—it doesn't matter. When he comes to me I'll send him to his hateful God."

And if Karl and the Lucattis were gone, her Master would pick up the reins to the Boston underworld. Control of Boston was a dream she'd harbored once herself, in some foolish long ago, when her skin had still been warm and she'd had no idea how free she really had been.

Without a word, she turned and ran for the stairs, desperate to get to Karl. She managed two sprinting steps before the sudden burst of agony dropped her. She writhed on the cold cement, smelling the lingering stink of mildew as the rough surface dug into her face, but Master Delgado wouldn't let her scream.

He wrenched her up by the hair and jerked her head back, then pressed the black dagger to her throat. The touch of it was warm, almost wet, like sticking a hand inside a decomposing body. She groaned.

"One more act of defiance," he said into her ear, "just *one*—and I'll unmake you and have done with it. My patience has deserted me."

"Please." She tried to arch her head back, to get her skin away from the disgusting feel of the blade, but he held her steady. A sob escaped her lips. "Forgive me, Master."

"Better." He let go of her hair, withdrew the blade and walked away. She clambered to her feet and hurried to keep up, lest he keep his promise. All thoughts of escape had been banished. Another touch of that blade would drive her mad.

She dared not even hope of Karl, dared not even pray.

Karl moved quickly past the rows of rose bushes toward the burning façade of the Lucatti mansion. The explosion had blown a gaping hole where the double doors had been, peeling open the interior of the manse. The inside of the foyer was ablaze, flooded with shifting red-yellow firelight. A hanging light swung back and forth, spitting sparks. The Hummer looked like a piece of abstract metal art a sculptor had set aflame. But as Karl neared the hole, he sensed something and stopped short.

A male vampire dropped from the roof and landed on the patio directly in front of him. Karl had no time to see anything but glowing red eyes before the vampire slashed at him, trying to open up his throat with his claws. Karl's swipe with the dagger opened the vampire's arm from shoulder to elbow. The vampire staggered back from him, cursing. His red power tie hung loosened and askew, dangling like a noose over his rumpled suit, while smoking black blood began to seep from the wound.

Karl advanced, his silver dagger glinting gold in the fire's blaze. Xiesha was quicker. She swung the shotgun and pulled the trigger. The shotgun bellowed and the silver slug ripped into the vampire's face, taking its head off above the nose.

Two more vampires sprinted out of the scatter of trees around the house and hurled themselves at Karl. He dodged a swipe of claws and snapping fangs. The female vampire laughed and tossed her head, a whipping braid of blonde hair, and then she cut at his eyes with black claws. Karl slipped aside, but the male vampire was on him again, pressing him backward.

Karl drove the silver dagger into the vampire's chest, and

he arched his back with a lingering howl like a dying wolf. The female kept close to Karl, putting him between her and the shotgun barrel, so that Xiesha couldn't get a clear shot. But Karl sprang at her and, with two quick strokes, opened her throat. She clutched at the wound, eyes wide, but her fingers started to disintegrate into swirling black specks. She stared at her vanishing hands in horror, unable to scream with her throat cut, as the black motes mixed with the smoke pouring from the front of the mansion.

Another two vampires leapt out of the fires of the doorway, untouched by the flames or heat. Xiesha shot one down as it leapt, an instant before it was upon her. A massive hole opened in the vampire's chest and it dissolved into a cloud of swirling black particles that fell around Xiesha like snow.

The other vampire turned and fled back into the mansion. Xiesha shot at it but missed, racked the slide and cursed in disgust.

In the distance, Karl could hear sirens. Lots of them, as though the entire Boston PD and every fire truck within a twenty-mile radius was on the way.

"Well, they know we're here," she said with a smile as she slipped new shells into the shotgun.

"Good. I want Delgado's full attention."

The strip of holy fire that guarded the threshold still burned with bright blue fire, but Karl merely walked around it, through the new doorway the Hummer had made. The smoke and fire had spread everywhere in the foyer and the anteroom. They ran past a burning piano and a fountain whose water had started to boil. The smoke was like a thick black curtain pressing down from the high ceilings, coiling and swirling as if made of a thousand serpents.

He heard shouting from somewhere, but it was hard to pinpoint in the smoke and roar of the fire. Karl and Xiesha advanced through the ground floor hugging the walls, moving in a low crouch to see through the smoke. He had the 9mm out in his right hand and the dagger in his left, as Xiesha brought up the rear with the 12 gauge. More shouting, this time from upstairs and further back in the house. Somewhere a little girl screamed and someone else, a little boy, perhaps, was crying. The sounds went through him like a stake.

"Children," Xiesha warned.

"I know." *God help us.*

"We have to hurry."

"Double check your targets."

She nodded, her mouth set in a grim line.

A man dressed in sweatpants and wearing a silver cross around his neck came running down the hall with a shotgun in his hands. He spotted Karl and raised the shotgun, but Karl shot him in the heart, the whisper and ratchet-click of the silenced pistol drowned out by the fire. The man rebounded off the wall, leaving a bright red smear on the wallpaper as he slid to the ground.

At the end of the hall, an obese man in a stained Harvard sweatshirt yelled something and fired a revolver at them. The bullet shattered an antique mirror. Glass rained down into the potted ferns arranged below.

Karl's shot clipped him in the leg and he toppled over with a shriek. Karl's next shot got him in the head.

"Stop him!" someone screamed. The voice of an old man, but still sparking with command. A flurry of coughs followed. "Get my family out of here!"

The sound of the fire behind them had grown until it was a constant roar like a massive ship furnace. Smoke curled along the ceiling of the hallway, and the air was hazy and blistering hot.

Karl came to the end of the hall and stepped over the body of the obese *mafioso*. A bullet whizzed by his head and plowed into the wall. Another shot missed wide and struck a family portrait, knocking it to the ground.

Karl dropped to a crouch and fired at the smoke-obscured shape across the room. The shape turned and ran, firing back over its shoulder. Karl followed slowly, the silencer barrel sweeping from side to side as he advanced.

The next room was a private theater with a large screen at the far end and twenty leather recliners all arranged in rows. The smoke was relatively light, little more than a haze, and there was no fire. A black-haired man dressed only in trousers stood at the far end of the theater, between Karl and another older man in a paisley dressing gown. The older man, perhaps sixty, overweight and bald, but with a grandfatherly face, locked eyes with Karl for one long moment.

Stefano Lucatti. Don of the Lucatti family.

Stefano fled out the door, leaving his bodyguard behind. The bodyguard fired. Karl took the hit in his shoulder and steadied his own aim. The bodyguard started to pull the trigger again, but Karl dropped him with a bullet in one brown eye, painting the wall in his blood.

The shotgun roared behind him, and he glanced back at Xiesha, who was holding the smoking shotgun to her shoulder, peering down the barrel toward the room they'd just left. He heard a shriek and saw the black particulate of a vampire burning away to nothing.

Karl turned and sprinted for the door Lucatti had taken, running down the inclined theater floor after him. The night outside sang with the wail of sirens. Inside, the fire's greedy crackle and roar filled his ears.

The door he ran through opened into a glass atrium leading out onto a veranda. The atrium was roughly octagon shaped, the walls ahead all floor-to-ceiling windows lined with Grecian stone benches and potted palms, with wide glass doors at the far end. A fountain filled the center of the room, but the water in its gray stone basin was still.

A woman and two children cowered near the double doors. Outside, darkness pressed its face to the glass, peering in. Stefano stood between them and Karl, unarmed, his hands out to the sides to protect them. The little girl, maybe eight years old, stared at Karl with terrified eyes, soot striping her face like a quarterback. The pretty young woman clutched the small boy in her arms, trying to turn his eyes away from Karl, but the boy kept squirming around to look as he coughed. Snot and tears ran down his round face.

"You." Stefano Lucatti's voice seethed with hatred, churned with fear.

"Where's Delgado?" Karl asked. He lowered the pistol to his side.

The floors trembled as if struck by an earthquake. Somewhere nearby, part of the house collapsed with a tremendous rending and breaking. A wraith-cloud of gray smoke began to pour into the atrium from the opposite interior door, creeping along the ceiling. The sound of the fire was suddenly much louder, much closer.

"Where's Delgado?" Karl demanded again.

Sweat poured down Stefano's face, and his skin was

reddened, appearing sunburned. "The basement!" he yelled over the roaring fire. "In the cellar—"

A shape crashed through the latticed window to the right of him, scattering glass everywhere, red eyes and fangs set in a twisted, inhuman face. The vampire shoved through the mother and children and seized Stefano.

"You betray him?" the vampire screamed. "You *dare*?"

The vampire's head darted toward Stefano's neck, but seemed to hit a glass wall and rebound. The silver crucifix around Stefano Lucatti's neck blazed like a star, and the vampire shrieked and let go of him. It whirled back to the children. A smile dripping with lust curled the vampire's lips.

Karl moved as fast as he ever had, knife raised to pierce that red eye, but he was too far. Stefano ripped the crucifix from his neck and swung his fist at the vampire, the crucifix wrapped over his fingers. He hit the vampire below the eye with a resounding *smack*.

The vampire screeched, its face smoking, its cheek half-melted. It knocked Stefano's fist aside. The crucifix flew from his fingers and splashed into the fountain.

Karl leapt over the fountain. Five steps to the vampire. Too far.

It drove its fangs into Lucatti's throat and shook its head like a wolf tearing at the carcass of a deer. Blood sprayed out in an arcing pulse as Stefano screamed and was hurled aside.

The vampire spun and lunged at the little girl. Her mother shrieked and yanked her backward just as Karl landed beside them. He batted aside the vampire's grasping claws and drove his dagger into its eye and out the back of its head.

The mother backed away from Karl, shielding the children with her body as best she could. She stared at Karl as a mother might stare at a pit viper that had crawled into her child's crib.

Karl turned to Xiesha. It was an effort to speak. "Help them to safety, Xie."

Xiesha walked to the woman and tried to take her hand, but the woman backed up another step. "Get the hell away from my children!" she screamed. Tears streamed down her cheeks and terror danced in her eyes.

The little girl sobbed, hitching in breath, shuddering it out. The boy was silent, his eyes wide.

"I won't hurt you," Xiesha said.

The woman didn't answer, she just continued backing away, her gaze darting from Karl to Xiesha and back again.

"Go with my friend," Karl urged her. "She'll keep your children safe until you can get to the police."

A hesitation.

"Do you want another one of those things to get to you first?"

A violent shake of her head, yet when Xiesha said, "Follow me," she turned and hastened after her, carrying the boy and shepherding the girl along.

Karl looked at Stefano's body. Dressing gown drenched in blood. Blood pooling on the marble floors, the smell of it stronger than the reek of smoke.

It all came down to time. Time pouring away, spilling out of a broken hourglass. The police had encircled the mansion. A helicopter had arrived and swept back and forth overhead, the chop of its rotors and whine of its engines fading as it circled away. And Delgado was still loose, and with him, Maria.

He had no more time for this family, but he watched anyway as Xiesha led them out through the double glass doors out onto the veranda, her shotgun at her shoulder, tracking back and forth for any of Delgado's rampaging vampires. Bad enough that those kids had seen such horrible things tonight. There was nothing he could do about it now except try and keep them alive.

They were painted with firelight as they ran the hundred or so meters toward the sea of flashing red and blue lights. Police spotlights found them and cops swarmed all over them, pulling the woman and children to safety.

Xiesha had broken off as soon as the spotlights had found them. She sprinted back toward the house, and Karl caught glimpses of her silhouette against the headlights and spotlights. Three shots were fired, but someone on a bullhorn yelled, "Cease fire! Hold your fire!" and the shots stopped.

A beam of light lit her up from above, and the intensity of the light made her appear ghost-like and translucent. The pounding *thump thump thump* of rotor blades drowned out even the roar of the fire as the police helicopter kept her illuminated. Xiesha leapt onto the veranda and another flurry of bullets kicked up dirt and followed her over the stone rail until she leapt back through the destroyed window into the Atrium.

The helicopter searchlight flared into the room, blindingly bright. Karl and Xiesha fled back into the theater. Its eastern wall had caught fire and the wood panels were burning, flames licking at the ceiling. The movie screen caught and disintegrated like film melting in a projector. The smoke reached down to Karl's chest, and they were forced to crouch and feel their way along the wall.

Time. Not enough time.

Around them the mansion burned, and with a terrible rending crash part of the second story collapsed in a rain of fire and burning debris, blackened dressers and beds and televisions tumbling in flaming rain, while smaller bits of debris fluttered down like burning snow.

Chapter Twenty-Four:
Silver Heart

The seven bay garage was set off from the main house and connected by an enclosed hall. Maria stood near a Corvette, watching the firelight and emergency lights reflecting along the roof from the large windows set high in the wall opposite the garage doors. Master Delgado sat cross-legged on the hood of a sapphire-colored Bentley Continental. The black knife lay next to him on the car's hood, the paint blistered and peeling where it touched.

The rapid back and forth of gunfire had tapered off. The fire's voice had become ever more insistent—a stadium crowd roar punctuated with crackles and small explosions. An officer on a bullhorn started bellowing demands for surrender, but only the fire roared back an answer.

"The Lucattis...?" she asked.

"Dead or dying. It matters not."

"They only gave us shelter."

Delgado smiled at her. "Your father's dead. With Stefano Lucatti dead, the Boston underworld will be open for bidding."

She shifted restlessly and looked away. A moment later she paced to the door leading to the enclosed hall and then back to the car. "Why is it taking so long?"

"Patience, *querida*. I'm shielding against him and he has to search the old-fashioned way. Let him kill to his heart's content."

"And the Order of Thorn?" she asked. "Boston won't be yours for long."

"I'll set the humans against them. Bring in shooters from

New York, if necessary. I'm not particularly concerned."

She had the feeling he didn't expect any of his sirelings to survive this—perhaps not even her.

One of her Master's beautiful female sirelings opened the door leading to the house. Her eyes glowed a soft red. "He's near, Master."

"I know he's *near.* Don't waste my time."

The vampire flinched and disappeared behind a closing door.

"The garage will catch soon," Maria said. "Will you stay if it burns?"

"We have time."

Maria looked back to the dancing lights along the walls and ceiling, listened to the riot of destruction so very close. Soon it would be over, one way or the other. Master Delgado would send her against Karl. She couldn't defy him again. Her refusal to slaughter her own father and his retaliation had leached all free will out of her. Karl would drive that silver dagger into her undead heart. And there would be peace.

Or so she hoped.

The police started to speak through bullhorns, but the sound was obscured by the riot of other noises—the helicopters, three now at least, the fire, the gunshots as ammunition cooked off. Karl and Xiesha crouched as a gas line suddenly exploded, shaking the walls like an earthquake. Ash and embers drifted like pollen. They passed the charred wreckage of the Hummer again. It was little more than a twisted heap of metal, half of it missing—driven as shrapnel into the walls.

Karl's skin blistered and burned more than once, his clothes smoking, but he healed as quickly as he burned. His shoulder still throbbed from the silver wound and the teeth of the spirit wolf, but the pain did not slow him. He slipped the 9mm into the holster beneath his shoulder and switched the knife to his right hand. No humans could survive in this inferno without fire-fighting gear. They'd either fled or died. Either way, they were no longer his concern.

"What now?" Xiesha asked, close to his ear so he could hear her.

"Lucatti said the basement." The house gave an ominous groan, loud even over the constant roar of the flames.

"And when we find him," Xiesha asked, "what then?"

"Kill his sirelings, if any live. But Delgado is mine."

"What if he sends Maria against you?"

"Let me worry about Maria."

The main stairwell and balcony collapsed in a flaming hail of wreckage. Karl and Xiesha sprinted away, burst through the doors into the kitchen as much more of the second story came crashing down in an apocalypse of noise and ruin.

The kitchen had been half-destroyed by an explosion and the partial collapse of the ceiling. One wall was completely engulfed in flame. Debris lay everywhere. Dagger-shards of the marble countertops. The contorted remains of the oven door, blackened and smoking. Half an overhead light fixture hung by its wires, spitting a rain of sparks. And hanging on a hook by the wreckage of a massive stainless steel refrigerator was an un-singed oven mitt decorated with bright brown and red roosters.

The door handle to the basement seared his hand when Karl grabbed it. He tightened his grip and pulled, but the door had warped in its frame and wouldn't budge. He scowled and tore it from its hinges. It twisted free with a tortured *skreek*.

The basement was a scene from Hell, the frenzied dancing flames so bright that looking at them was like staring at the sun through an unshielded telescope. Smoke roiled and churned along the support beams, pouring up through holes burned in the basement ceiling. Karl could feel the soles of his boots smoking. The heat pushing up through the column of gray-black smoke forced him back a step.

At the bottom of the basement stairs he could see a weakly thrashing vampire buried under flaming rubble. Only his head and one arm were free, but his skin almost seemed to shiver as the flames ate at it. The vampire stared up at Karl with horribly aware, hate-filled and desperate eyes. A long spear with a silver blade lay broken by his hand. Karl motioned to Xiesha. She stepped forward and raised the shotgun. The shotgun bellow was shockingly final, the *click-clack* of the slide one final curse.

Karl turned away from the basement inferno. There was no way Delgado was still down there. And with the second floor already collapsing and the rest of the house swallowed in flames, Karl's options were running out. Only one place remained.

He could see the garage from the cracked kitchen windows. Together Karl and Xiesha ran to the access door to the garage, dodging a rain of sparks and leaping pockets of flames. He ripped the door from its hinges and slung it aside only to find another corridor—this one lined with windows on either side looking out into the gardens and the pool area. A light haze of smoke stirred in the air, but no fire yet. The walls shimmered with light from the fire eating away at the house and danced with the red-blue-amber from the sirens, or exploded into brilliant angelic white when the helicopter ran its searchlight across.

A voluptuous woman stood in the shadows at the far end of the hall, her eyes glowing embers. She saw Karl and fled through the far door into the garage, slamming the door behind her. Someone had painted an eye in blood on the white panel of the door.

Xiesha sidestepped him, the shotgun raised. She stared down the sight and tracked right to left. He gritted his teeth, but the shotgun's roar was still agonizingly loud when she pulled the trigger. A two-inch hole burst chest-high in the door panel, below the painted eye. A scream and then nothing. Xiesha racked the slide, and the red shell casing bounced on the tile floor with a hollow clatter.

The police helicopter swooped in low again, drowning the world in the roar of its blades. They pressed themselves to the walls until it circled away.

Karl risked a glance out the windows. The ground sloped down toward the gate, and from here he could see just how much trouble they'd stirred up. Dozens of squad cars and fire trucks, ambulances, two SWAT vans and a sea of news vans had formed a wall of motor vehicles around the estate. A cacophony of noise filled the air: engines, helicopter rotors, radios, bullhorns, phones, conversation, the hum of lights—too chaotic to discern much, he had to work to shut it out. More searchlights swept the house, bright as lightning.

Karl and Xiesha crawled beneath the long row of windows to avoid the searchlights. They stood again at the far end of the hall, each taking position on opposite sides of the door. He could hear nothing within, but that meant little with all the random noise. He took a risk and peered through the hole she had blown in the panel, but he couldn't see much, only rows of cars parked between support beams.

He glanced at Xiesha and she nodded. He stepped back, stared at the painted eye for a moment, and then kicked the door in.

The garage was huge, with seven bays and seven sleek, expensive cars. A Ferrari 550 Maranello, a sapphire-colored Bentley Continental GTC, a black Cadillac Escalade with rims that gleamed like liquid silver, a Porsche 911 in metallic gray, a Chevrolet Corvette sitting next to a sleek and elegant Rolls-Royce Phantom, and finally a vintage 60s era Alfa Romeo. Someone had a lot of money and a love of rolling iron.

A row of huge windows lined the garage's back wall, and the place was thrown in stark shadow and brilliant illumination by the police floodlights. The circling helicopter's searchlight pierced through every so often, making it look as if some alien ship were searching for someone to abduct. The far wall held shelves and Stanley Vidmar tool cabinets and row upon row of gleaming tools. The floor polish shone like water reflecting moonlight, and the chrome on the vehicles glowed like white-hot coals.

Alejandro Delgado sat cross-legged on top of the sapphire Bentley. He grinned at Karl and motioned him in. "Welcome. Quite the apocalypse. You've never been guilty of doing things halfway, have you?"

Karl moved silently across the floor toward him, dagger held loosely in his right hand. The blade flashed in the passing light from the searchlights.

Xiesha followed, slipping around the doorframe and pressing her back to the wall, shotgun to her shoulder, sighted on Delgado.

Movement caught his eye and he glanced toward it. Maria slowly stood from where she'd been crouching on the hood of the Corvette in the shadow thrown by one of the garage's wide, weight-bearing columns. She stepped to the fender and down onto the floor, the bottom of her short red dress gripping the curve of her thigh. Her face was impassive. No recognition. Certainly no joy.

"She is lovely in the moonlight, no?" Delgado said. "I so enjoy how she looks in silver when her body is moving against me."

Maria flinched, but her eyes remained a dull glowing red as she walked toward him with one hand behind her back.

Karl heard Xiesha slip shells into the shotgun's magazine. He held out a hand toward her, without turning.

"Maria," Karl called softly.

She flinched again, but kept coming toward him. Pain writhed across her face, her lips pulled back from her fangs in agony. When she brought her hand around he knew why. In her bare hand she held a silver dinner knife, probably taken right out of Lucatti's dining room. It probably wasn't sharp, but it wasn't the edge that Karl worried about. He could see a thin trail of smoke wafting upward from where the silver handle burned into her hand.

She was closer now. Twenty feet away and moving with that silent deliberation.

"All your children are dead, Alejandro," Karl said. "You have nothing."

"On the contrary, I have all I need. Maria is still mine." Delgado laughed. "I can always make more slaves."

Maria halted. Her hand trembled, and the light shivered on the surface of her silver knife. Her mouth opened and her lips moved, but no sound came out.

Delgado's smile widened. Karl sensed something pass between them, and Maria started to whip her head back and forth. Delgado laughed again and Maria convulsed, becoming rigid, her teeth slamming together in a hard clack as if she had stepped on a downed power line. She sagged suddenly, her head lolling, but she never let go of the knife. She straightened and took another step toward him. Tears glistened on her cheeks.

"I'll kill you for that," Karl said to Delgado. His hand crushed down on the dagger hilt.

"Promises, promises." Delgado's eyes glowed.

Maria leapt at Karl, slashing with her knife. He slipped aside, out of her downward stroke. She cut back across him, trying to disembowel him, but again he dodged her. She left her guard open for a second, overextended from the strike, but Karl didn't press his advantage. He circled back away from her, and the look in her eyes told him she was very aware he had ignored the chance to kill her.

She stopped and raised herself from her fighting crouch,

the knife falling to her side. Again she tried to say something. Delgado clenched his fist, and Maria's back arched and her head whipped backward. She stood rigid on her toes, every muscle convulsing, but Delgado let no scream escape her lips.

Karl sprinted for Delgado, his knife cutting silver arcs in the air as he ran.

Delgado remained seated on the hood of the Bentley and smiled.

Maria threw herself in front of him, forcing him to slide to a halt a dozen feet from Delgado. Her knife blurred in slash after slash that he barely avoided. She drove him back steadily, away from her Master.

Delgado's laughter echoed from the rafters. The helicopter searchlight pierced through the windows, trailing over the cars. Karl hid behind a support beam and Maria crouched down behind the Rolls-Royce. Delgado didn't bother to move from his seat, and the searchlight, by chance or luck, never found him. The searchlight moved off, the rotor thump diminishing.

Karl slipped along the shadow of the column, then stood and sprinted for Delgado again. Maria leapt in from the side, knife thrusting toward his ribs. He had to twist in mid-stride, seizing her wrist an instant before the knife pierced him. *Forgive me.* He spun, using strength and momentum to fling her away from him.

She twisted like a cat in midair. Instead of slamming into one of the support columns, she hit it feet first, and then sprang off it again, launching herself back at him. Karl braced himself.

The shotgun roared.

The blast slammed Maria into the side of the Porsche, crumpling the door and shattering the window into a million cubes.

For a moment no one moved.

Maria peeled herself out of the huge dent in the side of the car. The world spun wildly for a moment and she clutched her head while she stumbled to her knees. She could feel her broken ribs realigning and healing.

"*Get up, you bitch,*" Master Delgado's voice screamed in her mind. Then it went mercifully silent.

She shook her head to clear it and groaned as the garage

wobbled. She had felt every pellet hit her, ripping through her flesh as she flew backward. But she'd also felt herself pulling back together, every tattered bit reknitting itself almost as quickly as it had been blown away.

That couldn't be. Xiesha used solid slugs in that shotgun. Silver. She'd seen Xiesha use it before, and she'd seen what those slugs did to vampires. She should be dead.

Carefully, she got her feet under her, crouching in the shadow of the wrecked car. The wooziness faded. A clash of metal on metal sang out, followed by the eeriest wail she'd ever heard, a sound like the wind across a battlefield strewn with corpses. It lifted every hair on her arms.

The light streaming in from the spotlights was so bright she winced and shaded her eyes. Karl and Master Delgado were silhouetted against that brilliant light, fighting atop the Bentley. Both had daggers. Karl's silver blade flashed and sparked every time Master Delgado parried a slash or stab with his cursed black steel.

She'd thought that Karl's dance with her had been graceful, but that was nothing compared to the deadly contest that took place on the Bentley hood. Strikes, parries, kicks, blocks, twisting, dodging, slashing, all so amazingly fast.

Her Master's voice had disappeared from her mind as he fought. She could still feel him, but his presence was small and far away, like a dim and unpleasant memory. The night was a riot of noise—the helicopters, the sirens, the police bullhorn, the hungry roar of the fire eating everything. Inside, no one breathed, and the only sounds were the hiss of blades cutting air or the creak of springs and the impact of boots on metal as they leapt from car to car.

Maria looked at Xiesha, who stared back evenly. She appeared untouched by soot or stains, unrumpled, her hair perfect, skin pale as Minsku's spirit wolf. Screw being a vampire, Maria wanted to die and come back as Xiesha.

Maria stood slowly from her crouch, feeling no pain from the buckshot, though her hand pulsed with agony where she'd been burned by the silver knife. Xiesha held the shotgun in one hand, barrel pointed down at the floor, and her other hand glowed with an aura of unearthly green light.

After a moment Xiesha began to walk toward her, deliberate and steady, not paying attention to the ferocious battle between Karl and Master Delgado behind her. On her way, she stooped and picked up the silver knife that Maria had dropped when Xiesha had shot her. Maria's hand throbbed again, as if in dread of touching it. A deep red burn had seared into her palm.

"I think you dropped this," Xiesha said, holding it out to her handle first. Xiesha's eyes flicked to Delgado, and then came back to Maria. One perfect eyebrow lifted in question.

Maria took the knife. Swallowed the pain.

"Go slowly," Xiesha whispered. "Don't let him see you."

Delgado had always been good with a blade. Karl had found himself on the other side of that blade before, back when they'd both been slaves to Cade and fencing had been in fashion. His black dagger was something new, however. It pulsed with a dark evil, the metal seeming to breathe on its own. Every time their blades met in direct contact there was a shrieking wail, like a tormented soul in hell.

Karl slipped beneath Delgado's slash and sliced upward, but Delgado threw himself backward. Karl rushed him, punching Delgado in the face with his left fist, hitting with such force that he hurled him backward. Delgado hit the windshield of the Corvette, and the glass shattered and the hood crumpled like a crushed beer can.

Karl smiled as Delgado pulled himself free. That was the key then. Delgado couldn't grab him or block him effectively with that stump on his left arm.

Delgado launched himself at Karl, fangs bared, dagger a blur. Karl caught his blade with his own and seized Delgado with his free hand. He hurled him into one of the garage's support columns, which shattered into splinters as if someone had hit it with a missile. Delgado crashed to the floor, but bounced back into a crouch. He sprinted toward Karl and jumped back onto the hood of the Alfa Romeo.

They locked their blades together. That mournful wail filled the air as the silver sparked against the strange metal of Delgado's dagger. Delgado glared at him over the crossed blades, hate burning in his eyes, his lips pulled back from his fangs as he fought Karl's unyielding press.

Then Delgado shrieked.

The scream bled agony. Delgado staggered, but something

had his foot and he almost fell.

Maria stepped back, her silver knife protruding from Delgado's instep where it pinned it to the hood of the Alfa Romeo. Wisps of smoke curled from her palm and from the impaled foot.

Maria smiled the most beautiful smile Karl had ever seen— a smile that was all peace and satisfaction.

Delgado bellowed—an animal rage that rattled the windows in their panes. He lifted his black dagger over Maria's head. The blade blurred down, a black streak, and Karl caught it in his left hand, stopping it a scant inch above Maria's upturned face.

Delgado's muscles bulged, but Karl's arm was unmovable. He slowly twisted Delgado's hand upward. He felt a smile stretching his face, something more snarl than smile, vicious and dangerous and half-mad with triumph.

Delgado's arm and hand bones broke when Karl wrenched the black dagger back toward Delgado's gut, turning the blade back on its wielder. He felt Delgado's bones shifting, trying to set and heal, but Karl drove Delgado's broken hand, still clutching that foul knife, back into his stomach. Delgado hissed out breath that reeked of blood and decay, his dark eyes fluttered and came back to Karl. But then he looked back toward Maria.

"She won't be like you," Delgado whispered. He grunted and his body shuddered as spasms ripped through it. "She'll always be mine. I taught her well."

"Let me show you what she knows," Karl said, leaning very close. He ripped Delgado's black dagger free, feeling scant resistance as Delgado's flesh tried to pull away from the cursed blade. It came free of the wound with Delgado's black blood hissing and spitting on the blade. Karl hurled it across the room where it buried itself to the hilt in the cinderblock wall.

Delgado drew in breath to shriek, but Karl grabbed Delgado's face in his left hand and shoved him backward into the hood of the car. The hood cratered beneath him and all four tires blew out, axles shattered, and the car frame dropped to the floor. Karl shifted his grip to Delgado's throat, pinning him, as stinking black liquid seeped from the gut wound.

Karl turned to Maria. "Free yourself." He held out his own silver knife, hilt first. Pain sizzled up his arm like electric current, but he held the blade steady.

She stared at it for one long moment, her silver-burned hand opening and closing. Opening and closing. She grabbed the dagger's hilt and turned to Delgado.

She froze as she met his gaze. The knife trembled in midair, halfway toward Delgado's heart, as if it had met a solid wall and stopped cold.

Karl watched her as Delgado bent all his will upon his slave.

"Free yourself," Karl said. "Make the choice. End it."

The silver knife wavered, and then she started to draw it back. The glow in her eyes grew duller, less focused. A grim smile split Delgado's lips, and his gaze grew more predatory.

"Want it more than being alive, Maria," Karl said quietly, his lips near her ear, remembering the feel of her skin as they made love, willing her to remember it as well, to remember her freedom, to remember her spirit before Delgado had taken her. "Want it more than anything else."

The knifepoint moved slowly, as if underwater. It descended toward Delgado's heart. Every muscle in her arm and back and neck stood out in sharp relief.

Delgado thrashed against Karl, but Karl's grip was unyielding. He dug his claws deeper into Delgado's neck. Crushing. Cutting.

Delgado started to scream something. All the power working against her seemed to vanish. Maria drove the silver blade downward into his black heart with a vicious thrust.

Delgado's body lifted from the crumpled car wreckage, floating upward, his arms thrown wide, his head thrown back, the dagger's hilt protruding from his chest and his unbeating heart.

Karl grabbed Maria's hand and pulled her backward, away from the energy he could feel spinning around the room. Dark light—that was the best Karl could describe it, as if shadows or the non-light of some black hole absorbed the illumination from the floodlights—streamed from Delgado's mouth and his wounds, and then seemed to split his body apart. The ground shook and the floor buckled as though a train had been dropped off a building to impact below Delgado. Every window shattered into glittering shards. An explosion of that same dark light filled the air, pulsing into a black sphere that consumed the center of Delgado, spread out to envelop him, and then collapsed in on itself, leaving nothing.

The silver dagger clattered to the floor and lay there gleaming, not a speck of gore left on its blade.

Maria sagged against him, shivering, trembling, her eyes still on the spot Delgado had died. Karl wrapped her in his arms, kissed her hair.

Xiesha came up beside them. She smiled that half-smile of hers and shook her head. She nodded to the twisted wreck of metal and the impact crater in the concrete floor.

"A little messy," she said. "But it sure saves on funeral expenses."

He couldn't help but smile back.

Alejandro Delgado was gone.

Maria could hardly believe it. Gone from her mind completely. No sense of his invasive presence. No phantom hand gripping her mind, ready to crush down without mercy. Freedom.

Well, as much freedom as a vampire could have as an enemy of the sun and a slave to blood.

But she didn't want to focus on that. Right now it was enough to feel Karl's arms around her. It was as if the hole that had opened up inside her had suddenly sealed itself shut.

"You let me kill him," she said quietly.

He pulled her tighter against him, kissed the top of her head. "We did it together."

"But...all those years...your revenge..."

"I found something more important." He leaned down and kissed her on the lips.

One of the middle garage bay doors began to slide upward, clanking and rattling as it went. Karl pulled back, but his arms remained protectively around her. Xiesha moved between them and the bay door, slipping a silver slug into the magazine and lifting the shotgun to her shoulder.

A woman stood in the middle of the garage bay. Behind her in the driveway and gardens swirled a kaleidoscope of colors from the emergency vehicle lights. The night was still filled with noise, but it felt as if they stood in a bubble of quiet, the eye of the hurricane, a sea of deceptive calm.

She was taller than Maria, hair graying at the temples and

framing a plain face. Warrior eyes, skipping across shadows, weighing, measuring threat. Lean, dressed in a strange combination of what looked like a SWAT uniform and medieval chain mail. Silver crosses at her neck and wrists lay hidden beneath her armor, but Maria could sense them. A blue shimmer circled her neck—some kind of holy water or blessing. She bore a sword on her left hip and a very big gun on her right.

The Order of the Thorn. Had to be.

Would this shit never end?

A half dozen more Thorn knights seemed to appear out of nowhere behind the woman, bearing every kind of weapon she could imagine.

"And look," Xiesha said. "Here's the cavalry. Just in time."

Karl let go of Maria and took a half-step toward them, shielding her from them. There was a hint of threat in the way he carried himself.

"Lady MacKenzie," he said. "I'm afraid it's a bad time."

The Thorn knights spread out in a loose crescent around Lady MacKenzie. She glanced around the garage, her eyes resting for a long moment on the car wreckage and the crater in the floor.

"Delgado?" she asked.

Karl gave a sharp nod.

"We killed two of his sirelings trying to escape through the police cordon. I assume you dealt with the rest?"

"All that we came across."

"All but one, it would seem." Lady MacKenzie's gaze fell on Maria, considering. It was like being watched by a mountain lion, and Maria shifted under the scrutiny.

Karl made no reply.

If it comes to bloodshed after all we've been through... Maria thought.

"Did you find what was taken from you, Karl?" Lady MacKenzie asked.

Karl put a hand on Maria's shoulder. "Yes."

Lady MacKenzie glanced at Maria and then at Xiesha. She smiled, and the winding tension seemed to dissipate a little. "I am Lady Kimberly MacKenzie of the Order of the Thorn. You may have heard of us. Our Order traces its roots back before the Knights Templar, to the fall of Camelot."

"Maria Ricardi." She walked around Karl to stand in front of Lady MacKenzie. "You may have heard of us too. Ruling family of Boston since I just killed this bastard."

Karl frowned at her, but she'd be damned if she were going to cower before these people. Delgado was dead. There was no more fear left to feel.

And she'd never be a slave again.

"Ricardi," Lady MacKenzie said. "Interesting."

"And I am called Xiesha. It appears we did most your work for you." She swept a hand back toward the mansion.

Lady MacKenzie smiled again, and it made her lined face seem almost kind. It didn't last long. "There isn't much time left. The main house is lost and this garage is starting to catch. The police finally let the firefighters start to move their trucks up the driveway behind the SWAT teams. The SWAT officers might not understand what went on here."

Not much time indeed. Maria glanced out the bay door and could see dark forms advancing from the street. A fire truck rolled along behind them.

"Don't worry," Lady MacKenzie said. "They can't see us yet."

Maria didn't bother to ask how that was managed. Evidently the Order of Thorn had tricks of its own.

"So what do you want?" Karl asked.

"We have another job we'd like you to do for us."

Maria felt the sudden tension in his arm. His mouth was set in a grim line.

"What are you paying?" he demanded. Maria moved close to him, but he didn't look at her.

"Generous terms." Lady MacKenzie glanced at Xiesha, then at Maria. "Pardons for your friends. The same terms as your own. To never interfere in any political process or seek to enslave, dominate or rule human beings to any degree. To feed only upon violent criminals—murderers, rapists, child molesters—but not those guilty of petty crimes. To never act against the Order or against any knight in the just performance of his duty."

"I shudder to read the fine print," Xiesha said. Karl glanced at her and she subsided.

Lady MacKenzie turned her head toward Maria. "You must

make a choice, and quickly."

"I go where Karl goes."

Maria could feel the stares of the knights on her like cold knives on her skin. Lady MacKenzie's gaze was by far the most piercing. The eyes of a hanging judge.

Lady MacKenzie opened her mouth to say something, but Xiesha interrupted.

"I agree to those terms." Xiesha's face was as serious as Maria had ever seen it. "I have lived by them so far. It shouldn't be hard to continue. I thank you for the amnesty, and for the sharing of this world." Xiesha bowed low.

A curt nod from Lady MacKenzie. Her eyes shifted back to Maria.

Did she want a bow too? A little kowtow to seal the deal? A little abasement to show her gratitude? Like hell.

A rending crash filled the air and a drift of sparks floated by the open garage bay. More of the mansion must have collapsed. At the same time, flashlight beams began to appear, stabbing along the walls of the garage, sweeping back and forth. The helicopter hovered low and its searchlight blazed through the garage bay.

"There's no more time!" Lady MacKenzie yelled over the roar of the rotor blades. She motioned them toward her. "Come!"

They hurried over and the knights encircled them. Maria could feel the power as the knights did something to the light— bent or warped it somehow. The helicopter searchlight swept over them but didn't pause. The helicopter circled off, searchlight stabbing down into the gardens, looking for survivors.

"Don't leave the circle," one of the Thorn knights said. "Make no noise."

There were a few shouts from the SWAT officers and a flurry of radio chatter. Lady MacKenzie took advantage of the moment to lead them out of the garage and away from the advancing police.

The mansion was little more than support beams, rubble and fire. A massive pillar of smoke curled up into the sky, blotting out the stars. Sections of the garage roof smoked and the annex between the mansion and the garage had started to burn. The gardens and yard were bathed in the fire's red-orange glow, and places close to the front of the house were illuminated in that stark white of the police flood lamps.

They moved through the back of the property, which had to be an acre wide at least. A team of heavily armed police officers passed them, advancing with the precision of a military unit, but none of them saw through the Thorn knights' circle.

In the end it was almost too easy, but she sure as hell deserved that after what it had taken to drive that knife into Delgado's heart. The police had a perimeter all the way around the property, but Lady MacKenzie moved around its edge, between two patrol cars with officers who never saw them and kept on down the street. They passed milling crowds of people in their nightclothes and more reporters and more news vans with cable laying everywhere like the tentacles of some stranded squid.

Too tired to think about anything but the feel of Karl's arm around her shoulders, she didn't even care who they wanted Karl to kill. Delgado was gone. Maybe she'd start dancing on cars like it was a musical or something.

Lady MacKenzie brought them to three black SUVs parked a block from the mansion.

"Snazzy," Maria said.

They loaded up, nobody saying much else. Maria didn't look back as they pulled away from the curb and off into the night, or when Karl took her hand and held it in his own.

Epilogue

The Order of the Thorn allowed him one last visit with Maria Ricardi before he boarded the ship for Constanta, Romania. A freighter. He'd ride in a coffin in the cargo hold, a corpse headed back to the old country for burial. From there it was on to Sarajevo by train. Also in cargo. He'd have handlers from the Order carrying the necessary documentation and bribe money to make sure no enterprising customs official pried open his casket in daylight.

Tonight, Lady Kimberly MacKenzie was his chaperone, but she stayed inside the SUV while Karl and Maria stood together in the backyard of his second house in Cambridge. It was snowing again, a soft fall of large wet flakes that made even his under-cared-for yard seem a mysterious and magical place.

"How long will you be gone?" she asked, her head on his chest. His arms felt good around her. She fit against him perfectly.

"I don't know."

"Why won't they let me come?"

He shook his head. She'd asked that several times, but Lady Kimberly had refused each request. They wanted Karl. No one else.

"Did they tell you who they want you to kill?" She turned her large eyes up to him. They appeared brown, the red vampire glow now hidden.

"They'll tell me when we get there." Not knowing didn't please him at all, but he didn't have many options at the moment. This client held all the cards.

"I don't want you to go." She kissed him, then put her forehead on his chest. "But I'll stop whining about it."

He smiled and said nothing.

They stood there for a long time in silence. He lifted his face and looked up into the falling snow. Flakes touched down on his cheeks and eyes but didn't melt.

"I'm taking over for my father," she said. "I'm rebuilding the family."

He looked down at her. "Are you sure?"

She nodded and looked away.

"The Order's pardon—"

"I agreed to follow you," she said. "Nothing else. A girl has a right to earn a living." A smile. "So to speak."

He remembered the conversation with Lady MacKenzie in Lucatti's burning garage. Xiesha had agreed to the terms, but Maria had sidestepped. He was surprised it had been overlooked, but time had been running out. Her father would have been pleased. "You think the family will accept you?"

"They won't have a choice."

He started to say something but she held a hand up.

"I know there'll be bloodshed," she said. "What sudden ascension is free of it?"

"And this is what you want?"

"Want?" She laughed. "Since when did anyone ask me what I want? I want a heartbeat. I want you. But I don't see anybody standing in line waiting to give it to me."

"You already have me."

"Not for now, I don't. Not until the almighty Order decides they're through with you."

He bent to her ear. It was cold against his lips. "Be careful. Remember what I taught you."

"I will."

The memory of Delgado's last words still lingered: *She won't be like you. She'll always be mine. I taught her well.*

Yet she was Delgado's slave no longer. She would have to decide for herself.

And Karl had faith.

The silence settled in again. The snow drifted down around them and the quiet was so deep it seemed they were the only people in the city. If only that were true.

In the street, the SUV's engine started with a jarring, beast-like rumble. They both glanced that way.

"No more time," she said.

"When I return—"

She leaned up and kissed him. Her lips were soft and cold. He broke away first, touched her face. Brushed off the snowflakes dusting her eyelids.

Neither of them said goodbye.

He turned up the collar of the coat he did not need, shoved his hands in his pockets and left her behind.

About the Author

Keith Melton was born in Arizona, but has careened around the country from Oregon to Alaska to Rhode Island. He's landed back in Oregon, where he lives with his writer wife, daughter and son, and a demon-possessed cat. An escapee from the bowels of the corporate world's lower dungeons, he now writes urban fantasy in the tower of a castle that normal people, including licensed health professionals, assure him is completely imaginary.

To learn more about Keith, please visit www.keithmelton.net.

To stop a killer, would you become one?

Even for Me
© *2008 Taryn Blackthorne*
An On the Prowl story.

Aislyn used to have a life, a family and a home until a witch on a mission shattered everything in one night with a spell. Now Aislyn is on the run, holed up in Denver, and fighting the Changes that ravage her body and mind while struggling to keep her humanity.

Jackson Havens is a ghost hunter short on cash. All he needs is quick proof that Aislyn is the Ghost Cat Killer, and he can get back to his day job. One pair of handcuffs and a double-crossing employer later, Jackson finds himself bound to the sexy Aislyn—and racing to catch the real killer before someone puts Aislyn down. For good.

Available now in ebook from Samhain Publishing.
Also available in the print anthology On The Prowl from Samhain Publishing.

GET IT NOW

MyBookStoreAndMore.com

GREAT EBOOKS, GREAT DEALS . . . AND MORE!

Don't wait to run to the bookstore down the street, or
waste time shopping online at one of the "big boys." Now,
all your favorite Samhain authors are all in one place—at
MyBookStoreAndMore.com. Stop by today and discover
great deals on Samhain—and a whole lot more!

Samhain Publishing ltd

WWW.SAMHAINPUBLISHING.COM

GREAT
CHEAP
FUN

Discover eBooks!

THE FASTEST WAY TO GET THE HOTTEST NAMES

Get your favorite authors on your favorite reader, long before they're out in print! Ebooks from Samhain go wherever you go, and work with whatever you carry—Palm, PDF, Mobi, and more.

WWW.SAMHAINPUBLISHING.COM